# Echoes
## The Affinity Saga Book 2
## Eddie Dee Williams

Rebirth Publishings LLC

# Contents

N
The Spine Mountains
The Serpent Flats
North Gate
MERIDIAN
Tech & Finance
HIGHGARDEN
Luxury & Agri-tech
East Gate
West Gate
MIDTOWN
Government District
GENESIS LANDING
Industrial & Port
THE UNDERBELLY
Low-income
LEICESTER
Residential & Commercial
South Gate
OCEAN BAY
MAP KEY
River direction
River direction
Maglev lines
Monorail
Bridges
Transport
URI CITY:
THE WALLED METROPOLIS
5 km

# The Defender's Oath and the Three Laws of the Uri City Contract Defense Agreement

**I am a Defender.**  The citizens are my people.  I swear to protect Uri City when called upon to defend it from any and all threats – foreign and domestic.  **I am a Defender.**  I humbly acknowledge the power I wield and the station I have been granted.  I swear to use my skills, powers, and abilities for the betterment of the populace I serve.  **I am a Defender.** As I stand as part of our city's last line of defense, I swear to be a watchful guardian of the health and welfare of my fellow Defenders and to never place myself or my agenda above the team, the Division, the Company, or the city.  **So help me Akan.**

<u>Law 1:</u> People are citizens, not the enemy.  Unless authorized otherwise, our aim is to subdue combatants using the path of least resistance.

<u>Law 2:</u>  We are to act on behalf of the Company *only* when authorized to do so.  Any action taken without authorization may result in termination from the Company and criminal prosecution.

<u>Law 3:</u>  As agents of Uri City, we must never abuse the position we hold nor abuse the powers we wield for selfish gain or ulterior motive that may jeopardize the overall goals and objectives of the Company and Uri City.

For all my heroes who ever went in the back yard, stood in battle formation, and screamed at the top of their lungs, "It's morphin' time!"

# Prologue

*Y**ou can do this.*

Darkness surrounded her on all sides as the rock formations hid and isolated her from the outside noise. She sat cross-legged in the deep, dark cave, her hands gently palming her knees. The only sign of life was a small fire she set in front of her a cycle prior. She wore a wide-legged, black jumpsuit that flowed loosely on her body. Seated next to her on her left side was a black journal and a gold pen. She had the journal turned to a page that read, "'Be still. Master your emotions. Feel the energy and tell it what to do.' Armitage." Scribbled all over the page were small pictures of flames, lightning bolts, arrows, asterisk stars, and the planet Uretha.

Her head faced forward, eyes closed and relaxed. Her wavy black hair rested on her shoulders. She took in a deep breath and released it slowly through the small circle of her parted lips while thinking, *Empty your mind, focus your thoughts, feel the energy coursing through your veins.* She slowly lifted her arms up and flexed her palms to face the fire.

She thought about the ice power rushing through her. She could feel the cool sensations throughout her entire body as the power flowed through her arteries, but she could also sense it slowly fading away and pushed herself to keep it alive within her. She thought, *Come on, you can do this. Come on!* She tensed her fingers more tightly, and her hands began to tremble. She grimaced as she tried to manifest the power within her. *Put the fire out. Put the fire out!*

Her entire body tensed up. She flexed every muscle she could summon. Her head began to send pain signals to her temples, but she continued to strain herself, determined to bring this power to life. Old memories flashed before her eyes – the countless power manifesting retreats she attended, the gurus she studied under, the training she underwent, the endless notes she took and read and reread, over and over again. She channeled years of scientific theories and spiritual affirmations to try one more time to extinguish the fire.

But the fire in front of her paid her no attention. The kindling continued to smolder as the dancing flames burned the contents within the rock circle with glee, taunting her. A single hot tear streamed from her right eye. She gritted her teeth and let out a high-pitched growl. Still, nothing materialized. She screamed with all her might and shot her hands forward again.

Nothing.

She fell forward and palmed the ground. She breathed heavily and rapidly, and she trembled in anguish. Another tear escaped her right eye. *Why? Why can't I bring it out of me?* She looked at the journal, grabbed it and slammed it shut, then threw it across the cave. *Day after day, it's the same result. I can't bring it out of me! I can't use it! I can't use any of them! Why? Why was I made like this? Why was I given this curse?!* She silently beat herself up while her chest tightened, and her throat began to swell.

She recognized that she was losing control. "This cannot be my purpose. Refocus, breathe." She closed her eyes, slowed her breathing for twenty seconds, and concentrated again. "Remember, do not get emotional. Silence your mind. Feel the energy flowing within you and bring it out of you. You can do this, Nova."

She raised her hands once again, and she concentrated on the energy signature that continued to decay within her. Nova was running out of time before the power would disappear completely. She flexed and tensed her fingers and attempted to manifest the energy outside of herself. Same effort, same result.

Her fate was the same as it always had been. She wouldn't fully accept it. But she understood that on this day, as in days past, she lost once again. Her mantra birthed in the crucible of childhood ambition reverberated in her ear.

*You are destined for glory.*

She knelt her head and closed her dark brown eyes once more, damming up the deluge of tears that begged to be freed from their ducts.

Nova didn't notice a bright light that shone behind her. Nova felt a presence creeping her way but paid it no mind. A long-haired, thin, dark-skinned woman with white pupils saw Nova and thought, *Oh, no, it didn't work again. I wish she would stop torturing herself like this. I'm strong enough on my own to fight for her. I don't understand why she doesn't just stand behind me, all of us. Does she not trust us to take care of her? Does she not trust me?*

She walked and stood behind Nova. "Boss?"

Nova silently cleared her throat to not draw any unwanted attention to herself. "Yes?" she responded.

"There's someone here to see you."

Nova wiped her cheeks and fought through the urge to sniff her nose. She lifted her head forward, and her eyes popped open. "Fantastic. Right on time." Nova reached to her right and picked up a black wristband connected by a small black tube to a gold ring with two gold tops. She slid her left hand through the wristband, and the band connected to her stripe. Her stripe lit blue from her wrist to the end of her forearm. Suddenly, the band hummed and began to siphon the ice power she felt within her, and the gold ring expanded as the essence of the ice power left her. The gold ring became a glowing white canister about eighteen inches tall. Once it filled, Nova took the wristband off and lay it on the ground.

Nova stood up and turned around. The woman standing in front of her was wearing a white shirt with a jean vest and pale-yellow leggings. She was holding a black mask in her hands.

"I thought you might want this," she told Nova. She offered the mask to her.

"Thank you, Ashanti," Nova replied. "Get Mason and meet me at the entrance." Nova took the mask from Ashanti. "Suit up, just in case things get a little interesting."

Ashanti raised an eyebrow in concern. "Are you sure? I thought this was going to be simple."

"Yes, well, with this guy, one can never be certain," Nova replied. "We have to be on guard. This trade can go sideways. I don't think it will. But be ready."

Ashanti thought through her stripe and summoned Mason. She heard Mason's voice in her ear say, "What's up?"

"Boss wants us at the entrance to meet her visitor. See you in three."

"See you there." Mason was sitting in the living room of his messy residence watching the holoscreen. The four hairy tentacles protruding from his back erected from excitement. He shot up from his couch, knocking over a food tray and spilling half his meal on the trash-ridden floor under his feet.

He walked around his couch, kicking some of the trash, and walked ten feet toward his door. He grabbed a button from a shelf on the left wall next to the door and spun it into his chest until it locked. He then double-tapped the button, and nanites flowed from the button and covered his body, turning him into a metallic gray and yellow man-spider. He opened the door and ran down the corridor to reach the elevator.

Nova, meanwhile, said, "AI, kill program." The cave that she and Ashanti stood in began to dematerialize, and the dark rocks and the fire on the ground all disappeared. All that remained was a gray room with stripe lights running vertically every ten feet on the walls. Nova looked at Ashanti and said, "Shall we?"

Ashanti double-tapped herself, and nanites began to flow onto her body, enveloping her into a blue, yellow, and white uniform. She left her visor off. Ashanti answered Nova, "Let's go."

Nova and Ashanti marched down the corridor and met Mason at the elevator. Mason asked, "Are we going to get Xander and Heinrich or...?"

"No," Nova replied. "We don't need them. We'll be fine." Ashanti hit the UP button, and the elevator rode down the shaft to meet them. Nova double-tapped her chest, and nanites began to envelop her in an all-black uniform. The silver elevator doors parted to reveal a 7x7 lift. Inside the well-lit box was a long, black trench coat hanging on the back wall. Nova walked in first, then Ashanti, then Mason. Nova grabbed the coat and slid her arms into it, then pressed it onto her body. It conformed to make her appear androgynous. She finally slid her head into her mask and locked the three clasps.

Nova spoke, and her voice was heavily distorted. "Lady and gentleman, destiny awaits."

Ashanti and Mason nodded in agreement. They looked forward and awaited reaching the top of the elevator shaft. The elevator slowed to a halt, and a ding indicated they reached their destination. The elevator opened, and they stepped off. The corridor was brightly lit with recessed white lights spaced every ten feet on the ceiling, and cyan-green lights recessed in the headboards and floorboards on the wall. Every twenty feet on either side were recessed cases with glowing white canisters floating within them. The black marble floor echoed with every step they took.

They reached the entrance of their lair. Nova said, "You two ready?"

"Ready," Ashanti declared, silently wishing for something to go wrong so she could unleash a lightning storm.

"Ready," Mason said as he locked his tentacles above his head, ready to strike.

Nova placed her palm on the reader on the right wall near the door. It scanned her print and lit white for approval. The door popped backward about half an inch, then slid to the right into the wall. The brilliant light of the three suns flooded the hallway. Their visors adjusted immediately so as to not blind them.

In front of them stood a tall, slender man in a cargo uniform, wearing a tan-colored field jacket. His beady eyes and crew-cut fade made him less intimidating than both Ashanti and Mason anticipated. He raised his arms wide and yelled, "Collector! It's great to see you! Streak, Mygalo, good to see you, too!"

"I can't say the same about you, Dante. You're late. Very, very late," the Collector responded, arms crossed.

"Well, what can I say?" Dante responded as he lowered his arms and smiled. "Do you realize what you asked me for? It's not every day that someone just has a nullifier lying around in a dump or a garage or a flea market." Dante patted his left hand on a gold box about three feet tall, deep, and wide on a dolly.

The Collector did not flinch. "Yes, that may be true. But I asked you for that nullifier two quarters ago, Dante. I knew we had to be patient with you, but Akan, this took too long, even for you."

Dante rubbed his chin. "Listen, Collector, you and your crew are playing a dangerous game, everybody on Uretha knows that. This nullifier you asked for is high-grade, as in, Asylum-for-the-Uncontrollable-grade. You don't realize the shit I had to go through just to retrieve this thing without sounding off any alarms or putting a target on my back. Had I gotten you some knock-off nullifier, you would have knocked me off my rocker and ended my precious life. So, forgive me if I didn't meet your timeline."

Dante placed his hands on top of the gold box and adjusted his feet to make an about-face. "I can just take this to somebody else, I'm sure this will fetch me a pretty payday on the dark net."

Streak let a spark fly from her hand. The tips of Mygalo's tentacles cocked forward. The Collector noticed them and placed a hand on both of their chests to calm them down. "Now, now, let's not lose our cool. How about we all come inside, you teach me how this thing works, and I give you the money you need to finally get out of Uri City for good like you've always wanted."

Dante smiled and answered, "That sounds right." He got behind the dolly.

"Follow Streak and me. Mygalo, cover his rear." Dante pushed the nullifier inside the doorway. Mygalo placed his hand on the reader, and once it lit white for approval, the door slid from the wall and sealed the corridor. Mygalo then followed Dante as he followed the Collector and Streak to the elevator.

Dante's curiosity piqued. "So, I never asked you this when you asked me to get this for you."

The Collector caught on. "I figured the question was going to come up at some point. I'm surprised it's taken you this long to finally ask me."

"What do you need a nullifier for?" Dante inquired.

"In order for my plan to work, we have to even the playing field by an incredibly large margin. This nullifier will ensure that we have the tactical advantage."

They rode the elevator to the bottom floor. Once the doors opened, they walked to the Collector's training room. Streak slid the training room door open, and they all went inside. Dante inquired, "You said 'tactical advantage,' and wanting to 'even the playing field.' Just who exactly are you going to use this on?"

The Collector and Streak stopped. The Collector turned her head to the side, then turned her body to face Dante. Without flinching, she answered, "You wouldn't believe me if I told you."

# 1

# Meltdown

The Uri Mega Mall was bustling with patrons. Some on a mission to spend as much money as they could, others just looking for a spot to hang out with their friends. A few single onlookers were perched in various places people-watching, while others were staring at their holoscreens as they waited for their shopping partners to finish rummaging through the clearance racks. Such was the typical rush of the weekend after Jubilee, Uri City's week-long celebration of the new year.

The center of the mall was one hundred feet in diameter and marked by four massive columns, each representing one of the four quarters of the year. Those columns anchored the seven floors that housed the stores. A blue, thirty-foot diameter stage was in the middle of the floor, three steps high. A spire was lodged in the center of the stage. It stood at least one hundred feet tall and helped hold up the glass ceiling that flooded the center with light. Many people were seated at several tables that surrounded the stage. Mall employees were still exchanging Jubilee-specific banners and advertising for Uri Mega Mall branding, some using scaffolding, some using their flight abilities, and some using either their abilities to stretch or to move things telepathically.

One family was walking through the bottom floor and arrived near the center of the mall. A mother, her husband,

and their son navigated the perimeter of the center, and they passed by Malachi Toys and Games, a very popular toy store in Uri City, and a particular favorite of their kid. As they neared the perimeter, the mother grimaced and stated with a low growl, "Lance, I told you we shouldn't have come this way. Jacob is going to see the toy store and flip out!"

"Kenya," Lance retorted, "we can't help that the jewelry store is right next to it. This was unavoidable. Besides, he can't learn that he can't get everything he wants if we don't teach him."

"True, but you know how he gets, and I don't feel like dealing with his tantrum today."

As they got closer to Malachi's, Jacob's parents tried to speed up and avoid it altogether. But Jacob's memory got the better of them as his six-year-old enthusiasm exclaimed, "Toys!"

Lance instinctually jerked Jacob's left arm with his right hand and reminded him, "No, no, Jacob, we're not going to the toy store today. We're here to fix your mom's ring, and then we're going to get ice cream at the food court like we said."

"But I want to go to the toy store!" Jacob yelled and planted his feet.

Kenya protested, "Jacob, no, you just got a mountain of toys for Jubilee and still haven't touched half of them yet."

Jacob began to pull away from his father as he demanded, "I want to go to the toy store!" His scream was so loud, it got the attention of everyone within twenty feet of them.

"Jacob, no, we're not going to the toy store today," his father pulled back while trying not to pull Jacob's arm out of socket.

Jacob's eyes flashed, and he scrunched his face, incensed by his parents' refusal. He yelled uncontrollably with a roar that rivaled a tiger. Lance remembered the calming technique their family therapist taught him. He knelt and hugged his son and declared to him, "Jacob, calm down, we're not going to do this today. We said no, and that's that."

Jacob huffed and yelled. He contorted his body to try to break from his father's grip. He kicked Lance in the stomach. Lance let out an *oomph* while still holding on to Jacob. Jacob cried and slowly enunciated, "I want to go to the toy store!" Jacob's body temperature rose exponentially, and his eyes menacingly glowed yellow.

Kenya got worried and said, "Lance, let him go." Lance didn't listen, and Kenya pleaded, "Lance, let him go! Something's wrong with Jacob!"

Lance opened his eyes and let Jacob go. Jacob stood on the ground, fists balled up, head bowed down. Jacob huffed and puffed faster and deeper. Lance said, "Jacob, buddy, look at me. What's wrong, buddy? What's happening? Kenya, what is this?"

Onlookers whipped out their holoscreens and began recording. Others got worried and started walking in the opposite direction. Security guards received signals from the surveillance team and were instructed to converge on Jacob. The guards began running and flying in their direction.

"I don't know what's happening. Lance, what do we do?" Kenya started crying.

Jacob lifted his head up and articulated once more, his voice having morphed from a six-year-old to a menacing dark lord, "I want to go to the toy store!" He unleashed a howl from the depths of his soul, and his skin turned orange and yellow. Smoke covered his body, and his clothes caught fire from the heat his body radiated.  His parents and the onlookers backed up in fright.  Onlookers shrieked, "We gotta get out of here! Let's go!"

Kenya pressed her hand on Lance's shoulders as security guards cut through the crowd running in the opposite direction.  She said, "What's wrong with our son, Lance?"

He let out a sigh and said, "He's powered.  We should leave, right?  Let security handle this?"

"No," Kenya declared, "I'm not leaving my son behind." She walked up to Jacob and said, "Jacob, come on, son, it's okay, we can..."

Jacob's body was suddenly covered in molten lava flowing from his pores.  He let out a shriek, and he unleashed a massive blast two hundred feet in every direction.  He incinerated his parents, the toy store, the stage, the tables, the pillars, the onlookers, and the security guards.  The glass ceiling shattered, and the energy blast knocked against the cloak designed to protect the mall from outside destruction.  The blast rode the cloak and began burning the ceiling of the mall. The mall began crumbling and imploding on itself while also turning into a furnace with nowhere for the heat to escape. Lava flowed from Jacob's entire body, and what was once the center of the mall was now a growing nuclear sinkhole.

Alarms blared in Intelligence.  Dax and five other analysts looked up from their holoscreens at their desks and toward the big holoscreen at the front of Intelligence.  Dax scanned the reports coming in from the Uri City Police Department, the Uri City Fire Department, and Uri City Medical Center stacked one behind the other regarding the incident at Uri Mega Mall.  Dax marveled, "Damn, not even a week after Jubilee, what on Uretha?"

Dax tapped on the keys of his console and commanded AI to pull up all video footage that could be gathered. AI followed his commands and pulled up the little footage that wasn't destroyed in the blast and could be retrieved without performing a deep dive. All he could get was camera footage from outside the building that showed the fire and energy flowing underneath the cloak. He could not yet retrieve anything from the inside.

The door to Intelligence slid open, and Stephanie, wearing a black pencil dress and her white lab coat, walked down the steps. "What's going on?"

Dax replied, "A massive explosion just took out a huge chunk of the Mega Mall. It looks like the director is dispatching a Super team to handle it. I'm gathering intel just in case they call the Elite in."

"Okay," Stephanie responded as she placed her hands on Dax's shoulders. "I'm going to get in touch with UPD and UFD. How much footage do we have on the incident?"

"Not a lot," Dax lamented as he rolled up the sleeves of his black button-up shirt. "The blast took out every camera and every person with a holoscreen, so all I have is what was around its perimeter and the outside. Apparently, the heat signature was strong enough to knock out the black boxes."

"Anything from surveillance yet?" Stephanie inquired as she walked toward the center of the Intelligence floor to sit at her desk.

"No, the power's knocked out, so they are currently off the grid. It'll take about two cycles for us to get through their firewalls and tap into their footage remotely."

"Makes sense. Okay, team, press pause on your assignments and start data mining as much intel as you can on this situation. Primarily, was this an act of aggression or an accident? Who are we dealing with? And do the Elite need to get involved? Focus up, and let's make sure they don't go in blind."

"Understood," the other members of Intelligence echoed to Stephanie.

Stephanie sat at her desk and tapped on the keys of her holoscreen. Running her fingers through her straightened, bob-cut hair, she felt immediate heartache thinking about the lives lost and the families who would have to live with that pain for years to come. She fought back tears and continued typing, determined to gather as much as she could to help with the rescue effort.

A cycle went by. The Elite exited the elevator, clad in their nanotech uniforms and cloaks, and they marched to the hoverpad atop the Company base where the Eagle's hoverbus was perched. The Mammoth, Ammo, Starburst, K.C., Enchantra, the Eagle, and Blitz prepared themselves for an intense afternoon. They climbed the steps and entered the hoverbus from the back hatch. The Eagle walked ahead while the other six took their seats, K.C., Starburst, and the Mammoth on the left, and Blitz, Enchantra, and Ammo on the right.

The Eagle stood at the countertop in the cockpit and pressed her hands atop it. The bus responded by lighting up all over the cockpit, and several holoscreens displayed flight information. The Eagle instructed, "Everyone, buckle up, preparing for take-off. T-minus 4 minutes to the Mega Mall."

Everyone pulled their belts from behind their shoulders and clasped them in their buckles in between their legs. K .C. stated, "Alright, Stephanie, recap us, what are we getting into?"

Back at Intelligence, Stephanie sat atop her desk, legs crossed with her left foot planted in her desk chair, staring at the big holoscreen. She relayed, "What we know is that the target let out a massive blast that engulfed the mall from the center about two hundred feet. Because of the cloak, the blast had nowhere to go and has incinerated the roof." The holoscreen showed a 3D blue and white wireframe model of the Mega Mall and displayed the blast and its impact on the building itself. "The heat caused floors five through seven to collapse on themselves. Massive structural damage."

"What's the report from Super Team III?" Enchantra asked.

"They said that they went toward the center, and they saw a pool of lava-looking nuclear energy that is rising and falling at the same time. They sent Aqua in to try to cool it down, but the energy is too hot, and he said that the steam being produced was only turning the mall into a sauna. It's too hot in there, and the team's cloaks were severely damaged by the heat and the radiation."

"Shit," Ammo chimed in. "So how do we stop this guy?"

"Their report gets worse. While the rescue mission is going well and they have gotten a lot of the survivors out of the building, with the lava falling as they described it, we're assuming that the target is creating a nuclear sinkhole underneath the mall. We're not sure how far down he's gotten, but if you don't do something quickly, he's going to cause several blocks of Highgarden to collapse."

K.C. declared, "Understood. Eagle, how far out are we?"

"Not far, maybe two minutes," the Eagle announced.

"Good. Okay, team, once we get down there, we'll get an assessment from Super Team III, then we'll lay out our plan of action."

The Eagle applied more pressure from her right hand on the console, and the hoverbus sped faster toward their destination. Blitz pondered out loud, "This couldn't have happened at a worse time, just a week after Jubilee. It's just awful."

"Tell me about it," the Mammoth agreed. "What a start to the new year."

Starburst lifted her head and responded, "All we can do now is save who we can and stop this guy from doing more damage. Stephanie, any confirmation on who started this?"

"Negative, Starburst. We still haven't cracked their security mainframe, so we don't have access to their camera footage yet. But from the reports we received from III, the energy is concentrated in the center of the mall, so there's no indication of a secondary threat."

"Copy that," Starburst stated. She gently planted her skull on the headrest of the chair.

The Eagle announced, "We're here." The hoverbus slowed its velocity and landed in the middle of the crowded parking lot. Ambulances, fire trucks, police vehicles, and emergency staff from the UPD, UFD, and UMC had turned the lot into their command and triage centers. The team unbuckled their belts and rose from their seats. The back hatch opened, and the Elite ran forward toward the entrance. Sirens and screams filled their ears as survivors, families of the missing and fallen victims, and personnel scrambled to make sense of the carnage and recover from it.

Another defender uniform-cloaked in black and white vertical stripes met them halfway and said, "K.C., Elite, you guys couldn't have come fast enough. We have to hurry. The mall is beginning to sink." The defender pointed at the entrance, and they noticed that the door was about six inches lower than normal, and the ground that once was flat was now sloped downward.

"How far along are you with the rescue, Blink?" K.C. asked as they ran toward the entrance.

"We have searched about 40% of what we can access. I'm sure we will be able to get to all of them before the energy envelops the whole mall," Blink answered.

K.C. stopped everyone about twenty feet from the entrance and said, "Okay, here's what we're going to do. Mammoth, Ammo, Blitz, you three are on rescue. Assist Team III and lift and blast all this debris apart. Grab as many people as you can and get them out of here. No point in trying to salvage the building. If you have to create a door, blow a hole through this place. Star, Enchantra, Eagle, you're with me. We've got to stop this guy before he does any more damage. We'll get to the center and assess and figure out how to do that. Everyone understand their assignments?"

"Understood," some said as others nodded.

"Alright, Elite. Let's get it."

Blitz flexed her legs and whisked past everyone in the blink of an eye. She surveyed the landscape, and the deeper she traveled into the mall, the greater the damage became. Stores that once glittered with lights and color were now charred relics and smoldering embers. She noticed a bright yellow light toward the center of the mall, and as she approached it, her cloak responded to the presence of dark energy in the air and began shimmering all over, yellow replacing the red and silver that her nanites danced in. A blue percentage number showed up in the right corner of Blitz's visor. It read, "100%, 99%, 98%."

Blitz stopped about one hundred yards from the center of the mall. "Oh shit, my cloak's declining." She immediately about-faced and ran back to the team who had just gotten to the door of the mall. She shocked them when she reappeared. "Listen, guys, the energy he's emitting is as powerful as Frimas. The radiation is no joke. Be cautious. I'm going to travel the upper floors and get whoever I can from there. Mammoth, Ammo, I think you'd do your best work on the ground."

"Copy that, Blitz," Ammo answered. "Mammoth, you ready?"

"Frimas yeah," the Mammoth bellowed. "Let's go."

Blitz disappeared again as Ammo and the Mammoth ran ahead of the team toward the charred areas of the mall about three hundred yards away.

K.C. said, "Okay, Blink, your crew is on the other side of the mall, you guys stay there and keep getting survivors out. We're going to head to the center."

"Sure thing. You guys need a ride?" Blink offered.

"Yes," the Eagle said.

Starburst was confused. "A ride?"

Enchantra smiled behind her visor. "Hold hands."

Everyone clasped hands, and Blink touched K.C.'s back. Suddenly, they disappeared like a vapor, and they reappeared near the edge of the center of the mall. Starburst nearly fell, shocked at Blink's power and how swiftly they arrived. "Whoa, that was a rush," she said as her eyes glowed.

"Good luck, guys," Blink declared, and she instantly disappeared and returned to her teammates.

Enchantra, Starburst, K.C., and the Eagle's cloaks started shimmering, and the same blue number from Blitz's visor appeared in theirs. "Alright, ladies. Let's see what we can do."

They looked over the edge of the crater, and all they saw was yellow light and felt intense heat radiating from the lava flowing from the hole. Their visors calculated that the energy began about fifty feet below the edge.

K.C. asked Enchantra, "Hold me up." Enchantra's eyes glowed green, and green mist emitted from her hands. It surrounded K.C., and he leaned forward, held by the mist from falling into the hole. He then pushed his hands forward and felt the energy below. He could feel the particles within the lava flowing freely and multiplying underneath the surface. He attempted to harden the surface. The team could see the lava slowly turning into solid rock. But by the time the rock would appear, it would instantly be swallowed up by more lava.

"It's no use, there's just too much lava to turn," K.C. said. He noticed the cloak's integrity down to 87%. "Bring me back up." Enchantra pulled him back to the cliff's edge. He then issued to the Eagle, "Can you see anyone down there?"

The Eagle attempted to adjust her vision within her eyes, switching from infrared to electromagnetic wave, contrasting as much as possible, and changing thermal frequencies. "It's no use," the Eagle sighed. "It's too much nuclear energy, and it just keeps growing and sinking."

K.C. shook his head while the cloak's integrity fell two more percentage points. "Enchantra, can you sense anyone down there?"

"I can try." As she was about to activate her telepathy, the ground beneath them shifted, and the cliff they stood on began to splinter. They all backed up about ten feet and noticed the rim of the crater crumble into the pit.

"The mall's growing more unstable, we're running out of time," Starburst declared. "Blitz, how is the rescue going?"

Blitz was scrambling from floor to floor as she, the Mammoth, and Ammo continued searching for survivors. "I've cleared the second floor and have started on the third. The fellas are still finding and securing survivors on the first. We're sinking, though, I can feel it."

"Alright, Enchantra," K.C. stated. "Give it a shot."

Enchantra closed her eyes, then opened them, her eyes glowing green. She tried to cut through the lava and see something, underneath the cistern. The lava's nuclear make-up proved too much for Enchantra's telepathy. "Ugh, I'm useless. The nuclear material is blocking my ability to reach whoever is underneath it all. It's just too thick and deep."

Their cloaks' integrities continued to steadily fall from the radiation. "Okay, we gotta stop this shit. Somehow, we've got to cut through the lava," K.C. reasoned. "Starburst, what about you?"

"I can try blasting it, but I honestly don't think it'll make a difference. It's energy on top of energy."

K.C. walked to the edge once again and looked down the glowing abyss. He thought through the ground shifting under them, the energy and its radiation, and the survivors and civilians on the street. *Okay Malcolm, think, how can we get down there without killing ourselves and stop this? Think, brother, think!*

"Okay, Enchantra, create a bridge for us to stand on while also encasing the Eagle, Starburst, and me with the nuclear material. That should at least stop the ground from crumbling under the mall. Starburst and I will combine our powers to create a lance that can cut through and part the nuclear material all the way to the bottom of the pool. As we're doing that, Eagle, you will see if you can find the people responsible for all this. Once you see them, praying that they're not cloaked, you'll hit them with tranquilizers, I will jump in the hole and grab them, while Starburst, you'll jump in with me and lift us out of the hole before the nuclear energy can swallow us whole or burn out our cloaks."

Enchantra nervously nodded her head. "Okay, I'm ready," she lied.

"Build the bridge and hover us over the middle," K.C. instructed.

Enchantra concentrated, and green mist flowed from her hands and onto the ground. A green translucent walkway about seven feet wide appeared over the nuclear abyss. K.C. and the Eagle confidently ran across the bridge toward the center of the pool while Starburst levitated, following them. Once they made it to the center, K.C. and the Eagle lay flat on the bridge and stared down. Their cloaks were down to 64% integrity.

"Okay, Star," K.C. said. "Blast a stream."

"Copy," Starburst understood. She directed her hands underneath her and shot a steady stream of star energy into the pool. It penetrated the surface. K.C. then concentrated on the star power near the surface of the nuclear energy and thought, *ice, the coldest ice the universe has ever known.* The star power suddenly froze at the edge, and the ice lance began to cut through the pool.

Meanwhile, Enchantra closed her eyes again, and she placed her right palm onto her left palm directly in front of her. She then shifted her hands to where the left palm was on top of the right. She then placed both hands in front of her in a prayer stance, then parted her palms, and the tips of her fingers touched, her hands now in the shape of a ball. A prismatic sphere appeared in between her hands. She opened her eyes and said, "Case!" She then shot her arms straight up, and the prism expanded, slowly enveloping the entire abyss and her teammates.

The lava began to rise, now having nowhere to go but up. The radiation intensified, and their cloaks responded in kind. Starburst and K.C. didn't flinch. They continued to cut through the lava. As the hole they created deepened, the Eagle began to make something out toward the bottom of the crater. "Keep going, guys, I can almost see something down there."

K.C. stayed focused despite the radiation damaging his cloak to 43%. He could finally sense what felt like a person underneath all the energy. "Eagle, do you see anything? I can sense someone down there now."

The Eagle tried again, switching to thermal, and could make out a heat signature underneath their ice lance. "Yes, I can see someone down there, about three hundred feet down. I'm zooming in now." She zoomed in and could make out Jacob's height. "He's a short guy, body makeup is under-developed. It's got to be a kid."

"A kid?" K.C. asked.

"Guys, there's no time, can you separate him from the power?" Enchantra asked as she was losing her grip on the bridge.

"Right, parting the energy now," K.C. remembered. He took the blast and began widening the hole. The ice lance hardened the energy to create a temporary cylindrical ice wall. The Eagle had a perfect visual on the kid. She took out her pistol, placed her fingers on the handle and tapped them to activate a tranquilizer round, then aimed at Jacob. She fired, and the round traversed the hole they created and struck Jacob's neck. His eyes widened, and he screamed then crumpled to the ground.

"Enchantra, drop the bridge and grab the Eagle," K.C. said.

Enchantra released the bridge, and K.C. and the Eagle began to fall. Enchantra clutched the Eagle and pulled her out of the encasement and onto the edge of the crater while K.C. flipped himself and fell head-first into the hole Starburst and he created. As he fell, he pulled the kid to him. The ice wall was cracking from the heat of the nuclear energy around him. Starburst fell into the hole, too, to rescue them. About two hundred feet in, the limp kid finally reached K.C., and he held him tightly while the nuclear energy broke through the ice at the bottom of the abyss and started rising again. Starburst grabbed K.C. by his armpits and blasted herself upward. The ice around them shattered, and nuclear energy rose and spilled from everywhere.

"You got this, Star, get us out of here!" K.C. yelled.

Starburst pushed her energy as their cloaks reached less than 20% integrity. The nuclear energy was about twenty feet under them and rising. She pushed, and pushed, and they finally reached the surface before the hole completely collapsed. They left the encasement and landed on top of the crater rim where Enchantra and the Eagle were waiting for them.

"Sheesh, that was a close one," the Eagle said. "You guys okay?"

K.C. said, "Easy peasy, just fine. You were right, Eagle," he stared down at Jacob's naked body. "He can't be older than seven. His body feels like it's on fire!"

"Man," Enchantra stated, "he caused all this damage?"

"Looks that way.  How long is the case going to last?"

Enchantra looked up.  "Should last a few cycles.  Enough time for UFD and Team III to finally cool it down."

"Okay," Starburst responded.  "We should get out of here and let them know."

"Agreed," K.C. said.  "Mammoth, how are you guys?"

"We're good on our end, probably could use some help on the upper floors, but most of the survivors have made it out as far as we can tell."

"Okay, let's get outside and let UPD and UFD handle final containment."

The Elite made it back to the entrance and walked outside. They noticed the larger crowd in the parking lot, people hugging loved ones, others wailing.  Survivors lying and sitting in gurneys, and news crews interviewing anyone who could talk.  Police and fire crews were drawing up plans.  Enchantra noticed a familiar face and yelled out, "Captain Banks!"

Captain Banks turned around and saw the Elite, then turned back to his crew and said, "Excuse me."  He turned and ran toward the Elite.  "Hey guys, what's up?"

K.C. said, "He was just a kid, it was probably his first time his powers ever activated."

Banks stared at the child in K.C.'s arms.  "Aww man, poor kid, what a way to find out you're powered.  Well, we'll take him and have him transported to the Asylum.  Any idea who he is?  His parents?"

Starburst replied, "I'd assume they died in the blast.  We haven't done a scan on him, so we don't know who he is."

"Roger that.  How about the mall?"

"The energy is contained in an enchanted case.  It'll last a few cycles, which should give UFD and Super Team III a chance to finally cool it.  The radiation is high, so make sure their crews are cloaked and take shifts until the radiation dies down.”

“Okay.  Good job, you guys,” Banks declared.  “Akan be praised.”

Banks took Jacob from K.C. and covered his body with his police jacket.  He then carried him off to an armored truck and instructed a couple of medics and the drivers to take him to the Asylum for the Uncontrollable for evaluation and placement.

K.C. looked at his crew and said, “Okay, team, let’s roll out.”

As they walked toward the Eagle’s bird, the Eagle said to Starburst, “Not bad for your last day, huh?”

Starburst smiled underneath her visor and answered confidently, “Not bad, not bad at all.”

# 2

# The End and the Beginning

One could barely see the stars in the night sky as the strobe lights scattered across the rooftop put on a dazzling show. The music pulsated through the loudspeakers, and the DJ was determined to get everybody on the dance floor. Several tables hugged the edge of the glass railings topped with a round metal bar. Loud laughter and chatter cut through the music. The party at Leicester's Switch club was in full swing.

The Elite sat together in a white lounge booth that overlooked the street and easily accessed the dance floor. A small blaze on the table in front of them illuminated their alluring physiques and danced in their eyes.

"How did you get us in here again?" Malaysia, holding a cocktail in her hand, marveled as her purple pencil dress glittered from the lights.

Alexia uncrossed her legs, lifted her arms, and declared, "Somebody owed me a favor, and I thought tonight would be the best night to cash in on it."

"No kidding!" Duncan yelled. "Do you know how hard it is to get into Switch? Let alone get on the roof. This is lux!" He lifted his glass from the table and downed his drink.

"I know! We can't waste this night at all," Alexia responded, pressing her thighs that were covered by her green and black romper.

Karl sat up in his seat next to Alexia and replied, "Right, so let's get this over with, Malcolm."

Malcolm, seated across from Karl and next to Symone, drank from his frosty mug, then set it down on the table. He looked at Symone, and she looked back at him and smiled. Malcolm, fighting to maintain his steely composure as excitement surged in his veins, smiled back, patted her thigh, then looked at the rest of the team and said, "Okay, first things first, how are we all doing after today's mission?"

"Really? We're about to debrief?" Daisy cut her eyes. "Can't that wait until tomorrow?"

Everybody stared at Daisy. Alexia was the first to respond, "Whoa, who is this? Daisy doesn't want to talk shop?"

"I'm with her on that," Malaysia chimed in. "That's new, even for you."

"Guys, we're wasting time, and I want to wild out tonight. Let Malcolm run it his way. I didn't whip out my blazer and fedora for nothing," Duncan stopped everyone from spiraling.

"Right, as I was asking, how's everybody doing?"

"We're doing great, Malcolm, as you can tell," Daisy waved her arms outward, annoyed that they were about to talk about work. "The mission was so sad, though, he was just a kid. The Asylum said he's only six years old."

"Right," Symone continued. "Intelligence finally cracked the security tapes, and it looks like he just had a meltdown. He wanted to go to the toy store, and his parents didn't want to go, and it made him mad. Nobody knew he was powered."

"Casualties were around the mid 500's, and scores more injured," Karl added. "By the time we got there, all we could do to help was grab the few who were still in, get the kid before he could do more damage, and contain the nuclear waste he put out."

Malcolm rubbed his beard and said, "Right. The mission was a success. They were able to contain and cool the energy down. The waste is now just a hardened rock. The radiation is still high, so they'll have to sanitize and neutralize that site for quarters before anyone can think of trying to bring the mall back."

The team agreed. As they chatted a little more about the mall, Malcolm lowered his arm to make sure his stripe could not be seen. He then sent a signal to Switch's staff to bring out Symone's surprise from the team.

Malcolm then stood up and silenced his crew. He tried to act cool, but he couldn't stop smiling from the joy bursting from his heart. "Alright, guys. So, for the past three quarters, our presence has been graced by the amazing, talented Symone Watson." He turned to look at Symone, admiring her physique perfectly accentuated by the black and gold pencil dress she donned. "And without her, we might have had our asses handed to us more than once."

Everybody laughed. Symone slightly shrank in delightful embarrassment.

Malcolm continued. "So, on this day, her last day, we want to wish her a very special 'Congratulations!' So, from us, to you, Miss Watson, we want to say thank you for an incredible three quarters with the Elite!"

The team started clapping while a woman wheeled over a large white cake with strawberries dotted all over it atop a cart. The woman stopped the cart in front of them. She stared intently at everyone for a moment, then stared at Malcolm. She thought, *He's right here. They're all right here, right next to me. And they don't suspect a single thing. This is almost too easy.*

She declared, "Hey guys! On behalf of the staff here at Switch, we just want to say 'Congratulations' to you, Symone Watson! Hope you enjoy!"

Malcolm glanced at the woman, and his senses suddenly heightened. He thought, *She feels familiar to me. Do I know her?*

"Thank you so much!" Symone and Alexia cheered simultaneously, snapping Malcolm out of his thought bubble.

*If they only knew,* the woman congratulated herself as she slinked away.

Alexia stood up and said, "Okay, okay, it's story time!" She walked from her seat and stood in front of the team. She then emitted green mist from her hands, and the mist traveled through everyone's ears and took over the synapses in their minds. Alexia said, "Let's recap Symone's glorious time with us!"

The club pixelated and displayed Alexia's point of view of Symone's time with the Elite. With each story, the team could see what Alexia saw at the time of the event. Alexia narrated, "Symone first arrived in the conference room as we were getting chewed out by Mallack after the DD mishap. She introduced herself to us, and what a show she put on. The Sentinel Bank was getting robbed, and we suited up. She took on her first in-field battle and forgot to cloak."

Symone rolled her eyes and chuckled, "Yeah, man, that double-tap was ridiculous."

"Don't we know it. But girl, weren't you determined! Not just to figure out your cloak, but to get a one-on-one showdown with your mentor. But first, you had to go through all of us. Well, all of us except Duncan."

"I was not about to get my ass handed to me," Duncan shrugged his shoulders and popped his blazer.

"You went through me, then Daisy, then Karl, then Malaysia (who almost killed you), then the final boss Malcolm himself. But not before we squared up with the Collector's henchmen first. They kicked our asses, then you kicked Malcolm's," Alexia laughed.

"Hey, last time I checked, I won," Malcolm crossed his arms.

"Yeah, but she didn't yield, either. Y'all just made a planet and walked away like nothing ever happened. Anyway, we went to the Power Party, then Malcolm and Symone convinced Malaysia and me to help them with Dredge, and we took on Dust. We had a showdown with the Collector's goons again, and we took down Trent Salazar."

"That was just the first quarter," Malaysia declared. "At that point, Symone had seen more action than all of us combined in our first quarters of Elite work."

"I second that," Karl agreed.

"And despite still being a trainee, seeing all that action pushed the Company and Director Mallack to request you to assist *us* with training, finally breaking Malcolm's long-standing tradition of watching us train from the observation room. We've been getting stronger as the quarters have passed. Meanwhile, we had to face a water monster that was about to devour the city's water supply."

Alexia's presentation pixelated again and displayed Enchantra standing in the middle of the street as Starburst, K.C., Blitz, Ammo, and the Eagle raced down a major skyscraper-lined corridor, being chased by a massive water wave twelve stories high in the shape of a dragon.

"Akan, how did we stop his ass?" Malaysia inquired.

"Remember, Alexia encased his ass in a box, and then Karl ripped power lines down and shocked the Frimas out him!" Duncan answered just as the water dragon slammed into Enchantra's crystal wall and the Mammoth pulled lines out of the ground, dragged them across the street, and slapped the dragon with the live wires. "Dude, that battle was so boss, we had to get him to chase us for miles before he finally felt like he had the upper hand, then *THUNK!* He was trapped."

"Too much fun!" Symone lifted her hands and cheered. "Hey, Malcolm, who won that race to Alexia's finish line?"

"Man, that's only because my bike's engine started taking on water and stalled for like half a second," Malcolm rolled his eyes.

Alexia continued. "Then there was the Brimstone Gang. They were like, what, twenty-five deep, fully cloaked, and knew how to manipulate fire unlike anything we'd ever seen."

"Oh, right, yeah, that was toward the end of Quarter 3," Daisy recalled, "it took us like two weeks to finally track them down and stop them before they burned out the lower quadrant of the Underbelly."

Alexia's presentation pixelated again, displaying the team in an open, dark, dusty brick lair facing twenty-five fire-wielding combatants. "Oh yeah, I remember that!" Duncan shouted. "Daisy, you did this sick move when you ran on the walls and dragged their fire with you, then ran up the ceiling and then crashed the ground, lighting all their asses up. Then Malaysia launched this sonic boom rocket thing that shook the ground from under them and covered them with so much dirt and sand that they literally didn't have any air to light themselves with."

"Malcolm then hardened the sand, and Alexia carted them all into UPD's holding cells," Symone continued.

"Right. Stopping them saved a bunch of people. And speaking of saving, remember the forest mishap?" Alexia reminded them.

"Yes!" Malcolm jumped. "Dude, those trees would not stop growing and multiplying. What was it, somebody was learning spells, and he got two of them crossed up and didn't know how to reverse them?"

The presentation pixelated again. This time, Enchantra was suspended in the air, chanting feverishly to create a massive shield as trees rose from the turf. "Yes, the trees rose so damn tall, they bucked up against the city's cloak!" Symone said. "The splinters were so big, they were crashing into buildings in Meridian. Alexia had to shield half the district, how the Frimas did you do that?! Duncan and Malaysia were making target practice out of the falling pieces. Daisy was moving people out of the way before they ended up crunched. Karl tried to knock the trees down, but they kept growing and multiplying like a damn hydra. Malcolm and I combined powers and turned the entire forest into dust."

Symone smiled as she recalled her time with the Elite. She could still feel the butterflies in her stomach from the first time she met Malcolm. She flashed back to her climb up Elite Mountain to get him to fight her. She couldn't forget when she lay on top of him after saving him from Mygalo's deathblow. Her heart still stung from the Affinity Theory cover-up, but since then, she had moved on, so much so, that when Malaysia finally revealed to her about a quarter after they rescued Duncan that she knew about and was partly to blame for the cover-up, it barely fazed her. Symone was content, and finally glad that she had reached this point in her career.

Alexia's eyes stopped glowing green, and Switch pixelated back to reality. Alexia said, "It's been a Frim of a ride, Symone. The Elite wouldn't be the Elite without you."

Symone shrugged her shoulders and replied, "I know." She chuckled, "But, honestly, I didn't really do anything."

The team all responded, "Whatever!"

Malaysia continued, "Come on, Symone. We all know that the Elite Unit would not be the Elite Unit if Symone Watson wasn't on it. You have made this team the most complete it has ever been. You pulled Malcolm, of all people, out of his shell. And you've made all of us better in ways we can't even begin to count. Face it, you've made a difference, and we'll never forget it. I think it was Malcolm who said this team, the Company, and the city is better..."

"...because you are a part of it," Malcolm finished.

"Aww, guys, stop it!" Symone grabbed her right arm with her left hand.

"Alright, Symone, stand up," Malcolm gently clutched Symone's left arm and pulled her to stand next to him and her cake. "So, I can finally say that after three quarters, several battles, immense training, and all the ups and downs that came with it, you, Symone Watson, have completed the Company's Mentorship Program. You are *officially* a Defender of the Uri City Division of the Company."

The team hollered with glee. Alexia jumped from her seat and gave Symone a big hug, nearly barreling them into the cake.

Malcolm silenced them one more time, "Last thing, last thing, and then I'm finished. Symone, you are free to join any team of the Company, to become a UC, or whatever you wish to do. Still, I will be recommending to the director that you stay on board with us, not that I really have a say in the matter, because this team isn't going to just let you go without a fight."

"Damn right!" Daisy yelled. "You're stuck with us!"

Symone's heart was overwhelmed. She flashed back to her prizefighting days when her crew and she would celebrate victories and talk about sticking together forever. It felt surreal, that she found her a new family again.

"Okay, gang, let's party!" Alexia exclaimed.

"Frimas yeah!" Duncan agreed.

The Elite marched their way to the dance floor and left everything on it, gyrating, twerking, two-stepping, grinding, and pop-locking like tomorrow wasn't promised. The bystanders joined in with them, and they all got lost in the thrill of the night for what felt like cycles. They forgot about all the issues of the day, being the Elite defenders, and let loose on the dance floor.

Sometime later, Duncan made his way over to the bar. He recognized the bartender and admired her beauty. Slightly slurred, he said, "Hey, you're the woman who brought the cake to us, right?"

The woman walked over and stood in front of him, eyes locked on him tightly. "Yes, that's me. What can I get you?"

Duncan tilted and shook his head, "Oh, no, I can't do another drink, I might pass out right here on your floor."

She leaned forward, smiled, and propped her head up with her right hand, "Oh, I'm sure we could find a way to pick you up. Sure I can't make you anything?"

"I'm sure. I'm trying to keep up with my crew anyway."

"You talking about the people you're with?  They seem like a great bunch of people."

"Yeah, that's my family.  Wouldn't be here without them."

She cracked a wry smile and answered, "I can imagine." She locked eyes on Malcolm as she noticed him dancing with Symone.  "The tall, slender fella with the girl you all celebrated tonight, what's his deal?  Are they together?"

"Oh, yeah, they're going strong.  Why? You checking for him?"

She laughed, "Who, me?  No, no, not if he has a girlfriend. I just assumed you did, so I didn't bother asking."

Duncan was taken aback and tried to fix his blurry eyes. He noticed her piercing brown eyes, her ponytail reaching the middle of her back, and her black, one-shoulder strap, sleeveless crop top conforming to her slender body.  He wanted to look over the bar to see how her ass looked but didn't want to seem too thirsty or pompous.  He did not want to fuck up this opportunity that stood before him.  He thought, *Okay, Duncan, get it together, she is a hottie!*

"No, no, I don't, I don't have a girlfriend."

She smiled.  "Well, I get off in about three cycles.  If you can stay up that long, wanna take me somewhere?"

"Girl, I'll take you wherever you want to go.  What's your name?"

"Nova.  What's yours?"

"Duncan," he replied and stuck his hand out.

Nova shook his hand and said, "Let me get you a drink, on me."

She slowly twisted around, and Duncan got a full display of the perfectly shaped bubble that was Nova's ass.  He believed he hit the jackpot.

Nova, meanwhile, thought, *Got 'em.  Dumbass.*

Malaysia was seated back at the team's table.  She locked onto Malcolm and Symone dancing in each other's arms and thought, *I am so happy for them two.  I can only imagine how difficult it has been for them the past few quarters.  Now they can finally be together without that whole mentor/mentee bullshit affecting them so much, well, affecting Malcolm so much.*  She suddenly felt a buzz from her arm, and her stripe read, "Call from DISASTER."  She sighed.

"Hi," she answered playfully.

A man's sultry, deep voice on the other side of the call responded, "Hi."

"What do you want?"

"If you have to ask, then you'll never know."

"Maybe I just want to hear you say it," Malaysia calmly replied as her body recalled how great riding his saddle felt.

"Fine, ask me the question again."

"What do you want?"

A few seconds of silence, then, "You."

Malaysia breathed deeply and shivered delightfully. "When?"

"A cycle ago," he admitted.

"Be there in twenty."

"See you soon."

Malaysia got up, her body starving for attention and an intense, explosive release.  She started walking toward the elevator, hoping to not bring attention to herself.  Daisy noticed her, and Malaysia was cut off by a red and brown blur.  "Hey, where are you going?"

Without skipping a beat, Malaysia replied, "Girl, my man's calling.  Gotta take care of my big baby.  He can't be without me for long."

"Right, right. Well, have a good night! We'll see you tomorrow during the debrief," Daisy gave Malaysia a hug.

"See you tomorrow, Daisy." Malaysia hit the down arrow, and the elevator immediately opened. She walked in, then closed the door. *This is terrible, just terrible. I can't keep doing this. But damn, he just feels so damn good inside me. This will be the last time, I promise.*

Malcolm and Symone pranced off the dance floor and found a quiet corner of the rooftop. Symone bellowed, "Whoo, my Akan, this was so much fun! I'm so thankful you guys did this for me."

Malcolm was a bowl of emotions. The liquor in his system didn't help, but he managed to keep it together. His mind ruminated from the beginning of their involvement together to now. He remembered how intoxicating their beginning was, how one secret almost tore them apart, and how amazing things had been since. He marveled at how Symone was now an inseparable part of his world and was surprised that letting her in didn't backfire on him.

They stopped at the edge of the rooftop. He stared into Symone's deep brown eyes and noticed one of the locs of her hair draped in front of her. He gently slid his fingers down the loc and moved it to the left side of her face. Symone said softly, "What?"

Malcolm then gently clasped Symone's left arm with his left hand so that their wrists lined up. Symone's eyes glowed as she stared at Malcolm, gazing at his physique poking through his black t-shirt and white jeans. His stripe turned green, and Symone's stripe responded in kind. Symone looked down, then looked at him and said, "What's going on?"

Malcolm said, "Shhh." A few seconds later, their stripes turned blue, and Malcolm let Symone's arm go.

She looked at her stripe, and words scrolled across it saying, "Symone Watson, codename Starburst. Status: Defender, Elite Unit. Congratulations! – Company HQ."

She looked at Malcolm, and Malcolm smiled. He leaned in and kissed Symone passionately and deeply. They locked lips for a few seconds as he pulled her into him and rubbed on the small of her back while she wrapped her arms behind his neck. He then pulled away and said, "Symone, I am at a loss for words for how happy I am that you stayed. With the Company. And with me. This doesn't fully capture how I feel about you, but I hoped you would appreciate this as a symbol of my love."

Malcolm pulled out of his pocket a gold necklace with a crimson, 9-pointed star pendant with the tips dipped in gold. He held it in front of Symone's face, and her eyes lit up and her rosy-red lips made a perfect O. She declared, "Malcolm, you didn't have to get me this, it's beautiful! Will you...?"

"Of course!" Malcolm chuckled. Symone turned around and pulled her locks forward, and Malcolm took advantage of the opportunity to gaze at Symone, marveling at how her skirt conformed to her frame. He lifted his arms over her shoulders and draped the necklace atop her chest, then fixed the clasp and lay it on her neck. Symone lifted the star off her chest and stared at it, then turned around and lay it across her chest again.

"What do you think?" she asked.

"Absolutely stunning," Malcolm smiled.

"Who, the pendant, or me?" Symone raised an eyebrow.

Malcolm pulled Symone into him again and kissed her once more. He then said, "Symone, I never thought I'd say these words to anyone, but I care about you so deeply. You are literally the best thing that's ever happened to me, powers be damned. I wouldn't be the man I am today if not for you. I truly admire you and consider myself the luckiest man alive because you are by my side. I love you, and I thank you for staying."

"Aww, Malcolm, I love you and thank you for riding the elevator down to fight me," Symone reminded Malcolm of their first spar after fighting Trent Salazar.

They hugged each other like they didn't want to let each other go. Malcolm's sense of peace resonated deeply in his soul, a satisfaction he bathed in for quarters now.

Symone, though, felt this overwhelming sense of panic within hers. She recalled Daisy saying, "You're stuck with us," cycles prior. She also remembered Malcolm saying, "I will be recommending to the director that you stay on board with us," and Malaysia and Malcolm saying, "better because you are a part of it." Now that Malcolm said, "luckiest man alive because you are by my side," Symone's emotional threshold had been reached. She felt this incredible urge to blast off into the night sky and run away, believing that Malcolm and the Company were tethering her to permanence, and she was suddenly unclear whether commitment was something she could commit to.

Eyes wide open, she stared at the twin moons shining in the midnight sky.

*Shit.*

# 3

# Consequences

The following rising, Daisy, Karl, and Alexia were sitting in the brightly lit conference room waiting for Mallack and the rest of the team to arrive for the debrief. The UNN news anchors on the holoscreen provided white noise as they chatted about nothing. Soon, a relaxed, glowing, deeply satiated Malaysia entered the conference room, sat in her usual seat, and bantered with the others. A minute later, Malcolm and Symone walked through the door.

"There she is," Alexia announced, "the newest *Defender* of the Company!" Everyone cheered for Symone once again as she pranced and twirled around, sparks of her energy swirling around her body.

"Thank you, thank you, it's a good feeling," Symone responded. She walked with Malcolm behind the table, and they took their usual seats in the middle.

"So, how's everyone today?" Malcolm asked.

"No complaints, brother," Karl answered. "Just been sitting here waiting."

"Right. What's the game plan for today?" Malaysia asked.

Malcolm crossed his arms and leaned back, "Well, I don't have any plans. Symone, you got anything for us today?"

Symone put her hands on the table, "Well, after the debrief, we have a team sparring session we have to do, and that's about it."

"Ugh, that's today?" Alexia shrugged. "Shit, I forgot all about that."

"You must have had plans today or something," Malaysia looked at Alexia.

"No, I just wanted to get a good seat for today's zintol match in Intelligence," Alexia told the team.

"Oh yeah! That's right, the UZL playoffs, that is today," Malcolm remembered. "It's who, Highgarden and Leicester's teams to set the championship match against the Underbelly?"

"Yes!" Alexia answered. "And the Underbelly needs an opponent they can beat if they're going to make it out of the Uri City division and play for the Uretha crown."

"Well, you better hope Highgarden finds a way to beat Leicester," Karl replied. "Leicester is the seven-time city league champs. They don't know how to lose."

"Got that right," Malcolm agreed. "As long as they have their speedster who can catch that damn ball and throw it in the rings faster than anyone else in the city, no one really stands a chance."

"Ugh, Malcolm, don't say that!" Alexia said. "I really want the Underbelly to represent this year."

"Speaking of representing, look, guys," Daisy pointed at the holoscreen, "we're on the news again."

The Elite turned their attention to the holoscreen. Daisy commanded the screen to turn the volume up. A woman wearing a red dress talked next to a screen playing a video of the Uri Mega Mall as it collapsed. "...the tragedy at the Mega Mall yesterday as reports allege that a small child unleashed a storm of nuclear lava that leveled half of the mall, killing and injuring hundreds and causing millions in damages."

"Aww, poor kid," Symone sighed, recalling the times she nearly burned down her family home during her early years of being powered. "He didn't know any better."

"Captain Banks was in charge of the rescue efforts and had this to say," the screen cut to Captain Banks standing behind the dismantled entrance of the mall.

He shook his head as he reported, "It appears that the kid used his powers for the first time, an unavoidable accident no one could have prepared for."

"Joining me now are Senators Dariuz and Wimberly. Senator Dariuz, the Senate will vote in three weeks on whether to put Proposition 1 – allowing the powered to run for offices – on the ballot in the general election. You believe that this tragic accident is a warning for the city regarding the Proposition. Can you tell us why?"

Alexia, having heard Senator Dariuz's anti-powered rhetoric more times than she could stomach, rolled her eyes and crossed her arms. "Oh, shit, here he goes."

Dariuz, a bald, pruny, slender man, sat on the left side of the holoscreen. He was a ruthless, unpowered politician who staunchly opposed any progressive measure in favor of the powered population. As the broadcast centered to him, he stated emphatically, "What happened at the Uri Mega Mall is precisely the reason why we cannot afford to allow the powered to hold office in our city. What if a powered official gets angry about a decision that doesn't go his way, and he loses control and unleashes Frimas on all of us? What if, to show his brute strength and incite fear, he powers up and shows his chest within the chambers? It's the mall today, but it can very easily be Midtown, your neighborhoods, all of Uri City, that goes up in flames because some idiot gets angry and has an uncontrollable temper tantrum..."

Senator Wimberly quickly interjected, "Senator Dariuz, how dare you try to use what happened at the mall to bolster your platform!" The broadcast switched to Wimberly, a dark-skinned, gray-dreadlocked woman who, despite being unpowered herself, fought alongside Chancellor Croft in his effort to advance progress for the powered in Uri City. "We know that these things happen all the time. It's what happens when over 70% of your population are powered, and that number continues to rise. The powered are not dangerous people. Individuals make the choice to become dangerous..."

"Exactly!" Alexia yelled, happy to see Wimberly not pull her punches.

"...and use their powers against the city. Now, what happened at the mall is a tragedy, no question about it. But that's not an excuse to exclude the powered from seeking to represent or be represented by those who are powered like them. Come off your high horse and stop trying to score political points. There's no warning here. When the Senate votes in three weeks, we *will* vote to let the people decide what they want to do."

"See, it's that kind of naivety that keeps the city in danger!" Dariuz yelled. "We cannot let the powered back in power. It will spell the end of Uri City as we know it."

The senators went back and forth for another three minutes while the anchor woman tried to bring order to their chaos. Daisy turned the holoscreen back down.

Alexia was not amused. "What an asshole! Using a kid to prove his point, which he doesn't have one."

"You sure he doesn't?" Daisy agreed with Dariuz, who was her political hero.

"Oh boy, here we go," Karl rolled his eyes, having seen the *Alexia vs. Daisy* movie before.

"What?" Daisy turned and looked at Karl, then back at Alexia. "He's not wrong. Can you imagine if someone powered got mad and went ham on everybody in the room just because he didn't get his way?"

"Shit, Daisy, here you go again," Alexia chomped down hard. "That's *fear* talking, and makes it seem like all of us who are powered should never be trusted to do a job we're elected to do."

"No," Daisy rebutted, "I'm not saying that. I'm saying that our elected officials should not have powers that they could use against us. We know what happened over a century ago."

Malaysia sighed, "Yes, Daisy, we all remember what happened. You only remind us every single time we have this conversation. Shit, you sound just like Dariuz."

"I only remind you because it's true. It took half the city's powered people to finally take down Chancellor Holland because of his bullshit. You all know how many of us had to die just to get him out of office, let alone locked up. Frimas, he's the reason the Asylum exists in the first place."

Malcolm chimed in, "Okay, that's a stretch. The Asylum wasn't built for him, that's just propaganda. Still, you're not wrong, it took a whole damn army to fight him off. But it's not fair for us to keep paying for his mistakes because officials continue shackling us all to the past."

Symone spoke up. "Malcolm's right. It's not fair that we don't get to choose from the best people, powered or not, to represent us. If someone who has powers wants to run for office, we should be able to see whether he or she measures up and choose for ourselves if we want them to represent us in Midtown."

Just then, Duncan stumbled in the conference room, ridiculously hung over from the night before. He hobbled toward his seat while nursing his head with his right hand. "What's up guys," he grimaced.

"Shit, Duncan, you look like Frimas," Karl noticed. "You wilded out, alright."

Duncan plopped in his seat as he narrated, "Man, I don't know what happened last night. I remember drinking and dancing at the club with y'all. After y'all left, I stayed and waited for Nova to get off..."

"Ooh," Alexia chimed in, "Duncan scored last night?!" She rolled her voluptuous body around in her chair.

"Well, I think I did, but I honestly don't remember whether we hooked up or not. We got to my crib, had a couple more drinks, and then my mind is a complete blank. I woke up with the biggest headache I've ever had. I didn't think I had that much to drink. Nova was gone, and I don't have any way to reach her, like a dummy."

"Just hit it and quit it, huh?" Symone laughed.

"It wasn't like that. At least, I don't think it was like that. I don't know, I don't want to think about it. Getting back inside Switch is a near-impossibility, so I probably won't see her again anytime soon," Duncan lamented.

"Well," Alexia offered as she waved her hand, "you could camp outside of Switch until she gets to work, you know, if you're the stalker type."

He shook his head, then hissed in pain. "No, no, not going to do that. I saw the bouncers there, and they looked like they would strip me for parts. Anyway, did I miss something, sounded like you guys were in a heated debate."

"Oh," Malaysia crossed her arms and recapped, "just talking about the vote in three weeks and how foolish Dariuz is."

"Oh, that bullshit?" Duncan chuckled. "Who cares? They're going to do what they want to do with us anyway."

"Is that how you really feel?"

"I'm not alone. Karl feels that way, too," he pointed at Karl.

Karl perked up and cut his eyes. "I never said, 'I feel like they're going to do what they want to do.' I just know that the decisions they make are not going to affect me, so I don't really have a dog in the fight."

"You can't be serious, Karl. I never thought you felt that way," Alexia interjected.

Karl shrugged his bulging shoulders. "Well, it's the truth. Listen, we work for the city, right? So as long as we work for them, they will make decisions that are in their best interests and keep me paid and taken care of. Do I think the powered should get to sit in office? I don't really care one way or the other, as long as their decisions don't fuck with my money."

"That's actually a very good point," Symone reacted.

Daisy grew more annoyed with her team's opposing and indifferent views. "You guys don't get it. We can never know a person's motives, and a good person could turn evil on a dime and use every resource he has to force his will upon us. And that can affect decisions on a city-wide scale. We should limit a person's ability to have absolute power as much as we can."

"So what?" Malaysia countered. "We just let them continue to take the choice away altogether? That's not fair! How is Symone always saying it? 'Don't take my choice away from me.'"

"Damn right," Symone agreed as she reached over the table to hi-five Malaysia.

Director Mallack walked in the room as Malaysia slapped Symone's hand and finished her thought. "Let *me* decide if I think an *individual* should hold that office, not some bogus rule written generations ago that doesn't reflect how we think or feel today."

Mallack, wearing a white dress and a red pearl necklace, said, "Ah, so you all saw the news, I assume. Yeah, yesterday's event did not help Chancellor Croft with his agenda. Clearly you all have different views on his push for the rights of the powered to be restored. And while you are entitled to your opinions, regardless of whose side you fall on, always remember, when you're on the battlefield, you will put those differences aside and fight for *all* of Uri City. We fight for everyone and will continue to stay neutral to the cause. Is that understood?"

Everyone nodded their heads. Mallack was not convinced. "Understood?"

"Yes, Director," everyone declared in unison.

She sat down in her usual chair in front of the team. "Alright, so, take me through it."

Everybody looked at Malcolm. Malcolm then looked at Symone and said, "You know what? Symone, why don't you start us off."

Symone shook her head, "No, no, by all means. Just because I'm a defender now doesn't mean I have to take on additional responsibilities. You got it."

The team laughed along with Malcolm, "Okay. Um, Intelligence gave us the call after Super Team III couldn't contain the energy in the mall. We assembled and arrived about twenty minutes after receiving the call."

"We landed in the parking lot," Malaysia tagged in. "Many of the survivors were out already. We met Laila, Blink from Super Team III, and after a brief assessment, Daisy, Karl, and Duncan were assigned to continue with the search of survivors while Alexia, Symone, Malcolm, and I were assigned to contain the energy and detain the threat."

Daisy said, "I went in and did a quick analysis of the building. I realized our cloaks would be severely damaged by the radiation from the energy and ran back to the team to let them know. Karl, Duncan, and I then searched the building for any survivors still remaining."

Alexia continued. "Laila teleported us to the energy source, and we each tried to cut through the lava and couldn't find the kid, who we didn't know was a kid at the time. The ground then shifted, and Malcolm scrambled and instructed me to build a bubble to contain the energy and to build a bridge for them to stand on."

"Malcolm and I used my star power to create an ice lance to cut through the energy and create a shaft that finally revealed the kid," Symone reported.

Malaysia continued. "Once I had the shot, I tranquilized the kid. Alexia dropped the bridge and grabbed me."

"I fell in the hole and grabbed the kid. Symone then grabbed us and blasted us out of the hole before the energy melted the ice and swallowed us whole," Malcolm said. "We transferred the kid to Captain Banks and the UPD, and we cleared them to take over the scene."

Mallack nodded. "Great job, Elite. Your assessment matches the account from Intelligence. I have just a few items here, and then I'll let you go.

"First, congratulations again to you, Symone, for completing your mentorship and Elite training. It feels good to see your title changed from Trainee to Defender on the roster."

Everyone cheered and banged on the table as Symone replied, "Thank you, Director!"

"Second, as you all know, I am preparing to transfer to Brilliance in the next couple weeks. I'm sure I'll be saying this again to you all multiple times before I finally depart, but it has been my greatest honor to lead you. I have watched you all grow and mature over the years, and I am so proud of you. As much as I have taught you, I have also learned so, so much from you as well," she nodded at Malcolm.

"Brilliance is going to be in good hands with you at the helm, Director," Malcolm responded.

"So, have they decided who will take over here?" Daisy asked.

"No, HQ has not made a decision, as far as I can tell. What I do know is that Malcolm is a heavy favorite to take over in the interim until they make their final call, and there's no better candidate for the job than him."

Everyone cheered again, except Daisy, who silently grimaced over not being considered worthy of being director by her team. Alexia could sense Daisy's angst but said nothing.

Malcolm slowly fanned his hands to try to silence his teammates. "Hey, now, nothing is set in stone. We don't know whether they'll give me the bump or keep me on the Elite. Either way, know that you're leaving us in good hands, and we've got some big shoes to fill."

Mallack smiled with mixed emotions swirling in her heart. "Thank you, Malcolm. Alright, one last item. HQ has been in talks with me over the last few weeks. They decided, and I agreed, to add an eighth member to the Elite Unit."

The Elite's jaws dropped. "What?" Duncan asked. "We're getting another teammate?"

"Really?" Alexia's eyes flashed green with excitement. "Did they say why?"

Mallack shook her head, "Not entirely. They didn't come right out and say it explicitly, but I inferred it's because they believe Malcolm's departure will leave a hole in the Elite that will need to be filled. So, the Company preemptively struck and chose her."

She summoned the holoscreen to pull up a dossier of the team's newest recruit. The Elite studied the dossier intently. An avatar of a tall, slender woman with hazel eyes and long black hair bundled into a ponytail, appeared in the middle of the screen. She was covered in a light-blue and silver nanotech uniform. Duncan's natural inclination to perk up was hit with a wave of headache-induced resistance.

Karl immediately recognized her and stammered, "For real? That's who the Company chose?"

"You know her?" Malaysia turned and faced Karl.

"Frimas yeah!" He pointed at the screen, "That's Kaminari!"

Alexia looked at Karl, puzzled. "Karl, I haven't seen you this excited in ages."

Karl looked at everyone and wondered why they weren't as hyped as he was. "Guys, that's Kaminari! You don't know who she is?"

Malcolm nodded his head, "I do, but apparently not like you do."

"I can't believe it," Karl buried his forehead in his massive palms, "you guys obviously don't read the scouting reports. Daisy, I'm surprised you're not as hype as I am."

Daisy shrugged her shoulders. "I don't understand. Who is she to you?"

Karl huffed, "She's not anyone *to me*. But guys, she's Kaminari, one of the most dangerous lightning-wielding defenders in the city. Please tell me you have the tape, Director."

Mallack was amused by Karl's reaction to her revelation and eagerly summoned the holoscreen to display a highlight reel of Kaminari's field experience. Clip after clip showed Kaminari summoning lighting from her body and unleashing it onto her opponents, blasting others' powers and falling debris. She boosted herself in the air, overloaded an electrical grid and blacked out a city block, and launched several opponents in the air all at once. The team immediately understood Karl's excitement as they marveled at her prowess and relished the opportunity to work alongside her.

"Damn," Symone's eyes glowed as she was slightly aroused by Kaminari's dominance. "She's a force of nature."

"You got that right," Malaysia agreed. "Where has the Company been hiding her?"

"Seriously? Guys, she's on Super Team VI!" Karl educated his teammates.

Mallack relayed, "Joy Olivier, codenamed Kaminari, has been the leader of Super Team VI for the past three years. Most of VI's work has been taking down crime bosses and maintaining stability in the Underbelly and Leicester districts."

"Right!" Malaysia finally remembered how she knew her. "VI needed us to take over for them with Brimstone last year. That was her crew that dealt with that Flower Power situation in Leicester."

"Yes," Mallack declared. "She single-handedly blew their base of operations apart and got her entire team out alive. She is one of the best assets the Company employs, and she is going to be incredibly difficult to replace on VI's team. But she is one of the fiercest warriors and greatest people you'll ever meet."

"Well, Frimas, who will train her? Seems like she already has the goods to be on this team. She's going to make us unstoppable!" Malaysia pondered.

Malcolm immediately shook his head, "No, no, no, no, no. Please don't make me train someone again. I'm all trained out."

Daisy perked up, hoping this might be her chance to prove herself.

"Oh, no, no, Malcolm, the Company decided that Joy will be trained by Malaysia."

Everyone looked at Malaysia. Malaysia looked stunned. "Me? Me, why me?"

"Why not? You've been with the Company long enough, been an Elite long enough. It's only right that you get to mentor somebody. Congratulations!"

"I don't know if I should say thank you or run," Malaysia retorted.

Daisy shrank in her seat. *Dammit, what do I have to do to get noticed around here?!*

Malcolm's mind started tinkering. *I see what the Company's doing. If they are indeed going to move me up, Malaysia's going to take over as the leader of the Elite. That's so boss!*

"Okay, Elite, that's all I have. Anyone have anything for me?"

"When is Kaminari going to get here?" Daisy asked, trying not to sound snippy.

"Her first day will be tomorrow. She's spending today saying goodbye to VI."

"Copy that," Daisy responded.

"Alright, Elite, dismissed." Mallack rose from her seat as the team all rose from theirs. She left the room.

The team began digesting the news they received. "Wow," Duncan started. "So much change is happening. I picked the wrong night to go all out."

"Yeah, you did," Daisy agreed. Jealousy and resentment churned in her chest, but she tried her best to suppress the feeling of being overlooked again. "Wow, so Malcolm, you're about to be our boss. How are you feeling?"

Malcolm shrugged his shoulders as he crossed his arms, "Um, I haven't really processed it yet. It's weird. I've always wanted to be a director, but now that the time is nearing, I don't know, it just feels weird."

Malaysia walked over and patted his shoulder. "Well, you better get ready, because in a couple weeks, we're going to start calling you 'Director Bennett,' and you're going to have to figure out what to do with all that power you possess."

Malcolm laughed. "Don't be surprised if I decide to go on missions with you guys just to get a fight or twelve out of my system."

Symone chuckled, "If you get time. Do you know how many phone calls you're gonna have to deal with every day?"

"Not to mention having to take the heat for our all bullshit," Alexia smiled. Everybody laughed.

"Aww Frimas naw, I didn't even think about that. Maybe I shouldn't take this job," Malcolm joked.

Daisy clasped her hands, a shock to her own system to celebrate her friend's victory. "Whatever, you're going to take it, and you're going to nail it. Uri City is in good hands with you at the helm. Gonna be the easiest transition in the history of transfers of power."

Malcolm grinned, "Thanks, Daisy. Well, guys, let's get down to the training room and get this exercise over with. The game starts soon, and I don't want to miss it."

Alexia grinned. "Yes, yes, yes! Let's go!" She bolted for the door. Everyone followed suit except for Malcolm and Symone, who stayed in the room.

Malcolm sensed a slight change in Symone's energy flow. He gently clasped her arm and asked, "Hey, are you okay?"

Symone's uneasiness slowly churned in her gut. She answered, "Yeah, I'm good. Just finally hitting me that you're about to be my boss."

"What's on your mind?" he probed.

"It's just, we spent all this time worrying about *you and me* while you were mentoring me. And though that wasn't a problem, it still felt weird. Now we're going to have to navigate you being my boss and my boyfriend. HQ isn't going to have a problem with that?"

Malcolm tugged Symone's arms and replied, "Not at all. I've already alerted HR and kept them up to speed about our relationship. Mallack sent it up to HQ, and she assured me that we're good. We have nothing to worry about." He hugged her and kissed her forehead.

"Are you sure? I don't want to screw things up for you," Symone inquired.

He pulled her back and said, "100%. 'You and me' is a non-factor in the decision the Company makes. And Frimas, even if they pass me up for somebody else, I'll still be right here fighting alongside *the* greatest Defender I've ever known. It's a win-win for me either way."

Symone smiled, raised her right eyebrow, and said, "The *greatest*, you say?"

"Well, I mean, after me, of course," Malcolm bantered.

Symone pranced toward the door, Malcolm's ego boost having lifted her spirit. "Oh, well, I guess we're about to find out.  Let's go, so I can pop that bubble over your head and remind you who you're dealing with."

"Yes, ma'am," Malcolm followed her out of the conference room.

## 4

# Civil War

The Elite reassembled in the dark grey training room, everyone wearing their nanotech training uniforms, all colored gray, visors off. The team huddled in a circle and stared at Symone as Alexia asked, "Okay, Symone, what are we doing?"

Symone stepped in the middle of the circle and gleefully informed the team, "Alright, today is the last day of training with our enhancements before we take them into the field. So, we're completely unlocked."

Karl pounded his right fist into his left palm. "Alright, so y'all are unleashing the pain today!"

"Aww, Karl," Daisy patted his back, "don't worry, you'll get enhanced at some point, too."

"It's no biggie," Karl confidently assured them, "just means that I'm already at my best." He flexed his pecs and biceps as he squinted his eyes.

"Not true," Symone patted his back, "we're going to figure something out for you. Anyway, we're going to be split into two teams chosen by AI. The objective is to disable the other team's cloaks. They will be set at 25% power. The team whose cloaks are disabled first loses. Easy peasy."

"Seems simple enough," Malcolm declared as he folded his arms. Everyone else nodded.

Symone did a little jig. "I thought we'd mix things up a bit, so I programmed the scenario to place us somewhere exotic."

"Ooh, I like where this is going," Daisy's eyes widened.

"Everybody ready?" Symone asked.

"Let's do this," Alexia quickly reacted.

Symone looked up. "AI, load Training 5.7."

The training room began to morph according to Symone's specifications. The drab, cold, steel box transformed into a lush oasis, a vast shoreline on a sunny day, with vibrant, green vegetation, tall palm trees, and crystal-clear water washing the sand underneath their feet.

Malaysia's mouth popped open, and she marveled at the vast color array that played with her eyes. "Okay, so can we plan a vacation to Brilliance soon? Because this is amazing!"

"Less aww-ing and more fighting, come on, the game starts in half a cycle," Alexia rushed them.

"Right. AI, choose the teams," Symone ordered.

Their uniforms glowed white, then flickered between red and blue. Malcolm's uniform stopped on blue, Malaysia's on red, Karl's on red, Alexia's on blue, Daisy's on blue, Duncan's on red, and finally Symone's on red.

Alexia and Daisy cheered, "Yes!" Duncan sulked.

Malcolm smiled and offered, "So, should we just quit now and declare my team the winner?"

"Fuck you, Malcolm! We're taking you down today," Malaysia declared.

AI announced, "Battle begins in three minutes." They split into their teams and marched through the sand about one hundred feet away from each other.

Alexia, Daisy, and Malcolm huddled, and Alexia immediately griped, "They have all the guns on this one. For real, guys, how are we going to win?"

Daisy looked at Malcolm, who answered, "They have all the offensive power, so that means we'll have to use both a defensive strategy and their own powers against them. Alexia, your telekinesis will be our greatest superpower. But don't forget that you can project things now, too. Throw things in their way, regardless of how they respond to it. Being thrown off by the tiniest bit may prove useful."

Malcolm noticed that Alexia was staring off to her side and a bit spacey. "Alexia, hey, you with us?"

Alexia snapped back, refocused, and nodded her head, "Okay, yes, projections, I got you."

"Good. Daisy, speed over strength. Rush, rush, rush! Remember what Symone taught you," Malcolm encouraged her.

"I can do this," Daisy encouraged herself and shuffled her feet.

Meanwhile, Symone hyped up her troop. "Just because we have all the firepower does not mean that they're just going to lie down and take it. We have to overwhelm them with everything we have. Duncan, don't forget that you can fly now. Use that to your advantage."

"Shit, today of all days, you're asking me to fly, too?" Duncan winced from his headache.

"Nut up!" Karl rallied. "No one has been able to beat Malcolm yet. I want today to be different."

"I second that," Malaysia chimed in. "He knows us too well. No matter what we throw at him, he's able to adapt and kick our asses."

"That's why we're going to fight smarter, not harder today," Symone instructed, relishing the thought of besting her former mentor. "Malaysia, perch yourself in the forest and strike as much as you can. Try not to engage hand-to-hand.

Remember to adjust your vision to find the weaknesses in their cloaks and strike smart."

"Right," Malaysia understood. "Karl, come with me and throw me into one of the trees."

"I got you," Karl flexed his arms.

"We got this, guys. Stay light, shine bright!" Symone declared.

The four stood in battle stance and faced their battle-ready opponents. AI made the sun pulsate to the countdown, "You have fifteen minutes to disable the other team. Good luck. 10, 9, 8, 7, 6, 5, 4, 3, 2, 1, fight!"

Daisy sprinted toward, then around Symone's team, kicking up a dust storm that no one could see through. The red team adjusted their visors to get a visual on Daisy. Just as Duncan made the right adjustment, Daisy pushed her fists into his stomach and launched him into the training room wall that shimmered upon impact. She then pummeled him with a series of successive strikes, his cloak shimmering in response to the damage. Duncan managed to grab one of her arms. His palms whirred as he powered the plasma cannons now embedded in them and instantly popped her arms with plasma blasts. The momentum dropped her to her knees. She zipped backward from Duncan, then charged toward him. Duncan's visor attempted to lock onto her, and he held his palms forward and blasted multiple shots at her. His shots missed her, but as she was about to punch him again, he launched himself in the air with the boosters now attached to his heels. Daisy bounced off the wall, slightly stunned. Duncan immediately slammed into Daisy's shoulders, locked her head with his thighs, and latched his legs onto her back. Daisy instinctively clawed at Duncan's legs, and Duncan leaned to his left, causing them to slam into the floor. He then used his boosters to slide away from her, spun himself around on the floor, then blasted Daisy twenty feet away with plasma shots. Daisy was fuming, pissed that he got the upper hand on her like that.

Symone launched into the air while Karl and Malaysia ran out of the dust storm and into the woods. Symone observed Malcolm and Alexia standing together in the same spot they were in before and Duncan and Daisy sparring each other. She decided to help Duncan and take Daisy down. Malcolm read Symone's mind and said, "Got her. Alexia, launch me toward Daisy."

"Here you go!" Alexia lifted her arms, and green mist swiftly clutched Malcolm. She then threw her arms forward, and Malcolm flew prostrate and pointed his palms toward his ally. Symone twisted her arms in the air, and a star grew above her head. Daisy was still stunned and trying to recover her bearings. Symone took the star and launched it at Daisy. Malcolm, though, caught the star and deflected it. Duncan had no idea it was coming his way. The star crashed into his cloak. Duncan flew across the sand and splashed into the knee-deep water. His cloak shimmered and dissipated, and his uniform turned gray.

"Shit! I'm out, Symone," Duncan yelled. Symone got upset and threw more stars at Daisy. Malcolm made it to Daisy just in time and began collecting Symone's star power above his head.

"Daisy, you alright?" Malcolm assessed.

"Yeah, I'm good, I'm good. Just dazed," Daisy shook her head again, trying to recalibrate.

Malcolm extended his hand, and Daisy clutched it to lift herself off the ground. Malcolm ordered, "Go to Alexia now.

Figure out where Karl and Malaysia went. Pretty sure they're in the woods, Malaysia needs a perch."

"Right, I'm on it." Daisy zoomed to Alexia.

"Went for the kill shot, I'm impressed, Symone!" Malcolm noted coyly. He effortlessly threw Symone's star power at the wall and awaited her next move.

Symone figured she wouldn't break his cloak shooting him head on. She turned and focused on Alexia and Daisy instead. Alexia saw Symone floating closer to them. Daisy said, "Okay, keep her distracted while I go look for Karl and Malaysia. I think I can pummel Karl if I can isolate him."

"Okay," Alexia confirmed. "Watch your cloak." Daisy sped away. Meanwhile, Symone began a star blast assault on Alexia. The stars bounced off Alexia's mind shield and crashed into the sand.

"Come out of there," Symone declared. Alexia brought her hands together and focused her mind. She opened her eyes, and they glowed green behind her visor. She raised her hands slowly, and multiple sand Alexias rose from the beach. Unfazed, she quickly created a star and pushed it into the ground, obliterating the Alexias. Having fallen for her trap, Alexia hovered her hands together. The sand around Symone rose like a tidal wave, and the wave smashed Symone into the ground. Alexia continued to hover and roll her hands, and the sand layered over Symone, burying her deep under the beach.

Malcolm, meanwhile, watched Daisy run into the woods and chased after her. Daisy searched the bushes, trees, and brush and couldn't find Karl or Malaysia. As she hurdled a fallen tree trunk, she was suddenly grabbed by Karl, and he tightly squeezed the air out of her lungs. Karl yelled, "Malaysia, now!"

Malaysia, fifty feet in the air, scanned for the weak point in Daisy's cloak. Once she found it near the center of her chest, she aimed her rifle and fired. Karl released Daisy once he heard the gun go off. Daisy's cloak was hit with an electromagnetic pulse disabler designed to overload cloaks for extended periods of time. The shock it delivered caused Daisy's cloak to shimmer then dissipate. Her blue uniform turned gray. "No! Damn it!" she said after she landed on the ground.

"We got you!" Karl yelled. He didn't see Malcolm behind him, who took a tree branch, hardened it, and swung hard at Karl's back. Karl stumbled forward and managed to stay on his feet. Malaysia locked onto Karl's position and began searching for Malcolm. Karl turned around and charged at Malcolm. Malcolm shifted his feet and waited for Karl to meet him.

"Karl, don't!" Malaysia yelled, knowing what Malcolm was about to do, but her warning was issued too late. Karl launched his right fist at Malcolm, and Malcolm dodged his right fist, grabbed his right arm, then launched his head into Karl's stomach. Karl doubled over, and Malcolm used the momentum to flip him over.

Malaysia steadied herself and aimed her rifle. She locked onto Malcolm, breathed, and fired. The disabler stopped just short of hitting Malcolm's back. Alexia stopped the disabler after coming from behind her shield and entering the woods. Malcolm turned around and said, "Put that on Karl."

Alexia obeyed and ordered the disabler to attach itself to Karl's arm. The disabler overloaded the cloak, and Karl's cloak shimmered then dissipated. "Aww man, you're kidding me," Karl lamented. "I was doing good, too." Karl's uniform turned gray.

Alexia placed a shield around Malcolm and her and said, "Okay, so it's Malaysia and Symone. What do we do?"

"We gotta get Malaysia off the board, which will leave Symone and us. If we can keep you on the board, we can take Symone easily. Where is Symone?"

"She's buried under sand. I'd say in about ten seconds she'll finally blast her way out of it."

"Okay," Malcolm hatched a plan. "Meet Symone in the sand. I'll get Malaysia to strike at me, you distract Symone long enough for me to figure out how to overload Malaysia."

"Alright. Dropping the shield now, see you on the beach!" Alexia blitzed away, and Malcolm ran forward away from the foliage. When the shield fell, Malaysia looked and saw no one. She looked at her stripe, and it read 9:19. She descended her perch and aggressively tracked Malcolm on the ground.

Symone finally burst from the sand pit. She scanned the area and saw Alexia charging forward toward her. Before she could ignite her hands, Alexia created green storm orbs and launched them from her hands. Symone created circular shields from her hands and blocked and deflected multiple orbs before Alexia floated ten feet from her. Symone created an energy beam and launched it toward Alexia. Alexia created a mind shield and deflected the star energy. She flew around Symone, and Symone followed her with the beam. As Symone kept shooting, Alexia quickly placed her palms in front of her and created a prism, then said, "Darkness," and shot her arms upward.

The prism enlarged and encapsulated Symone and her energy beam. Within the floating prism, Symone was trapped in complete darkness. The only thing she could see was her body. Symone flew upward and banged her head against the encasement. She shot several stars around to see how big the encasement was.

Malaysia finally stepped out of the greenery and saw Malcolm running backward toward the shoreline. Malaysia whipped out her pistol and zoomed her eyes in on Malcolm. She shot several rounds, and Malcolm froze each round in front of him. Malaysia kept firing as she crept closer to him, hoping to outsmart his power set and strike a weak point. She fired seventeen total before giving up and pressing on the handle to switch to an explosive round. Malcolm sensed her making the switch. He took his hand and raised the rounds upward. Malaysia fired the explosive. Malcolm took one of Malaysia's suspended bullets and hurled it toward her explosive, and upon impact, Malaysia's round exploded.

Malcolm used the distraction to launch the other sixteen bullets toward Malaysia. As he hurled them, he stretched them and melded them together. Malaysia didn't see the steel box hurdling toward her, and before she could zoom her eyes out to notice, Malaysia was swept into the steel box, and Malcolm sealed her shut.

"Hey, Alexia, get down here and overload her cloak with your energy!" Malcolm yelled.

Alexia saw Malcolm and looked for Malaysia and didn't see her. "Where is she?"

"In the box over there," Malcolm pointed. Alexia saw the box and flew over to it. She created a green energy storm in front of her and launched it into the box. The box lit up from the storm, and Malaysia had nowhere to go. Alexia's energy popped Malaysia's cloak repeatedly, and within seconds her cloak overloaded, shimmered, and dissipated.

Malcolm dismantled the box and revealed a defeated Malaysia in a grayed-out uniform. "One to go," he declared. "Seven minutes. Let's go, Alexia."

"You two are punks!" Malaysia yelled. Malcolm and Alexia grinned and ran toward the prism.

Symone intensified her heat and descended to the bottom of the prism. Her hair glowed white, and she unleashed a heat beam from her hands that flowed around the entire prism. She pushed the energy but made sure not to touch it, fearing that the intensity would break her own cloak.

Alexia hovered toward the prism, then looked at Malcolm and said, "What do we do, we're running out of time!"

"I have no idea, I guess drop the prism?" Malcolm reasoned.

"Okay," Alexia replied. Alexia stood about seven feet from the prism and placed her hands forward. Her eyes lit green, and she said, "Dispel."

The prism disintegrated, and Symone unleashed her star storm. It swallowed Alexia, and her cloak couldn't handle the load. It shimmered and dissipated as she fell to the ground, her now-grayed-out uniform and the sand breaking her fall.

"Damn it!" Malcolm yelled. "That was a good shot!"

"You and me, Malcolm." Symone blasted toward her boyfriend. Malcolm raised a wall of sand twenty feet high in front of him. Symone crashed into the wall. He then swirled the sand and rolled his hands in front of him to keep Symone trapped within the sand.

Symone charged herself and released a burst from her body that obliterated the sand. She then launched stars toward Malcolm. He captured them, pushed them together, then shaped them into a lasso. He threw the lasso at Symone, and she dodged it, landing in the sand. She ran toward Malcolm.

The rest of the team left and went into the Observation Room. Malaysia stood at the window while the others sat in the chairs near the holoscreen desk. "Less than five minutes, who do you think will win?" Malaysia pondered.

"Between those two?" Karl asked. "Please, they're going to fight for the next cycle, neither of their cloaks are going to break."

Alexia shot out of her chair. "I'm glad she had this one timed, because I don't want to miss a second of the zintol match."

Malcolm and Symone traded punches and kicks. Symone heated her palms and her feet, reasoning that as long as she didn't fire any shots at him, he couldn't use her powers against her. Malcolm morphed the dust under Symone's feet into quicksand, and Symone sank about two feet in. He then lifted some of the sand and morphed it into a lance. He thrusted his right hand forward, and the lance hurled toward Symone. Symone blasted out of the sand and hovered just enough for the lance to miss her. She then hurled herself toward him and delivered a series of haymakers at him. He lifted his arms to block her assault. He then grabbed her arms and head-butted her. She fell backward, and he thrusted his boot into her stomach. He tried it again, but she grabbed his foot and flipped him backward and quickly blasted a star into his back. He face-planted into the sandy shore. Symone thought, *This is my chance.*

She charged up and fired a steady stream of star power at Malcolm. Karl, Malaysia, and Duncan looked at each other as Karl said, "She might do it!" Symone then blasted fifty feet upward, and with one minute to go, built the biggest star she could in five seconds, and launched it at Malcolm. The shockwave the blast produced shook the room, dust from the sand rising past Symone.

*Finally! I did it!* Symone twirled in the air. Her eyes embered brightly, and sparks flew from her hands.

When the dust cleared, Symone looked down and saw a silhouette surrounded by a white energy spiral. Malcolm's uniform still shone blue, cloak still intact. Symone grimaced in disgust and defeat as the seconds counted down.

AI declared, "10, 9, 8, 7, 6, 5, 4, 3, 2, 1, time!"

"Aww man," Duncan said, "I thought she did it. Oh well, at least we didn't lose." He lay his head on the table and shut his eyes.

Symone landed on the ground next to Malcolm as their uniforms and cloaks powered down and melted off them. The sand, the trees, and the water all pixelated and disappeared, and the room returned to its cobalt gray hue.

"You good?" Malcolm asked sarcastically.

Symone rolled her eyes. "Sure, I'm good," she punched him in his shoulder. "I knew I had you, damn it!"

Malcolm chuckled. "Yeah, a trick I picked up from Alexia last quarter. Surprised I was able to pull it off."

"What trick?" Symone was curious.

"Last quarter, Alexia took someone's power and commanded it to spiral around her before finally unleashing it on her opponent. I went into the practice room and taught myself how to do it. So, I pool the energy around me so that it doesn't touch my cloak. It's my first time applying it in battle. What do you think?"

"Whatever," Symone rolled her eyes and sulked toward the exit, annoyed that once again, she was unable to defeat Malcolm in combat.

As they walked out of the training room, they saw the Analyst prancing from the elevator toward them. "Ah shit," Symone remembered, "I forgot today was Report Day."

The Analyst sped up. "No worries, Symone. I was watching the footage at my desk and figured I'd come down here to meet you. Are you ready?"

Symone shook off her annoyance and turned to face Malcolm, gently planting her hand on Malcolm's chest. "Save me a seat in Intelligence?"

"Right next to me, you got it," Malcolm replied.

Symone walked with the Analyst. As they walked toward the elevator, the Analyst asked Symone, "So, let's talk about the team's progress this week."

# 5
# Zintol

Alexia was the first to burst through the quarters entrance and blast toward Intelligence, leaving a trail of green mist dissipating behind her. Daisy and Karl laughed and fanned the mist from their faces as they followed after her. Duncan, Malaysia, and Malcolm left last. Malcolm noticed that Duncan was still nursing his head and patted his shoulder.

"Hey man," Malcolm inquired, "are you okay? You really do look like Frimas."

Duncan shook his head, "I'm telling you, man, I really don't know. My head is pounding." He held his right temple.

"You sure you want to watch with us? Maybe you should park it in the commons or your residence."

"Nah, nah, I'll be alright. I can lay my head down and watch the screen," Duncan replied.

Malaysia took a quick peek into Duncan's cybernetic wiring and noticed swelling near his temple where he held it. "Looks like you might have had a bit too much fun last night, Duncan. You've got a bruise right there."

"Really?" Duncan asked. "Maybe she liked it rough? Maybe *I* like it rough?"

"I guess. Maybe you should get medical to look at that, just check you out," Malaysia proposed.

Duncan shook his head again. "Naw, I'm good, I promise. Just need to get some real sleep tonight, no booze, a couple pain meds, and I'll be good as new."

Malcolm said, "Alright, but if you're acting the same way tomorrow, I'm gonna order you to get a full workup."

"Yes, *boss*," Duncan joked.

As they arrived at the entrance to Intelligence, Duncan walked in while Malaysia pulled Malcolm's arm and held him back. "You sure we don't want to get him checked?"

"Why?" Malcolm wondered. "You think something's really wrong with him?"

Malaysia folded her arms. "Well, no, but you and I both know he hasn't been the same since he got captured by the Collector last year."

Malcolm scratched his head. "Yeah, he didn't feel too good getting caught by Sonic. But I haven't seen a decline in his performance. His attitude, maybe. I just assumed seeing Psych was helping him modify his 'shoot first, ask questions later' way of life. He mentioned he wanted to adjust that the day of the Power Party."

Malaysia nodded in agreement. "True that. I don't know, I just got a bad feeling, that's all. I don't want him to get hurt or worse. Having that bad a lapse of memory can't be good for any of us, especially since we're the Elite."

"You're right," Malcolm nodded and tapped Malaysia's shoulder. "I'll push him to go to the Infirmary and get checked out after the game."

"Good deal. Alright, let's get inside," Malaysia answered.

She slid the door open. Intelligence was almost a packed house. Alexia had found a seat in the front row, and the rest of the team were scattered around the room. The holoscreen flashed replays of the zintol match's most recent activity. The announcers analyzed the teams' strategies. Malaysia walked down the steps in the middle of the auditorium and found three chairs. She signaled to Malcolm to follow her. She slid to the third chair, and he sat next to her.

Alexia yelled, "Alright, enough talking, go back to the game!"

Karl joked, "Now you know how these games go. They gotta reset the board since Leicester scored. Give them another thirty seconds."

"Wait, they scored already?!" Malcolm asked.

"Yeah, you already knew that was going to happen," Karl replied. "Their speedster is determined to end this quickly."

"Shut up, Karl!" Alexia slammed her hands on the desktop, and green mist puffed from her body. "I won't accept that!"

"Speedy might not give you a choice," Malcolm retorted with a smirk.

Highgarden and Leicester were playing in the NextGen Coliseum in the heart of the Leicester district, a 200,000-seat oval arena built for the Divine. Capacity was maxed out to witness the glory of the game, and the mingled sounds of joy and rage were deafening. On the green field, three ten-feet-wide, red-glowing rings floated at the edge of the left side, while two blue-glowing rings floated on the right. Each team had ten players on the field. Three of Leicester's team members stood on the left side to guard the rings, two of Highgarden's on the right, while the others were scattered across the field. Highgarden was clad in green and silver, while Leicester donned the ominous black and purple.

Soon, the field began to shake, and huge patches of the turf began to rise and fall. A furry creature the size of a small dog with wings like an eagle fell from a portal in the sky and howled gleefully as it landed in the middle of the field. The crowd screamed even louder.

A field announcer yelled through the loudspeakers, "3, 2, 1, go!"

The zintol raced away from the combatants, and they chased it down. The ones guarding the rings held their positions as they prayed that the rings would not move before someone scored. Some of the competitors hurdled across the broken field and climbed the terrain, while others used their flight abilities to hover over the field to get their hands on the elusive beast.

Leicester's speedster shuttled closer to the zintol than anyone else. One of Highgarden's athletes held down the middle of the field, and as the ground lifted, she aimed her hands at the speedster and hurled several fireballs at him. The fireballs threw him off course, and the zintol took a sharp turn and flew away from him. Another Highgarden combatant took advantage and got in front of the zintol. The zintol was caught off guard, and he caught him. The zintol, known for its friendly demeanor, lowered its wings and calmly curled into a ball.

"Oh, Highgarden's Liftoff now has the zintol!" the announcer proclaimed. "He's looking around, getting his bearings straight, and is now making his way toward Leicester's rings!"

As Liftoff hastened to the goals, suddenly, the rings began to glow. "Uh oh," the announcer declared, "looks like the goals are moving!" The rings for both Leicester and Highgarden vanished, and the goalies suddenly rushed the field while Leicester's crew rushed to get to Liftoff and make him release the zintol. One of Leicester's competitors aimed his hands and unleashed a wave of water toward Liftoff. A big warrior from Highgarden motored and rushed into him, knocking him to the ground and stopping his assault. The rings had not returned, and Liftoff was suddenly face-to-face with the speedster.

"Ah shit!" Alexia yelled. "What are you going to do?!"

Liftoff suddenly plummeted to the ground. He yelled, "Holey, move this!" He threw the zintol at his teammate thirty feet below him.

"Oh my goodness!" Alexia closed her eyes and held her head down in dread.

As the zintol began to pop open its wings, Holey opened a portal in front of him. The zintol thought it was a ring and squealed. He flew through the portal, and on the opposite side was another Highgarden teammate who grabbed the zintol. The zintol curled up again. This Highgarden competitor then whispered, "Invisible," and she and the zintol disappeared.

Just then, the rings reappeared and were randomly scattered across the field. The ones closest to the rings ran as fast as they could to their assigned colors to guard them. Everyone then started looking around to see where the zintol went. No one could see it, and everyone looked at each other confused.

One of the Leicester teammates made it to a red ring and started guarding it. About thirty seconds later, the ring suddenly started glowing white. As the crowd and the teams looked confused, the Highgarden player revealed herself, and she was holding the zintol through the ring. The crowd exploded with raucous praise and agony.

Alexia shot out of her seat and yelled, "Yeaaaaaaaaaaaaaaaaaaaah!" She ran around the front of the room in a burst of green sparkles while others banged on the tabletops, clapped their hands, hi-fived their co-workers and friends, and celebrated Highgarden's first score of the game.

"Wow, that was a sick move!" Malcolm cheered.

Symone entered Intelligence and noticed everyone cheering. "What just happened?"

Daisy returned, "Highgarden just passed the zintol through one of the goals, and the crowd's gone nuts!"

Symone walked down the steps and sat next to Malcolm. "I take it, then, that it's a good game so far?"

Malcolm answered, "Highgarden isn't going to just lie down, it looks like. They got some tricks up their sleeves. They're going to make this game interesting."

"That's awesome," Symone replied, her mind rummaging through what she just learned from the Analyst.

Malcolm sensed that something was off with Symone again and inquired, "Everything okay?"

Symone tried to snap herself out of her funk and lied, "Yeah, I'm good."

"Mmm, no, that doesn't sound like you're 'good,' love. Talk to me, what's going on?"

"Mmm, not here, not yet. Let's wait until after the game, I don't want to think about it right now," Symone replied, feeling like a corked champagne bottle ready to explode but choosing to keep her composure and get lost in the reactions of her friends to the game they loved.

Malcolm chose not to push the issue. "Alright. *After* the game, okay?" he proposed as he reached for Symone's hand and softly interlaced his fingers with hers.

"Okay." Symone and Malcolm faced the holoscreen and listened to the commentators react to Highgarden's scoring sequence while NextGen reset itself.

Before round two, Leicester's coach was interviewed, and she said, "We've been down before, but I told my team to stop being passive and stop leaning on one person to win the match. We still have to strike as a unit!"

For thirty more minutes, Highgarden and Leicester battled on the field. The crowd's cheers intensified. One by one, the rings fell until only one remained, surprisingly, on Highgarden's side. Highgarden had scored the first point of the first-to-five match. Everyone reveled in watching Alexia's uncontainable joy, her spontaneous reactions becoming a spectacle unto itself the more she burst into yells and screams.

Leicester took heed to their coach's rallying cry and launched the zintol into two straight rings. Everyone went insane. Karl kept patting Alexia's back, consoling the inconsolable. As the field reset itself again, the commentators reported, "It is obvious that Leicester is looking to tie this game up and end the match as quickly as their speed demon can run. If they score this next go—"

Without warning, the holoscreen went black.

"What's going on?" Malaysia's eyes flickered. "Dax, did you touch the button?"

Dax turned and faced Malaysia, "No, that wasn't me. All the tables are disabled. The channel is still on. The camera in the arena must have shorted." Dax tapped keys on the pad and changed the channel to another station covering the zintol game, and its coverage, too, had gone dark.

"We're experiencing technical difficulties, so while we wait to get signal of the match between Highgarden and Leicester, let's talk about how the game has gone so far," a commentator stated as the camera switched to a studio feed, and he and his co-host sat at a desk to discuss the game.

"Wow, I can't believe this!" Alexia lamented. "This game is too damn important for the cameras to be cutting out!"

Back at NextGen, the players and the spectators looked around the arena, trying to understand why everything in the arena had suddenly powered down. Security personnel tried using their stripes, but they looked at their arms and saw the gray color denoting a lost signal. The players noticed that the field had not finished resetting itself, and some of the turf was elevated while other parts were depressed. They decided to walk toward their coaches' sidelines.

The speedster looked down and noticed that the turf started looking glossy. The others noticed it, too, and one of Leicester's players asked, "Are any of you doing this?"

"No, none of us can freeze things," Holey answered, bewildered. "Who's doing this?"

The speedster noticed frost suddenly accumulating on his feet, and he instinctively ordered the athletes, "We gotta get off the field. Now!"

The crowd above them observed the players' sudden retreat and wondered out loud what was happening to the field. The competitors rushed and flew off the field as fast as they could. Highgarden's gargantuan ran too slowly, though, and the frost covering the ground was now enveloping his legs. "Holey, a little help!"

Holey turned around and saw his teammate getting trapped in ice. He opened a portal next to his teammate. With all his might, he broke the ice by jumping into the portal and landing on the opposite side of the field near the tunnels. Holey saw the others and opened portals near all of them and helped everyone escape to the tunnels. As he tried to create a portal for himself, the frost beneath him gripped his legs, and he couldn't lift himself out of it. The ice entombed him, and he stood a lifeless statue on the frozen tundra.

The crowd realized that this was not a part of the game, and they began to rush toward the exits in a panic. Security tried to calm everyone down, but there was no stopping them from running, stomping, hopping, and flying away to safety. Just then, booms could be heard outside of the arena. The crowds trying to break out of the arena screeched to a halt. Walls of fire blocked off any possible way of getting out. Everyone backed up. Security personnel looked for fire extinguishers and water hoses to put the fires out. Meanwhile the crowd continued to search for a way out of NextGen, stuck between the walls of fire outside and the frozen tundra inside.

A tidal wave suddenly engulfed the seats from one side to the other. The patrons slipped and slid across the stands, banged into chairs and each other, and were swallowed by the waves of water that rushed from one step to another until it overflowed onto the frozen turf and crystalized along the outer wall of the field. The waters rose on the field, and the crystal blocked off the tunnels, making escape a near-impossibility.

As the security teams tried to put the fires out, a massive gust of wind blew into the exits, fanning the untamable flames into the tunnels and pushing the security team and the patrons farther back into the tunnels. The wind howled, and everyone struggled to stand.

Back at Intelligence, the Elite and the Intelligence analysts were waiting for the game to come back, listening to the announcers as they blathered on about Highgarden and Leicester. The man cupped his ear to listen to what his news team was reporting to him, and he relayed, "We're receiving word that NextGen is under attack. They're saying that the entire arena is under siege, and no one knows who or where the assault is coming from."

Alexia stood up. She turned to look at Malcolm, who looked down at his stripe and noticed that he hadn't received a notification. Stephanie, seated in the front at the right, said to Dax, "Turn the screen to UNN."

Dax tapped a couple buttons on his countertop, and the screen switched to UNN. The Elite observed live helicopter footage of the assault. Stephanie hurried to her desk and contacted Director Mallack.

Mallack was sitting at her desk in her office, tapping on her holoscreen with her eyes closed, when her stripe buzzed. Her eyes popped open, and she responded, "Yes?"

"Director," Stephanie began, "we have a situation. NextGen Coliseum is under attack."

Mallack quickly switched her holoscreen to UNN, and she saw the carnage unfolding just as the ground underneath the arena quaked, and glass panels, scaffolding, beams, and concrete shook and broke apart. She said, "Thank you, Stephanie." She then ended the call and contacted Chancellor Croft.

Croft answered instantly, "Are you seeing this?"

"Yes, Chancellor, what do you want us to do?"

"What you do best."

"Understood. Consider it handled," Mallack ended the call. She pulled out her mini-holoscreen and tapped on an application. She commanded her tablet to do a quick analysis of the NextGen Coliseum and the damage being done there. The holoscreen informed her that ice, fire, water, terrain, and wind were being deployed. She then ran the analysis through a risk assessment tool to determine which team would be best equipped to handle the situation. Fifteen seconds later, the holoscreen suggested the six Defenders who made up Super Team V, and she pressed the "Summon" button.

Mallack received a call from the leader of V, and she answered, "You got your assignment?"

"Yes, we received it. Do we know who we're dealing with?"

"No sign yet. Still waiting to receive any intel we can gather. Take your team and handle the situation. No kill order from UPD as of yet, but exercise extreme caution."

"Understood, we're on our way," the voice ended the call.

Malcolm grew concerned that his stripe hadn't lit up. "Shouldn't we be getting the call right now?"

Malaysia looked at Malcolm and responded, "Knowing Mallack, she did a risk assessment and sent a super team to assess what's going on. You know, path of least resistance."

Alexia overheard them and remarked, "Ugh, I hate it when she does that! We should be the ones out there right now!"

"You know they can't give us *all* the assignments," Karl reasoned.

"Yeah," Daisy chimed in. "It's the only way they'll learn and grow, just like us."

"I want this one, though," Symone agreed with Alexia, her eyes glowing with yellow embers.

"Let's hope they can handle it," Dax said. "Just got word Super Team V got the call."

An individual finally emerged on the center of the icy field, donned in all black with the initials POC in shiny silver letters across his chest. Five other people followed suit and descended from the sky and landed next to him, all wearing the same garb with the same initials. They looked at each other. The one in the middle said, "And now, we wait."

The UNN helicopter flew over the field and zoomed in on the six. The reporter announced, "We now can see six people dressed in all black with letters across their chests. We're going to get a closer shot at them," and the camera zoomed in more. "It looks like POC is across their chests. We cannot confirm what that means, so we won't speculate here. It does appear, though, that they are the ones responsible for what's happening at NextGen right now."

Sirens blared as UPD, UFD, and UMC responders rushed to NextGen. Super Team V's hoverbus scrambled to the scene. Minutes later, the bus rose above the shaken and torn coliseum and lowered onto the field.

The back hatch opened, and Super Team V exited the bus. Saber, Flora, Spark, Talon, The Major, and Metallica assumed battle formation. Talon, the team leader, declared, "Okay, surrender peacefully, now!"

"I don't think so. We came here to fight, so let's fight!" the leader declared. His team assumed battle positions and rushed toward them.

V mirrored them and rushed forward. The leader suddenly stopped, and he blasted a wave of ice from his hands toward V. The team immediately split up to avoid getting hit. As they split, the other assailants charged up and threw their various powers toward the super team. Talon alerted, "Okay, they tipped their hands. Everyone, pay attention to Intelligence's analysis and split the team up, take them one-on-one."

Spark, wearing black and yellow nanotech, used his ability to create bursts of electric energy and blasted the wall of ice away. He charged forward toward the ice warrior. Saber was alerted by Intelligence's report that she had the advantage over the one who controlled fire and unsheathed two purple energy lances from her arms, which color matched her all-purple uniform. Flora donned a green and red compilation, and she controlled plant matter. Intelligence assumed one of their opponents knocked the power out and reckoned that her ability would tip the scales in her direction against that specific assailant. Intelligence advised The Major, a small, dense, powerful brute clad in bronze, to take down the one who manipulated water. Metallica, wearing all silver, immediately recognized that the wind controller would be powerless against him. And Talon's natural wings clad in red and white nanotech gave him the tactical advantage over the one who controlled terrain.

Spark rushed to the ice man and hurled two spark bombs at him. The ice man threw up an ice shield, and the shield took the blasts. He then swiftly crafted an ice sword and swung it toward Spark. Spark dodged the swings as the ice man sliced air twice. Spark launched a bomb at the ice man's torso, and the ice man backed up, his cloak taking damage. Spark threw two more bombs at him, and they landed on his chest and legs. The ice man backed up and unleashed an ice wave at Spark's legs. It grew difficult for Spark to move, and he jumped before his legs completely froze over. He stood atop the wave and hurled another bomb at the ice man. The ice man spun to dodge the bomb and threw ice daggers at Spark. The daggers pierced Spark and launched him backward. Spark's cloak took the damage while he flipped on his back and landed in a three-point stance. He launched himself toward the ice man again, and they traded jabs, punches, and kicks before Spark shot a small bomb at the ice man's feet, popping him upward. Spark then launched both of his hands in the air, aimed at the ice man's head, and shot a pulse of electricity at him. The ice man spun in the air and landed prostrate on the ground.

Flora placed her hands on the ground and summoned her energy. She concentrated and felt for the turf below the block of ice underneath her feet. Meanwhile, the electronic controller looked around for anything that she could manipulate on command. She saw the hoverbus fifty feet in front of her. She, too, concentrated her energy and began scanning its codes, deciphering them to gain control of the hoverbus. Flora finally sensed the grass. Her eyes lit up rose pink, and she commanded the grass under the controller's feet to rise and multiply exponentially. She searched for any other plant life that might be able to germinate on command. The controller broke the code for the hoverbus, and she commanded it to lock onto Flora and fire laser rounds. Flora received a warning from her Intelligence division that the hoverbus was locked onto her position. She turned around and saw the lasers locking onto her. Without breaking her concentration on the vegetation, she reasoned to run toward the controller. As she ran, the hoverbus fired rounds of lasers at her feet while Intelligence fought feverishly to regain control of the bus. Flora raised her hands up, and the ground underneath the controller's feet shook and shifted. Suddenly, large blades of grass, roots, trees, and bushes broke through the ice and began swallowing the controller's position. The controller got lost in the overgrown weeds. Flora ran into the woods so the hoverbus would lose her within it and cease firing at her.

Metallica looked up at the one who controlled the wind who had surrounded himself with a strong whirlwind that suspended him about twenty feet in the air. The opponent shot his hands forward, and a mighty gust blew down upon

Metallica. Metallica increased his body density and planted himself on the ground. He then pulled a crossbow from his back and aimed it at his opponent. He calculated the wind resistance and fired a percussion round. It pierced the sky and fought through the wind surge and hit its target. The percussion round exploded, and Metallica's foe tumbled to the ground. Metallica ran to meet him, pulling out a plasma pistol and firing several rounds at him. The wind controller pushed himself upward a few feet before meeting the ground, turned himself straight, and aimed his hand at Metallica and pushed a massive air column at him. Metallica was caught off guard and spun away. He regained composure and increased his density once again, plummeting to the ground. He landed, and as the wind continued to push him, he turned to face the direction of the wind, and he swung his arm upward and fired a shot in the air. The wind caught the round, and as Metallica calculated, the round looped with the wind and exited the storm. It circled back, and unbeknownst to the wind controller, punched him in the face and spun him to the ground. The wind immediately ceased.

The fire setter got to work on Saber, unleashing a wave of fire from her hands. Saber used her lances to form an X and shielded herself from the assault. The fire setter switched to fireballs, and Saber blocked and sliced each of them. Saber then whipped her right lance at the fire setter, and it corralled her. Saber spun her around, then took the left lance and corralled her again at her legs, then whipped it away and caused her to fall to the ground. The fire setter pushed a fireball from each hand to propel herself away and flip herself around. She knelt, then created a fireball in front of her and pushed it in the air. That fireball exploded into a hailstorm. Saber took the lances and spun them above her head to protect herself from the hail, then launched herself in the air and summoned the lances to stretch out to clutch the fire setter. Once she clutched her, Saber dropped to the ground, using the momentum to swing the fire setter in the air and crash her head-first into the turf. Still clutching the fire setter, she spun around five times and then released the fire setter, launching her into the outer wall of the field.

The Major was in the middle of a bath as the one who controlled water hit him with a high-powered assault of water pressure. The Major began clapping his hands. Each clap bent the air and created a sound wave that the water would skip to, causing the blast to jump over him. The water controller switched to the ground, and the Major lifted his right leg and stomped the ground so hard, it split the ice between him and the water controller, and the water flowed down the crevice. Major cracked the ice again, and the water controller slipped inside it. The tundra was still cold enough to where he ended up freezing himself inside the crack. Major then rushed and rammed his arm into the water controller's head, knocking him unconscious.

The terrain controller summoned the frozen turf to rise upward as sharp lances toward Talon who was in flight. The lances missed Talon as he spun around in the air. He then plummeted and latched onto the terrain controller, crashing her into the ground. He punished her with several strikes to the head. She summoned the ground below them to rise, and they launched upward. She then made the ground reach above her and punch Talon in the head, knocking him off her. She then reversed their direction, and they shuttled to the turf they came from. Talon was about to whisk away, but the terrain controller caused the ground he was on to surround him, and he was stuck. She then caused a piece of the turf to meet her, and she jumped off the piece of terrain and onto the other, watching as Talon crashed to the ground. She floated toward the impact point, and when the dust settled, she didn't see Talon anywhere. Suddenly, Talon grabbed her, and they blasted into the sky. Talon punched her several times then speedily rushed toward the ground. At the last second, he let her go and floated above the ground while her greatest strength became the force that knocked her out.

Meanwhile, back at the Elite Grand Hall, Malcolm and his team cheered as they witnessed Super Team V taking down the elemental powers. "Good for them, wow, they made it look easy!" he declared.

Symone agreed as she clasped her hands. "Yeah, looks like Mallack made the right call."

"That was almost better than the game," Alexia said. "But damn it, man!"

"Yeah, looks like the game will have to be postponed," Karl responded.

Malcolm looked at Dax and asked, "Hey, what can you get on these guys?"

Dax was pressing on keys like his life depended on it as he replied, "You already know I'm looking into it."

Back on the field, Talon looked around and asked, "How's everybody doing?"

"I'm good, placing the disabler on my guy right now," the Major answered.

"Still looking for my guy through the brush," Flora answered as she pushed through the forest she created to find her opponent.

"I'm making my way over to my target now," Saber informed.

"Placing the disabler on my target now," Spark said.

"Same here," Metallica responded. Just as Metallica was about to pull out the disabler from his pocket, a hand grabbed his arm. He turned around and jerked his arm. He saw another masked individual, different from the rest of them, dressed in red and purple nanotech. Metallica grabbed the individual's hand and said, "Hey!"

The individual spun him around. Metallica then tried to strike the person with his left hand, and the person blocked his punch, then struck Metallica with his left hand. Metallica charged and delivered a series of punches and kicks toward him. His opponent dodged every strike, then delivered the same series of punches and kicks toward Metallica in the same exact order. Metallica was hit with the last three moves and stumbled backward. Metallica was stunned. He charged again and delivered another series. His opponent dodged them again and hit Metallica in the head, then in the chest, then in the abdomen. Metallica increased his density, and the moves didn't affect him. Metallica then delivered a powerful punch to his opponent, and his opponent's face felt like punching into a steel column. Metallica let out a yelp, despite being cloaked. His opponent then kicked Metallica in the stomach, launching him several feet across the tundra. Metallica crashed into the ground. He groaned as he lay on the ground, "Hey, yo, we got another powered in the field. Don't know where he came from."

Talon looked around to see where Metallica was. Meanwhile, before Metallica could regroup, his opponent stood over him and put his foot on his chest, then increased his density, crushing Metallica under his weight. His cloak was the only thing preventing him from meeting his demise. His adversary pulled out a disabler from his pocket and lay it on his arm, and Metallica's cloak overloaded, shimmered, and dissipated. The disabler then delivered three electric shocks to Metallica, paralyzing and knocking him unconscious.

The Major was closest to Metallica and rushed toward the unknown challenger. He aimed his head at the man's back, but the opponent quickly slid to his right, and as the Major missed, the man grabbed his right arm and planted his feet, jerked the Major to a halt, and released his arm and swept him with his leg. The Major tripped and fell backward, hitting the ground hard. The assailant then stood up and stomped the ground, cracking it underneath the Major. He mimicked the Major's clap attack and produced a sound wave that pushed the Major farther into the turf.

Talon scanned the field and saw Major getting pummeled. He said, "Team, we're down two! Disable your people and converge on this guy!"

The Major was disoriented, and his opponent looked over the edge. As he pulled out a disabler, Talon suddenly kicked him in his back. He fell forward into the hole he created, turned his body to face the sky, and spread his arms to reveal wings that mirrored Talon's. He flew out of the hole and followed Talon. Stunned, Talon stopped and began swinging his fists at his opponent, hitting only air as every attack was dodged and blocked. His attacker repeated his moves and landed every punch, then raised his hand upward and delivered a tomahawk at Talon's forehead. It dazed Talon, and he crashed to the ground.

The Elite was awestruck as the mimicker had tipped the balance of the scales against Super Team V. Daisy was standing up, and she said, "Malcolm, what is happening? Who is that guy?"

"I have no idea," Malcolm shook his head. He was leaning forward on the tabletop trying to make sense of what they were witnessing.

"It's just one guy, they can't take one guy?" Malaysia pondered.

"It's one guy, but he's acting like three! You see this shit?!" Malcolm explained.

Symone examined the holoscreen, locked onto the new opponent. Silence gripped her throat. Her heart sank deep into her gut, and a sharp pain pierced the space where her heart sat. She wondered if her eyes were deceiving her. *No way, it can't be.*

Saber hastened to help Talon. She ran toward their foe and unleashed her lances upward at him. He saw her coming and dropped below her lances. His arms lit up purple, and he unleashed lances of his own at her. Saber retracted her lances and placed her fists in front of her face. Her lances spun in front of her like a propeller and cut his lances into pieces. He landed on the ground and pursued her, but he suddenly was hit by a bomb, and it knocked him sideways. Spark left the ice man after having placed a disabler on him and came to Saber's aid. The man tumbled on the ground, then popped back up and threw a continuous lance at Spark and threw electric bombs at Saber. Spark shot several bombs at the lance and slid to his right to avoid it, while Saber swung her lances at the bombs.

"Who is this guy?" Saber asked Spark.

"No idea, it's like he owns all our powers and knows all our moves!"

Flora was still sifting through her forest and said, "I'm coming, guys!" She summoned the forest to shrivel up and die. All the foliage turned brown, the leaves and grass all cracked and turned to dust, and the trees became twigs. She didn't notice her previous opponent standing about twenty feet behind her. She shot a disabler at her, and her cloak overloaded, shimmered, and dissipated. The disabler then shot three electric pulses, and Flora crumpled to the ground. The electronic controller ran toward Saber and Spark.

The mimicker flew upward and released several bombs at Spark and Saber. As they dodged the barrage, the fire setter regained her composure and unleashed a wave of fire toward Spark and Saber. They were surrounded by a ring of fire and could not escape the flames or the bombs. The mimicker finally clutched them both with Saber's lance power and lifted them above the flames. The electronic controller aimed her disabler gun and fired two shots, hitting Saber and Spark and disabling their cloaks and shocking them unconscious.

The Major climbed out of the hole. The fire setter noticed him and delivered several powerful fireballs at him. The wind controller had regained his composure and fanned the flames with devastating gusts. The Major tried to clap the flames out but was unable to do it. The mimicker flew above him and grabbed him by the lances, lifting him out of the flames. The electronic controller repeated her gunfire, and the Major's cloak overloaded, and the Major was shocked three times and rendered unconscious.

Everyone in Intelligence looked at the holoscreen in shock and fury, wondering if Mallack was going to call them next.

The UNN cameras continued rolling. The mimicker landed on the ground. He commanded, "Okay, it's showtime. Get everyone together quickly. Wake Terra up and get her to tear a hole in the ground. Ignatia, you and Cypher will push them into the pit, Wave will fill it up with water, and Frostbite will freeze them in place."

"Won't that kill them?" Ignatia, the fire setter, asked him.

"No, Frostbite has been working on freezing them quickly enough to put them in cryo-sleep, or something like that. We have to hurry before someone else shows up, we're running late."

"Didn't expect them to send a team," Cypher, the electronic controller, reasoned.

"Go, now, get the team! Cyclone, help them!" the mimicker demanded. Ignatia ran to the Wave and used her heat to free him from his ice trap. Cypher shook Frostbite a few times, then slapped his face. Frostbite's eyes spun around, and he slowly rolled to a kneeling position. Cyclone moved to wake Terra up from the nasty drop she endured from Talon's assault.

"Hey, Terra, you alright?" Cyclone knelt and shook Terra.

Terra groaned as she replied, "Yeah, never felt better. Didn't see him coming at me. How we doing out here?"

"We're almost done. Come on, time to finish the job."

He grabbed her hand and pulled her up. They each picked up a member of Super Team V and dropped them at their leader's feet. Terra then stretched her hand forward, and the ground underneath V turned into mush, and they sank ten feet below the surface. Wave then stuck his hand out, and water flowed from his hand into the pit, quickly becoming a watery grave. Frostbite, still a bit woozy but functional, stuck his hand out, and the water quickly hardened and turned into a glacier. Super Team V was defeated and entombed.

The six stood with their leader in between them. Cypher's eyes turned yellow, and the loudspeakers, the cameras, and the displays within the crumbling stadium all sparked and lit up.

The UNN commentators stated, "We're now seeing NextGen powering back up. The lights are all shining on the attackers."

The leader of the team stood boldly, proud of what he accomplished and unafraid to flaunt his achievement in front of the world. He had Uri City's attention, and he relished it.

"Citizens of Uri City, we are members of the Powered Order Coalition, and you have now witnessed our emergence from the shadows as we are making final preparations to become full citizens of this city-state. For far too long, we have cowered under the direction and influence of the unpowered, made to hide behind their fear and only engage in activities that bolster their position of power over us. We pay our share of fares, entertain them with our abilities, rescue them when they are incapable of saving their powerless selves. And yet, they believe that we do not have the right to govern ourselves, let alone them. We, the Powered Order Coalition, stand united to say, 'No more!' We will no longer stand for the unpowered to wield their powerlessness over us. When the Senate gathers to vote in three weeks, they will vote in favor of placing the decision of allowing the powered to hold offices in the hands of the citizens of Uri City. We guarantee that nothing will stand in the way of the powered taking their rightful places in this city. And if anyone chooses to stand in our way, they will be eliminated."

"We are the POC," the seven lifted up their left fists, "and we approve this message."

Cypher activated Super Team V's hoverbus, and it began its launching sequence. The seven dashed into the bus, and it lifted off and away. The UNN and other news stations and UPD attempted to follow the hoverbus, and Cypher, holding down the cockpit, reported, "We've got an entourage."

Their leader ordered, "Frostbite, Cyclone, put some distance between us and them."

The back hatch opened, and everyone braced themselves against the forces trying to pull them out of the bus. Frostbite and Cyclone held onto the wall on either side of the back hatch, and they shot their free hands forward and summoned their energy. They unleashed a devastating wind and snowstorm behind them that pelted the news crews and police's aircraft. The pilots were forced to give up the search and retreat to prevent the ice from further disabling their machines and causing them to crash into buildings or the pavement.

# 6

# The Powered Order Coalition

The avenging spirit stirred up Malcolm's soul, and his mind immediately switched to warrior mode. Someone's ass needed to be kicked, and with clenched fists, Malcolm craved a target. "Hey, can you track that bus?" he asked Dax.

Dax was one step ahead of Malcolm, already tapping feverishly to lock onto the getaway plane. He growled, "No, whoever's on their side was able to disable the tracking device within it. That bus is theirs now. It'll take me about seven minutes to regain control of it, and that's if they're not actively trying to keep me out like before."

"Shit," Symone sighed, still discombobulated and struggling to keep it together. "Shit, who were those guys?"

Malaysia stood up, "Whoever they are, they just declared war against Uri City."

"This is not good," Stephanie snapped her fingers to realign her frazzled mind to the matter at hand. "Um, okay, everyone, we got to get to work. We need a surge in data analysis. We need to figure out who these people are, where the Frimas they came from, and what they want. We have to assume that Mallack is going to get a call from the Chancellor, and we're going to get assigned this mission. So, let's make sure we give Malcolm and his team the advantage. I want to take these assholes down before they can even sniff a whiff of our presence."

Stephanie expected immediate movement from her analysts, but no one budged. They instead locked onto the holo-screen behind her. Puzzled, she asked, "What?" She looked at her clothes, then noticed everyone's attention had shifted. She turned around and saw the talking heads on UNN.

Senator Dariuz was split-screened with the host, a woman in a blue dress. He was chomping at the bit, impatiently waiting for his turn to speak about what happened at the zintol match. Dax turned the volume up. "Senator, thank you so much for meeting with us on short notice. What are your thoughts right now regarding this terrible tragedy that has just taken place?"

Dariuz's raspy voice responded, "First, to the victims' families, our thoughts and prayers are with them as our incredible team of officers, fire/rescue, medical staff, and our contract defenders are out there putting their lives on the line to restore order and save as many lives as they can."

A disgusted Alexia crossed her arms, "'Thoughts and prayers.' Ugh, this train is never late."

"This senseless act of carnage that the Powered Order Coalition has unleashed on these innocent people is exactly the reason why we cannot, *we must not* allow the powered into office."

Alexia growled and shot her arm out, "See, there it is."

Dariuz continued, "They said it themselves. They feel like they've had to 'cower under the direction and influence of the unpowered,' when that has not been the case. We, the powered and the unpowered, came to an agreement over one hundred and fifty years ago, and it has held this city together in steady peace. If we allow the powered to have the right to enter offices, what deterrents will we have in place to stop monsters like the POC from wielding their power for their own purposes and at the downfall of all of Uri City?"

The woman shook her head, "Senator, are you saying that the POC are monsters?"

Dariuz chuckled, "Listen, for the past several years now, they have paraded as a peaceful organization bent solely on granting full rights to the powered. I have long held suspicions that the POC's true intentions were domination, and now, they have exposed themselves and revealed the truth. If we don't stop this now, then we will expose our city to a level of destruction that we may not be able to recover from, and we will only have ourselves to blame. Yesterday, it was the Mega Mall. Today, it's the NextGen Coliseum! How many more innocent people have to suffer before we wake up? How much more proof do we need? I ask my fellow senators, let's not make this a powered vs. unpowered issue, but a safety and security issue for the future of our city."

"Thank you, Senator Dariuz," the blue-dressed woman stated.

Dax muted the holoscreen.

Malaysia sat back down, massaged her temples, and huffed, "That guy really gets on my nerves."

Symone agreed as the room got quiet. "Yeah, see how he used the kid again? Like he had something to do with today. Such a fucking opportunist."

"No kidding, that's what I've been saying for years," Alexia reminded the team. "All he does is try to win political points. He doesn't care about anything but being on TV, staying in power, and using whatever advantage he can to win votes."

Daisy shook her head, "Well, that's just not true. Dariuz has actually done a lot of good for the city over the years. He's a showman, sure, but behind the scenes, he's really a good guy."

Alexia fought the urge to mind wipe her. She quickly spun her chair around to face Daisy's direction. "Look, I know he's your boy, Daisy, but you can't be this naïve. Dariuz is a problem for the city, always has been. Genesis Landing, Leicester, and for damn sure the Underbelly, have all suffered greatly because of people like him. And the more people keep supporting him, the worse off those districts will be until they're completely wiped off the map and restructured like Meridian or, worse, Highgarden!"

Everyone could feel the room shift slightly. Karl recognized Alexia's power and stood to try to interject, but not before Daisy retorted, "Say what you want, Alexia, but the truth is our city has never been better. The data speaks for itself. Hate his rhetoric all you want, but you cannot deny that because of him and 'people like him,' our city continues to shine as an example for the world to see. I don't like that he used the kid any more than you do, but I can't sit here and say that he's wrong about what he thinks."

Malcolm knew their conversation wasn't going anywhere, and he sensed Alexia's power churning more intensely. Before Alexia could keep the fire alive and tear through the holoscreens, desks, and chairs, he put an end to the debate, "Ladies, right now, we got bigger problems to deal with than Dariuz and his attitude toward the powered. Seven terrorists just leveled NextGen and froze Super Team V. Mallack is going to call us, and when she does, we have to be level-headed. So put your differences aside and let's focus on the task ahead."

Alexia sulked, "Fine." Her anger raged, but she quelled her energy, and Malcolm felt it, a signal that he had regained control of his team.

Duncan silently lamented, *Damn, should have let them fight, Malcolm.*

Malcolm continued, "Stephanie's already got Intelligence ready to go, so we'll do the same, Elite. Let's get out of their way and head to the quarters."

Just then, a call rang through Intelligence. Stephanie answered, "Yes, Director?"

"Is the Elite Unit there?" Mallack asked.

"Yes, they're all here," Stephanie replied.

"Good, this won't take long. You guys all saw what happened. I just got the call from the Chancellor, and you're up. Stephanie, get as much intel as you can on the seven and the POC. Figure out who these punks are and how to stop them from doing this again. Malcolm, looks like you'll be going out with a bang."

Malcolm replied, "I was just thinking the same thing about you, Director."

"Soon as Intelligence has anything, Stephanie, alert me and the team."

The Elite rose from their chairs. Alexia was pissed, unable to understand why Daisy loved Senator Dariuz so badly and could side against her kind so easily and fervently. She walked past Daisy and rolled her eyes at her. Daisy shook her head and gently grabbed Malaysia's hand. "Did I do something to Alexia?" she asked.

Malaysia snorted, then spoke her mind, "Now Daisy, you know she has never aligned with your views. She wears her heart on her sleeve more than anyone else here. And you *choose to challenge her* every single time, knowing she's not going to back down. Don't play dumb. You know why she's mad at you. But she'll get over it. I mean, I will never understand why you support Dariuz as hard as you do, but you're still my girl, and I respect your views regardless."

Daisy sighed, knowing that Malaysia was right about everything. "I get it. I just hope this doesn't cause a rift between us as a team."

Malaysia grabbed Daisy's hand. "We're a team, Frimas, a family. We're supposed to have rifts, as long as we heal them back up as quickly as they show up. Now come on, we gotta get ready."

"Thanks Malaysia," Daisy answered. She hoped with every fiber of her existence that the attack on NextGen would help people see that Dariuz was right and that the powered should stay out of office. Malaysia and Daisy walked out of Intelligence, following their teammates to their quarters.

Across town, Captain Stewart slowly marched in the aisle of the darkened UPD hoverbus carrying twenty of his Special Operations unit on board. Stewart stared at the holoscreen in his hands, quickly sifting through the orders he'd received from his commanding officer a cycle prior. "Alright, let's go over this one more time. We are infiltrating the Powered Order Coalition office. We do not know who or what we are going to encounter, so make sure you are cloaked at all times. The primary suspect is Mitchell Daniels, whose power is, um," he swiped through the pages again, "mysticism and optical illusion. Wait, is he like a magician? Anyway, we are to apprehend him at all costs, so make sure your blasters and sticks are set to 'stun.' Let's get this right, for NextGen and Uri City. Understood?"

"Sir, yes, sir!" the battle gear-clad officers acknowledged.

The hoverbus and several other UPD vehicles descended to the streets of the Underbelly, blitzing by people, other hovercraft, and low-rise buildings that encompassed the commerce sector of the district. The citizens noticed the oversized craft and wondered why the UPD was showing such a menacing presence within their district limits. The closer their blaring sirens got to the POC office, the more chatter picked up among the civilians.

"Oh no, they're going to take the POC down," one man said to his friends as the UPD rushed past them.

"It looks that way. If they destroyed NextGen, then the UPD is going to make them pay for that," another man said.

"Frimas, if the POC did that, what the Frimas can the UPD do about it? They're gonna get their asses handed to them," a woman posed.

"You're right about that," the first man said as they all laughed. "They're about to fuck around and find out on live camera. No doubt the news crews are already there. Look!"

They turned around and stared through the store window to watch the holoscreen. UNN was already on the scene just as the UPD landed on the street. In the bus, Captain Stewart declared, "Alright, people, let's lock and load. Remember, apprehend everyone, including Daniels. Move, move, move!"

The back hatch of the hoverbus opened, and twenty pairs of black-suited boots swiftly hit the pavement in lockstep. They formed a straight line on the sidewalk parallel to the POC office, a two-story orange building with glass covering the first-floor walls.

Silently, Captain Stewart prayed, *Please, Akan, don't let any of my crew get trigger-happy today. Remind my crew of their training and control their reflexes. Whatever we face today, let everyone on both sides make it out alive and well.* He stood in front of his crew and set his stripe to speaker mode. He declared, "Mitchell Daniels, this is the UPD. We have a warrant for your arrest. Come out with your hands up!" UPD officers stepped out of their vehicles, blasters drawn, ready to strike if any surprises arose.

Stewart instructed his unit, "Everyone, take a breath. Do not make a move unless ordered, understood?"

"Understood!" his officers replied.

Two minutes went by, and Stewart announced the UPD's presence again. "Mitchell Daniels, come out with your hands up in thirty seconds, or we will enter the premises!"

Inside the brightly lit POC office, several people stood at their messy desks across the room, terrified that they were about to be slaughtered. They looked at their leader, Mitchell Daniels. One of them asked, "Mitchell, what are we going to do?"

Daniels, a tall, light-skinned man with beady eyes and textured brown hair, stood at the windows and noted the UPD's show of force. He could feel the tension in the air, apprehension from his team, and the cops' anxiety and subtle thirst for justice and vengeance. He knew that one wrong move could result in unnecessary bloodshed, remembering the countless videos on the airwaves of innocent powered persons being senselessly harmed due to a subtle flick of the wrist, an accidental release of energy, or a squint of the eyes. He did not want to give anyone further ammunition to fuel Dariuz's narrative, thwart the POC's cause, or incense an officer's instinct to go ballistic in the name of life and safety.

"Okay, guys," he calmly turned around, "we are not going to fight, we're not going to use our powers." He placed his hands on his waist, "They are going to take us all in, and more than likely, we are going to be placed in the Asylum."

Another pleaded, "But, Mitchell, we didn't do anything! That wasn't us!"

Mitchell raised his hand to calm everyone down, "I know, but whoever they are made it seem that they were representing us. We all knew that something like this might happen someday, and we planned for it. We stick to our script. We're going to walk out of these doors and surrender peacefully. Be honest, don't hold anything back, answer all of their questions. What they choose to do will be on them."

Everyone nodded, and their hearts grappled with the harsh inevitability of spending the rest of their lives nullified, rendered powerless in a white box.

The UPD stared at the glass entrance scanning for any movement. Thirty seconds later, Stewart fanned his hand forward, signaling to his team to move in. They took a few steps forward when the glass door finally slid open. Stewart swiftly raised a closed fist to stop his team, and they trained their weapons on the entrance. Seventeen people walked out of the building, and they quickly raised their arms in the air to signal their surrender. Several officers demanded, "On your knees, down on your knees, hands on your heads!"

The seventeen complied, and Stewart ordered his team to flex-cuff them, then stand them all up. Stewart moved through the crowd and found Daniels. Stewart stood in his face and said, "You know why we're here?"

Daniels remembered his own words and calmly replied, "I've seen the news, yes, I know why you're here."

"So, you admit that you are responsible for NextGen?" Stewart asked.

"I didn't say that. We don't claim responsibility for what happened there. But those bastards wearing POC shirts sure made it look like us. So, we understand why you're here. But you're not going to find anything here linking us to NextGen."

Stewart was stunned at how easily Daniels gave up but maintained his steely resolve. "Take them into custody. The rest of you, search the premises. Box everything up and bring it back to HQ."

The officers pushed Daniels and the others forward, and they walked to the UPD hovercraft in peaceful surrender to the city. The officers inside the building grabbed every document and holoscreen they saw. They carted off data-filled whiteboards, hordes of pages that could fill libraries, anything they felt was pertinent to building their case against the POC.

Once they finished their seizure, the UPD ascended to the skies and blasted to Midtown, where their headquarters was located.

Director Mallack was sitting in her office watching the seizure unfold on UNN. She listened as the news anchor reported, "The members of the POC office in the Underbelly have just been apprehended without incident. All seventeen suspects walked out of their office unarmed and hands raised. The UPD captain was seen speaking to Mitchell Daniels, the leader of the POC, and after their brief exchange, the suspects were placed in UPD vehicles as the officers initiated and later completed their seizure of evidence."

Mallack reasoned that the apprehension and seizure operation was too simple. She stood up and activated her stripe. She contacted Malaysia and Alexia on a three-way.

Malaysia and Alexia were sitting on the couch in the commons watching the holoscreen. Malaysia felt the stripe buzz first, and she answered, "Yes, Director."

"Alexia, you there, too?" Mallack summoned.

"Yes, Director, I'm here."

"UPD has just apprehended Mitchell Daniels, the leader of the POC."

"Yes," Malaysia concurred. "We just saw it on the screen."

Mallack knocked twice on the desk and continued. "I want you two to head to UPD and interrogate Daniels before they bury him under the Asylum. I'm going to get clearance from the chancellor. I get the feeling that Daniels didn't have anything to do with this, but we won't get the chance to find out if they lock him and his crew down."

Malaysia stood up and looked at Alexia. "Understood, Director. We're on our way."

Alexia stood up. "Let me get changed real quick, and I'll meet you in the garage."

"Gotcha," Malaysia answered.

Just then, Karl walked from his residence to the commons and noticed the two of them moving about. He saw the look of concern in both of their faces and said, "Hey ladies, what's up?"

It took everything in Malaysia and Alexia to not fawn over the rugged chocolate mountain that was Karl, his remarkable, impeccable physique accentuated by his tight A-shirt and gray sweatpants. Malaysia noticed the bulging print from the pelvis of his sweatpants and resisted the urge to switch to X-ray as she responded, "Um, yeah, Mallack wants us to interrogate Mitchell Daniels before UPD tries to asylum him and his crew."

"Hmm," Karl crossed his ripped arms. "Sounds like she doesn't think he's bad news."

"You're right," Alexia reacted, struggling to keep her eyes on his face. "She's usually the first person to let UPD have their way with the bad guys."

"Exactly," Karl agreed. "Y'all want some company?"

Malaysia swung her arm. "Sure, come on with us."

"Alright then, let me put something on, and we can bounce."

Malaysia and Alexia's thoughts synced, *Yeah, you do that before I bounce on you.*

# 7
# Order 816

Malaysia piloted the black hovercar into the bustling Uri City skyline toward Midtown. Alexia rode in the passenger seat while Karl dozed off in the backseat. Still angry with Daisy about her strong stance against the powered taking office, Alexia used this car ride as an opportunity to blow off some still pent-up steam.

"I just can't understand how anyone could side with Dariuz the way she does. Isn't it obvious that he does not care about us or what his decisions cost the city?"

Malaysia kept her eyes on the skies and shrugged her shoulders, "Yeah, clearly Daisy has a crush on the man. We have to remember, though, she's not from the Underbelly or Leicester. She's Highgarden-borne, so her struggles are different from the rest of us."

Alexia shook her head, clenched her fists, and enunciated slowly and emphatically, "But she's fucking powered! Doesn't that count for anything? Why wouldn't she want her own kind to be free to do whatever they want without restriction?"

"Just because we're powered doesn't mean that we are all on the same side. What should unite us divides us, too. You know how many big-time people keep their powers under wraps? How many powered people say they wish they didn't have powers?"

"They only feel like that because they don't feel backed by their own government," Alexia retorted.

"There are other reasons, too," Malaysia countered. "Some feel like our powers make us useful pawns in others' games, and they want to be measured by something other than their power sets. And I can't tell you how many people I've talked to who've told me their boyfriends or girlfriends only got with them because of their powers." She recalled her own history – living in the Underbelly and being used by others because of her powerful eyesight – and quickly deflecting to take the attention off herself. "Frimas, you remember how messed up Symone was after that whole Affinity Theory thing. She almost quit the Company because of that." Malaysia's left arm suddenly buzzed.

Alexia waved her hands with annoyed understanding. "I mean, okay, I get it. I wouldn't have liked that, either. Still, Malaysia, we should all be free to do what we want and not have to capitulate to the imaginations of others, especially those who don't even know what it feels like to be like us, don't you think?"

Alexia noticed an awkward silence and looked over at Malaysia, who was preoccupied by the message she received on her stripe and the lustful feelings her lover produced. Alexia said, "Um, Uretha to Malaysia?"

Malaysia snapped out of her licentious daze. *Oh shit,* she recoiled, *I hope Alexia doesn't read my mind. No one can know that I'm seeing him.*

"Everything alright?" Alexia asked, tempted to probe but shutting down the urge just as quickly as it appeared.

"Oh yeah," Malaysia answered, chuckling slightly to relieve some of the tension gripping her spine. "Just my man, you know."

Alexia's eyes glowed. "For real? Hey now, Malaysia, that's good, right?"

*Huh? Good?* "What do you mean?" Malaysia kept her eyes on the skies.

"Well, I remember a while back, you and I were talking about how you felt like things between you and Dennis were looking bleak."

Karl, eyes shut but ears wide open, agreed, "Right, I remember that, too. Have things changed?"

"Yeah, things have certainly changed," Malaysia deflected. "One day he's not paying me any attention, the next, he can't stop thinking about me. It's like a switch flipped, and now he's giving me what I need, and we're better off now than we've ever been." Malaysia thought, *Ugh, I hate this. Now I'm lying to my teammates.*

Alexia's senses could feel the tension all over Malaysia's body. *Why is Malaysia's lying to me? I should probe her. No, nope, not gonna do that anymore, remember?*

A voice in Alexia's head gently protested, *But she'll never know you looked under the hood.*

Alexia replied to the voice, *No, we can't, not to her, not to our team.*

The voice growled, *Ugh, fine. You never let us have any fun.*

Alexia responded to Malaysia, "Well, I'm happy for you guys. We'll have to get together again sometime soon."

The three Elite got a buzz from their stripes. Intelligence passed them information about Mitchell Daniels and the members of the POC office. Karl swiped through the information on his pocket holoscreen and deduced, "Looks like everyone from the POC is clean as a whistle. Not even so much as a parking ticket."

"Right," Alexia did the same thing and hypothesized, "there's no way any of these pulled this off. Right?"

"It doesn't look that way. None of them carry the powers that the suspects wielded. None of their connections could have given them the capability to pull NextGen off."

"Then we need to hurry. The Chancellor's gonna want heads to roll, and it'll be Daniels and his team if we don't stop the UPD." Malaysia stepped on the accelerator, grateful to Dax and Stephanie for their timely diversion.

About ten minutes later, they arrived at the entrance to the Uri City Police Department, a massive, seventeen-story concrete palace surrounded by a green laser fence about twenty feet tall. Malaysia slowed the hovercar and approached the access gate. An officer stepped out of the booth to the left of the car and tapped a transparent badge on the car's window. The badge scanned the occupants and determined they had permission to enter, lighting white for approval. The officer stepped back, and the gate in front of them rose. Once it fully opened, Malaysia accelerated then put the car on autopilot to find a spot to park. They landed about five spaces in front of the glass-paned entry to the department. The hovercar's doors swung open like wings, and they stepped out and walked into UPD.

They pushed through the unusually crowded lobby and approached the reception desk. Several visitors were annoyed that they cut in line and protested, but the Elite paid them no mind. Malaysia said to the officer standing at the desk, "We three are with the Elite Unit of the Company on official business. We need to see Captain Stewart at once."

Malaysia planted her palm on a reader, and the officer read Malaysia's dossier and replied, "One moment," and pushed a button on the holoscreen. "Captain Stewart, you have guests at the front."

Alexia turned and looked at the white-lit lobby with most of its chairs occupied by citizens and officers. She still disagreed with the color clash of burgundy flooring with orange walls, recalling talking with an administrator once about making their scheme at least match their patrol officers' red and white uniforms. She reminisced further on her tenure with the UPD, the years she had walked those floors and utilized her mystic prowess to help the department put scores of bosses away.

The officer instructed, "You guys can head back, Stewart is waiting for you on the second floor, room 3A."

"Thanks," Karl acknowledged. The three walked around the reception desk and to the door at the back of the lobby. The light around the door lit white for approval, then swung open. They walked through and traveled about twenty feet to the elevator. Karl pressed "UP," and the elevator lowered to meet them.

"You two ready?" Karl asked.

"Of course!" Malaysia's eyes squinted.

"This is what we do," Alexia's eyes glowed green.

"Alright then," Karl said. The elevator doors opened, and they went in. Karl pressed "2," and the doors closed. The elevator carried them to their destination, then opened again. Malaysia, Karl, and Alexia observed the chaos that the NextGen disaster generated. Officers and detectives scurried across the floor passing holoscreens around from one place to another. Scores of witnesses sat at desks giving their accounts of what they survived. Alexia wished she could have been there to help and wondered if she could have saved some of the ones who were lost in the tragedy.

"Let's go, 3A," Malaysia ordered.  They walked through the middle aisle to the interrogation rooms.  They reached 3A and opened the door.  Captain Stewart and two of his detectives assigned to the case stood inside a dark observation room with a one-way mirror looking at Mitchell Daniels in the interrogation room next door.  The Elite felt like they were back at the Company in an observation room on the training floor, noting the holoscreens on desks at the back wall.

"Ah, here they are.  Elite, these are Detectives Holloway and Fletcher," Stewart introduced them.

"Pleasure to meet you.  I'm Malaysia Jones, and this is Karl Luther.  I think you all know Alexia Montague."  Everyone shook hands.

"So," Stewart began, "what do you guys have on Daniels?"

"Well, we honestly have nothing on him.  Have you talked to Mallack?" Malaysia inquired.

"Yes, she *requested* you guys get first bite of the apple, so I've gotten you guys cleared for seven minutes in the room.  After that, he and the POC belong to us," Stewart informed them.

"Captain, I still don't think this is a good idea," Holloway griped.

"Well, this comes straight from the Chancellor, so we have to stand down," Stewart reminded Holloway.  "You two, observe them, make sure nothing gets out of hand."

"Alright, Alexia, Malaysia, do your thing," Karl hyped them up.  "Seven minutes."

"I've done more with less time," Alexia batted her eyes.

"So have I," Malaysia agreed.  Both of them chuckled.

"Y'all are nasty.  Get in there," Karl laughed.

Alexia and Malaysia put their game faces on, left 3A, and entered 3B, a white room brightly lit with near-blinding LED lights in the ceiling. Daniels sat cuffed to a metal bar attached to his end of the table. He gazed as Alexia and Malaysia positioned themselves at the opposite end and thought it was his birthday, marveling at their radiant beauty. "Oh wow, now you two are probably the loveliest bruisers I have ever laid eyes on."

"Aww, you think we're lovely?" Alexia scrunched her body and twirled her hair. "Thank you!"

"Quite welcome," Mitchell returned. "I assume you're here to get information out of me, so I'm going to tell you like I told the captain in there. I don't have anything to hide, so you can pry all you want. You won't find what you're looking for from me."

Malaysia looked at Alexia and replied, "Oh, so this should be easy then."

"I agree," Alexia responded.

"Easy?" Mitchell pondered.

Alexia turned a chair around and slowly squatted into it, gently folding her arms onto the backrest. "Yes, well, we could ask you a round of twenty questions, but we decided instead to just look for ourselves and see whether you're lying. Trust us, this won't take long."

Mitchell tensed up, having heard stories about offenders being transferred to contract defense organizations to suffer a fate worse than death. "Wait, what are you going to do?"

Malaysia relayed, "Oh, we're what you could call *living lie detectors*. We are going to strap you to Alexia's mind here, and I'm going to scan your biorhythms, and we'll decide whether you're telling us the truth. If you lie, I suggest you get your affairs in order, because you will have lived your last day as a free man."

Mitchell's mind eased. "Okay, then, let's have at it, I'm game," Mitchell sat up straight.

Karl deduced, "Yeah, there's no way he did this. He's too calm."

Alexia's eyes glowed green, and green mist flowed from her hands through Mitchell's ears to his mind. Malaysia then began, "You say that you had nothing to do with this, correct?" She switched her eyesight to thermal to check for changes in his body temperature.

"Yes, that's correct," Mitchell stated. Alexia could feel Mitchell steady his mind.

"If that's the case, then why did these terrorists say they were the Powered Order?"

"I don't know why they said that. I don't know why they dressed in garb with POC draped across their chests. But I know for a fact that they do not represent the Powered Order."

"How do you know that?" Malaysia asked.

"Do you know what the POC stands for? We want to engage fully in the world in *harmony* with the unpowered. We have no desire to dominate the unpowered. Take out your holoscreen and play their speech. I'll prove it to you."

"Alexia, you good?" Malaysia checked on her partner.

"I'm good, holding steady," Alexia answered.

Malaysia pulled out her pocket holoscreen and looked up the speech from the terrorists at NextGen. She found the clip and pressed "PLAY," and the tape sounded, "For far too long, we have cowered under the direction and influence of the unpowered, made to hide behind their fear and only engage in activities that bolster their position of power over us. We pay our share of fares, entertain them with our abilities, rescue them when they are incapable of saving their powerless selves.

And yet, they believe that we do not have the right to govern ourselves, let alone them. We, the Powered Order Coalition, stand united to say, 'No more!' We will no longer stand for the unpowered to wield their powerlessness over us."

"Play the end of the speech," Daniels requested.

Malaysia forwarded to the end of the speech, "We guarantee that nothing will stand in the way of the powered taking their rightful places in this city. And if anyone chooses to stand in our way, they will be eliminated."

Daniels explained, "See, right there, that part about 'the powered taking their rightful places' and 'they will be eliminated,' that is not us. We do not condone violence. We choose to live in harmony with all mankind. Even though we, the powered, are incredibly special, we should be treated as equals with the non-powered, period. We don't want to dominate anyone. That's how the unpowered have treated us for over a century. We do not want to flip the script. That shit is what Dariuz and his kind want Uri City to think. But that is not the POC, that is not what we are about. We want peace and harmony, not power and domination."

Alexia probed Mitchell's mind. She observed a younger him walk into the office in the Underbelly for the first time. He read the mantras of the POC that were etched on a plaque on the wall and felt an immense sense of pride. She fast-forwarded through a highlight reel of his rise through the ranks of the POC to eventually become its leader three years later. She witnessed him holding meetings with several business owners in the Underbelly and Leicester districts, hosting rallies across Uri City, and delivering speeches to Chancellor Croft and his executive board. Nothing she observed read *domination* or *power*. Meanwhile, Malaysia checked Mitchell's body and recognized no abnormalities.

Alexia released Mitchell's mind. Malaysia switched her eyesight back to normal. "So, then, why would someone want to put your name on this?"

"I have no idea. What I do know, though, is that my crew would not jeopardize two decades of work like this. We have never been this close to restoring full citizenship rights to the powered. No one in the POC would do this. This was not us."

Malaysia turned and looked through the one-way mirror at Karl. Karl understood her signal and established a call between him and Director Mallack. "This is Mallack."

"We're at the UPD. Daniels and the POC didn't do this," Karl responded.

"Okay. I'll get the Chancellor. Tell UPD to release Daniels and his team to the Company's custody, order 816. They'll know what that means."

"Copy that, Director." Karl disconnected the line. He then looked at Captain Stewart and said, "Order 816."

Stewart looked at Karl, then said, "Roger that, letting the Deputy Commissioner know now." He sent a message through his stripe that read, "Attention: Daniels and the POC released to the custody of the Company per order 816."

Holloway said, "Just like that?"

Stewart replied, "Just like that. Chancellor's orders."

Fletcher stated, "Let it go, Holloway. You know how these things go."

"Shit," Holloway cried. "We can't ever keep the good ones."

"Nothing personal, buddy," Karl assured him. "We got bigger fish to fry, and the UPD isn't equipped to handle these jokers."

"Ugh, fine." Holloway stormed out of the interrogation room.

Stewart walked to Karl and said, "816 is approved. We'll escort the POC to the Company at once."

"Good deal. Can we take Daniels ourselves? We have more questions to ask him and could use the ride back to the Company to get answers."

Stewart agreed, "Sure thing. I'll clear it with admin. Good luck, guys. Make those assholes pay for NextGen."

"Thank you, Captain," Karl shook his hand.

Karl walked out of the room and entered 3B. He said to Malaysia and Alexia, "Order 816 was enacted. Daniels, you and your team are coming with us."

Mitchell looked up. "I am? What are you going to do to us?"

"You're going to help us find these assholes and make them pay for NextGen. You say you're not the ones who did this, and we believe you. So, we need your expertise to find these guys and stop them before they do something worse to the city."

"Oh, good."

Malaysia said, "Once they get you out of the cuffs—"

Daniels laughed, "Oh, these things? Here," Daniels flicked his wrists, and the cuffs fell off his wrists and onto the table. "They couldn't hold me if they wanted to."

Alexia's eyes glowed slightly, turned on by Mitchell's bravado. "You let them hold you in custody?"

"Like I told you, the POC does not condone violence." Daniels stood up and continued, "Shall we go?"

Alexia looked at Malaysia, and Malaysia looked at Karl, then at Daniels. "Sure, let's go," Malaysia answered.

# 8
# Change

Symone's thoughts spun faster than the spinning blades of the ceiling fan her eyes locked onto. She lay naked under the thin sheet covering her bed, her hands clasped behind her head. The light through the windows could not cut through the cloudiness in her headspace. The softness of the sheets could neither caress nor comfort Symone's body enough to deter her mind's rapid pace. She vacillated between the NextGen nightmare, Malcolm's imminent promotion, her own rise in the ranks, and the deepening bond between Malcolm and her. She lifted her head up slightly to free her hands, placed her left on the nine-pointed star, and her right on the ribbon tied around her waist, the same ribbon Malcolm crafted out of her star many quarters ago. Her temples tensed up like someone was pushing their thumbs into them.

Convinced that she was not going back to sleep, she sat up and looked at the clock that read 27:04, a little under a cycle before the rising. Symone said aloud, "I have to get these thoughts out of my head. AI, new journal entry."

AI responded, "Acknowledged. Audio or video?"

"Video."

"Acknowledged. Recording video journal in 3, 2, 1, begin."

A blue line swiftly scanned the room from top to bottom, then Symone began.

"I struggled to sleep last night, again. So much is going on right now, and I'm trying so hard to ride the wave like I always do. But I don't know, I feel like it's becoming too much for me."

She lay back down. "The Analyst and I were talking yesterday, going through the team's stats, and everyone seemed to be holding steady in their progressions. He then said something to me that I don't think he meant to say because he then said, 'Oops, I shouldn't have said that,' like he does about pretty much everything he is thinking about. Anyway, I asked him what he was talking about, and he said, 'Well, I think we might have been wrong about the Affinity Theory.' I was like, 'Wait, what do you mean?'

"He then revealed to me that he thinks it's not my closeness to people that's changing them. He said, 'I've been watching how close you've grown with the team. Obviously, you're not dating any of them but Malcolm, but you're still very close to the rest of the team. And I've been careful to, with your permission, monitor your interactions outside of battle and training. And your connections with the rest of the team have not affected their evolutions.' I pressed him, and he said, 'I don't have solid proof of it yet because we weren't monitoring it from this perspective, and I'm not sure if we're too late, but I think it's either purely battle-related or star power-related.' Long story short, he thinks everyone is evolving because of my star power.

"While it is kind of exciting, it has me thinking a lot about my past relationships with every person I've come into contact with, especially in battle and training. Like, what if he's right? What if I made everyone evolve and never knew it?

Has anyone ever known what was happening to them and wrapped their heads around the fact that it was me, or rather, my power? Were the people who have come and gone in my life ever using me for what I did for them and never told me?"

Symone sat up again and scooted to her headboard to rest her back against it. She ran her fingers through her locs and continued, "It's got me in this really dark place. Malcolm's talking about the future, his promotion and us being together despite being my actual boss. I know he said he never knew about the Affinity Theory shit that Mallack, Malaysia, and the Analyst pulled over us, but how do I know that he's not using me now, now that he knows? Has he talked to the Analyst about me? Has the Analyst slipped out to him that he doesn't think it's the Affinity Theory?

"Never mind the fact that Malcolm seems to be making plans about us. I should be happy, right? Right?! Alexia and Malaysia both talking about how happy they are that I am staying with the Elite, with the family. I can feel everyone tying themselves to me, and it's eating me alive. I feel like I'm losing my freedom. Training my teammates has made me more responsible for them. Being with Malcolm is making me responsible, no, accountable to *and* for him. And if the Analyst is right, then anyone I've battled with, sparred with, accidentally used my powers around, I am responsible for what happened to them."

The images of the NextGen disaster flashed through her mind. The terrorists' leader, his cadence, his chameleon-like power, his fighting style – Symone gasped, and a lump emerged in her throat. "Oh Akan, what if I'm right about that guy at NextGen? Shit, I should have talked to Malcolm yesterday. He had to stay with Mallack to deal with all this stuff going on with NextGen from the director's perspective.

I'll tell him today.  If I'm right, he and the others have to know what we're up against.  Akan, I hope I'm wrong.  Akan, I *have* to be wrong.  This shit's too much to deal with."  Symone buried her head in between her knees, trying to convince herself that she was not responsible for creating a monster.  She then pulled the sheet over her face and wished to be swallowed by her bed.

Two cycles later, Symone rode the elevator to the Elite Grand Hall.  She had received a message that she was needed in the Conference Room without delay.  The elevator door opened, and she walked out and to the left, then turned the right corner.  She saw the rest of the team all waiting outside the Conference Room door and grew concerned.

Malaysia was the first to see her and said, "Here she is."  The rest of the team turned to face her.

"Great rising, everyone," she slowly articulated.

"Great rising indeed, Symone!" Alexia rushed and hugged Symone.  Symone was surprised and squeezed her back.

"Somebody's happy to see me.  Everything okay?" she asked.

"Yes, everything is great!" Alexia let her go.

"Alright, so, why are we all standing out here?  The message said our meeting was urgent," Symone worked to compartmentalize her thoughts and emotions to absorb whatever intel she was about to receive.

Malcolm, heart full of joy, stood in front of Symone and said, "Yes, it is urgent.  But, before we get in there, we all saw something highly unusual, and we need your eyes to see if you see it, too."

*My eyes? Isn't that literally what Malaysia's role on the team is for?* While Symone wrestled with her rebuttal, the team looked ahead of Symone and gazed at the wall behind her. Malcolm gently clasped Symone's shoulders and positioned her to where her back was parallel to the wall. Symone was confused but didn't want to be rude. "See what?"

He leaned in, kissed her forehead, then whispered in her ear, "Turn around."

"Okay?" Symone complied and turned around. Her avatar stared back at her – her locs floating and falling perfectly in slow motion, her uniform aglow in crimson and gold. Symone's mouth agape and her mind utterly blown away, she backed up three steps to read the words atop her avatar's abdomen, "Symone Watson, Codename Starburst." Affixed to the left of her avatar was Symone's bio, which read, *"Symone Watson is the brightest star in the galaxy. A living energy generator, Watson brings both the power of the three suns and her extensive prizefighting prowess to every battle she engages in. She has served with the Company a little under a year and is the newest Defender of the Elite Unit."* Scenes of her battles with the Elite over the past three quarters played to her right.

The team clapped and cheered for Symone in celebration of her achievement, elated that she was officially an Elite Defender of the Uri City Division of the Company. Symone felt proud, emotional, accomplished, and victorious. *Yes! Yes! I did it! I'm Elite! Finally!*

But that pride was suddenly engulfed by dread. She fought back tears while thinking, *Akan, I've longed for this spot on the wall! Why am I feeling like this?!* Symone looked for a reason, *any* reason, to sprint for the exit.

But Malcolm hugged her from behind and smiled while saying, "Congratulations, love."

She grabbed his hands and bathed in his gentle yet consuming embrace to rid herself of the anxiety crawling on her skin. *Don't leave. I can't leave this. I can't leave him.* She closed her eyes and mustered up the energy to reply, "Thank you."

Malaysia could tell that Malcolm and Symone were about to have a moment. "Alright, let's head inside, guys, before Malcolm and Symone start making out in front of us," Malaysia redirected the team. "Mallack's ready for us."

Alexia stood flat-footed, playfully staring at Malcolm and Symone, and remarked, "What's wrong with watching them making out in front of us?"

"I second that," Duncan stood next to her and joked. They fist-bumped each other and smiled.

Malcolm and Symone snorted and chuckled. Malcolm replied, "Let's move, team."

The Elite entered the conference room and recognized the director and Stephanie. They also noticed two unfamiliar faces in the line-up. The team silently counted the number of chairs at the table and immediately figured that one of the new faces was Joy Olivier, and the other was Mitchell Daniels. They took their seats, leaving one space in between Alexia and Malaysia.

Mallack stood up and said, "Great rising, Elite. We have a lot of ground to cover today, so I'll get right to it. First, Elite, meet Joy Olivier, codename Kaminari. Joy, please stand up."

Joy pressed her hands against her skin-tight jeans and stood up. Joy's jet-black straight hair flowed down her spine in a ponytail, her caramel skin sharply contrasting with her sil-ver-white eyes and her white sleeveless shirt.

Mallack continued. "Some of you know, Joy has been with the Company for four years, spending a year in training be-fore joining and eventually becoming the leader of Super Team VI for the past two years. Joy worked closely with the UCs, taking down many of the Underbelly and Leicester's crime lords. As stated in our last meeting, she single-handedly took down the Flower Power base of operations while getting her entire team out alive, and assisted with getting you guys the access you needed to take down Brimstone. Joy, welcome to the team."

The team clapped for her as a bashful Joy scrunched her shoulders in and saluted, "It is an honor, Director, Elite. I am grateful to be fighting alongside you all. I won't let you down. Thank you for this opportunity."

"Well, don't just stand there, Joy," Karl interjected. "Take your seat."

Malaysia motioned her hand toward the empty seat next to her. As Joy walked over to take her seat, Symone pon-dered silently, *Something doesn't add up. If Joy is as gifted as everyone says she is, then why did the Company choose to put me on this team last year, and not her? She clearly has the power and the body count. No reason that I should have been chosen over her. That doesn't make any sense to me. Am I overreacting?* Symone thought to say something but kept quiet, not wanting to spoil the moment or throw the meeting off on a tangent.

Joy sat down, and Malaysia stuck out her hand. "Good to see you again, Joy! Welcome to the Elite!"

"It's good to see you, too," Joy returned as she shook Malaysia's hand. "Thank you so much, I'm excited!" Joy thought to herself, *Akan, I can't believe I'm here among these giants! I don't belong here, how did I get here?!*

Mallack continued. "Now, onto the matter at hand. Everyone, this is Mitchell Daniels, the head of the Powered Order Coalition. Yesterday, he and his team were arrested and taken into UPD custody. Thanks to Malaysia and Alexia's 'lie detector test,' we were able to determine that the POC are not the ones we are hunting. Under Order 816, Daniels and his team are under our custody until we can gather evidence to prove their innocence. I asked him to talk to us about the POC and how he distinguishes his organization from the crew that hit NextGen. Daniels, the floor is yours."

Daniels, wearing a blue jumpsuit he picked out of Weapons and Wardrobe, rubbed his goatee as he stood up and began. "Great rising. Thank you for bringing us here and giving me the chance to share what information I have regarding the incident at NextGen. My team and I worked with your Intelligence team well into the late cycles of the night and were able to develop a working manifesto for the attackers.

"The Powered Order has seven mantras that govern what we do, bound by a code of peace and harmony among all mankind, powered and unpowered."

Daniels used the holoscreen in front of the room to display and read the POC's mantras:

1 – The Powered are people, worthy of dignity, honor, and respect because of their existence.

2 – The Powered are people first, not tools or commodities to be used or exploited.

3 – The Powered have aided in building Uretha into what it is today.

4 – The Powered are not dangerous because of their powers, and therefore should be afforded every opportunity to

pursue their interests unhindered by restrictions based on fear and ignorance.

5 – The Powered have the right to live as freely as the Unpowered by virtue of their existence alone, not by permission from the Unpowered.

6 – The Powered have the right to exercise their opinions, values, and morals as individuals. No one Powered person speaks for all, and no one person's actions reflect the opinions or beliefs of the Powered as a whole.

7 – The Powered desire to live in harmony with all mankind, and though the Powered are incredibly special, we should be treated as equals in all of life (not as tokens, chattel, entertainment, or subhuman) at all times, not just when it is convenient.

Daisy's blood boiled, and she started tapping the table. *I can't believe we have to listen to this bullshit. I could* blitz *his ass right now and do this city a huge favor.*

Daniels paced the floor while keeping steady contact with the Elite. "As I explained to Malaysia and Alexia yesterday during their interrogation, the POC has spent the past two decades fighting for the powered to have full citizenship in Uri City, and because of how close we are to achieving it, it would be foolish for any of us to jeopardize that. So, using the speech the attackers gave yesterday, we determined that if they had a manifesto, it would sound like a negative imprint of the POC's mantras, something like this."

Daniels used the holoscreen to slide the POC's mantras to the left while displaying a second set of mantras titled "The Extremists' Manifesto." He read –

1 – The Powered are people, worthy of dignity, honor, and respect because of their existence as a new, better species of humanity.

2 – The Powered are heavily responsible for building the world into what it is today.

3 – Akan has chosen the Powered to be special in this world, and they should be treated as such by those without powers.

4 – Evolution demands that there be a dominant and subordinate species. Therefore, the Unpowered should be dominated by the greater species.

5 – The Powered have the right to live freely by being the greater species and should not answer to the laws of the Unpowered nor seek permission from the Unpowered to exist.

6 – The Powered have the right to use their powers to exercise their dominance in the world and seek compliance by any means necessary.

7 – The Powered will live in harmony with the Unpowered, as long as the Unpowered recognize their place as the subordinate species.

Malcolm was awestruck. He crossed his arms. "Damn, Daniels! You guys were able to pull all that just from the speech?"

*You're actually falling for this shit?!* Daisy couldn't believe her ears.

"Well, we figured that this crew, whoever they are, is probably inspired by Chancellor Holland and his attempt to assume absolute dominion over Uri City over a century and a half ago. We know that his actions then inspired the government to put the laws in place which limit powered individuals. Combined with their threat to eliminate anyone who stands in their way, we can only assume that these are the rules they will play by."

Alexia gently patted the table and ran her fingers through her long, wavy hair. "It's obvious they are unafraid to attack anyone, even the powered. So, who exactly are these guys, and where the Frimas did they come from?"

Stephanie uncrossed then recrossed her legs and answered, "Intelligence has been working since NextGen to pull any intel from these guys. So far, we've retrieved nothing. Biometrics, power analysis, nothing has proven fruitful. It's like these guys are super ghosts. They do not exist on the grid. Preliminary theory is that they are not from Uri City. We've gotten permission from the Chancellor's office to enlist In-CiP and pull their data for further analysis. It will take us about two days to sift through it all, and we're hoping we will be able to provide something of substance at that time."

"Until then, Elite, prepare yourselves," Mallack instructed them. "We are in for a long three weeks. Chancellor Croft wants the vote to go through, so he has made these extremists our top priority. Malcolm, make sure your team is ready at a moment's notice. Everyone, make Joy feel at home, and use Daniels and the POC however you can."

Daniels raised his hand, "Might I make a suggestion? More like a request?"

Mallack looked at Daniels and said, "What is it?"

Mitchell cleared his throat. "If Croft wants to secure the vote, it might be beneficial for me to get in front of a camera and make a statement on behalf of the POC. Even a joint statement between him and me."

Daisy rolled her eyes, sat back, and crossed her arms as Mallack asked, "How so?"

"The narrative is that the POC have become extremists, but Croft has been working tirelessly with the POC to secure his interests. If he and I were to appear on UNN, we can at least shift the narrative and separate ourselves from the extremists. At the very least, we can make a clear distinction between the

POC and them. Your hunt, then, could be solely focused on the extremists, and not the vote."

Malcolm tapped his forehead while his mind rapidly analyzed Mitchell's approach. "Boss, that might not be a bad idea. It could even force their hand, make them come out of hiding."

Mallack rubbed her chin and answered, "Okay, Daniels. I will speak with Chancellor Croft and see how he wishes to proceed. Right now, technically, you are still in UPD custody given Order 816. I'll keep you informed once things change. Alright, Elite, you're dismissed. Symone, may I have a word with you in my office?"

Symone thought, *I don't want to talk to you right now, the fuck?* but answered, "Sure thing, Director."

Mallack and Stephanie left the room. The Elite came over to Joy and introduced themselves to her. Karl could hardly contain his excitement as he proclaimed his admiration of her work with Super Team VI.

Symone shook Joy's hand, and then gently grabbed Malcolm's arm and said, "Hey, I need to talk to you about something, something to do with the attackers. Once I'm done with Mallack, can we go somewhere?"

"Sure, and hey, we didn't get to talk yesterday, either."

"I know. Everything with NextGen, you and Mallack had a lot to deal with. I knew it was going to be a long night for you two. Thank you for your messages, though, they were really thoughtful," Symone levitated a few inches off the ground and kissed Malcolm's lips.

"You're welcome. Go see what Mallack wants. I'll meet up with you later."

"Okay," Symone answered. She walked out of the room.

Malaysia, meanwhile, saved Joy from her fan club. "Alright, everybody, Joy and I have a lot to talk about, so if you don't mind, can you leave us here?"

Alexia answered, "Fine, but don't keep her to yourself all day. We want to get to know her, too!"

"Second that," Duncan agreed. The crew motioned for Daniels to follow them out of the room, and they left Malaysia and Joy behind.

"So, Joy," Malaysia sat atop the table and crossed her legs, "how did it feel leaving Super Team VI?"

Joy put her hands atop the chair in front of her and said, "You know, it was really hard. That team has been my family for two and a half years now, and we've been through Frimas and back so many times. But this is the Elite! I could not pass this up. I've worked so hard to get here."

"I know the feeling," Malaysia briefly reminisced. "Trust me, there's nothing like fighting on the Elite. We don't get as much action as the super teams, but when we do, like right now, we bring the heat."

"I'm psyched! I won't let you down," Joy assured Malaysia.

"Of course you won't! I'm your mentor! We're going to make you the best Elite Defender in the city!"

"Oh, now I don't know about all that. You guys are fucking legends. I saw the wall. You all make me look like a trainee."

"Well, we're about to experience just how powerful you are, and you'll have your own spot on that wall with the rest of us in no time. Quick test!"

"Ooh, a test already? Let's go, I'm ready!"

Malaysia hit her with, "What's the Defender's Oath?"

"Oh damn, Orientation 101," Joy chuckled. "Okay, ahem."

Joy stood at a pseudo-attention, locked eyes with Malaysia, and declared, "I am a Defender. The citizens are my people. I swear to protect Uri City when called upon to defend it from any and all threats – foreign and domestic. I am a Defender. I humbly acknowledge the power I wield and the station I have been granted. I swear to use my skills, powers, and abilities for the betterment of the populace I serve. I am a Defender. As I stand as part of our city's last line of defense, I swear to be a watchful guardian of the health and welfare of my fellow Defenders and to never place myself or my agenda above the team, the Division, the Company, or the city. So help me Akan."

Malaysia nodded, then asked, "And what are the three laws?"

Joy recited, "Law 1: People are citizens, not the enemy. Unless authorized otherwise, our aim is to subdue combatants using the path of least resistance. Law 2: We are to act on behalf of the Company *only* when authorized to do so. Any action taken without authorization may result in termination from the Company and criminal prosecution. Law 3: As agents of Uri City, we must never abuse the position we hold nor abuse the powers we wield for selfish gain or ulterior motive that may jeopardize the overall goals and objectives of the Company and Uri City."

"Very good, Joy! Well, let me show you around the hall, and maybe before the day is over, you can show me what you got in the training room." Malaysia popped off the desk, and as Joy breathed a sigh of relief, they walked out of the conference room.

Karl, Malcolm, Daisy, Alexia, Duncan, and Mitchell were walking the halls toward the quarters. Daisy, fuming because of Daniels's suggestion to Mallack, decided to press him. "Daniels, how can you be so confident that the attackers are not POC?"

Alexia attempted to cut her off at the pass. "Oh Akan, Daisy, don't start, alright?"

The team stopped walking as Mitchell said, "No, it's alright, Alexia, I can answer that." He stood a few feet in front of Daisy and continued, "I'm confident because what happened at NextGen yesterday took months of planning."

Daisy's eyes cut through Mitchell like a pair of sais. "And how do you know that?" she questioned.

"Well, over a year ago, my team put on an event at NextGen. It was the culmination of two years of planning. There's no way that something like this was a spontaneous attack. Every step they took had to be precise."

Daisy crossed her arms. "Just because it took forever to plan it doesn't mean that they weren't your people. Maybe they were working under your nose the whole time and you just didn't notice it."

"Oh boy," Karl muttered.

Mitchell, having engaged opposing views like Daisy's more times than he could count, did the mental calculus required to argue his position, and retorted, "You assume that there are shadowy figures working for the POC. Sure, every political group has some variant lurking around. Because of that possibility, we, the *real* POC, have taken every measure we can conjure to ensure that no variant will interfere with or undermine our agenda."

Believing that Daisy had finally met her match, Malcolm whispered to Alexia, "I think he can handle himself. Let's let them argue."

"I agree," she said. They slowly started walking backward. Alexia silently crafted a mental lasso, roped Karl and Duncan, and gently tugged them backward. They both felt the tug and turned slightly. Alexia motioned them to come with them into the quarters, and they slinked away, unnoticed by either Daniels or Daisy.

"Let me ask you," Daniels pivoted, "what are you so upset with the POC about?"

"I'm not upset," Daisy retorted and cut her eyes. "I just don't think the POC knows what's best for the city."

"And let me guess who you think does: Dariuz?"

Daisy pursed her lips. "Yes, he and his side of the aisle know how to run this city better than anyone else can. Croft and his 'Powered in Office' agenda is a danger to the city, not a help."

Mitchell found Daisy's political doggedness refreshing and her body alluring from head to toe. He lowered his head and chuckled. Daisy squinted her eyes. "What's so funny?" she pressed.

"You're from Highgarden, aren't you?"

Daisy was taken aback. "How did you know that?"

"Well, statistics show that most of Dariuz's backers are from Highgarden and Meridian. Some support comes from Genesis Landing, right along the boundary between them and Meridian. Leicester and the Underbelly hate Dariuz with reckless abandon. So, it makes sense why someone as stunning as you would follow him."

Daisy was speechless, hanging onto Mitchell's use of the word *stunning* to describe her. Mitchell immediately noticed the slight tick of her right eyebrow and the way her lips slightly parted. Mitchell stepped to Daisy and closed the gap to mere inches between them. Staring into her eyes like a live camera, he delivered, "As long as you're fighting for your own interests, it will be nearly impossible for you to see the other side and come to the right decision that benefits everyone. And that's too bad, because sometimes the right decision can be staring you right in the face, but you can't see it because you're stuck looking in the mirror instead of past it."

Daisy could see her reflection staring back at her through Mitchell's eyes. He backed up and walked away toward the quarters. While he walked through the open door, Daisy stood like a gazelle gazing at headlights. Her mind escaped her body, still stuck on the word *stunning*. Once her mind's circuitry reconnected, she scrambled to understand why her body was suddenly on fire. The only person she could think of to help her make sense of it was Alexia. She paused for a moment, knowing how divided they were lately, but she remembered what Malaysia told her the day before. She said, "Fuck it," and sent a message to Alexia.

"So... I think Mitchell made a pass at me. What do I do?"

# 9

# Stuck

Symone opened the door to Mallack's office. Inside, she noticed several boxes scattered around the floor, some of them filled, others empty. Symone remembered that Mallack's departure was looming, and despite her animosity toward her last year, Symone cared for Mallack and admired her leadership and care for her and the entire division. A lump inside Symone's throat attempted to take her breath away, and she coughed to clear it. Mallack, seated at her desk, motioned Symone to sit down.

"I'll try not to keep you long," Mallack said.

"It's fine," Symone assured Mallack. "What did you want to talk about?"

Mallack leaned back and rocked her seat. "I wanted to get an update from you regarding the team's evolution. The Analyst has given me his report, and now I want to hear from you what you've observed from your teammates."

"Where do you want to begin?"

"Let's start with Malcolm and work our way down the list." Mallack tapped on a few keys on her countertop, and the holoscreen to Symone's left displayed Malcolm's black and blue Kingdom Come avatar and his demographics and statistics.

"So, Malcolm is getting closer to being able to create objects out of thin air. He said something to me about being able to feel the particles in the air a lot more keenly than ever before. Though he hasn't been able to produce anything right away, I believe in time, with the right push, he will manage turning air into solid objects of his own design."

Mallack's eyes widened. "Symone, that's impressive!"

"Absolutely, Director," Symone agreed. "We already know Malcolm is capable of reshaping solid objects. If he can re-shape the air?! Who, tell me, *who* can beat him?"

"Why hasn't he attempted to do anything like that in the field?" Mallack asked, knowing the answer, but wanting to hear Symone say it anyway.

"Malcolm has to concentrate longer to perform high-level manipulations, so in-field transformations this complex would require defending his position long enough to pull it off. Besides, you know Malcolm. 'Exercise restraint.' Even in training, he's still holding back, and it makes no sense because he still wins every single time. Every. Single. Time," Symone growled and gritted her teeth, still ticked that he got the best of her the day before.

"Right you are," Mallack stated. "His Ability level is maintaining well above Elite level. At some point, he'll have to unleash all that power on somebody."

Symone's eyes flickered, but then she remembered, "Well, maybe not, if he becomes the Director."

Mallack nodded, "You have a point there. Okay, so next is Malaysia."

Mallack swiped to Malaysia's purple and black Eagle avatar as Symone explained, "Right, so with Malaysia, we have been working very, very hard on getting her to see past cloaks. In our battles these past quarters, we realized that part of our tactical disadvantage has come from us needing her to see through cloaked buildings and other guarded things. We have to break the cloak first, then she can see whatever we need her to relay to us. So, she's been working on seeing past them. Double W and the Analyst haven't found a solution, but I feel like Malaysia may figure it out before they do anyway. Once she does, she will be able to scan targets and get demographics off them long before we have to engage."

"What's her issue with seeing through the cloaks?" Mallack inquired.

Symone scratched her head, "The way the Analyst said it, every cloak is designed to withstand all kinds of powers. Their adaptive properties are near-impossible to beat without overloading them first. Malaysia has to zoom in and zoom out at the same time. See the cloak, then see the particles, then see what's beyond them, all at the same time. The Analyst can tell it better than I can. My head hurts trying to recall how he explained it."

"I agree. Okay, What about Karl?"

Karl's black and gold Mammoth avatar appeared on the holoscreen. Symone narrated, "Now, Karl is a head scratcher. There's no way I can help enhance him because his power is healing. He himself said that he used his healing properties to rip his muscles apart and make himself stronger. A few weeks back, I toyed with the idea of body mods."

"Body mods, huh?" Mallack pondered.

"Yeah. Since his body can heal faster and easier than anyone else, he can withstand several modification processes with ease. Not only would he be strong as Frimas, but he could also be a weapon wielding weapons, kinda like Duncan."

"I see. Speaking of Duncan," Mallack swiped to Duncan's silver and gold Ammo avatar.

"Speaking of Duncan, not gonna lie," Symone perked up and started dancing around in her seat, "I've had the most fun with him because he's like a block set you can keep building on, right? Zoom in on his hands."

Mallack typed on a few keys, and Duncan's hands dominated the view. "In his previous configuration, his hands retracted back and forth when he wanted to switch to blasters. I told him, 'You're wasting time retracting. Why not put the blasters in your palms? That way, you can keep your fists and beat the shit out of people, and when you need to blast, you don't have to waste seconds doing so.' Since then, he's been much more effective in combat. Also, we added thrusters to his feet, and he's mastering flight. Duncan's going to be a real problem. He might decide to finally fight me one-on-one, even give me a run for my money."

"Yeah, he's already got a hot head, now giving him the firepower to go along with it? Might prove dangerous," Mallack suspected.

"Exactly! Besides, Duncan's calmed down a lot the past couple quarters. I don't know, I think getting captured by the Collector last year woke him up to how serious he needs to take being an Elite."

"I can agree with that, you make a good point." The director swiped to Alexia's green and blue Enchantra avatar.

"After Alexia broke Hex's cloak last year, she was motivated to become more powerful in the field. Training wasn't cutting it, so about two quarters ago, she started studying an ancient Chioro tome, and it has been helping stabilize and enhance her abilities. She can break cloaks given enough uninterrupted time to interfere with them. But, more importantly, she's learning how to project her thoughts onto the material world without having to penetrate people's minds. She's getting really, really good at it, too. She said at some point, she hopes to be able to make people feel her projections, not just see them."

"Wow, if she can do that, she'll be a living training room," Mallack declared.

"I never looked at it like that, but yeah," Symone agreed.

"Daisy?"

"Okay, so at first, I thought the main thing we should do with her is just teach her how to fight with weapons. Malcolm and Malaysia have been working with her on hand-to-hand combat training, putting some knives in her hands and turning her into a human sawblade, or a gun and blasting things from random places on a wall. She's also learning how to hover in the air better. But the Analyst said something to me that neither he nor I have made complete sense of yet."

"What is it?" Mallack asked.

"He said that when he reviewed Daisy's training footage, he noticed she's been 'skipping.'"

"Skipping, like kids in the park?" Mallack looked confused.

"No, skipping like, how did he say it? She's showing up somewhere before she's supposed to be there. Like, if she's traveling from point A to point B, and it takes her three seconds to get to point B, she's at point B at the 2-second mark, while still running to get there."

Mallack's eyes popped wide as she gazed at Daisy's red Blitz avatar. "What the Frimas?!"

"That's what I said, Director! It makes absolutely no sense to me. We asked Daisy about it maybe three weeks ago, and she told us she has no idea how it happens, that she doesn't even recall doing it. She's just running, and when she gets to where she's going, she's there. She and the Analyst are supposed to do more tests and training on that at some point.

But we don't know what that means or how we can harness it."

"Wow, just, wow! I almost don't want to leave, just to see what that materializes into. Okay, so that leaves you, Symone."

Symone's crimson and gold Starburst avatar appeared on the screen. Symone looked down at the ground as she felt a heat flash, wondering if Mallack could see past her steely demeanor and sense her increasing dread. She looked back up at Mallack and said, "Me, I've just gotten hotter. I fight smarter. But nothing's really evolved with me compared to the others. I think I've spent so much of my life evolving my abilities that there's nowhere for my powers to really go, know what I mean?"

Mallack sat up and leaned on her desk. "You really believe that, Symone?"

"I mean, I know I can grow in other areas of my life, sure. But powers-wise? No, I think I've maxed that out since learning how to glow blue. With all my fighting experience, only Malcolm has given me what I feel like might be my last 'challenge,' my last 'conquest' worth enhancing for. And I haven't figured it or him out yet."

"May I offer a piece of advice?" Mallack softly said.

"Sure."

"Don't underestimate yourself. There is always room to evolve. You kinda already said it, evolution is not just connected to our powers, but evolution will always affect our powers."

Symone looked at Mallack and smiled. "That was very profound."

Mallack shrugged her shoulders. "Well, every now and then, I can spit a few bars." Symone chuckled. "Symone, I am proud of the work you have been doing with the team. After the Analyst discovered what was going on with the team three quarters ago, you took on the task of pushing their enhancements, and your methods have proven effective in ways we couldn't have envisioned."

"Yeah, about that, though, Director," Symone recalled what the Analyst said to her. "The Analyst said to me yesterday, before NextGen, that he suspects the Affinity Theory has nothing to do with the team getting better or stronger."

Mallack sat up straight in her chair. "He did, huh?"

Symone looked at Mallack's straightforward, unchanged face. "You already knew, didn't you?"

She rolled her eyes. "Well, he mentioned it to me, and I wanted to be the one to tell you first. But leave it to him—"

"Yeah, he can't hold anything," Symone laughed, "but when did he tell you?"

"He told me about five days ago, right around the time HQ and I were in talks about you becoming an official Defender for the Elite. I figured I would combine what I want to tell you today with what he said to me."

Symone shook her head. "What? What do you want to tell me?"

"Obviously, the heads of the Company have closely monitored your work with the Elite, and they are supremely impressed with you. Your teammates are stronger, fight smarter, and are the most cohesive unit Uri City's Division has employed in the three decades of the Company's existence. You have contributed greatly to that, and so, the Company wishes to promote you to Tactical Trainer after this mission."

Symone couldn't think straight, her thoughts swirling once again, and the vise of commitment clamping on her heart. "I don't know what to say, Director."

"If the Affinity Theory was not what made your teammates stronger, and you and Malcolm were just a unique situation, then your training methods made them better, and that has not gone overlooked."

"But, Director, I haven't really done anything," Symone downplayed her accomplishments as her heart thumped harder than a bass drum.

"Symone, did we not just go over every person on your team and what you were able to do with them? That, that was all you, all your work. Take the win! You deserve it! I won't be here to make your promotion official, so once the mission is over, Malcolm will get everything pushed forward, and he will give you the details of your new role. You will have additional responsibilities, but you won't leave the Elite, and anything Elite-related will take top priority."

Mallack sensed Symone's shifted mood, the giddiness on display mere minutes ago suddenly overtaken by anxiety and dread. Mallack put on her maternal hat and offered, "I feel like I've dumped a lot on you. How are you feeling about all this?"

Symone was succumbing to the ropes binding her heart and mind. Her unresolved feelings toward being responsible for others were making her skin crawl. Hot flashes ran up and down her back, her lungs tightened, and her nostrils flared. She was drowning in an abyss of accountability. The only word that she could come up with in her mind was, *Run. Run. RUN!*

"It's a lot to process," Symone calmly responded. "Thank you, Director, I'll think on everything and get back to you, or Malcolm, whoever's sitting in your seat once the mission is complete."

"Good deal. Congratulations, *Defender*, I am so, very proud of you. Dismissed."

Symone fought the urge to burst from the chair. She calmly stood up and began walking out of Mallack's office. She then remembered something she was gnawing on in her head since their briefing. "Actually, Director, can I ask you something?"

"Of course, what is it, Symone?"

Symone turned to face her boss once more. "I know the Company does things however they choose to. We rarely ask *why* something happens here, just accept the missions and assignments as they are appointed to us. But I'm just curious, why was I chosen for this team *before* Kaminari?"

Mallack sat back, "What do you mean?"

"Well, okay," she sat back down. "Don't get me wrong, I know *I'm* great! But Kaminari is a bona fide star. The reports, her missions, sheesh, her powers, she absolutely belongs here. I guess I'm trying to understand why HQ chose me over her."

Mallack understood Symone's question. "I know you're not one to doubt your ability, Symone."

"Right, and this is not about that. No one can kick ass better than me, damn the training exercises. But if Kaminari's been here for almost four years, why did the Company put me on the Elite Unit as a rookie and not on a Super team first?"

Mallack stood up and walked to sit next to Symone as she replied, "The Company is an impeccable, scary judge of talent. And even though Joy is supremely talented, so are you. And the Company knew that this team needed you *before* it needed Joy. I am confident that without you, the Elite Unit would have been decimated by the Collector's forces last year, and the team would not be as cohesive or powerful as it is now had they not chosen you.  If you think about it, you *know* I'm right."

Symone thought through Mallack's rationale, and she responded, "You're right.  This team needed me, as much as I've needed them.  Thank you for reminding me."

"Anytime, Symone.  Listen, you belong here.  Don't doubt it."

"Yes, Director."  Symone wanted to believe it, but hearing the words from Mallack did not soothe her soul.  She rose and walked out of the office.  Scurrying through the corridor, she panicked, *I'm stuck. I'm stuck. I can't do this. I have to leave. I can't stay here. I can't be a part of this.*  She stopped at the elevator and lifted her finger to hit the UP button to blast herself off the roof and away from her feelings.  But before she pressed the button, she recalled that she needed to talk to Malcolm about the leader of the POC extremist group, and somehow, thinking about the mission was enough to take the edge off.

She floated to and entered the quarters.  Malcolm and Karl were watching a sports channel on the holoscreen from their favorite spots in the commons.  The commentators were discussing their thoughts on NextGen's collapse and what that meant for the Zintol playoffs.

"See, Malcolm, I told you, they're gonna call that game and give the win to Highgarden," Karl lamented as he rubbed his forehead.

Malcolm hunched forward, chuckled and replied, "Oh yeah?  Alexia would love for them to do that.  That'll give her the matchup she's looking for and give the Underbelly a chance to represent Uri City in the global playoffs."

Malcolm heard the door close.  He turned around and saw his girlfriend walking up to them.  He could feel the distress coursing through her body. He stood up and saluted, "Symone, hey."

"Oh, hey Symone," Karl recognized her.

"Hey guys, what's going on?" Symone asked as Malcolm walked up to her.

"Nothing much, just watching UCSN, waiting for the Zintol league to make up their mind about yesterday's match." He leaned in and gave Symone a hug. Symone hesitated to return the hug to Malcolm, and he could tell. "Hey, what's going on with you?"

"Malcolm," Symone began, "I need to tell you something."

"Yeah, I remember," Malcolm pulled back and looked into Symone's deep brown eyes. "You wanna get out of here so we can talk?"

Symone summoned the strength to say, "Please?"

"Sure, let me grab a jacket, and we can go," Malcolm agreed. *Something's wrong with my girlfriend. We definitely need to talk. Something's off.* He walked away to his residence to pull one of his jackets from the closet.

Symone paced the floor a little bit, clutching her arms to try to settle her nerves. Karl started to say something when a breaking news marquee flashed on the holoscreen. The commentators were holding their ears, and one of them said, "We are receiving word from sources that the attackers at NextGen are issuing a statement to all the major news networks as we speak. We are a sports network, so we advise everyone who is following this story to tune in to your preferred news station to receive coverage of this statement and more from there. As we receive more information, we will relay what we know regarding the NextGen tragedy."

Karl immediately switched the channel to UNN.

"...attackers at NextGen have just released a video, and we are about to play that video now. Standby, this is the Powered Order Coalition's latest announcement to Uri City. We're playing the footage now."

The tape played by UNN began with a man dressed in a suit and tie bound to a chair in a dark room, sitting in front of six of the extremists fully masked and armored in black nanotech. As Malcolm returned to the commons, the seventh extremist, donning his red and purple, walked into the camera's view. Karl saw Malcolm and said, "Brother, look," and pointed to the holoscreen.

Malcolm turned around and witnessed the leader of the group standing in front of the camera. "Ah, shit," he groaned and threw his hands up in frustration.

Symone stared at the leader and wondered, *Is that him?*

The leader said, "Citizens of Uri City, NextGen was just the beginning of our pursuit of securing the ballot in the general election. We are taking every precaution necessary to ensure that the powered are restored to their rightful place in this city. Behind us is Senator Berkeley from the Meridian district, a staunch opponent against the powered. His loyalty to Senator Dariuz and his ilk is commendable, but like Dariuz, he poses a risk to our cause, and thus must be eliminated. In two cycles, if we do not hear from the Chancellor's office that the vote is secured, Senator Berkeley will be killed. Every day until the numbers are without question in our favor, a senator will be taken. Chancellor Croft, we await your response. We are the POC!"

The screen cut to black, and the commentators on UNN returned, discussing what transpired. Meantime, Malcolm looked at Karl, then Symone, and said, "Mallack's going to call us soon. We need to be ready. I imagine she'll get Intelligence to retrieve their coordinates, and we'll assemble soon."

"Yeah, that sounds right," Symone responded, deflated.

"Hey," Malcolm said, "come on, Symone, let's get out of here."

Symone looked at Malcolm as he walked up to her. "But wait, shouldn't we be here?"

"We won't go too far. Something is eating away at you, and you need to tell me what it is. Karl, let me know if I miss anything before we get back."

"You got it, brother," Karl announced as he got up to go to his residence.

"No, Malcolm, let's just go to my room," Symone changed her mind. "The right play is for us to be on the grounds. I can tell you here."

"You sure?"

"Yes, let's just go to my room."

"Alright," Malcolm complied. Symone and he walked to her room, and he shut the door. Malcolm didn't let his worries consume him or show up on his face. "What's going on, Symone? I can feel the anxiety crawling all over your body."

Symone walked five steps forward, then turned around, awkwardly rubbing her fingers together. "Okay, so, this team we're up against, this POC extremist group? I think I might know one of them."

"Really?!" Malcolm was floored. "How?!"

"Um, well, I think I might have dated their leader," Symone rubbed her right shoulder with her left hand.

Malcolm chuckled as he lowered his head slightly and walked up to Symone. "That's it? Okay, so, then, who is he?"

Symone was slightly surprised by Malcolm's nonchalant response. *Wait, why am I surprised? Did I expect him to be mad? Why did I expect him to be mad?* "I don't know, it might not be him. He's masked, and like Intelligence said, they haven't been able to confirm him through biometrics. But I can't unsee what I saw."

"What do you mean? What did you see?"

"It's the way he fought Super Team V at NextGen. I swear, I've only seen one person be able to do the things he did."

*You're circling. Please land your plane.* Malcolm gently pressed his hands on Symone's arms and rubbed them to soothe her nerves. "Symone," Malcolm calmly inquired to not show his irritation, "who is he? What's his name?"

"Jason. Jason Xavier," Symone mumbled.

Malcolm hugged Symone and replied, "Jason Xavier, okay. Well, then, what are we up against with this guy?"

Before Symone could continue, Malcolm's stripe buzzed. Malcolm looked down and saw it was Director Mallack. He opened the call to Symone and answered, "Hey boss, I got Symone on the line with us."

"Great, listen, I've talked with UPD, and they agreed to post officers at every senator's home for the foreseeable future."

"Does that include Dariuz?" Malcolm joked.

"Yes," Mallack didn't hide her disdain, "even that asshole Dariuz deserves to be alive to see the vote go through," Mallack responded. "Intelligence is running a trace and should have a location within the next five to ten minutes. Gather your team and meet in Intelligence, ready to move once the location is secured. This has to go perfectly, Malcolm. We need the senator returned to us alive. Otherwise, everything Croft has worked toward will be brought to ruin."

"Understood, Director, we're ready," Malcolm said.

"Good." Mallack disconnected the call.

Malcolm looked at Symone and asked, "So, Jason Xavier, you sure?"

"No, I'm not sure at all. We won't know unless we can confirm it. Still, I can't see it being anybody else."

"Okay, then, that's what we'll go to Intelligence with. I'm so sorry you felt like you had to hold onto that for so long."

"It's my fault," Symone chagrined, "I've been such a mess lately, and I don't like it."

"Well, as long as you know that it is okay for you to be a mess around me," Malcolm assured her. "Are you sure that's all that's bothering you?"

Symone hugged Malcolm and said, "No, I'm not sure. But we don't have time to deal with it right now. Let's get ready to rescue a senator. We can talk later tonight."

Malcolm slightly pulled Symone back and passionately kissed her lips. Symone became enthralled with passion, wound up tightly like a shaken up corked bottle in desperate need of a release, a temporary fix to combat the whirlwind of swirled emotions and the pendulum of doubt that swung from assurance to uncertainty. Symone ferociously kissed Malcolm back, and they locked lips as they rubbed on each other's backs.

Malcolm pulled back and smirked playfully, "You sure we have time?"

The embers in Symone's eyes glowed red, and she was never more certain about what she wanted than in that moment. "We have time. Shut up and fuck me."

Symone was desperate to forget her feelings for a moment and feel pure pleasure. As Malcolm lifted her by her ass cheeks, her legs popped open and clutched his waist as they locked lips once again. He planted Symone on her couch, and as he proceeded to undo her belt, eager to satisfy his woman, one thing kept ringing in her mind.

*Make me forget.*

## 10
# Kaminari

The elevator stopped on the training floor. With each passing minute, Malaysia's enthusiasm toward being a mentor grew. *I got this! I can do this!* They stepped off the elevator as she said, "I'm sure you've been down here plenty."

Joy fought to contain her happiness and anxiety as the newest recruit of the Elite unit. She nodded. "Yeah, this is probably my third home. I spend a ton of time down here honing my skills."

"Usually, we use the rooms down this main hall," Malaysia pointed forward.

"Great, so, when do we get started?" Joy faced Malaysia.

"The way things are going, I don't think it'll take too much time before you see some action in the field. Might actually get some today," Malaysia bantered.

"That'd be good for me, I haven't gotten any in almost three weeks," Joy chuckled, hoping her double entendre landed as she imagined in her mind.

Malaysia caught what Joy threw, smirked, and countered, "So we shouldn't waste any more time, then, huh?"

"Like I said earlier, I'm ready for anything, *anytime,*" Joy cracked a half smile and squinted her eyes.

Malaysia belted a jovial laugh and patted Joy's shoulder, then said, "I like you! We can drill another day. Right now, I want to know your story. Who exactly is Joy Olivier?"

Joy blinked twice, not expecting to go deep so soon, "Which version do you want, the long or the short?"

"Let's ride the elevator to the lobby and walk the street while you give me the long version," Malaysia answered.

"Cool," Joy pushed the up button for the elevator as she crossed her arms and began narrating. "So, um, my story actually doesn't start here."

"Obviously," Malaysia replied.

"I meant, I'm not from Uri City."

"Really? That's a rarity," Malaysia was taken aback. "How'd you get to Uri City?"

The elevator door opened, and they walked in. As Malaysia pushed the "L" button for the lobby entrance, Joy continued, "I was born in the Bari Grove district of Maldola."

Air escaped Malaysia's lungs, and she put her hand to her chest. "Maldola? *That* Maldola?"

Joy nodded her head, "Yeah, the city that basically cannibalized itself twenty years ago. *That* Maldola."

"'Cannibalized' is being nice," Malaysia countered. "That was a straight-up genocidal annihilation. How the Frimas did you make it out of that massacre?"

Joy slightly shuddered. Vivid images of fire, explosions, static shocks, smoke, and destruction flashed violently before her eyes. She could hear wailing ringing in her ears as if it happened yesterday. "To be honest, it was divine intervention. My parents put us on a ship and told us they would find us in the next city. The ship lifted out, and then the bombs went off. There's no way our parents made it out of that alive. Between the bombs and the powers, Bari Grove became an incinerated graveyard."

The elevator opened, startling Joy slightly. Malaysia picked up on Joy's jitteriness and changed demeanor. She wondered whether she was pressing Joy too hard, but she shook the thought. They walked out to the vast glass atrium of the Company's lobby. They walked through the corridor toward the reception desk. Malaysia circled back, "'Us?' You said, 'us,' and, 'our.'"

"Yeah, right, I have a twin sister."

"Really? There's two of you?"

"Yeah. We both got out of Bari Grove alive that day. We got to the port, and the crowd of survivors was so massive. Everything was happening so fast that my scared, jittery mind couldn't keep up, and one moment we were together, and then the next, we weren't. I fought through that crowd for what felt like eternity looking for her, kept calling for her, 'Tee, Tee,' and never heard her call back to me. Our stripes were busted due to the fallen towers, so I couldn't call her or pinpoint her location. At some point, somebody grabbed me and put me on a bus." Joy's chest tightened. "I kicked and screamed, scared shitless. I thought I was being kidnapped, but whoever threw me on that bus saved my life because as the bus blasted off, whatever took Bari Grove took the port, too." Tears began to well up in Joy's eyes.

"Joy," Malaysia lamented, "I'm so sorry." She patted Joy's back as they walked out of the building. "I shouldn't have pressed you so hard."

Joy sniffed, "No, it's okay. You were gonna hear my story sooner or later." She pressed a finger toward the corner of her right eye to keep the tear from falling out and ruining her makeup. "The ships that escaped all went to different cities. Mine ported in Uri. For years, I've searched for my sister and had absolutely no luck. Frimas, I even worked up the nerve to go back to Maldola a couple years ago, thinking maybe she had returned there. Bari Grove is still a wasteland, though, so I really believe she died in the blast.

"Anyway, that's how I got here. I ended up in an orphanage in Genesis Landing for a few months. I was nine at the time, and that's the age when my powers activated. It was a really bad storm outside that day. I stood on the roof, and I could feel the electricity in the clouds calling out to me. I raised my hands. A bolt of lightning fell from the sky, and without warning, a bolt of lightning shot from my body to meet it. The bang that followed scared the shit out of me! Once I saw that I was okay – aside from my clothes being burned and still smoldering – I jumped up and down from excitement. I then shot lightning from my hands and feet and launched bolts into the sky one after another.

"A few weeks later, the teachers at the orphanage enrolled me into the Powered Academy in Meridian, and that's where Kaminari was born. I got hired by a private security firm once I graduated, and I worked there for several years before getting the call from the Company."

"Well, from the looks of things, you overcame Maldola very well and turned that tragedy into a testimony."

Joy smiled, "I didn't have a choice. I was always afraid something bad was going to happen to me, so I had to learn how to take care of myself. Once I found out I had powers, I could do that and then some. I'm just glad I can help others along the way." She let a couple yellowish-white sparks fly from her hands, and her eyes sparkled.

They continued walking down the street as Malaysia continued to praise Joy. "You really have. I read the reports and watched film, Joy. You are a beast in the field!"

"I guess," Joy chuckled.

"No, no 'guess,' the way you handled Flower Power, that was legendary stuff!" Malaysia cheered.

"I had to save my team. The Analyst said that had it not been for me forgetting something in the hoverbus that night, that shock bomb might have taken me out, too – though probably not because I'm electric – but we all would have had our asses handed to us." Joy shook her head, then grabbed the end of her ponytail. "I didn't want to blow up the whole building, but once I got everybody out and back on the bus, they were attacking me so hard. I don't think I've ever let out a charge that big and held it that long. I just knew I was gonna get suspended after that."

"But, instead, you got a commendation!" Malaysia reminded her.

"I know!" Joy squealed. "Hopefully I can measure up to you guys and help out. Don't want to stick out like a sore thumb."

"Trust me, you'll be just—"

Malaysia and Joy's stripes lit red and buzzed. They looked at their stripes which read, "Mission brief imminent. Report to Intelligence immediately."

"That's us, something must have happened. You ready?" Malaysia asked Joy.

"Frimas yeah! Let's go." Malaysia and Joy turned around and sprinted back to the Company.

A moment later, Malaysia and Joy got off the elevator and walked across the hall to Intelligence. Malaysia and Joy walked through the door, and they observed the room glowing red. Stephanie and Dax were up front analyzing the details pouring onto the holoscreen. Karl, Daisy, Alexia, Mitchell, and Duncan were seated around the room waiting for the rest of the team to assemble.

"Hey, where's Malcolm and Symone?" Malaysia asked.

Karl covered, "They went off to talk about something, I suspect they're on their way."

"Oh, okay," Malaysia replied as she took a seat on the second row. She accurately pondered, *They're probably having sex.* As Joy took her seat next to Malaysia, the door opened, and Symone and Malcolm walked through.

Malcolm started, "Okay, Dax, Stephanie, what can you tell us?"

Dax turned around and answered, "Okay, Elite, we were able to do a trace of the footage that was played on the news. Intel concludes that the extremists are located in Genesis Landing, about ten blocks from the gateway port. We were able to get aerial footage of the location, and this is what we captured."

Duncan scoped Malcolm's shirt and noticed the buttons were misaligned. He whispered to him, "Hey, what happened to your shirt, homie?"

Malcolm looked down and realized he buttoned up wrong as Symone and he rushed to get redressed after their soiree. "Good catch, bro," he whispered back and swiftly fixed his wardrobe malfunction.

The holoscreen shimmered and displayed a live feed of a man in a suit and tie suspended by four ropes, two tied to his arms, and two to his legs. The feed then zoomed out, informing the team that he was suspended several feet from the ground.

"That's got to be at least one hundred feet, if not higher," Daisy examined.

"That's right," Stephanie confirmed. "I don't know what Croft is going to do. Mallack is in talks with him now. According to the extremists, we have about 90 minutes before they kill Senator Berkeley."

"Okay," Malcolm began, "Stephanie, Dax, load the information to our stripes. Team, suit up and gather in Malaysia's bus in the garage. Oh, and one more thing, Dax, look up the name 'Jason Xavier.'"

"Jason Xavier?" Dax parroted.

"Jason Xavier," Malcolm returned. "Gather as much information as you can off that name. Symone and I will explain why when we return. Joy, you ready?"

Joy gleefully looked at Malcolm, "Yes, I'm ready."

"Elite, let's get it."

# 11

# The Emulator and the Elements

Malaysia shuttled the Elite to Genesis Landing, soaring high above the skyline to avoid the traffic below, locked onto their target location. The two minutes of silence were deafening within the cargo bay. Stephanie and Dax delivered an update of what Intelligence analysts had captured with their aerial drones. Malcolm examined their report on the red-lit holoscreen latched to the side of the bus. He relayed, "Alright, team, it looks like the senator is strung up by tension cables, one for each appendage. Duncan, come look at this."

Duncan looked up, surprised he was being tagged in. "Me? Me, why me?"

"Just get over here and look at this," Malcolm swung his right hand swiftly. Duncan rushed over to the screen. "What is that on his neck?" Malcolm took his fingers and stretched them to zoom in on Senator Berkeley's neck. The senator was wearing a collar that Malcolm was unfamiliar with.

"Oh shit," Duncan scanned, "that looks like a proximity shock collar. It's like an ankle monitoring bracelet that will shock you if you cross a line. No doubt it's set to kill."

"Damn," Malcolm's jaw clenched, "so where is the line?"

"Zoom out," Duncan said as the team paid attention to their conversation. Malcolm pinched the screen until it showed a panoramic view of the senator. "The cables are attached to the sides of these buildings. Looks like tracks." Duncan poked at the screen, and circles appeared on the snaps the lines were attached to. "Those tracks are sliding downward. I bet there's a line those tracks are set to pass, and once the collar crosses it, boom!"

"Alright, I can imagine that's where our timeline comes from, and right now, we have about 75, 74 minutes before he explodes. That should give us plenty of time to rescue him before the chancellor has to do anything. We'll land the bus about a block away from him, roll to the floor parallel to him, disable the collar, then cut him down. Should be easy peasy, but let's make sure that we're not walking into a trap. Can't afford to make things worse beforehand."

"You can bet we're walking into a trap," Karl reasoned.

Malcolm sighed, "You're right. But this is what we do. Dax, are all the civilians out of the area?"

Dax replied in Malcolm's ear, "Affirmative, no signs of civilians in the area, and UPD is posted half a mile away in silent, unmarked vehicles on standby as requested."

"Good deal," Malcolm confirmed.

Malcolm's random request to Dax during the briefing lingered on Alexia's mind, and she was itching to understand why Malcolm made it. Upon hearing Dax's name, she raised her hand, "Um, Malcolm? Hi, it's me, Alexia. Just curious. Who is Jason Xavier?"

Malcolm, slightly annoyed but knowing it was a fair question, turned and looked at Symone. Symone looked at Malcolm, and Malcolm nodded his head while saying, "Symone, give them the short version."

Symone sighed, leaned forward, and propped her elbows on her knees. "Jason Xavier is my ex-boyfriend, and I think he's their leader."

"What?!" Alexia shrieked while the rest of the team was stupefied. "Why do you think he's their leader?"

"It's how he fights. He mimics powers. We don't have time for me to explain it fully, but if we can confirm that it is him, it might give us a leg up on his crew."

"30 seconds to touchdown," Malaysia reported from the cockpit.

"Alright, team, visors up, cloaks on, let's get it," Malcolm stated as his visor enveloped his head. The others followed suit. "Joy, you ready?"

"Um, yes, I'm good to go," Joy stated as her visor enveloped her head, opened in the back to let her ponytail flow. Joy donned a yellow uniform with white streaks cascading from her shoulders down to her boots.

Everyone double-tapped their chests, and their cloaks shimmered and disappeared.

"I promise," Starburst declared, "I'll explain everything I know when we get back."

K.C. suddenly remembered Starburst's reports on the team and how close the Eagle had gotten to seeing past cloaks. "Eagle, I know this might not be the best time to ask, but if the extremists do appear, and you get enough time, see if you can scan past the leader's cloak and get a visual confirmation. We just need a picture of his face, and you might be the only one who can get it."

"That's assuming we don't kick their asses, which we will," the Eagle declared confidently.

"I second that," Blitz declared.

"That's right," the Mammoth punched his right fist into his left hand.

The Eagle's hoverbus descended onto the streets of Genesis Landing. Enchantra pondered aloud, "Isn't it weird that this happened in the middle of the day? Like, where is everybody?"

"Good point," Starburst agreed as she noticed how abandoned the location appeared despite their gratitude for no civilian presence.

The back hatch opened, and the Elite rushed out of the hoverbus. They looked up and saw the silhouette of the senator against the backdrop of the three suns shining brilliantly in the sky. K.C. ordered, "Starburst, go up to him and see what we're up against. Eagle, scan him."

Starburst launched from the ground toward Senator Berkeley as the Eagle telescopically scanned the senator. Starburst got close to the senator and noticed that he was blindfolded. She said, "Senator Berkeley, I'm with the Company. My team and I are gonna get you out of here."

Senator Berkeley whimpered and sighed, "Oh, thank Akan, I thought for certain I was going to die. Please, help me, get me out of here!"

The Eagle finished her scan and said, "He's cloaked, and it's pretty high-powered. We could shock the cloak, but it might set off the charge around his neck."

"Okay, so we need to disable the cloak, then the collar," K.C. instructed.

Starburst looked at the tension cables attached to the senator and the tracks on the walls of the buildings. Her visor scanned the connections on the wall, and she reported its findings. "It gets worse, K.C. Those cables are wirelessly attached to the collar around the senator's neck. I've seen something like this before. I thought we could just cut the cables and take him, but if those cables are cut, then it will set off the collar and could kill him."

Just as K.C. was about to give another order, he saw three silhouettes in front of the team rushing toward them. He then turned around and saw three more coming from behind. "Shit, it's them. Okay, listen up team! Enchantra, Mammoth, come with me to the top. We're going to get the senator. Star, you, Ammo, and Kaminari, run the Triangle. Blitz, get out of here now and get behind them so they don't see you coming. Eagle, come with me and perch yourself at a window. Everyone copy?"

"Copy," the Elite reacted.

Starburst descended as ordered. Ammo and Kaminari positioned themselves next to her, all standing back-to-back-to-back. Blitz became a red blur and disappeared through a side alley in between buildings. The Eagle, K.C., Enchantra, and the Mammoth ran through an open bay of the left building. Enchantra ascertained that the building was unfinished, and a gaping hole was in the middle of the ceiling. She instructed her teammates, "Run to the center, guys!" They all ran to the middle, and she looked up and saw that the hole went all the way to the roof. Her eyes lit green, and mist surrounded and corralled them. She then lifted them thirteen stories up and landed them on the fourteenth floor – a dusty, unfinished slab of concrete with metal pipes scattered everywhere.

"Alright, Eagle, post up on a perch and help the ground unit. The rest of you, let's get the senator," K.C. declared.

On the ground, Starburst's eyes and hands lit yellow. Kaminari charged, and electricity spiraled around her body. Ammo placed his palms in front of him, and white plasma glowed from his palms. The six elemental powers stood about twenty feet from them. Starburst quickly instructed, "Okay, play to your strengths."

Frostbite, the Wave, and Cyclone faced Starburst head-on, while Ignatia, Terra, and Cypher stood in front of Kaminari and Ammo. Frostbite took the first shot by blasting a wave of ice toward the three to try to trap them. Starburst immediately shot a star wave at the ice that disintegrated his ice blast. Ignatia threw three fireballs at Ammo and his teammates, and both Kaminari and he shot electricity and plasma at the fireballs, and they exploded on impact. The Wave unleashed a river from his hands, and Starburst created a shield to part the blast and avoid impact. Starburst then pushed the shield forward, and Frostbite and the Wave rolled to opposite sides while Cyclone quickly spun a whirlwind to launch himself upward. He then summoned a massive wind column down toward the Elite just as Terra shifted the ground underneath them, cracking the street slab and launching them upward to meet the column.

"Ah shit, we gotta jump!" Kaminari screamed. They jumped off the slab just as the wind column decimated it and continued to hunt them down. They diverged away from the column's path. Kaminari shot lightning from her legs to slow her descent while unleashing a lightning strike upon Ignatia, Terra, and Cypher. Ammo remembered his training and summoned his feet's jets to propel him, slowing his descent to a float. He then shot several plasma strikes from his palms.

Ammo and Kaminari's combined assault struck their targets, and their three opponents flew backward, and their cloaks shimmered as they landed on their backs.

Starburst launched several stars at Cyclone. Cyclone used the wind to divert the stars away from him. Starburst created a large star in front of her and flew behind it. Cyclone used the wind to push it away, not realizing that Starburst used the diversion to get directly in front of him and punch him in the head. She then punched him in the chest, kneed him in the stomach, clutched her right fist into her left hand, crafted a star, and tomahawked Cyclone in the head. The explosion blasted Cyclone into the pavement. Frostbite and the Wave combined their powers and launched an ice column toward Starburst. She saw it coming and spiraled around the column, flew above it, then auraed star energy around her, and drilled through the column. She landed in the space between Frostbite and the Wave, pushed her arms out, and launched two stars simultaneously at them, blasting them through the buildings on opposite sides of the street.

K.C., Enchantra, and the Mammoth looked outside the window near the track holding the senator's left leg and arm. K.C. said, "Okay, Enchantra, you can break cloaks faster than I can. I'm going to create a bridge in between the buildings. Mammoth, get on the bridge and hold the senator up so that the collar doesn't drop anymore. Enchantra, do what you do, break the cloak, then I'll break the collar."

"Sounds like a plan to me," Enchantra said.

"Let's do it, brother," the Mammoth agreed.

K.C. looked out the window and looked at where the track ended. He noticed that it was about ten feet below where the bottom cable was attached. He concentrated on the exposed brick right below it and stretched his hand out. The exposed brick began to stretch toward the opposite building. He then stretched out his other hand, and the brick under the opposite track began to stretch to meet in the middle. A brick road about ten feet wide stood outside the window.

"Alright, Mammoth, go. When you get to the middle, I'm going to raise you up to meet him. Place him on your shoulders."

"Copy that," the Mammoth jumped from the window and landed on the bricks. *K.C. is so good, man, how does he come up with this stuff?*

"Alright, Enchantra, break the cloak," K.C. instructed her.

Enchantra flew out of the window and stood face-to-face with the senator. "Hi, Senator Berkeley, I'm Enchantra. You have a cloak around you that I'm going to break. Don't be afraid, I'm not going to hurt you."

"Okay, I hear a bunch of explosions going on around me, though," Berkeley relayed.

"Oh, that, it's just my friends fighting off the extremists. It's normal, we're fine. My partner, the Mammoth, you're going to sit on his shoulders to keep the collar from shocking you to death."

The blindfolded senator nodded his head and said, "Okay."

K.C. raised the bridge the Mammoth stood on, and it became an outlined trapezoid. Once the Mammoth met the senator, he moved his head in between the senator's legs, and the senator straddled the back of his neck. Enchantra's eyes glowed, and green mist flowed from her hands and surrounded the senator. She began listening to the cloak as it shimmered in resistance to the mist resting atop it.

Meanwhile, Ignatia rose from the ground and shot a wave of fireballs into the air. They exploded, and hail fire rained down onto the streets and hovercars parked along the sidewalks. Explosions banged all over, and some of the hail fire hit Ammo and Kaminari. They dodged as many as they could, hiding behind an out-of-range hovercar. The hovercar suddenly activated and levitated. It then slammed into the two of them.

"The Frimas?!" Ammo held his hands out atop the hood of the car and pushed it as the car revved up and pushed back. Kaminari rapidly shocked the car. The engine blew up, and the car slammed back onto the ground. They looked around, and without warning, several hovercars rushed toward them. Ammo and Kaminari stood back-to-back and began blasting cars one by one before they could slam into them. Cypher took control of a streetlamp and increased its intensity, turning it into a laser. She pointed it at them and launched a blast at them. Kaminari didn't see it coming, but Ammo did, and he grabbed her and spun her into his arms. They spun around twice, and Kaminari swooned and shivered in delight. He then let her go, and instinctively, she transmuted the quick shot of horniness into energy, supercharged herself, and launched a lightning storm at Cypher.

Ammo shot two pulses at Cypher's lamp. While he destroyed the lamp, Terra took a slab of the building next to Ammo and slammed the bricks into him, pinning him to the ground. Cypher dodged the electric storm and directed three more hovercars to attack Kaminari. Kaminari waited for the cars, then at the right moment, she shot herself upward as the cars crashed into each other. She thrusted her right arm upward and her left downward, then shot a current into the air and into the ground. She swung her arms in front of her, and the bolt in the sky cracked forward. She then swiftly swung her right arm downward and her left upward. The bolt in the sky came crashing down, and the bolt in the earth split the ground to meet the bolt from the sky, causing a massive pop to ignite the ground with yellow electricity. Cypher couldn't dodge the energy, and her cloak took on massive damage as she flew an entire block away from the epicenter of the fight.

Ammo blasted himself from the bricks and launched toward Terra. Terra built a tunnel out of the asphalt that surrounded Ammo. She then sealed the tunnel. Ammo charged up and blasted through the tunnel, but he didn't see Ignatia on the other side. She launched a wave of fire at Ammo, and Ammo blocked the wave with his arm as his cloak took on damage. He switched his cannons to monoammonium phosphate. He shot the chemical forward to keep the fire off him and kept pushing it. Terra used the distraction to throw more asphalt at Ammo.

Suddenly, Terra flew twenty feet to the side, then was launched upward, then slammed into the ground. Then, Ignatia was pushed in her back violently by a blur, tripped, uppercut in her head, then slammed in her back into the pavement. Ammo stopped what he was doing, and suddenly, Blitz was standing next to him, her golden braids flapping and floating to a halt.

"Damn, girl," Ammo was mesmerized.

"Can you disable them?" Blitz asked.

"Shit, I have a couple disablers, but I'm not sure if they'll be enough for their cloaks, we didn't ask about that in the briefing or with Double W."

"We have to try."

Frostbite rose from the wreckage and placed his hands on the sidewalk. He began freezing the ground. Starburst noticed the ground getting slicker and hovered over it before her feet could get stuck. Just as she was about to launch a star at Frostbite, a wind column suddenly appeared and surrounded her. She started swirling around, unable to stabilize herself. The Wave rose from his hole in the wall and launched a massive water attack at the wind column. Starburst was now swimming in a whirlpool. Frostbite connected his ice sheet to the column, and the whirlpool began to freeze over. Starburst looked around to try to get her bearings but could feel the ice taking over. She instinctively let the whirlpool take her while surrounding herself with an aura, and as the whirlpool completely froze over, her tumbling momentum slowed to a halt as she lay stuck in the ice.

Frostbite, the Wave, and Cyclone walked up toward the column they created. Distracted by their own design, Frostbite suddenly felt a gatling of shots pop his side. He couldn't see where the barrage was coming from and tried to create a shield to stop the assault, but the bullets cut through his ice. His shield took damage when suddenly, a different round hit him, and his cloak shimmered and dissipated. The round then shocked him. He seized up and fell to the ground. Cyclone and The Wave wondered what happened and hid behind the ice column they created.

"What the Frimas was that?!" Cyclone asked. "Did you see where that came from?"

"We were standing next to each other, you know I didn't see it!" the Wave reacted angrily. "It definitely wasn't that chick, she's stuck in the ice!"

"We gotta get Frostbite," Cyclone scrambled. Cyclone came out of his hiding place and was immediately met with the Eagle's rapid gunfire. "Shit, shit!"

The Eagle trained her eye onto their location. She switched to thermal and saw through their ice column. Without taking her eyes off the target, she tapped her middle and ring fingers on the grip to swap out the rounds to element-piercing.  She aimed the long gun at Cyclone's chest, let out a slow, steady breath, then squeezed and held onto the trigger. She unleashed a barrage of gunfire on Cyclone that pierced through the ice column and slammed into his chest.  Cyclone flew backward, and his cloak took massive damage from the rounds.  She then quickly tapped her middle and ring fingers to swap to a disabler, and she charged the gun, then fired. The disabler landed directly on his chest, and it shocked the cloak.  It shimmered and dissipated, then the disabler shocked Cyclone.  He, like Frostbite, seized up and crumpled to the ground.

The Wave breathed heavily, fearful that he was next.

Starburst thought, *I'll let the Eagle get her gun off.  If I break free too soon, she might lose her target to the falling ice, and they'll get a chance to regroup.*

Enchantra began humming at the frequency that the senator's cloak was singing to.  The resistant cloak tried singing at a different frequency, but then Enchantra started singing to that one.  *Hey, I want to sing, too!  La, la, la,* a voice in Enchantra's head said to her.

*So do I, hey, I think I can catch it,* another voice chimed in.

*I'm trying to concentrate, calm down!* Enchantra ordered the voices.

The first voice protested, *I'm just saying, we can help!  Let us help!*

*Ugh, if I let you help, will you shut up?*

*Yes, yes, yes!  Let us help,* the second voice said gleefully.

*Fine, but then you have to let me work!* Enchantra reluctantly agreed.

The first voice latched onto the frequency of the cloak, and Enchantra's throat widened.  The second voice then harmonized with the first, and Enchantra's throat widened even more. The cloak couldn't resist as strongly as it had before. Enchantra then chimed in, and the three of them synced. They switched from three-part to five-part harmony, and the cloak shimmered yellow, then dissipated.

*Yay! We did it,* the first voice cheered.

Suddenly, the cables swiftly slid down the tracks. The Mammoth could feel a strain in his spine as he resisted the tracks trying to pull the senator's legs. "K.C.," the Mammoth strained, "Enchantra triggered the tracks, they're pulling the senator down!"

"Shit, okay, I'm on it!" K.C. looked out the window, and he concentrated on the collar. He could feel the components and recognized he couldn't just pull it apart without it sending something toward Berkeley's neck. *Okay, K.C., don't fuck this up!*

K.C. contacted Intelligence, "Hey Dax, tell me how to disable this collar!"

Back at Intelligence, Dax looked at the holoscreen. He tapped on the keypad and pulled up Enchantra's view of the senator. He said, "Okay, K.C., the collar is basically a dead man's switch. Someone will have to keep the collar from shocking him while you disable it."

"Enchantra, protect the senator's neck," K.C. informed her.

"On it," Enchantra created a protective green mist and swirled it in between the collar and the senator's neck.

"This hurts so much," the senator declared as his arms and legs were being stretched from the pull of the tracks. The tracks recognized that the senator wasn't coming down, so their programming instructed the cables to retract.

The Mammoth bear-hugged Berkeley's legs and said, "I'm not going to let you drop." The Mammoth could feel the bricks beneath him cracking under his weight.

"Okay, what do I do, Dax?" K.C. pleaded.

"With the senator's neck protected, you can just dissemble it. The shock that comes from it is rendered ineffective with Enchantra protecting his neck."

"Okay, cool," K.C. sighed with relief. Shots from the Eagle's long gun could be heard several feet from them. K.C. felt for the collar and ripped it apart. The electric energy blasted from the collar and hit Enchantra's shield as the pieces tumbled to the ground. The tracks disabled, and the senator's arms and legs were unshackled.

The Mammoth's back felt relief, and he said, "Alright, great work, let's get you out of here, Senator Berkeley."

Enchantra pulled the blindfold off the senator's eyes, and they marched back to the window they came from.

Ammo and Blitz disabled Terra and Ignatia's cloaks and shocked them unconscious. Kaminari, meanwhile, looked for Cypher in the debris caused by her lightning strike. As Kaminari was about to charge up, she suddenly was blindsided by a blur and launched twenty feet to her side. She then was uppercut in the head, tomahawked in her back, and slammed into the ground. Suddenly, Ammo was punched in his gut, pushed in his back, tripped, then kneed in his head upward, then slammed into the ground. Blitz got her bearings and trained her eyes to move as fast as the blur. She saw Ammo getting assaulted by the extremists' leader. She swiftly shifted her feet and, as Ammo was slammed into the ground, she sped into the leader and bear-hugged him, and they barrel-rolled into the ground. The leader kicked Blitz off him then rushed into her. They fought at lightning speed, using punches, dodges, and kicks to outperform the other. Blitz grabbed her opponent's left arm and swung him over her head, then let him go and scissor-kicked him four times in the chest. He slammed into a wall, but before Blitz could deliver a series of haymakers, he charged himself up with electric current and blasted Blitz away from him.

The Eagle scanned the area and recognized the leader. "Guys, he's here, Jason Xavier is here."

K.C. immediately ordered, "Alright, Eagle, get a scan of this guy. Blitz, once you've recovered, meet me in the building and get the senator to safety, then circle back here. The rest of you, your objective is him. Let's end this now!"

The Mammoth put the senator down, then jumped out of the window. Enchantra floated below to meet the extremist leader. Starburst understood the assignment and began to glow brightly. Her aura melted the ice around her, and she immediately burst from her ice chamber. The Wave looked up in disbelief and dodged the massive shards that crashed where he once stood. He rushed toward his boss.

Kaminari got up from her fall and charged up. She then shot two bolts of lightning from her hands and gripped them like lances. She spun them around and charged forward toward the leader. She then launched one of the lances toward him, and he blitzed away, then shot his right palm forward and shot a couple plasma shots toward her. She dodged them, and they engaged each other. She hurled the other lance at him, charged herself with electricity, and they exchanged punches and kicks. She hit him with an electric punch in his chest, then roundhouse kicked him in the head. He spun but quickly recovered and built a star and blasted Kaminari with it. She flew backward.

Starburst saw it and quickly flew toward him. She blasted a continuous star wave at him, and it dealt damage to his cloak. He then blasted star energy of his own, and something triggered in his mind.

*Wait, this energy, I know this energy*, he thought as he shot his shot toward her. He didn't notice the Mammoth charge at him, and the Mammoth knocked his shoulder into the extremist's side and slammed him into the wall.

The Eagle took that opportunity to begin scanning the cloak. She zoomed in on the particles within the cloak, and the cloak swarmed to meet her scan. She strained her eyes to get past the particles.

Enchantra met the leader and stretched him out in midair. Before she could perform a nullifier spell, he mimicked Kaminari's energy again and shocked Enchantra and the Mammoth with big bolts. Enchantra released him, then pushed an energy storm ball toward him. He used an electric whip to dissipate the ball. She threw more toward him, and he responded the same. Kaminari got up and used electricity of her own against him. Starburst landed on the ground and shot another wave of star energy at him. Ammo got up and shot plasma his way.

He realized that he was surrounded by four shooters and placed himself in a star shield. His eyes lit yellow, and he then unleashed the star shield at them all, blasting the Elite backward, their cloaks taking damage as they landed.

Blitz met K.C. and Senator Berkeley and said, "Okay, I got him, help them down there, K.C."

"No problem," K.C. jumped out of the window as the mimicker blasted the team. He grabbed some of the blast and turned it into a heated javelin. He took the javelin and threw it at the mimicker, and the energy exploded on the mimicker's chest, sending him tumbling. K.C. turned the ground underneath him into a sponge, and he bounced onto solid ground. K.C. grabbed a piece of metal debris and shaped it into a bo staff. The rest of the team got up and stood battle-ready.

The Wave unleashed a barrage of water onto the team, and they fell forward, surprised by his attack. Cypher took control of several hovercars and commanded them to slam into each other to create a barrier between the Elite and the mimicker and her. Cypher then declared, "Listen, Emulator, we gotta get out of here, they are going to beat us. We lost this round. Gather the rest of the team before you lose the fast girl's powers, and let's get the fuck out of here!"

"Are you kidding me?" the Emulator protested. "I can take them!"

"No, you can't! The plan is fucked. We gotta regroup. Get them now! We gotta figure out another way."

"Shit, fuck! Fine!" The Emulator sped away from everyone and grabbed Frostbite, Cyclone, Ignatia, and Terra and whisked them to safety in their hoverbus. He then grabbed the Wave and took him back to the hoverbus. He lastly grabbed Cypher and said, "I am so pissed off!"

"Be pissed. We'll get another shot at them. Get us out of here!"

He sped away. Just then, the Elite got back up and regrouped. They ran behind the wall of hovercars. Enchantra cried, "Where the fuck did they go?"

The Eagle declared, "They're gone.  He used Blitz's power to get away."

K.C. pounded the ground.  "Eagle, please tell me you got the scan."

The Eagle let out a sigh, then answered, "I guess Enchantra's not the only one who can break through cloaks anymore."

"Shit yeah!" Starburst yelled with glee.

"I'm sending his face to you now, Starburst.  Is this Jason Xavier?"

Starburst's visor showed a picture of the Emulator to her.  His brown skin, thick lips, beady eyes, smooth cheeks, and crew-cut hair sent Starburst down memory lane, a lane she didn't think she'd ever travel down again.

"Yes, that's Jason," she lamented.

"Dax," K.C. declared, "get the Eagle's footage and make a scan of that guy.  Starburst has confirmed that Jason Xavier is the leader of the extremist group."

"Already done, K.C.  Working on biometrics as we speak," Dax declared.

Blitz suddenly reappeared.  "What did I miss?"

"They got away before you could get back.  But it's okay.  We completed the mission.  Great work, everyone!  Let's get back to HQ."

In the opposition's hoverbus, the Emulator strapped his wounded and unconscious teammates in their seats and activated their recovery units in their stripes while Cypher manned the cockpit, and the Wave sat in his seat.  The Emulator then sat down and demolished the arm rest with his fist, having forgotten he still possessed the Mammoth's massive strength.

"Hey, man, calm down," the Wave said.

"Man, fuck you, Otis!" Jason barked while he summoned the nanites to melt the mask off his head.

"Fuck me? Man, fuck you!" Otis barked back, water droplets shooting from his face and hands.

"Hey," Cypher yelled from the cockpit, "fuck both of y'all! Damn it, who were those guys?"

"I don't know, Samantha," Otis said, "but those assholes were ready for us. It's like they knew exactly how to strike us. Frimas, they almost beat us."

"Do you know them, Jason?" Samantha asked.

"No, not all of them. Just one. The one with the star power."

"Well, who is she?"

"She's Symone, Symone Watson," Jason reflected.

"Symone Watson. Can we use her?"

Jason slammed back into the seat. He closed his eyes, the memories of a lifetime ago echoing in the chambers of his mind. He growled, rubbed his temples together, and let out an exasperated sigh. *I can't believe this shit. Seriously? Of all the fucking people on Uretha, Symone? Fucking Symone Watson?! Shit!*

"Well?" Otis piggybacked.

"Only if we fight her."

"What does that mean?" Otis was confused.

"I'll explain once we get the rest of the team up."

# 12

# Symone × Jason

Symone cupped water from the faucet and threw it into her face. She cupped water again and threw it in her face again. A third time. She then shook her hands and reached for the towel on the rack. She wiped her face clean, placed the towel on the counter, and turned the faucet off. Her hand still gripping the knob, she stared into the clone in front of her, peering into her eyes and searching for her soul. Her mind raced faster than Daisy's feet could dash on her best day, and despite the thrill of the fight she engaged in half a cycle prior, it seemed that no pleasure could erase the anxiety that gripped her heart like a bear trap.

*Jason. Damn it, Jason!*

Her hand charged up, and the knob grew hotter from her touch. She ruminated on the years they spent together, the good times they cherished, the fights they endured together, how often her parents would tell her that they liked him but were concerned about his motives, how supportive he was when she dealt with the prizefighter commissions, the amazing sex they had, the arguments they never resolved, and the future that never materialized. Symone was convinced that part of her life was closed, never to be revisited again. And yet, as Akan would have it, *Here he is, again! And he's stronger and more gifted than ever before. Is it my fault? Did I make him this way? Am I to blame?*

The knob's shape warped.  Its heat stung her hand and finally snapped her out of focus, and she looked down and huffed, "Great, that's gonna come out of my check."

Symone pulled her tactical romper off her body and threw it in the clothes hamper.  She then walked to her closet and pulled out a pair of jeans and a gold crop-top t-shirt and climbed into them.  She found a pair of sneakers, planted her sock-covered feet into them, and walked toward the kitchen.  She filled a glass with water and chugged it down.

*Shit, how does Malcolm feel about all of this? He has to face my ex? What kind of full circle shit is this?*

Symone walked out of her residence and made her way to the commons to meet her comrades.

**Jason flipped the switch,** and the lights flickered cyan blue around the dusty room.  Two small card tables and folding chairs sat in the middle of the floor.  A holoscreen sat on each table, and a holoscreen hung on the wall to the right.  Across the walls were pages of notes, plans, photos of different locations in the city – including NextGen and the port at Genesis Landing – portraits of different leaders, and calendars marked with different dates.

Jason decided to wait on Samantha and Otis in this room.  They managed to get the rest of their teammates into their beds.  He sat down and pulled out a deck of playing cards from his unzipped track suit jacket pocket.  As he shuffled them, he recalled that this deck was one of the last decks Symone and he played with before they broke up.

*Of all the people that would show up, it would be her, wouldn't it? Damn it, she's going to fuck everything up!*

Jason ruminated on his relationship with Symone, the time they shared, their spars in the gym, their conversations about ruling the world, and her body up against his.  Jason's emotions spun, his anger toward her incensed, and it further hardened his heart and locked his focus.

Samantha suddenly rushed through the dark hallway and into the room. Her skintight, highlighter green jumper made her stand out in the room and broke Jason's concentration. Her eyes widened in frustration. "Okay, start talking, Jason!"

"Damn, didn't I say I wanted to wait for the rest of the crew?" Jason retorted.

Samantha, dissatisfied, planted her feet and held her waist. "You know damn well they're not going to wake up for at least another eight cycles. Those disablers are meant to *dis-able*, and I want answers now!"

The holoscreens scrambled violently from Samantha's amplified intensity. On her command, the words "Start talking!" blinked and scrolled repeatedly.

"So do I," Otis popped from the corner, a trail of water following his footsteps.

"Fuck, alright, alright," Jason waved his card-gripped hands and conceded. "Here goes."

**Symone cleared her throat** and crossed her arms. Standing in front of the holoscreen facing the Elite and Mitchell, she began narrating, "He goes by the codename 'The Emulator.' His ability is mimicry. He mimics a person's powers and fighting style, and within seconds, you're fighting a carbon-copy of yourself."

Alexia leaned on the island and scratched her head, "So basically, we're fighting somebody who can become any one of us at any given moment?"

"Shit, not just any of us, *all* of us," Karl sat up in his seat. "It's almost like we're fighting Trent Salazar all over again."

"Damn," Malaysia almost choked on her drink, "I was actually thinking that."

"He's right," Symone said, "Jason is one of the most formidable fighters I've ever known, well, before I met you guys. He spent his whole life studying every fighting style that exists. His mind is his true superpower, it's sharp as a needle. He analyzes things so fast and can command his cells to replicate what he's studied – word-for-word, move-for-move, power-for-power – at a moment's notice. That's actually how we met."

**Jason planted his clasped** hands on his crew-cut fade and smiled. "She and I were matched up in a tournament, and she put up a good fight, but I kicked her ass good. But there was something about her power that drew me to her like a magnet. So, after the fight, I found her outside the locker room and asked her out. She told me, 'Frimas naw,' and walked away. Made a few calls and found out where her gym was, and for three weeks straight, I just kept showing up there until she finally agreed to go out with me, but only after we sparred in the ring."

Samantha chuckled as she sat down and ran her fingers through her slick magenta hair, "So, she's *that* girl?"

Jason replied, "Yeah, she's *that* girl, not one for glitz and glamour. A real, get down and dirty with you, 'ride-or-die' bitch. And still fine as Frimas when she does it."

"Cool, so, what's so special about her powers?" Otis turned his chair backward and sat with his teammates.

"Well, I figured out that I was getting faster and better at emulating the longer we dated and the more we sparred together. Being with her made me stronger, more than years of training at the best gyms in Uri City ever did. She was literally making me better at mimicking. I thought maybe she was just inspiring me to be better. Frimas, Symone can motivate a pebble to become a mountain, she's so encouraging.

But here's what Symone doesn't know: she has the power to *transform* that pebble into a mountain."

"What do you mean?" Samantha questioned.

**Symone sighed and lamented,** "In the five years we were together, Jason got better at mimicking people. I mean, crazy, stupid good. He admitted to me that before dating me, it would take him quarters to make a dent of progress with his skills, but I motivated him, pushed him harder than anyone ever had, and he got so good at mimicking that the commission almost stopped him from fighting because of how unfair his abilities were. Here I was, thinking that I was just motivating him to be great, but now I'm convinced it's not true."

"Why not?" Malcolm inquired.

Symone looked up and huffed, then relayed, "The day that NextGen was attacked, the Analyst said to me earlier that he believes my star power is the reason people around me have gotten better, no, 'have evolved.' You all didn't get stronger because of the Affinity Theory. Your evolution has nothing to do with the theory and everything to do with the energy that flows through my veins. And if that's the case, then my star power helped make Jason who he is today."

The Elite perked up as they wrestled with Symone's explanation. Daisy spoke up, "Damn, Symone, that's quite an assumption."

"It's the only rationale that explains why he's as good as he is."

**"You're telling me that** her powers made you who you are? And you never told her?" Samantha leaned her bare elbows on the table.

"That's exactly right," Jason declared. "I wasn't about to tell her that shit. She would have gone all, 'Don't take my choice away from me,' and probably wouldn't have sparred with me ever again. I kept that shit to myself and just kept getting better and made her feel like she was my inspiration."

"That's fucked up," Otis folded his dripping arms.

**"So, wait," Daisy interjected,** "that explains why he fights so well, but not why he's fighting to get the powered in power."

Joy agreed. "That's a good point. If I had his power, I'd just stay in the prizefights and make millions of creds. Why is he blowing up stadiums and kidnapping senators?"

**"I told Symone countless** times that she is an empress and deserves to be worshipped by the nations," Jason declared. "She, like us, deserves to be at the top of the food chain, not taking scraps from these non-powered motherfuckers who spend more time bossing us around and using us for their own interests and agendas. I told her that she deserved to be placed on a pedestal. But the more I tried to convince her of that, the more she resisted the idea of the powered taking over Uretha. I invited her to a couple meetings with some of my associates, and she immediately got up and left when we talked about what life would be like if we ruled the world."

**Symone sat down next** to Malcolm. "I told him, 'I can't build a life with you if this is what our life is going to be about, us trying to dominate the world at the expense of others. That's not what I represent. I love my people, but I won't elevate my people by tearing others down.' He said he understood, but the more involved he got with his 'kind,' as he put it, the more distant we grew. At some point, it was like we were living alone together, and I grew to resent him and what he stood for. I—" Symone hesitated, recognizing that she was about to say too much and edited herself on the fly, "broke up with him and left. Anyway, Daisy, Joy, I think that's why he's doing this. This is his play for global domination."

"If he takes Uri City, then he can take Uretha," Malcolm declared.

Karl shook his head. For him, the math wasn't *mathing*. "Wait a second. That doesn't make sense. Does anyone else get what's wrong here?"

"I see it," Mitchell's instincts kicked in.

Duncan stared at them and pleaded, "Well, can you help the rest of us get on the same page, because I don't."

"Think about it," Karl leaned forward. "If dominating the world is what he wants – putting the powered in power – then isn't what he's doing *counterproductive*? The POC are literally days away from achieving that. I'm with Joy. If I'm unbeatable, it'd be better for me to just sit back, beat folks up, and collect prizefighting checks instead of blowing up a zintol stadium and stringing up a senator for the Frim of it. Something about all of this just doesn't add up."

Mitchell agreed. "That's why I said in the beginning, this isn't the POC. We wouldn't throw all this work away right when we're about to throw the zintol through the ring."

"Well, one thing is clear," Symone said, "Jason doesn't want peace. He wants war. He doesn't want to live among the unpowered. He wants to control them. He's certainly not working for the benefit of the POC. We can only hope we can stop him and his crew before the POC takes anymore blame for their bullshit."

**Samantha stood up, "So,** what's the play, Jason?"

Jason rubbed his head. "We can't do anything until the others wake up, but as far as I can tell, we stick to the plan. Symone and her super friends have thrown a wrinkle in our agenda, but the timeline is still in our favor. We don't budge.

We're this close to the prize. Now that we know who we're up against, we'll be better prepared. Pull the tapes and let's do an analysis of Starburst and her allies. Let's figure out who she's working for."

"Are you sure you're up for this? She's not going to stand in your way, is she?" Otis wondered.

Jason's jaw clenched, and he pierced his eyes at Otis and barked, "Let's keep one thing clear, anybody can get it! I don't care if it's my own mama! We have a mission to complete, and anyone who stands in our way will get wiped off the board. Trust me, I'm focused. In fact, Symone might give us a better chance to pull this off now that she's in play."

"How do you figure?" Samantha asked.

"I'm going to make a call. If I can get the equipment, I might be able to enhance us and ensure that Starburst and her crew can't overpower us. Let's get some rest, and when the others get up, let's get back to work. We gotta prepare for the next phase."

Otis looked at Samantha, and Samantha shrugged her shoulders. "Why wait?" she declared. "Let's start prepping now, get a head start."

Jason nodded. "Good point."

**Malcolm stood up and** said, "Alright, Intelligence has Jason Xavier's information, and they are running it through every database on the planet. Once they have something useful, they will let us know. In the meantime, stay connected through the stripes, be mindful of the news, and stay alert. We don't know when the next assault will take place, but we will be ready. We almost had them beat, and they know it. We have to assume they're going to fight smarter next time. Let's not give them the upper hand. Oh, and one last thing,

Joy, excellent work out there today, you did the damn thing, and we are lucky to have you on the team!"

Everyone clapped and cheered. Joy scrunched her shoulders and said, "Thanks, guys!"

"Alright, everyone, dismissed," Malcolm declared.

"Yes, *Director*," Malaysia quipped.

Malcolm laughed as everyone stood up and nodded in agreement. Symone stayed behind while everyone else left. Malcolm turned to face her and softly inquired, "You alright?"

"Yes," Symone whispered while her head shuddered no, her eyes turning red and welling up.

Malcolm gently held Symone's hands, stood her up, then pulled her into his body and hugged her. He said, "Come on, let's go. It's time we talk."

"Okay," Symone agreed.

# 13

# Run. Run. RUN!

Malcolm and Symone landed their hoverbikes on the roof of her apartment complex. Symone wondered why Malcolm had chosen her place as the meeting place for their long-overdue conversation. But she was so exhausted from thinking that she just rolled with it. She unsaddled her bike and double-tapped her chest to turn her cloak off. Malcolm did the same, and he walked and stood next to Symone. He grabbed her right hand with his left, and they walked toward the corner of the building. The suns had finally set, and the crescent moons began to take center stage in the sky.

Symone looked at the rooftop they walked on and noticed a blanket draped near the corner. She looked at Malcolm and asked, "You did this?"

Malcolm smiled and said, "I might have had some help from Alexia. She doesn't know why, but she was more than happy to put it there for me, for us."

Symone awed, "That's what took us so long. I was wondering why we flew halfway around Uri City. I thought you were just trying to distract me."

Symone turned to face Malcolm, pulled his face into hers, and kissed him passionately. She then sat down on the blanket and patted her right hand on it, signaling to Malcolm to sit next to her. Malcolm eagerly complied. Symone then lay back on the blanket, her locks radiating from her head like sun rays. Malcolm followed suit.

As they stared at the sky, their eyes slowly adjusted to the darkening star scape, and little by little, the stars shimmered and glittered all over the darkness. Malcolm and Symone lay for five minutes, the silence binding their hearts together. She thought the natural wallpaper would soothe her soul, but as the minutes went by, Symone's mind began racing all over again, and her heart began beating rapidly. *Run.*

Malcolm could sense her body tensing up, could feel her heart thumping, the blood and fire raging in her veins like lava. He broke the silence. "Talk to me, Symone."

*Run.*

Symone opened her mouth, and nothing but air flowed from her vocal cords. She had been longing for this moment, but now that it had arrived, she couldn't find the words to explain her feelings. She had grown exhausted of feeling her feelings.

Malcolm figured that to get her started, he would have to ask her a question. "What did you and Mallack talk about the other day?"

Symone took the bait, silently saying, *Thank you, Malcolm, Akan, I didn't know what to say.* She slowly articulated, "She told me that the Company wants to give me a promotion. They want to make me a Tactical Trainer."

Malcolm was surprised and sat up. "Aye! That's great news, Symone! Congratulations!" He noticed Symone continued lying flat, unaffected by his cheer. "Right?"

"Well, yeah, I guess."

"You guess? What's wrong, Symone?"

"It's just, 'Tactical Trainer?' That's more responsibility, more people I'm responsible for. I'd be training new recruits. I didn't sign up for that."

"Well, no, you didn't," Malcolm agreed.

Symone finally had words. "And that's on top of finally making the Elite squad officially. Like, I'm a real Defender now. I'm responsible for the team. Like, my actions have consequences for all of you now more than ever."

"Yeah, being an Elite, on the team, that's true, too."

"Everyone's talking about me being here for the long haul, Alexia and Malaysia talking about me being a part of the family, not going anywhere anytime soon."

Malcolm grew a little concerned about the direction of the conversation but figured she needed to get all this off her chest, so he didn't allow his thoughts to spiral for the moment. He said, "Yeah, well, that's how we all feel about you. You know that."

Symone sat up, and the dam broke. "Then we find out that Jason is our target, that he's responsible for NextGen and Senator Berkeley, and Frimas, I might be responsible for his cockiness because of my powers. Frimas, who else am I responsible for?" Memories of every person she ever fought and interacted with since she first learned of her powers flashed through Symone's synapses. "All the people I've fought and sparred with, both good and bad, shit! Who has profited from my powers? How do I know that the Company truly wants me to train people because of my training skills? What if they just want my star power like it's a super juice or something? They want me to be responsible for every defender's evolution now?"

"It's possible?" Malcolm chimed in.

"And, then there's you and me," Symone had become a flood of consciousness.

"You and me?" Malcolm slowly bellowed. His heart tensed up and was pinpricked by a sudden, stinging trigger set off by his fear of being abandoned.

"Yeah. Like, we've grown so close, and I adore you, love you, so much," she grabbed his hands. "But you're starting to talk about the future. You've already made plans with HR about us being together if, no, *when* they make you the director. And, I don't know, Malcolm, I know you say I make you happy."

"But?" Malcolm asked.

"But," Symone froze, "but I..." Symone couldn't fix her mouth to say it.

Malcolm took a deep breath, preparing his heart for the worst while fighting back the urge to defend his love for her and dissipate his fears. He knew this wasn't about him, so he restrained himself from making the conversation about him, staring his fears dead in her deep brown eyes. He softly spoke, "Symone, say it."

A tear fell from Symone's right eye, encapsulating the pain she felt from the emotion she couldn't bear to let out of her heart. She slowly seized up.

*Run.*

*Run.*

*Run!*

Malcolm calculated, *Okay, Malcolm, don't panic, don't freak out. Give her a push, but don't act up. Shit, she's gonna break up with me. She's gonna break up with me! What did I do? Did I push her too hard? Did I not love her right? Did I move too fast? I knew I shouldn't have given her that necklace! Fuck! Malcolm, you're spiraling! Snap out of it. Get out of your feelings and stay in the conversation. Remember what your therapist said. Don't burn the bridge. Keep talking.*

"Symone, you've given me the facts." Malcolm hugged Symone and squeezed her as gently and firmly as possible. "Tell me how you're feeling. 'I...'"

Symone's mind spun, and her heart pounded her rib cage harder than a puncher. But she couldn't contain herself anymore. "I'm scared." She crumpled in Malcolm's arms and gave herself permission to fall apart.

Malcolm ran his hand through Symone's locs. "There it is. Now, why are you scared?"

Symone started weeping. Her voice broke. "I'm scared because I don't know how to take care of someone else. I'm used to being free. Free to do what I want, when I want, with whomever I want. This life, being responsible for other people, I don't think I'm capable of doing this. I'm not built for this."

Symone backed off Malcolm and wiped her face. She stood up and walked toward the edge of the building, her heart the heaviest it had been in years.

Malcolm gathered himself, stood up and walked next to her. "What makes you say that, Symone?"

"I mean," she sniffled, "by being responsible for others, I am chained to people. My actions impact you, the team, the trainees, everyone. What if I decide to do something you don't agree with, or you want me to do something I don't want to do? I won't be free to do what I want to do without worrying about how it's going to affect everyone."

Malcolm knew that Symone was still withholding something. His feelings attempted to get the better of him, but he pushed his feelings back and asked, "Symone, what decision did you make that impacted you like this? What are you not saying?"

Symone clutched Malcolm and stared at the stars. She noticed her favorite star in the cosmos shimmering in the night sky. She whispered, "Her name would have been Kali."

"Kali?" Malcolm parroted.

Symone spoke through her tears, "Yeah, like the star. Kali, that would have been the name of my child."

Malcolm's eyes widened, then became sorrowful. He gently planted his hand on her shoulder. "Symone, I'm so sorry."

Symone held herself as she narrated, "Jason and I, we were in love, you know? But, like I said in the quarters, toward the end, things were pretty rocky between us. I never wanted children, but I wasn't opposed to having one, either. Still, I was careful, so careful, except this one particular night. We were both drunk, he came inside me, and I carelessly forgot to follow up with contraception protocols. And those little swimmers, well…"

Symone wiped her face as she continued, "Anyway, Jason was well into his 'conquer the world' bullshit once I found out, and between that and my desire to continue prizefighting, I felt that bringing a child into this world would be the worst decision of my life. I made one already by creating her, and he was *not* the man I wanted to raise a child with. So, I made a choice."

Malcolm was perplexed. He couldn't believe that Symone, the queen of *don't take my choices away from me*, took a major choice like that from Jason. "You terminated your pregnancy?"

"What?! No! I would *never* do that! She didn't ask to be brought into this world. I'd never get rid of my child. No, I put her in cryosleep at a facility in Highgarden. She's been a frozen embryo for years, and I never looked back."

"Wow," Malcolm mumbled. "Did you ever tell Jason? Does he know what you did?"

"No," Symone admitted, "I never told anyone, not even my parents. I buried that shit. I broke things off with him a quarter afterward and vowed to never put myself in a position like that again, where my actions have these massive consequences for others."

Malcolm's heart grieved. He stared off into the skyline, not sure how to respond in this moment. Symone's tear-stained face broke his heart to pieces, and he struggled to find words or actions to help her. He knew that it was not his turn, but he couldn't help but wonder whether the end was near and if there was any way to avoid it.

Symone cut through the silence. "Malcolm, say something."

He wanted to reassure her, but reassurance wasn't what she needed. Malcolm decided to hit her with facts. *Don't be afraid, Malcolm. Give her the truth. She might decide to leave, but know that you did everything you could. Don't be a fucking hero. Don't save the day. Don't make this about you. Be a friend.*

He gently pulled Symone and hugged her. He then looked her in the eyes, took a deep breath to rid his lungs of the anxiety engulfing his heart, and declared with conviction, "Symone, hear me when I tell you, you are indeed free to do whatever you want to do."

"How do you figure that?" Symone sniffed.

"Because you are free to do whatever you want to do. Just as you did back then, you are still able to do now: choose. You chose to not have a child for the sake of the child, your career, and your failing relationship. That was the choice *you* made. Being on the Elite for the long haul, that's a choice *you're* making. You can choose to walk away from us right now, and yes, the team will suffer, but the Elite will find a way to fight on. *You* can choose to say no to the Tactical Trainer position, and it will be okay. Sure, the trainees will suffer because they don't get that prime training from one of, no, *the baddest fighter* in all of Uri City, but they will get trained nonetheless and move forward. Yes, you didn't know that you were enhancing Jason, just like you didn't know you were enhancing me with all that Affinity Theory shit, and because of that, you can cut and run, do your own thing, and never use your powers, if your powers are the reason we've all evolved, so no one else will ever grow again. That, too, is *your* choice.

"You could even break up with me." Malcolm breathed in deeply to clear the lump in his chest and the dagger in his gut. Symone's tear-filled eyes looked at Malcolm as he fought back tears of his own. "The thought of that alone is crushing me, but it is the truth. Breaking up will devastate the Frimas out of me, and I will probably never date again for a decade, but at the end of the day, that will still be *your* choice. Know up front that I will fight like Frimas for you, but eventually, I will respect your decision and move forward with my life."

Symone continued crying as she began to understand what Malcolm was saying to her. He continued, "Know, Symone, that one choice doesn't have to define who you are. Stop judging yourself for the decision you made back then. You do not have to be the same person you were when you were with Jason. If you do, that's a choice *you and you alone* are making.

"Everyone in your world, right here and now, wants you in our lives. You, *all of you*, powers be damned. Yes, your powers might have brought us together, but none of us love you because of your star power. We love you for *who you are*, and we all want to be around that energy you carry, not the star power, the *Symone* power. You have grown, and that has opened up opportunities for you. You have helped us grow, and that has opened up opportunities for you. You are an amazing girlfriend, lover, best friend, and partner, and that has opened up opportunities for us to grow in our relationship. But in the end, you, Symone, have the choice to take those opportunities and do something with them, to place roots down, or to cut all ties and run. Whatever you decide to do won't change a damn thing between you and me nor change one thing about how I feel about you. But at the end of the day, *being here* is your choice, and yours alone to make."

Symone's heart burst. She bear-hugged Malcolm. He squeezed her tightly and finished, "Take my advice, Symone. Be still."

"Be still?" she parroted slowly.

"Yes. Be still. Take the next couple days to really think through everything. Don't make any rash decisions right now. Just take time to get the clarity you need. When you're ready, say yes to the things you want, no to the things you don't, and be at peace, knowing that everything you're doing is by choice. Still your heart, and let it be your guide."

Malcolm and Symone held each other in comforting silence. Symone replayed Malcolm's advice in her head, and the spinning, ruminating, and repeating slowed down significantly. For the first time in the past few days, Symone could finally breathe.

"Malcolm?" Symone said.

"Yeah?"

"I love you."

"I love you, too, Symone, no matter what." Malcolm wanted to add, *I'm not going anywhere*, but he reasoned that now wasn't the time to affirm his place in her life. *Not until she knows what she wants to do.*

Symone's chest expanded, the jaws of the bear trap having finally released her lungs. Her mind finally stopped racing, and the peace that Malcolm referenced earlier had found her. She inhaled deeply, held it, then slowly released the breath. She held onto Malcolm, and they slowly rocked each other under the backdrop of the stars above.

Cycles went by.

Malcolm's eyes popped wide, waking up from a dream about the last battle with the extremists. He uncovered his chiseled, chestnut body, the moonlight streaming through his open windowpanes tinting him silver, much like any other night. The crisp air produced goosebumps on his skin. He planted his palms onto his forehead and gripped his textured hair. The skyline was bustling. The clock read 25:03.

Much like any other night, he sat up and planted his feet on the ground. He walked to his bathroom and turned on the light. Much like any other night, he turned on the faucet and cupped water in his hands, then splashed the water in his face. Much like any other night, he took the towel next to him and wiped his face off. Much like any other night, he then ran his fingers through the water.

But, unlike most nights, as his fingers wafted through the water, the water didn't follow him. Instead, the water flowed straight past his hands and into the drain.

Malcolm was confused. He tried to feel for the water molecules. He could only feel the water on his skin. He couldn't sense the water at all. Malcolm tried to dial up his senses to detect the glass in the mirror and couldn't feel it. He felt for the porcelain on the sink, the toilet, the bathtub.

He felt nothing.

Mortal dread began to fill his heart. He tried to sense the linoleum on the floor, the popcorn on the ceiling.

Still nothing.

He tried to feel the wood and steel mixed in the door.

Nothing.

Malcolm looked in the mirror and thought to himself, *What the fuck is going on with me? Did our conversation drain me that badly? No way!* He looked down at his stripe, thinking he should call the Analyst, but his stripe was grayed out, the sign of no service. *This can't be good.*

He looked back at the mirror to stare at himself, hoping maybe if he focused hard enough, he could summon his powers back. He looked over his reflection's shoulder and noticed a shadowy figure standing in front of the threshold behind him. He swiftly turned around and instantly recognized who stood in front of him. Mortal dread tore at Malcolm's insides while adrenaline shot through his veins faster than a sniper bullet from Malaysia's long gun. His eyes adjusted, and silver glints sparkled on his assailant's uniform.

"Hello, Malcolm Bennett," the distorted voice said to him.

"Collector," Malcolm growled back. Malcolm set his feet in battle stance, fighting to steady his breathing and slow the bass drum rattling his rib cage. He immediately understood this would be his last battle on this side of Glory, and, in his mind, since the Collector already took his powers, it would take everything in him to fight his way out of this.

*Okay, Malcolm, this is it. What you've trained for your whole life. All that time you spent in the training room, all the battles, prepared you for such a time as this, right here, right now. Powers be damned. If you're going to die tonight, you make sure you take her with you. Let's get it!*

# 14

# Malcolm V. the Collector

"**I**'ve waited a long time to finally get you alone," the Collector slowly, gleefully articulated to Malcolm. She sat at the foot of his bed, planted her hands on the sheets, and crossed her legs, the three-inch stilettos of her boots staked on the floor. "You've made it quite the challenge, but oh, this moment, your face, makes all the trouble I've gone through worth it."

Malcolm's rage fueled his focus, and his nostrils flared. "Realize that there's no fucking way I'm letting you out of this room," he growled.

"I'm absolutely certain," the Collector calmly replied. "In fact, I'm counting on it. I'm priority number one on the Company's hit list, right? Kill order still in place?" The Collector did not budge from her spot in Malcolm's bed. "Well, Malcolm, I'm not cloaked. Do your worst."

Malcolm saw red and lunged forward, determined to knock the Collector off her arrogant pedestal and save himself from her clutches. He swung his right fist, and the Collector swiftly lay back on the bed, flipped herself to a crouching position, then lunged forward and tackled Malcolm, pinning him to the ground. She landed a punch to his face with her right hand, and she tried to land another, but Malcolm raised his right arm to block her left swing. She straddled him tightly with her thighs and tried to pummel him. Malcolm grabbed both her arms and pushed himself off his back. Just then, his mind felt an echo, a faceless reminder of a battle's past. *Not now, no! Stay focused!*

He immediately shook it off and stood up straight, still latched onto the Collector's arms. The Collector swung her legs around his waist and sharply headbutted Malcolm in his nose. He released her arms, and she let go of his waist as Malcolm stumbled backward. Before he could regain his composure, the Collector kicked Malcolm in his side, the stiletto slightly piercing him. She then punched him twice in the chest, grabbed his arm, and flipped him over her head and into the floor.

Malcolm was stunned. He thought to himself, *What the fuck?! How is this tiny chick kicking my ass like this? Wake the fuck up, Malcolm!* Malcolm rolled onto his stomach and pushed himself off the ground. "Alright, Collector, nice moves. But this shit ends now."

The Collector was amused. "Ends? Oh, Malcolm, we're just getting started," she laughed. Malcolm and the Collector traded punches and blocks for ten seconds, moving toward the windows. Malcolm finally landed a blow to the Collector's head. He grabbed her arms and kneed her in the stomach, then swung her into his nightstand, smashing the lamp and knocking her head into the wall. Malcolm ran toward her and slammed her up against the wall as she sat on the nightstand with him in between her legs. She thrusted her arms upward to break herself from Malcolm's trap, then clasped her right fist with her left hand and tomahawked the crown of his head. As he let out an "Oomph," she then thrusted the same clasp into his chest. Malcolm stumbled backward again. The Collector then triple-punched him in his chest and kicked him. Malcolm crashed into his closet dresser, and several shelves broke under his weight.

The Collector cackled, "And you're supposed to be the best the Company's got? Come on Malcolm, stop *trying* to hit me and hit me!"

Malcolm grimaced from the splinters slicing his skin. He pulled himself up by a broken shelf board, emerged from his closet, and tried to land a strike. The Collector swiftly dodged his attacks. Malcolm managed to swing his right arm and get a grip on the Collector's mask. She grabbed for his hand, and Malcolm slammed her head into the window, cracking it at the strike zone. Malcolm used his left arm to deal several strikes at her right side, then kneed her in the stomach as he let her head go, then uppercut her with his right fist in her head. He grabbed her head again, and the Collector jumped and planted her feet on the glass, then pushed them onto the ground. The Collector straddled him again and hit Malcolm with haymakers. Malcolm sensed something eerily familiar about the woman who sat on his lap but cared more about his well-being than trying to solve that mystery. He took his arms and swung them to his left, swiftly knocking the Collector in her side and sending her barrel-rolling into the broken nightstand.

Malcolm was hurting, and he realized that he would not be able to take the Collector head-on. Despite not being cloaked, she was armored enough to withstand anything he threw at her. He reasoned that he needed to live to fight another day and calculated his path to freedom was through his bedroom door. Malcolm coughed a couple times and pushed himself off the floor. He tried to sprint to the door to his apartment, but before he could get to the door, the Collector had gotten up as well, and she jumped onto Malcolm's back, swung herself by her legs around Malcolm's waist, and hoisted herself upward to meet Malcolm face-to-face. Malcolm instinctually held onto her thighs, and the Collector used her momentum to clock him in the head again with her helmet.

Malcolm turned and slammed the Collector into his holo-screen. When he heard the screen split, he yelled internally, *Fuck! I spent three thousand creds on that! It was a gift to myself!* He pushed off the Collector. Unfazed, she ran back toward him and delivered several punches at him. He blocked them with his arms, and they sparred back through the kitchen and into his bedroom once again. Malcolm thought, *I'm going to have to choke her out.*

Malcolm grabbed the Collector's arms and swung them behind her back, pushing her body into him. His mind remembered her body, but he couldn't piece the memory together, the pictures coming from the fringes of his mind. He lifted the Collector up, swung her to where he was facing the bed, then slammed her onto the bed and straddled her fiercely. He then swiftly pinned both of her hands with his knees, grabbed the Collector by the neck and squeezed tightly, and reached for clasps of her helmet, convinced that he could win and identify his nemesis once and for all.

One clasp.

Two clasps.

Before he could pop the final clasp, Malcolm's arms suddenly jerked and spread outward. The Collector wheezed and coughed as her lungs gasped for air. Malcolm then rose from the bed, his legs spread eagle. Malcolm witnessed purple and gold symbols swirling around him. He knew at that point that the Collector had help, remembering Hex's color scheme. Malcolm laughed nervously, "So, you couldn't beat me in a fair fight? Had to get your lackey to help you?"

The Collector chuckled as her breathing slowed back to normal. She coughed a few more times before responding with a raspy voice, "You assume that I actually wanted to beat you." The Collector rolled off the bed and knelt to the ground to finish recovering her breath.

Just then, Hex unlocked Malcolm's apartment entrance and walked in. He floated in his pristine purple and gold robe and cowl to Malcolm's bedroom and said, "Love what you've done with the place. Very deconstructionist."

The Collector responded, "Gotta hand it to Malcolm, he put up a decent fight. I expected to kick his ass mightily, with him not being cloaked and all. But he still has the moves and intellect, I suppose."

Hex stared at Malcolm and said, "Well, well, we meet again. Last time you and I faced off, your girl nullified me. Very smart play on her part, I did not see that coming."

Malcolm was terrified of what was coming next, but he refused to display weakness to his opponents. "Yeah, well," he said, "that's what happens when you face off with the Elite. We find a way. And if we can't find it, we make a way out of no way."

"Such a Chioro cliché," the Collector replied. "But that actually makes sense. I was supremely impressed by you and your team last year. I bragged about you all for weeks."

Hex sighed, "She could not stop talking about how 'amazing they were in battle,' it was annoying."

Hex turned Malcolm around so that his back faced the headboard of his bed, then gently floated him to the wall the headboard rested on. The Collector and Hex stood at the foot of the bed as she dictated through her distorted voice, "Like I had said earlier, I've been waiting years to meet you face-to-face like this. You are everything I thought you would be."

Malcolm lamented internally, *Why hasn't the cavalry arrived yet? Shit, she probably disabled the silent alarm, too. How would she even know one was in my room?* Sternly, he remarked "Yes, Collector, it's me, Malcolm Bennett, Kingdom Come, the one you said needed a different name?"

The Collector laughed again, "You remembered?"

"Yeah, kinda hard to forget a homicidal psychopath Frimas-bent on selling powers and killing whoever's in her path."

"Homicidal psychopath?" the Collector gasped. "I didn't think that's what people were saying about me. Wow, that's a new one."

Malcolm started getting annoyed. "Well, you got me. You already took my powers, so what are you waiting on? Kidnap me, or kill me, or whatever it is you're going to do. But hurry on with it."

"Oh, you think I took your powers?"

Malcolm perked up. "I don't have my powers. I assume you took them from me."

"Hex, do you see a glowing canister around here?" the Collector asked sarcastically.

"Nope, not one that I can see," Hex answered.

"Malcolm Bennett, codenamed Kingdom Come, I don't have your powers. I don't want your powers. I nullified you with a high-powered, Asylum-grade, state-of-the-art, targeted nullifier. I figured, to be safe, we would nullify you while everyone in the building is asleep to not arouse suspicion. The one who has visions in her dreams, though, we had to move her out of the building by way of an all-expense paid vacation to the shores of Brilliance to make sure she didn't ruin our plans by seeing us here and possibly warning you."

Malcolm said, "You did your homework."

"Malcolm, I've gone to incredible lengths to set this meeting up with you. But I know you. You wouldn't have just met with me if I asked you to come over my crib for a lunch-and-learn. You would have brought the full weight of the Company to my home and locked me up, but then you never would have gotten the information I've longed to give you. I didn't go through all of this just to get your powers. Your powers are useless to me. I can't use them, and some wannabe gangster like Jackson Santana wouldn't know what to do with them. No, I am here to give you insight."

The Collector climbed into Malcolm's bed and stood face to face with him. "See, when you retrieved Dredge's drive and booted it up, I asked it to retrieve a specific set of information on you. I made sure Intelligence couldn't find out what I pulled, but that you would all be so afraid for your well-being by revealing that the information was all about you. Notice, though, we've been ghost ever since. No sequel to the Trent Salazar saga, no more killings, no more powers being taken. None of that. I got the information I needed from the Company and left you all alone. This information will change your life, Malcolm. And I will give it to you, free of charge."

Malcolm was stunned. "The Frimas? That's it? You're just going to give me this information?"

The Collector brushed her finger against Malcolm's cheek. He wanted to twitch away but was unable to move. "Well, yes, that's all I want to do. I want you to have this information."

"Then why not just send me a message through my stripe?"

She slid her hand down and caressed his chest. "Because Malcolm, I'm no fool. You're a do-gooder, hand-picked to deliver swift justice, even if it means making the idiotic, sacrifice play. You wouldn't have cared about the information, just beating me. And I need you to focus on the information. The Company has been keeping something from you, and you have the right to know what it is."

"What do you mean, 'the Company has been keeping something from me?'"

"Exactly what I said, Malcolm. And had you killed me, you would have never known. That's why I nullified you. I don't want your powers. I want you to know the truth."

"I could just ask the Company myself and get the answers from them," Malcolm reasoned.

The Collector spun around and gracefully lay on the bed, her head on a pillow, facing Malcolm. "You could, except no one in Uri City knows about this. The only ones who know about this are at the Company HQ. And we all know that the Company HQ is off-grid, impossible to reach, impossible to find. You wouldn't know where to look or who to ask. If you want the truth," the Collector reached in her right pocket and pulled out a thumb drive, "this is the only way to get it."

Malcolm rationalized that he had no choice but to comply, but he pushed the issue anyway. "What's the catch, Collector?"

"Ugh, you're impossible. I already told you, there is no catch. I'm going to place this drive on your kitchen counter, and Hex and I are going to walk out of here. Once we're out of range, you will regain your powers, and Hex will release you from the binding spell. Your stripe will turn back on, and all will be right again. At that point, you'll just have to decide whether you want to know the truth or continue being left in the dark."

The Collector turned her body and stood back up in the bed. She gently rested the forehead portion of her helmet on Malcolm's forehead. She breathed deeply as she said, "Akan, you smell so good." *Take the bait.* "Good luck, Malcolm Bennett. We'll meet again soon." The Collector walked out of the bed and onto the floor. "Hex, let's go."

The Collector and Hex walked toward the exit. True to her word, the Collector placed the black thumb drive onto Malcolm's kitchen countertop, and they walked out of his apartment.

Malcolm wrestled with what the Collector just told him. *The Company's been keeping something about me from me? What if she's playing games? But she went through an incredible amount of trouble to get here, and I'm still alive. The Collector's MO is not one for lying. She and Hex should have killed me. Why do all of this just to give me information? I need to see what this information is. And how does she know about our priority list? The kill order? Intelligence?! Nobody knows how we run things in the Company. Nobody.*

Two minutes went by. Suddenly, Malcolm's senses rapidly dilated, and he sensed everything in the room again. The data input overwhelmed Malcolm – he distinguished the textures and molecules like before the nullifier was turned on. His head spun as he scrambled to recalibrate his senses. Hex's symbols that swirled around him dissipated, and Malcolm slid to his bed. He rolled and stumbled out of his bed and sprinted out of the door in pursuit of the Collector and Hex while holding his head. He bolted up the stairs to the roof of his apartment complex and stared out into the distance. He scanned the streets and observed no sign of them. Malcolm grimaced and huffed, stunned at the flawless execution of their plan, and walked back down to his apartment.

Once inside, he closed his door and looked at the black drive on his kitchen counter. As the adrenaline thinned in his veins, he limped to the counter and picked up the drive, then went back to his room and pulled a holoscreen from the broken nightstand. He dusted it off and lay the drive on top of the holoscreen. He then opened a command prompt and said, "Open drive."

A flood of documents poured onto the screen. Malcolm struggled to make sense of what was in front of him and how the Collector pulled so many pages from HQ. He sat on his bed, groaning from the beating the Collector handed him, and began sifting through the information from the Collector's data pull.

*Shit. This is going to be a long night.*

# 15

# Trust Issues

Malcolm sat silently in the conference room as his comrades bantered. His usual steely demeanor had grown colder and harder, and his eyes turned into curt, piercing daggers. Arms crossed, back to his seat, he panned around the room to examine his teammates, interrogating them in his imagination as he bathed in suspicion, paranoia raging through his synapses.

*Malaysia Jones, is it possible? There's no way. She like my older sister, man. We've gone through way too much for her to do something like this. She wouldn't betray us like this. She did keep the Affinity Theory plan from me, but she was just following orders. Could she be following orders from the Collector, though?! I have noticed she's been on her stripe a whole lot more than usual. But she always says it's her boyfriend she's talking to, despite their near-breakup several weeks back. What if it's not her boyfriend? What if she's been communicating with the enemy this whole time?*

*Duncan Blake, he got kidnapped by the Collector. He is cybernetic, maybe she programmed him to do her bidding somehow. Did she fuck with his hardware and let us rescue him rather than keep him on her side? Now he's a gift-wrapped poison pill that nobody will see coming?*

*Karl Luther, no way, he's my best friend. He wouldn't do this. Or maybe he would? Maybe the Collector found out about our secret. Maybe she got in contact with him and told him she knows about them. Could she be holding his feet to the fire as ransom to keep them safe, and he can't say anything to me or anyone else without risking their safety? That's not like him, though. I'm sure he would have told me something by now.*

*Daisy Parker, she wouldn't do this. She is a princess of High-garden, and her family has quite a few connections with power-ful people in the city. No way she would sully their reputation like this and risk her family's clout. But maybe the Collector used those connections against Daisy's people? Exchanged intel for lives, power, or creds? The Collector is one of the most con-nected people we've faced, apparently. Could she have tapped into Daisy's connections and forced her to do her bidding?*

*Alexia Montague, I don't see her doing something like this. What would she have to gain from doing the Collector's dirty work? Did the Collector find out about Alexia's past? Her time with the UPD? Those records were supposed to have been ex-punged. Did she dig those files up and throw them in her face? No, Alexia would have just dismissed them all. Everybody knows about her past, she has nothing to hide, and nothing to fear. She can't be the Collector's accomplice.*

*Joy Olivier, sure, she's new, but she's been with the Company long enough. Maybe she has been working with the Collector this whole time. But why make their move against us all right now? Maybe they're using the Emulator as their cover to strike us while we're divided.*

*Symone Watson.* Malcolm's chest tightened. *Could the Collector have used her as a honeypot? Got close enough to me so she could extract secrets from me? Keep me in check? Direct me? No, I can't believe that. I won't accept that. It's too easy. But maybe that's what the Collector wants me to think? The one person I wouldn't suspect is the one person I should have kept my eye on the entire time.*

*Shit! This mental exercise got me nowhere.*

Symone could feel Malcolm's death glare but didn't say anything. Meanwhile, Malcolm's mind kept ruminating and dissecting the Collector's treasure trove of intel.

*I don't get it, though. That injury, it doesn't make sense with my time here in orientation. And I've never been scanned for any kind of recovery on it, from what I can remember. Why would the Collector have gone through all that trouble just to pull a medical file? But then, why would the Company keep a medical file, turn it into a red file, and bury it in HQ?*

Symone couldn't stand the silence anymore. She tapped Malcolm's shoulder and said, "Hey, Malcolm."

Malcolm's mind snapped back to reality. He turned to Symone and said, "Hey, what's up?"

Symone felt stung by Malcolm's shortness. "You haven't said much to me, let alone anyone else, the past few days," she lamented.

Malcolm attempted to deflect. "Yeah, just been trying to get my mind right for the next battle."

Symone shook her head, "No, that's not what this is. I know you better than that. What's wrong?"

Malcolm deflected again. "Nothing's wrong. I've just been doing a lot of thinking and trying to stay ready for what's coming next."

Symone sighed. *I wonder if he's talking about us. Did I say too much to him? Maybe I shouldn't have told him about Jason and me and the baby.* She had been doing a lot of thinking, too, taking Malcolm's advice and being still enough to listen to what her heart and mind had been trying to sort out. She had come to no conclusions and pondered what Malcolm was considering. She heard him say he intended to fight for her, but his coldness gave off a different vibe.

"What's next?" Symone asked.

"Yeah," Malcolm replied. "A lot of change about to happen, don't you think?"

Symone nodded slowly and said, "Yep, definitely a lot of change." Malcolm grew quiet again, and Symone got slightly annoyed by the silence. "Is it because of what I said the other night?"

*Damn, I forgot all about that. I've been so focused on this Collector shit, I forgot what we talked about. I can't tell her that, though.* He used that to deflect again, "You could say that. I'm in my own head about that, and you're in yours, and I just don't want to drag you down farther than where you already are."

Symone looked at Malcolm and responded, "While I appreciate that, don't think that I want you to distance yourself from me. We're allowed to have bad days, right?"

"I understand." Malcolm's heart and mind were pounding, and through the crack of his heart, he asked Symone, "Can I still trust you?"

Symone was taken aback. As her lips parted to answer him, Mallack, Stephanie, and Dax entered the room, and Mallack immediately spoke, "Okay, Elite, let's talk. Give me updates."

Daisy cleared her throat and said, "After all the hoopla from the past couple days, Chancellor Croft and Mitchell went on the holoscreen to do damage control. They've been on every major network and late-night show trying to reassure the citizens that the extremists are not tied to the POC and are acting independently as a rogue organization. They keep getting hit with the fact that they have no proof of an 'independent' organization, but Mitchell's doing his best to reassure the public that the POC have nothing to do with this."

Everybody stared at Daisy with half smiles glittering their faces. Alexia slowly crossed her arms and batted her eyes, "Mmm hmm."

"What?" Daisy asked.

"You certainly know a lot about Mitchell's goings-on," Malaysia smirked as she twirled a loc.

Daisy shrugged her shoulders. "Well, I'm the only one who watches the news like that."

"You get no argument from me on that," Duncan responded. "I can't stand being in the same room with you when you've got control of the holoscreen."

Alexia asked, "And you're sure your viewing preferences yesterday had nothing to do with him showing some kind of interest in you?"

Daisy blushed, "Alexia!"

"What? Everybody saw it, don't act like we didn't see it. He's into you, and I think you might be into him."

The team lowly chuckled. Daisy admitted, "Yeah, well, I'm only bringing him up because he asked me to speak for him today since he's still running the circuit."

"Oh, you're speaking for him now?" Joy chimed in.

"Oh yeah, that's what I'm talking about!" Symone let out a whoop. "Pretty soon, they'll be debating the city economy over a plate of linguini."

Mallack chuckled as she thought, *Yeah, I'm going to miss this crew.* She then cleared her throat and corralled the team. "Okay, Elite, let's get back on track. Stephanie, Dax, you're up. What can you tell us?"

Stephanie started, "I hate to admit this, but we haven't gotten anywhere with this Jason Xavier person. He is a straight-up ghost."

Symone spoke up, "That's impossible."

Dax countered, "Yes, Symone, you're right, it *is* impossible. And yet, we can't find anything on him. There is absolutely no record of his existence. In every way imaginable, Jason Xavier does not exist. He has been completely scrubbed off the grid on every level ever conceived. No birth records, no dental records, no hospital records. Even his fight record in the prizefighting leagues have been wiped. We tore through social media, including your pictures and postings, Symone. Nothing exists. No mention of his name or likeness on any database. Even a simple search renders nothing at the far end of the search results. Jason Xavier is a figment of our imagination."

"Can't we go through the other cities and get his information that way? What happened with InCiP?" Daisy asked.

"We tried that, too," Stephanie recalled. "And we got nowhere. Because he's a prizefighter, we went through possible mutual connections between both Symone and him, and even that was a dead end. We could send some UC's over to question them, but our analysis makes me certain they won't be able to point us in any direction."

Mallack leaned forward in her chair and inquired, "Who can do something like this, just wipe someone's entire existence off the map?" Malcolm perked up, heavily invested in the answer.

Stephanie sighed, "Something like this, only a government agency has this kind of pull. You're talking about a comprehensive identity removal. This is deeper than witness protection, because at least with that, they keep a record of your original identity. And it's not just for him. It's for his elemental teammates, too. We can't find anything on any of them, not their power signatures, past battles, nor biometrics. All of them have been completely scrubbed. An erasure like this takes clearance at unreachable levels."

"So, you're saying that one day they were here, the next they were gone, and then suddenly, they just reappeared?" Malcolm chimed in.

"Yeah," Dax answered. "One day they didn't exist, and the next, NextGen."

Mallack rubbed her hands through her hair, annoyed by the fact that they were hitting a dead end. "There has to be somebody who can find out who these people are. We have the smartest people and the most advanced technology on Uretha housed in this facility. There isn't a single person who can find them?"

Silence covered the room as the team couldn't come up with a response. A light bulb flashed in Malcolm's head, and he killed the silence with a snap of his fingers. "Yeah, yeah there is."

"Who?" Malaysia asked.

Karl suddenly knew exactly who Malcolm had in mind. "No, you're not serious."

"Yeah, I am," Malcolm nodded his head.

Daisy understood and said, "Malcolm, are you sure about that?"

The light bulb went off in Alexia's mind. "Aww shit, damn, Malcolm, for real?"

"What am I missing?" Joy looked around as the Elite's faces all shown awe and nervous wonder.

Symone's mind put it together. "You know what, he might actually be the only person who can."

"Who?  Tell me, please!" Mallack answered.

"Dredge," everybody but Joy answered.

The team patted the desk and waved their arms.  Malcolm said, "I told y'all back then we needed to give that man a job.  He might be the only person who can figure this out.  Probably can do it in a half-cycle without breaking a sweat."

"Wait a minute," Dax swiftly grew territorial and suspicious.  "We're actually considering recruiting the man who single-handedly hacked our entire system with a thumb drive?"

"You got a better idea, Dax?  If you and Intelligence can do it, we can take him off the table.  No offense to Intelligence, but we've hit a dead end.  And we're running out of time.  We don't know what Jason or his crew will do next.  Dredge may give us the upper hand to get in front of these assholes."

"Yeah, you're right," Dax swallowed his pride and checked his ego.  "So, we can locate him and relay his location to you guys."

Mallack stood up and said, "Malcolm, Malaysia, and Joy.  You three go and recruit Dredge."

Malcolm thought this might be an opportunity to resolve some of his paranoia.  "Duncan, you should come, too."

Duncan perked up.  "Yes, yes!"  His eyes instinctually darted at Joy, itching to get a chance to talk to her alone.

Malcolm immediately knew where Duncan's mind went.  "Don't get any ideas, loverboy.  We're working, not setting up your next conquest."

Mallack said, "Okay, you *four* get Dredge and bring him back here.  Malcolm's right, we're running out of time, and we don't know what this squad is going to try to do next.  We need to stay sharp and get ahead of them.  We'll reconvene once Dredge can give us something to work with. Dismissed."

Mallack, Stephanie, and Dax got up and left the room. The Elite stood from their seats, and Malaysia walked up to Malcolm and said, "Wheels up in ten?"

"Sounds good," Malcolm concurred. He told Duncan, "Ease up on the cologne, alright?"

Duncan rubbed his chin and remarked, "Man, let me be great!"

Malcolm laughed, "Negatron."

The rest of the team left, with Malcolm and Symone at the end of the line. Symone gently tugged Malcolm's arm and asked, "Hey, you sure you're okay?

Malcolm turned and faced Symone. "Yes, I'm sure." He hugged her, holding the embrace a little longer than usual. He sensed the fire and blood flowing through her veins.

"Yes," Symone declared.

"Yes?" he questioned.

Symone backed off and faced Malcolm, her deep brown eyes softening to match his gaze. "Yes, you can trust me."

Malcolm remembered the question he asked her and responded, "Okay. Thank you, Symone. I'll come find you after we bring Dredge back."

"Okay." Malcolm walked out of the conference room, leaving Symone to herself and her thoughts. *He's lying to me. He's not okay. He doesn't trust me. Shit, what do I do?* She sat atop the table for a moment, then she plotted, *I can't solve the issue right now. I should ask the others if they feel like sparring with me, something to get my mind off all this. He'll find me once he's ready to talk, and we can deal with it then.*

Symone stood up and walked out of the conference room. While standing in front of her avatar that was staring back at her, she activated her stripe and established a four-way with Daisy, Karl, and Alexia.

Karl answered first, "Yo, what's up?"

"Hey Symone," Alexia answered.

"Hi!" Daisy answered.

"Hey everyone, I was wondering if y'all felt like sparring together," Symone requested.

"Sure, I'm game," Karl didn't hesitate.

"Absolutely, yes, let's go!" Alexia replied.

"I'm good, just let me make this call real fast, and I'll meet you down there," Daisy planned.

"Ooh, I bet she's calling *Mitchell*," Alexia sang gleefully.

"Oh yeah?" Karl whooped. "Tell Mitchell we all said 'hi,' Daisy."

"Y'all, leave Daisy alone," Symone chuckled, "she deserves this win. Go talk to Mitchell and meet us down there. No rush. But hurry up!"

"You all make me sick," Daisy shot. "Bye!"

Everyone disconnected the call. Symone stared at her avatar for a moment, then walked down the corridor toward the elevator, itching to pummel something or someone and take her mind away from the abyss of the unknown.

# 16

# Pushing Past It

Malcolm and Malaysia walked ahead of Duncan and Joy on a relatively quiet sidewalk in the middle of the commerce sector of the Underbelly district. They could smell the aroma of aged brick and mortar steaming off the walls of the buildings and the asphalt underneath their soles. For the first time in a while, Malcolm noticed the clear sky above him and the suns' rays beaming on his face. "It's been a long time since I've noticed the heat from the suns," he said.

"Yeah," Malaysia agreed. "Not a lot of high rises to hide the suns within this area. Kinda miss this."

"You haven't been down here in a while, either, huh?"

"Nope, not during the day at least," Malaysia said as her recent memories sent echoes of ecstasy through her body.

"During the day?" Malcolm caught on quickly. He cocked an eyebrow, "What do *you* be doing down here under the cover of darkness?"

Malaysia chuckled and cut her eyes, "Don't act like *you* don't know what I be doing."

Malcolm clapped his hands and let out a snort while trying not to admire Malaysia's perky, shapely, hard-to-miss assets even in the baggiest of clothing choices, reminding him of a close encounter between them a lifetime ago that never materialized. "I hear that. Y'all doing alright?" he referred to her boyfriend.

Malaysia played along, "Yeah, we're alright.  I think we're coming closer to an understanding, but you know how this job can be.  Some guys say they can handle it, but then weeks like this happens, and they're all like, 'I need more.'  I thought he was going to break up with me, much like the others."

Malcolm continued, "What changed?"

Malaysia thought, *I got my needs met elsewhere and left his ass alone.*  "Well, I think he got the message when he felt me distance from him.  You know me, I'm not going to waste time.  Either you want me, or you don't."

"I hear you.  It's a shame it has to be like that sometime," Malcolm reacted.

"Right?!  I never understand why people can't just give us what we want or say that they can't.  No love lost.  We just move on."

Malcolm countered, "For some people, they have a hard time saying what's on their minds, not that that's an excuse."

"Certainly not one you can use on me.  And I'm not one for giving people too many chances before I ice them out.  Maybe that's something I need to work on?"

"Perhaps," Malcolm shrugged his shoulders.

The team's stripes buzzed.  Malcolm looked at his arm and read Intelligence's message, "Confirmed: Dredge is three blocks away from your current location.  We made contact with him, and he said he will meet you outside once you arrive."

Duncan said, "About five minutes away."

Joy replied, "Yep."  She then looked at the buildings again.

Duncan asked, "So, explain to me again how your powers work."

"Right, well, my body generates electricity at an incredible intensity.  All our bodies create electricity, but just so low that it can't really do anything beyond running them. Not me. I'm a damn everlasting battery."

Duncan was captivated, which he himself found uncharacteristic of him. "Cool, so, then, how do you control the current? Batteries don't just power themselves. They need to connect to a circuit to be useful."

"True," Joy agreed. "Maybe I'm the circuit, too? The battery in me is being used by me, so yeah, I'm the circuit. Should I change my name to 'Circuit?'?

Duncan laughed, "Nah, 'Kaminari' is badass, don't change that."

Joy instinctively pulled her slick black ponytail forward. Her eyes sparked as she thought, *I know what everybody has said about him, but gosh, he's dreamy.* She stole a glance at Duncan and noted his fair skin that glistened in the sun much like his silver eyes glittered. She just knew his muscles could carry her anywhere, and she slightly fawned over his chest that bulged through his dark charcoal muscle shirt.

Duncan hoped that Joy didn't notice him do the same thing, admiring her thin, toned physique from head-to-toe, admiring how her edges accentuated her glowing face like a crown on a queen. His eyes made a quick pit stop at her curves and highlighted her bubble butt that her skinny jeans could not hide. He cracked a smile as he noticed Joy's reaction and thought, *Yeah, she's digging me.* His bravado tried to break through, but he managed to tame it and instead continued to focus on her. "So, how do you do all that you do?" he continued. "Like, you don't just shoot bolts from your hands. It's like the lightning listens to you and obeys your commands."

"Well, over time, I learned how to sustain the current flowing through me. Since electricity can't hurt me, I can hold bolts as they run, make them swirl, push them wherever I want." She summoned a bolt from her waist, and the yellow stream swirled around her as it lightly crackled and sizzled. "It took a lot of practice, and I'm still learning so much about my powers, so I know I have a long way to go before I really have it down."

Duncan smiled. Joy noticed it and said, "What?"

"You are modest as Frimas, Joy."

"I'm just saying, there's always room for improvement, to be better than yesterday. Don't know what could come our way, always best to be prepared." Joy absorbed the bolt through her hand.

Malcolm and Malaysia overheard the two of them talking and looked at each other. They both chuckled. "Should we save her?" Malaysia asked.

"Nah, she's a big girl. If she's catching what he's throwing, let it happen," Malcolm expressed.

They stopped at the intersection and waited for the crossing light to change. Malaysia looked across the street, and jubilation overtook her like a flood. She clutched Malcolm's arm and gritted her teeth, exhilaration filling her throat. "Malcolm!"

Malaysia's grip began cutting off Malcolm's circulation, and he reflexively sensed the tension in her fingers tightening. "Ow, what is it?"

"Can we go? Please, just real quick, can we go in?" Malaysia pleaded like a kid at Jubilee.

"Where?" Malaysia pointed, and Malcolm followed her finger to the three-story building with signs in the windows that read, "Guns, Guns, Guns!," "All the ammo you need!," "Upgrade Here!," and more to lure patrons like her in.

"Oh, yeah, we got time, let's go!" Malcolm declared. He turned around and said, "Hey Duncan, Joy! Malaysia and I are gonna go across the street to the gun shop. Y'all coming with or staying out here?"

Duncan was enjoying Joy's company too much. He took a gamble and responded, "I'm good out here."

"Yeah, me, too," Joy answered, thrilled to see where their conversation would go.

"Alright, don't go off. We'll be out in a bit. Malaysia, shall we?" Malcolm opened his right arm.

Malaysia swiftly locked arms with him, then clasped her hands. "Yes, my king." The hovercars slowed to a halt, and the signal changed. Malcolm and Malaysia pranced across the street while Duncan and Joy found a bench and sat down.

The sign on the double doors read, "Benny's Emporium." Once inside, Malaysia's eyes widened again as she gazed at the treasure trove of weaponry that covered the walls and the floor. Every type of weapon was on display – artillery, hand-to-hand, short-range ballistics, even drones. The five-year-old in Malaysia came out to play. Her nostrils flared and inhaled the sweet aroma of gunpowder and steel. Malaysia looked around to see if there was a spare bedroom hiding in the store so she could become a permanent resident. *I have died and gone to Glory!*

Malcolm looked at her and smiled. But the paranoia crept into his heart again. *Is it possible? I don't think she could be. She wouldn't do this, she wouldn't be this calloused. She wouldn't turn on us, on the Company. Even if she did, she couldn't keep it up this long, she couldn't, not with me.  Am I just that naïve?  Is she that good?*

"Malcolm?  Malcolm?  Malcolm!" Malaysia snapped her fingers.  "You okay?"

Malcolm jolted and replied, "Yeah, I'm just in a weird headspace right now."

"Well, walk with me and talk about that," Malaysia reached for his hand.  Malcolm grabbed it, and they walked through the aisles.  She looked at the different types of weapons they passed by.  "Mmm, look at this," she said while picking up and admiring a knife with a four-inch handle and a ten-inch serrated blade.  "I've been reading up on this one, it's perfectly balanced, which is hard to achieve with medinure metal.  You have to be a master craftsman to achieve this.  Watch!"  Malaysia twisted her left wrist and pointed her index finger out.  She then placed the blade on her finger, in between where the handle ended and the blade began.  The knife balanced perfectly on her finger.  "See that?  See what I mean?"

"Oh wow, yeah, that is some serious craftsmanship right there," Malcolm marveled.  "Are you going to get it?"

Malaysia shook her head quickly as she grabbed the handle, "Oh, no, no, no, this blade would set me back six months.  Medinure is so fucking expensive.  I'd love to use one of these in battle someday, though."

"Why not just ask the Company to get it for you?" Malcolm asked.

"The Company?  Come on, Malcolm," Malaysia said.  She then admitted, "I tried, they said no."

"Wait, what?  That's surprising," Malcolm was slightly taken aback.

"Yeah, well, that's medinure for you.  They said, 'We already got you all these other weapons, we're way over budget now. You'll have to wait,' blah, blah, blah. Anyway," she put the blade back, "let's go upstairs. I want to show you my black zintol."

"What, this blade wasn't it?" Malcolm laughed.

"Shut up and let's go!" Malaysia laughed. "Besides, you still haven't told me what's got you in a funk."

Malcolm sighed as they kept walking toward the back of the store toward the staircase. Malcolm did not want to expose himself, but he was also bursting at the seams, clawing at the walls of his heart to tell somebody about his encounter with the Collector. *No, I can't tell her. She might be in on it.*

"Malaysia, what if you found out something that could change everything you know about yourself?"

Malaysia saw through Malcolm's deflection and pushed, "What did you find out that could change everything about you, Malcolm?"

*Damn it! See, I shouldn't have said anything!*

Malaysia started ascending the stairs. Malcolm walked behind her and was distracted by Malaysia's eye candy again, admiring how she fit in her jeans so well. Malaysia noticed Malcolm had gotten quiet again and said, "I know I have a nice ass. Don't let this thing throw your focus off. What did you find out, Malcolm?"

Malcolm replied, "It's something very simple, and it's probably nothing. It's just, the timeline doesn't fit, and I'm trying to figure out when this event took place and, more importantly, where I was when it happened."

They walked toward a massive gun display on the wall. Malaysia didn't let up, concerned that her friend was in trouble and needed her help. "When what happened?"

Malcolm felt cornered. *Okay, if I tell her, I risk exposing the position I'm in. But if I don't tell her, she's going to keep prying until she gets it out of me. Shit, fuck it. Just tell her.*

"A medical procedure," Malcolm admitted.

"Oh, that's it?" Malaysia breathed a sigh of relief. "Malcolm, you scared me half to death. I thought you were gonna tell me you killed somebody or some shit. I'm actually kind of bummed, thought we were going to have to fight somebody. Well, if there's a problem with a medical procedure, you can just ask the Analyst about that. He keeps all our records, you know that. He should be able to help you get all the answers you need."

They arrived at the glowing blue wall. Malcolm replied, "Yeah, the Analyst, that makes sense, actually."

"Of course it does, because I suggested it!" Malaysia turned her attention to the guns that stretched from one end to the next, arranged in five rows from the floor to the ceiling. Malaysia walked to the middle of the wall and stared at her black zintol. "See that gun right there?"

Malcolm followed Malaysia's eyes and immediately knew what she was coveting. "The purple one?"

"Yes," Malaysia fawned. "That one is called the Iris. See the yellow streaks along the barrel?"

"Yeah."

"Those are the charges that power the gun. Charged by light. That gun virtually has unlimited ammunition. It can fire anything that can fit the chamber, but it can also fire plasma, pyro, electricity, even hydro. But it gets even better. The gun can become an extension of yourself, kinda like Duncan before he upgraded his arm cannons, but in reverse. So rather than just firing from the trigger, your arm becomes the gun.

Whoo, it is a gunner's wet dream, and if I had that, I'd never wake up again."

Malcolm was mesmerized by Malaysia's enthusiasm, captured by her passion for her craft and fighting the urge to fawn over her like a fanboy. "So, are you gonna get it?"

"Nope, the medinure knife will set me back six months. But this gun will bankrupt me. I couldn't afford this even if I lived ten lifetimes. It can do way too much and never has to be maintained."

"But Malaysia, it's called 'the Iris.' The Iris, *the Eagle*, it's literally your birthright."

"Yeah, well, unless somebody gifts me my birthright, I'm not going to get what I deserve on this one," Malaysia lamented. "It's okay, I can always dream of going to town with this someday."

Malcolm understood. "I feel ya."

"Let's go before I start crying in front of you." They turned around and headed for the exit. "Malcolm, listen, whatever it is about this medical procedure that's got you shaken up, you owe it to yourself to see it through. Just make sure that you don't jeopardize the team, the mission, or your relationship."

"My relationship?" Malcolm asked.

"Uh, yeah! I've been noticing you two the past few days, and y'all don't seem to be doing so well right now. Are you two beefing?"

Malcolm thought, *I can't hide shit from you, Malaysia.* And yet, he felt a sense of relief that he could talk a little bit about Symone's worries. "No, I wouldn't call it beefing. It's just that Symone feels like things are getting too serious too fast, and it's freaking her out. I'm just giving her some space to figure out how she wants to proceed going forward."

"Proceed going forward, what does that mean? You two might break up?"

"Akan, I hope not! But right now, she's not in a good place to know what she really wants, and I'm not going to pressure her to do anything."

"Malcolm, did you ask her to be pledged to you?!" Malaysia gripped his hand.

"What? No! I'm nowhere near ready for that, not with what's about to happen at the Company."

"What, you don't want to spend the rest of your life with her?"

"Well, yes. I mean, no. I mean, I love her, but we're not ready for that step. I'm committed. She's just not sure she is. I'm waiting on her to let me know. No pressure."

Malaysia didn't mince words. "Look, you and Symone have a good thing going. Don't let this thing she's dealing with, or the shit you're dealing with, screw y'all up. Symone's my girl. I'll kill you myself if you let that happen."

"Hey, you were my friend first, don't forget that," Malcolm joked.

"I don't give a damn!" Malaysia laughed. "Girl code, brother. Chicks before dicks unless and until you're pledged. And even then, you can still get these hands and these bullets. I got plenty of both."

"Yeah, you do," Malcolm agreed.

"Do I need to get you two into therapy or something?"

Malcolm shook his hands, "No, I think I've had enough therapy for the both of us. For now, anyway."

Joy and Duncan continued getting acquainted with each other as they waited for their partners to return. Joy was taken by Duncan's swagger and felt comfortable enough to ask him about himself. "So, what about you? How does your power work? I can feel the current running through your veins and robotics."

"Oh, you can?" Duncan inquired.

"Oh, yeah! It's not like I can draw from you unless I touch you. If I shoot a bolt, though, I can attach it to you because of the current in you. Much like with anything in my purview. If it runs on electricity, I can sense it. Anyway, I'm talking too much about me. Answer my question. What does it mean to be cybernetic?"

"Right, right. Well, my power is not so much a 'power.' I'm code and mechanics."

"Code? Like, you're AI?" Joy worried that she was developing a crush on a machine.

"What? No," he laughed. "So, I got a lot of family in the military. My dad, mom, uncle, and a few cousins. I enlisted in the military straight out of the academy. And when it came to artillery weaponry, there was no one smarter than me. That sounded like a brag, and it was! I killed it in combat ballistics. Nobody understood or handled weapons like I did." Joy smiled as he continued, "So, I was recruited to work R&D, and I helped run a division working on experimental tech that would enhance soldiers and give our wounded ways to have excellent quality of life and, if they wanted, to return to the battlefield. One day, our base got attacked by hostiles. We rallied and defended the base, but most of us didn't make it out alive, including me."

"The Frimas?" Joy's eyes widened.

Duncan reeled, freshly recalling the shell that blew him backward and the pole that impaled him straight through his heart. He remembered telling the doctors to keep his full memory intact so that he would always guard his heart most of all. "Yeah, I died that day. 02-43-5719. But the government decided my knowledge was too valuable for my story to end like that. So, they found my body, at least what was left of it, took me to another base, and I became the first recruit for the experimental cybernetics program."

"Oh shit, so when you say you're code –"

"I'm saying I am a living machine, one hundred percent man, one hundred percent machine."

"That's fucking incredible, Duncan!"

"The two or so years after that, I was on the frontlines of several combat missions, taking down foreign enemies left and right. I racked up a pretty hefty kill count and got commendations and medals like crazy. Those two years were the best of my career."

"So, why didn't you stay with the military?"

"Shit, when the Company calls, you fucking answer! I put in my papers immediately, and the military did not hesitate to honorably discharge me. I couldn't wait to get my ass back over here, making triple what I was making there to do the exact same thing. Plus, with the Company's Double W department, we perfected the cybernetics program, and it has since helped enhance the soldiers and improve their mortality rates exponentially. Oh, there's Malcolm and Malaysia. Come on."

Joy and Duncan jogged across the street to meet Malaysia and Malcolm. "Did you get anything?" Duncan asked.

"No, not today," Malaysia sighed. "Just browsed. You two ready?"

"Yeah," Joy answered, "let's go."

"Alright." Malcolm seized the opportunity to talk to Duncan one-on-one before they met Dredge a block away. "Duncan, come walk with me, brother. I think you've schmoozed Joy enough for one day."

"Ha, ha, very funny," Duncan reacted.

He walked ahead to meet Malcolm while Joy and Malaysia stayed a few steps behind. Malaysia looked at Joy and asked, "So, did Duncan put the moves on you?"

"Honestly, no. I mean, if he did, it didn't seem like it to me. He seems really cool."

"What? *Duncan* seems cool?" Astonishment barely captured Malaysia's reaction.

"Yeah. We talked about our powers and where they came from and all that. Like, he didn't do the whole 'smooth operator' thing some of my former teammates warned me about."

"Fascinating," Malaysia replied. *Does he like her?*

Malcolm, meanwhile, investigated Duncan on an entirely different matter. "Hey brother, I want to pick your brain a little bit."

Duncan thought, *Oh shit, what did I do?* "Okay, about what?"

"Um, your time in the Collector's lair."

Duncan squinted his eyes and gazed at Malcolm. "Why?"

*To rule you out as a suspect.*

"I know we don't really talk about it, and I don't know, ever since we got you back from the sanctuary, you have been very mum about it. And I feel like it's my fault for not asking you about it more."

"I mean, it's cool. I don't really like talking about it."

"Why not?"

Duncan shrugged his shoulders. "I mean, who wants to talk about the lowest moment in his career? I got caught trying to help y'all out at the power party. Not a great conversation starter, if you ask me, 'Hey, so let's talk about your biggest loss.' Shit, that sounds like a job interview question. But you know what? Getting caught isn't even the part that pisses me off the most."

"What do you mean?" Malcolm's antenna picked up.

Duncan's irritation from the memory showed in his slow articulation of his explanation. "Malcolm, I sat in a room for days, and the Collector and her crew didn't do shit to me. I wasn't tortured. I wasn't prodded. I wasn't beaten. Like, the only thing they did was disable my powers. I basically camped out in their version of one of our residences in the quarters."

Malcolm was shocked as Duncan continued, "I ate three meals a day and had access to a big ass holoscreen to watch what was going on in the world. I didn't struggle at all while I was in her custody, or Frimas, how did she put it, her 'care.' It was infuriating!"

"Wait, you're telling me that she captured you just to treat you like royalty? Why is this the first I'm hearing about it?" Malcolm scratched his head.

"Because it was embarrassing as Frimas! Karl, Daisy, and Alexia asked me about it, but I didn't feel like talking about it when they did. I didn't want to tell anybody, 'Hey, the most diabolical woman on Uretha gave me cookies and milk and a bed with five-hundred thread count sheets.' I mean, come on, Malcolm, who does that shit? The Collector is a monster, but what monster you know treats her captives like kings?"

Malcolm was stupefied. *I wish I knew, Duncan. She should have killed me, too. She had me dead to rights, and she let me live.* "I'm just as confused about that as you are."

"I saw the therapist, and she wondered if I had my mind scrambled, or maybe I dissociated by 'creating a narrative to get through my trauma,' but I promise, I'm not tripping. My training experience at the Company was worse than what I experienced at the Collector's. In fact, preschool was worse than that shit!"

Malcolm patted him on the shoulder. "Well, I am glad you came out of there. But I never knew you had it that good. Did you learn anything about her while you were there?"

"Naw, just the whole 'destiny' shit I told y'all way back when. I couldn't tell you anything about the layout of that place or where it's located. No idea what her plans were or why she pulled your info. Nobody talked about anything important while they were around me. She's got her people trained well, that's all I know."

"What do you mean by 'trained well?'"

"Whatever it is they're doing, they are locked in, like a well-oiled machine. Between you and me, isn't it funny to you that we haven't heard a peep from them since last year? Like, they haven't done a damn thing since we beat Trent Salazar. Usually, someone who's taken a loss would have re-grouped by now, but, to me, her silence seems intentional, like Trent was part of something bigger than just sizing us up."

Suddenly, Malcolm's mind reflected on what the Collector said to him a few nights prior: *"Notice, though, that we've been ghost ever since. No sequel to the Trent Salazar saga, no more killings, no more powers being taken. None of that. I got the information I needed from the Company and left you all alone."*

"Right," Malcolm responded. "Nothing about the Collector ever makes sense." *He does make a valid point. But how do I know he's not just trying to spin my top? Ugh, this is driving me crazy!* "We won't know anything until she shows up again, that's for damn sure."

"That's what worries me. Her crew is biding time. For what, we may never know until it's too late."

"Agreed."

Malcolm felt some relief, believing that the likelihood of Malaysia or Duncan playing for the Collector's team was slim. Still, he couldn't shake Duncan's assessment that was dead on with the Collector's sentiments a few nights prior. He struggled to piece together what her endgame could be, and why she was so adamant to give him intel about a medical procedure and rehabilitation time. *What on Uretha is the Collector doing, and what do I have to do with it?*

The foursome made it to the target location. They stopped at another brick-and-mortar building with glass stripes across three floors. "Alright, this is the place," Malcolm reported. "Malaysia, make the call."

Malaysia used her stripe to call the number given by Intelligence. "Hello?" a voice answered.

"Hey, is this Dredge?" Malaysia asked.

"Yeah, this the Elite?" Dredge returned.

"Yep, come outside."

"Alright, I'm on my way." Dredge disconnected the call.

"He's on his way out," Malaysia pulled and adjusted her jeans and pulled down her shirt. "I had to have lost some weight, I can't keep these things up."

"We probably all have over the past few days," Malcolm reasoned, "all this fighting and stressing we've been doing."

Dredge stepped through the glass doors. He had lost some of the pudge that rested on his stomach, and his hair was spikier than before. He felt a nervous joy seeing the Elite in front of him again. "Yo, Malcolm, Malaysia, what's up! You two, I don't know you. You new?" He pointed at Joy and Duncan.

"Yeah, I'm Joy," she answered.

"And I'm Duncan," he mimicked.

"Nice to meet you," Dredge responded.

"How's Lana?" Malaysia asked.

"Oh, Lana? Man, she's great, in school crushing it! She's got her dad's instincts, so I'm trying to keep her mind occupied enough so she doesn't get bored and end up doing something dumb."

Malcolm couldn't help himself and still held it against Dredge that he assisted the Collector. "Speaking of, how are you doing? You're not getting bored and doing something dumb, are you?"

"Me, no, not at all," Dredge laughed nervously, still intimidated by Malcolm's moral resolve and terrorizing demeanor. "After you guys helped me get my daughter back, I got a job here. Fixing holoscreens and other electronics, all legit. You guys really had my back by convincing the Company to pay my debts off. I couldn't believe it when I went to my bookies and the bank and they were all like, 'Why are you here? You paid us already, accounts closed.' Then I got a call about this job and took it, for Lana's sake."

Malaysia, Malcolm, and Duncan recalled what the team did for Dredge to make sure Lana didn't grow up without a father. They all agreed they wouldn't say a word to him about any of it.

"I don't remember doing anything like that for him," Malaysia said. "Malcolm?"

"Naw, that didn't come from me. Maybe Mallack?" Malcolm responded.

"We can ask her when we get back. Right now, let's focus on the task at hand," Duncan turned the team's attention back to what they traveled there for.

"Right, why are you guys here? What do you want? A free holoscreen or something? We got good deals on 240-inches, perfect for the zintol—"

"No, no. Listen, you been paying attention to the POC stuff on the news lately?" Malcolm inquired.

"Oh yeah, those jokers mean business. What's up?"

"Well, how would you like to be the one who brings them to justice?" Malaysia offered.

Dredge was taken aback. "Wait, you want me to help you find them? Why can't you do it?"

"Well, to be honest, we tried. Our entire Intelligence unit tried, and they can't do it. All we have is a name, and no one can find him," Malcolm reported.

"Yeah," Duncan chimed in. "His identity has been scrubbed off the grid, a government-level scrub. We can't crack the code to find him or his crew."

"We need your help," Joy tagged herself in. "I heard about what you can do, and Malcolm is convinced that you deserve a job with us because of your legendary work."

"Legendary," Dredge whispered with glee.

"Yeah, okay, I wouldn't call it *legendary,* so don't get the big head," Malcolm rolled his eyes. "But for real, if you help us, if you can find this goon, I promise you, I'll put in a word for you to come on board. You are literally the only person we know who can do this."

Dredge didn't hesitate, "Yeah, I'm in, let's do this. I'll help you find these guys. But you gotta absolutely get me a job with you guys because this shit is boring as fuck. I want to gamble so bad because of how bored I am. If one more person comes in here talking about 'how do I get my holoscreen to change channels,' I will make it where everyone's screens in Uretha will play one channel for a month just for kicks."

Malaysia quickly reacted, "Okay, so let's get Dredge to the Company so we can all keep control of our holoscreens, right?"

"Agreed," Malcolm stated. "Malaysia, call the bus."

"Alright, alright, Dredge working with the Elite again, this is awesome!"

"I hardly call our last encounter 'you working with us.' Frimas, we were working *because* of you."

"With," Dredge incorrectly corrected Malcolm. He clapped and rubbed his hands together. "Let's do this! Hey, you guys got food at the Company, right? I'm hungry."

Malcolm rolled his eyes. "This better not come back to bite me in the ass."

"Title of your sex tape," Malaysia joked. Duncan and Joy snorted, then looked at each other and smiled.

Joy wished, *Akan, please ask me out!*

# 17

# Losing Control

Daisy consumed her rose-colored energy drink in a nanosecond. Her mind swam through a pool of emotions as she ruminated on her conversation with Mitchell, excited about their date scheduled for later that night. *I just cannot believe this is happening, and with him of all people. But gosh, he's so yummy! Oh Akan, I can't believe I'm crushing on the leader of the POC! Daisy, what are you thinking? My dad will kill me if he ever finds out.* Daisy's heart pounded around five hundred beats per minute. She recalled her self-soothing techniques and performed her breathing exercises. She mentally switched gears and prepared her mind for Symone's sparring exercise.

She exited the quarters, and she overheard Karl's baritone voice as she approached the elevator. He stood alone, and she surmised he was on his stripe. She heard him say, "...hopefully this weekend. Kiss those babies for me. I love you. Buh-bye."

Karl caught Daisy out of the corner of his eye and waved. "Daisy, you ready?"

"Always ready," Daisy answered. "Hey, was that your sister?"

"Sure was, just checking in on her and her kids," Karl responded and embraced Daisy. "Gotta make sure she's keeping them in line."

Daisy smiled as the elevator door opened. "I think it's great that you're so involved with them, Uncle Karl."

"Well, that's my family, you know? Since I'm here a lot, I don't get to see them like that, so I make sure they still feel my presence as much as I can."

"So, what do you think Symone is going to make us do today?"

"Who knows," Karl replied. "But if I know her, it will involve tearing a bunch of shit apart."

"Why do you think that?"

Karl crossed his arms. "Her presence and energy have been off the past few days. She's bottled up about something, and this will be her way of letting some of the pressure off."

"That's rather observant of you, Karl. Think we should say something to her?" Daisy wondered.

"No, not yet. This looks like something she needs to figure out on her own. Or, rather, she and Malcolm," Karl figured as he had been pondering why his best friend's behavior shifted, too, inferring that his relationship with Symone had hit a bump.

Daisy agreed, "Oh, yeah, right. Everything's about to change." Daisy tried not to let her envy seep through her statement. "I got you. Well, let's hope they both get it figured out soon, right?"

But she couldn't hide her feelings from Karl, who heard the inflection in her voice and pressed in, "Still in your feelings about Malcolm?"

"What, no!" Daisy shook her head.

Karl crossed his bulging arms and stared at her with a sub-liminal, *You do know who you're talking to, right?*

She growled and rolled her eyes. "Fine, yes, I'm still in my feelings about it. But I also know that there's nothing I can do about it, and Malcolm *is* the best choice to take over. If not me, then I'm glad it's him."

"Why does his promotion bother you so much, Daisy?"

Daisy sighed, "I guess I just don't know what he's got that I don't. Is it his speeches, his charisma? I can give a good speech. I can be suave."

"You know it's more than that, Daisy," Karl reasoned. "Malcolm has more combat experience than all of us, and he's been leading the Elite for years. Becoming the director is almost his birthright at this point."

Daisy tinkered with his praise of Malcolm and deduced, "You're saying I should try to lead a team first?"

*No, that's not what I meant.* Karl shrugged his shoulders, "I mean, it can't hurt. But first, you should at least think about *why* you want to lead so badly." The elevator landed on the training floor. "Ask yourself, '*Why* do I want to lead?' What is your *why*? Do you want to lead because you want the work, or just the title and perks?"

Karl walked ahead of Daisy, the subtle distance causing Daisy to pause and ponder over Karl's precise inquisition. Once they arrived, Karl placed his hand on the palm reader, and Symone's training room opened. They noticed Symone and Alexia in their training uniforms.

"Great, come on in guys," Symone pounded her right fist into her left hand.

Karl joked, "Hey, that's my move!"

Symone chuckled just as AI announced, "Karl Luther, codename the Mammoth. Daisy Parker, codename Blitz. Modifying room to powered state." The room hummed as the cloak on the walls recalibrated to match their powers.

"Alright," Karl bellowed, "what are we doing today?"

"So, I was thinking we would do a melee today," Symone replied gleefully.

"I told you she was gonna blow shit up," Karl laughed.

"That you did. We haven't done a melee in a while," Daisy reacted. "What are the terms?"

"We'll each have to tear through one hundred targets. Your targets will match your color, so only destroy yours, or else the ones that aren't your color will count for your opponents. The first to destroy all of their targets wins. Easy peasy!"

"I like it!" Karl said as he pounded his fist into his hand.

"You guys don't stand a chance against me," Alexia replied as her eyes lit green.

"Oh, y'all must have forgot who I am!" Daisy swiftly shuffled her feet.

"Oh, like my power just disappeared," Symone created an aura around her body, and her hair glowed.

"Let's do this," Karl announced. His training uniform shot out from the wall and latched onto him, covering his body, and Daisy's uniform did the same.

"Alright, AI, load Melee 3.7," Symone ordered.

"Initiating Melee 3.7," AI responded. The room pixelated and morphed from the sterile gray training room to a night scene in an abandoned parking lot. The twin moons shone brightly and served as the only light in the room. The team looked around as they noticed an abandoned, damaged five-story building about fifty feet away from them.

"Ah shit, Symone," Daisy declared. "I didn't think you were going to make it this challenging."

Symone smirked, "This is me you're talking to. I want to win!"

AI sounded, "Melee begins in 3, 2, 1, go!"

The foursome's uniforms changed colors: Karl to black, Daisy to red, Alexia to green, and Symone to gold. Daisy sped away in search of her targets. Symone blasted into the sky. Karl marched forward toward the building, and Alexia stood where she was. She closed her eyes and listened for movement across the training floor.

Doors secretly opened along the edges of the training room, and androids filed into the room, all color-coded to match their opponents. Symone noticed several bots flying toward her. She quickly charged her hands and launched stars at the bots. She hit a few of them, and the bots' cloaks shimmered as they flew backward, recalibrated, and continued their pursuit. Symone remembered that she programmed the bots to be cloaked and heated herself up from yellow to white. The bots got closer and engaged with her. They delivered a series of punches and kicks at her, and she dodged and countered with heated palms and feet, damaging their cloaks. She grabbed one of them and spun it around, then released it into some of her gold-colored targets. Symone then blasted downward, and two of the machines could not escape her star trail, and their cloaks dissipated, and the machines exploded. The other androids were unfazed and pursued her.

Daisy saw red machines racing toward her and thought, "Piece of cake." She rushed one of them and was shocked when her palm planted on the bot's chest, and they traveled together as the bot tried to make sense of its position and counter Daisy. Daisy said, "Damn it, Symone, I didn't know you cloaked these bastards!" Daisy released the machine, and it slowed itself to a halt. Meanwhile, the other droids hurried toward her like ants. Daisy said, "Alright, I need a gun," remembering her training from the past several weeks. She sped away requesting a blaster from AI through her stripe. She stopped near the edge of the training room, and a blaster appeared from the wall. She grabbed it and pushed a button on the grip to charge the plasma-powered weapon, then zipped toward the army formed in front of her. She squeezed the trigger rapidly, turned herself into a gatling gun, and blasted some of the bots until their cloaks dissipated and they exploded. The other droids regrouped and prepared to counter Daisy's assault.

Karl made it onto the abandoned building's splintered concrete floor. Several black figures ran his way. He shook his arms and said, "Alright, let's do this." He charged forward and raised his fist, then swung his arm forward and planted a punch on the lead android. The android's face shimmered from the cloak, and Karl continued his barrage, landing several punches and kicks onto the bots that surrounded him. He grabbed one of them and spun him into the others, knocking them all down. As those machines rose, more ran from the corners of the building toward Karl. Karl raised his fists high and smashed the ground, splitting the ground in front of him. Several of the machines fell into the fissure he created, but then propelled themselves out of the hole with their feet jets. Three machines grabbed him from behind and pushed him to his knees. Karl struggled to shake them off. He then pushed himself backward and flopped onto his back, crushing one of the bots under his weight, then smashed the two holding his arms into each other, then flung them into the androids flying toward him. He then flipped himself upright and turned to run toward the staircase at the back of the building.  He said to Symone, "Decided to make this a real challenge, huh?"

She replied in his ears, "Sure did!" He shook his head and kept marching forward as the black army raced toward him.

Alexia couldn't pick up the color signature of her machines like she wanted and realized the machines were cloaked.  The green machines hastily rushed toward her.  She placed her hands in front of her in a prayer stance, clasped them together, then swung and spanned her arms outward, and a green mist surrounded her.  Suddenly, one hundred Alexias appeared in a line.  They stood in battle stance, ready for the ensuing attack.

As Symone flew toward the top of the building, she noticed Alexia's tactic and said, "Ah shit, no fair man! Damn it!" She turned around and launched several stars at her gold-colored opponents and landed blows against their shields.

The Alexia army jumped and delivered energy storm strikes against her green counterparts.  Most of her opponents dodged the shots, but some of Alexia's blasts landed devastating blows against them, and fifteen of them fell.  The rest of her opponents reached the Alexias and began pummeling her crew one by one.  Those that remained used binding spells to suspend the green army in the air.  The Alexias thought they were getting the upper hand until some of them turned around and saw another group of green bots appear from behind them suddenly and strike them.  "Shit," Alexia cried, "how did I miss them?" Alexia herself turned around and suspended them all midair.  One of the first bots grabbed her leg and tripped her, slamming her into the ground and breaking her concentration.  The other Alexias struggled to break their combatants' cloaks.  The rest of the army were no longer suspended and began assaulting Alexia's team, and their blows reduced Alexia's crew to just her.

Daisy's gatling gun technique proved supremely effective. She ran to the rooftop, and as her opponents launched themselves toward her, she emptied clips of plasma energy at the machines until they exploded. Her visor indicated that she had destroyed twenty-two of her one hundred by the time they had reached her on the roof. At that point, she ran off the building and back onto the parking lot. The red machines changed course and made their way toward her, and she kept repeating this cycle, quietly scoring points and hoping no one would catch on.

Symone, meanwhile, landed on the roof and created a heat shield. She assumed the machines would either try to fly around it or go through it. She stood aways behind the shield, and her suspicions were correct. The gold wave barreled through the shield, damaging their cloaks, making it easier for Symone to then blast them to bits with gatling stars. Each machine that rolled through the shield ate Symone's star power and exploded. Symone reached thirty-one kills before the machines recalibrated and went around the shield. Symone caught wind of their approach and surrounded herself with a star dome and said, "Come get this!"

Karl made it to the top and ran to the middle of the slab. He noticed a couple twenty-foot, metal bars on the ground and picked them up like twigs. Just as the black ants arrived atop the staircase, Karl noticed gold bots flying through the walls. He thought, *Are they coming for me? Don't attack them, Karl, those aren't mine!* The black and gold bots crossed paths. The black bots launched their assault toward Karl as the gold army attached themselves to the ceiling and started picking it apart with punches and kicks. Karl wondered what they were doing, but then snapped to attack mode. He slammed the bots across both sides of the slab with his pipes. They crashed-landed and then got back up to try to come for Karl again. Karl continued to swing the bars, and as their cloak integrities fell, some of his bots exploded, and Karl's kill count rose to twenty-eight.

Symone wondered what had happened to her bots. The gold warriors pummeled the ceiling she stood on, and it crumbled beneath her. Symone's feet shifted, and without warning, the slab collapsed, and she fell through the hole the gold warriors created. Karl watched her land on the floor and get tackled by the gold army. She lay on the ground underneath a scrum of gold metal.

Alexia lay on the ground, getting punched and kicked by her army. Her eyes lit green, and she unleashed an energy dome and pushed all the bots off her, destroying seventeen more of them. She then suspended them in midair again and began stinging their cloaks. Her temples pounded like someone was drilling screws through her skull. She struggled to tear their cloaks off. *I can't break them like this. I'm not strong enough to do this, not with all of them cloaked.*

The voice inside her head yelled, *Let us do it! We can do it!*

Alexia cried silently, *No! I can do this!*

*You just said you can't!* the voice protested.

*I got this! Shut up!* Alexia demanded.

Alexia held them in suspension, flew about thirty feet away from them, then created an energy shield in front of her. She then released her grip on the machines and pushed the shield forward. The shield hit the androids and damaged their cloaks, but they continued to pursue her.

Daisy's bot count rose to seventy-four using her cat-and-mouse method. She admitted to herself that she had gotten bored, but she would not lose this opportunity to finally win a challenge, especially after all the weapons training she received the past couple quarters. She killed her seventy-fifth bot, and AI announced, "Daisy is in the lead with seventy-five machines destroyed."

"Damn it, AI! Why'd you have to announce it?!" Daisy yelled.

Symone heard the announcement and decided to end things before she lost the challenge. She heated up from white to blue, and she raised her adrenaline and sensation levels up, mightily charging herself. Her aura began to sting the bots' cloaks. Their relentless pursuit became their downfall as one by one, the cloaks of the androids closest to her body started dissipating, and they couldn't take Symone's heat. As those bots disintegrated, the next machines fell into her aura.

Karl saw the gold dome shrinking and pouted, "Aww Frimas naw, not today!" Karl saw two pillars about thirty feet behind him, and he ran toward them and knocked his entire weight into one, then the other, and the rooftop began to collapse. He dashed for the hole in the wall, and as he jumped through it, most of the black ants were crushed under the weight of the rooftop. He then gripped the edge of the wall and slid into the floor below. He then repeated what he had done, knocking out the two pillars holding the ceiling up, and that ceiling collapsed also, and he jumped out another hole in the wall, and he repeated this cycle until he had made it to the bottom floor and had toppled the middle section of the building. His number rose to eighty-eight.

Symone continued to lay on the ground as the bots continued to try to reach her to no avail. Her number rose to eighty-nine. The eleven remaining bots finally recalibrated and backed off her to try to figure out what to do next.

Alexia heard the announcement and lamented that she was only at forty-eight. *Shit! I'm going to lose again!*

*Oh no, you're not!* the voices in her head sternly countered. *We got this!*

"No, no, no!" Alexia shrieked.

She suddenly couldn't feel the armor on her skin nor the clothes covering her body. She attempted to move her hands and feet, to no avail. Her vision suddenly blurred and faded. She could no longer see the training room, the bots, nor her friends, surrounded by utter darkness. Her soul was yanked backward as the voices shuttled her into a deep dark pit of her subconsciousness. Alexia screamed and clawed at the air. She reached within herself for her powers, trying to stop herself from plunging deeper into the black chasm, but she could not retrieve them.

*Help! Somebody, please! Help me!*

The voices sank Alexia into the corner of her subconscious and assumed complete command of her body, mind, and powers. Eager to take their new vessel out for a test drive, Alexia's body inhaled deeply, then her arms shot out, her eyes slammed shut, her neck sharply craned upward, and her entire body stiffened as she levitated swiftly off the ground. Her eyes popped open, and her right eye was now orange, her left eye yellow. Alexia's vocal cords stretched and deepened, and her voices declared, "Finally! Let's destroy everything!"

Orange and yellow mist and bolts flew from her hands and surrounded, gripped, and squeezed every green android. "See, Alexia, *this* is how you do it!" The orange and yellow mist turned into static sparks, and the machines' cloaks could not withstand the damage for long. Their cloaks dissipated, and the bots wriggled and convulsed until one-by-one, they blew apart, turning into a heap of metal and wired rubble on the parking lot.

AI announced, "Winner: Alexia!"

Karl, Symone, and Daisy's bots immediately powered down. Symone cried, "What?! How?! That's crazy!"

Daisy lowered her pistol and lamented, "No way! I was almost there! Damn it!"

Karl clapped his hands, "Alright, Alexia! Way to go!"

Alexia's voices crossed her eyes to look at each other and said, "No, we're not done yet. Destroy the rest!"

Symone emerged from the building and landed near Karl. Daisy blitzed to them, and they walked in Alexia's direction. Meanwhile, Alexia's arms shot out, and orange and yellow mist and bolts surrounded the other bots, and Symone, Karl, and Daisy. They all levitated and wriggled to be free from Alexia's trap. The moons, the parking lot, and the building began to pixelate as a bewildered Symone asked, "Alexia, what are you doing?"

Alexia did not answer; instead, the voices continued to pulse power. The bots' cloak integrities fell to zero, and the bots began to dismantle. Symone saw her cloak's integrity plummeting and grew alarmed. "Alexia, you won, what are you doing?!"

Alexia could not stop. The voices tasted freedom and intensified their assault. "They're in our way!"

For the first time in decades, Karl felt a sting of sharp pain in his bones. He grimaced, "What the Frimas? Alexia, stop!"

Daisy could feel her insides turning against her. "Somebody's gotta stop her before she kills us!"

"Analyst! Initiate shock on Alexia Montague, now!" Karl desperately ordered.

The Analyst heard the distress call from Karl and rushed to his holoscreen to open Alexia's profile. He tapped her avatar and swiped to "STRIPE CONTROL," then scrolled to "SHOCK" and pressed the button hard.

Alexia's stripe turned red and connected to her uniform's nanites, and they delivered a high-voltage electric shock to her nervous system. Alexia's body felt the sudden surge of current course through her entire body. It knocked Alexia out, and she fell and crumpled lifelessly on the ground. The mist flowing from her hands immediately stopped. Symone, Karl, Daisy, and the bots' remains slammed to the floor. The three groaned from the stinging in their insides.

"Alexia, what was that?" Symone rolled onto her knees.

"She's never done that before, and that shit hurt," Karl reacted, terrified that he had lost his powers but feeling the pain rapidly subsiding.

Daisy rapidly shook her arms and legs to try to get the pain to rescind. "What do you mean?" she was surprised by Karl's statement. "She hurt *you*?"

"Yeah, through the cloak and everything." He stood up and shook himself. "I haven't felt anything like that since I was a teen." His mind attempted to flash back to a dark time in his life when killing himself seemed the only way out of the sorrows of his adolescence, but he quickly pushed the thoughts away. "Has she ever done anything like that before?"

"No, never like this. This was different." Symone noticed that Alexia didn't answer her call. "Alexia? Alexia? Come on guys, Alexia's not responding to me." They rushed over to her. Symone knelt and lifted Alexia's torso off the ground.

"Alexia? Alexia, come on, girl, wake up," she pleaded as she shook her. "Alexia!"

Alexia lay on a cold, wet surface. She batted her eyes and scanned her dark, entry-less tomb. She pushed herself off the ground. Her eyes scanned for any sign of life, a pointer to any direction, but she couldn't get her bearings. *Where the Frimas am I?* Hyperventilating, she tried to harness her powers but couldn't tap into them.

"What is this?! Where am I?! What have you done to me?!" she shrieked.

The voices responded in kind. Two pairs of glowing, piercing eyes – one set orange, the other set yellow – stared at her from a distance. They replayed for her the scene in which they won the challenge and almost took out her friends. Alexia knelt, mortified, embarrassed, and disgusted. "I can't believe that just happened. What have I done? What have *you* done?!"

"That," one voice said, "was true power. What you asked for. What you sought us for. You'll never experience this unless you set us free. Let us out!"

"You can have real, unlimited power," the other voice added.

Alexia gripped her skull and shook her head feverishly as anxiety clamped down on her heart. "No, no, I can't let you out. I have to stop this."

"It's too late. You can't stop what's already begun. We will come out, one way or another. Our time is coming, and you are the conduit." Orange and yellow mist flowed from their direction and pushed Alexia back. She reached deep within herself and thought, *Come on, Enchantra! Dig deep! Where are your powers? Kick their asses!*

Alexia's temples pounded, and she felt a glimmer of her essence. She pulled on it, and it ignited an inferno that resuscitated her powers. Immediately, she shielded herself with green mist and blocked their assault.

"You cannot resist us forever. Eventually, we will break free. The more you resist, the more painful this will become for you. Give up!"

Alexia strained, determined to not let them win. She planted her palms together, and as she levitated off the ground, she yelled, "No!" She unleashed her energy shield, and the darkness surrounding her shattered, shredding the veil and revealing the monstrosities residing in Alexia's head. Orange and yellow clouds of energy swirled violently around the twenty-foot, skeletal ghouls. Their eyes flashed from the rage they felt regarding Alexia's resurgence.

Alexia fought through her terror and blasted upward. Her captors chased her, and Alexia reached out her arms, straining for the bright light of her consciousness. She created a prism in between her hands above her head, then threw it at the figures and yelled, "Encasement!" A crystal wall stretched wide below her, and to her surprise and relief, the ghouls banged against the barrier, roaring deafeningly in frustration.

They yelled, "Magic always comes with a price! And soon, we will come to collect!"

As their sentiment echoed in her ears, Alexia raced into the light and set herself free from their mental chamber.

Alexia's eyes popped open, and she heavily inhaled, awakening to Symone shaking her. She shuddered and shrieked in fear, green mist puffing from her body.

"Hey, Alexia, Alexia, it's okay, it's alright," Symone lifted her and hugged her. "You're alright, you're okay. Shhh."

Alexia melted in Symone's arms, mortified. She always knew what she was capable of, but she never envisioned unleashing her powers on her allies – her family – like this *again*. She sobbed bitterly. "I'm so sorry, I'm so sorry."

"Hey, hey, it's okay, we're okay, it's all good."

Karl knelt, "Can you tell us what happened?"

Alexia raised her head and said, "I'm so sorry, y'all, I didn't mean it. I was trying out a new skill and I lost control. I'm so sorry."

"It's cool," Symone said. She looked at Alexia and noticed that she lost pigmentation in her face, then examined her neck and noticed the same thing. "Are you okay, though? You don't look too good."

"What do you mean?" Terror gripped Alexia's lungs tighter.

"Just, your face. You're pale as a ghost. I—"

Suddenly, their stripes buzzed. The nanites split the sleeve open, and their stripes lit red and scrolled: "ELITE: URGENT. Outlier group is uploading message on UNN. Meet in Intelligence at once."

"Ah shit, that's us. We gotta go. Alexia, can you stand?" Symone said.

"Barely, the nanites stung me good."

Karl reacted, "Here, I got you. I'll take you to the Infirmary."

"No, I'm good, I promise. Just wiped from using all that energy. I promise, I'm good," Alexia lied. She remembered what happened the last time she lost control of her powers, how the UPD was forced to let her go and erase any documentation of her work with them.  The threat of scores of apprehended bosses being released, open cases jeopardized, all because of a sniper's dart.  For the first time since that freakout, Alexia's heart wrestled with the possibility that her time with the Elite could end, that Enchantra could be terminated for losing control of her powers.  Alexia resigned, *Shit, I'm losing it.  I can't let what happened at that house happen again.  I've gotta get a grip on this shit.*

Karl and Symone helped Alexia stand up.  As they walked out, Alexia tugged Symone's shoulder.  "Symone, after we get done with Intelligence, can I talk to you?"

"Frimas, us, too!" Karl refused to be left out.

Symone faced Alexia.  "No, talk to us now, because I know you're lying to us.  What's going on with you?  What happened in there, for real?"

"Guys, I've got voices in my head," Alexia wept again.

"What do you mean?  Is that something Medical or Psych can fix?" Daisy offered a remedy.

"No, I don't think so.  See, I've been dibbling and dabbling in ancient Chioro mystic magic."

"I remember you telling me that, Alexia," Symone stated.  "What does that have to do with voices in your head?"

As the melanin slowly returned in Alexia's skin, she answered, "I don't know how it happened.  There was this one spell I used to try to tap into a deeper power source almost two quarters back, and these voices entered my head and have lived there ever since.  I thought they were just spiritual advisors.  They never wanted anything, so I've been working with them by my side for weeks.  But now they're talking about taking control of me, saying I'm a conduit to their freedom. They overrode me and made me do those things in the room."

Karl squeezed Alexia's shoulders. "Alexia, you should tell the Director. They almost destroyed us in training. Imagine what they might do in the field," he reasoned.

"I think you're right, Karl. I'll tell her once we get up there. I'm so sorry, y'all. I really didn't mean for this to happen," Alexia sulked.

"Well," Symone said, "nothing we can do about it now. We gotta figure out how to contain them, because we can't beat the Emulator and his goons without you. Go talk to the Director and see what she wants you to do."

"Understood."

## 18

# Split Decision

Malaysia landed her bird in the middle of the Company's hangar. Dredge stepped out of the bus and was awestruck by the vast array of hovercars, bikes, and buses across the floor. "Wow, this is amazing!" he gawked.

Malcolm, Duncan, Joy, and Malaysia walked past him, then Malcolm turned around and said, "Come on, Dredge, you'll have plenty of time to marvel later."

"Right, right, business first. After food, though, right?"

Malcolm huffed, second- and third-guessing his decision to bring Dredge on board. "Joy, go to the cafeteria and see if you can get him something to munch on."

"On it," Joy acknowledged. She sprinted to the exit and headed toward the staircase.

Their stripes lit red. They read the words, "ELITE: URGENT. Outlier group is uploading a message on UNN. Meet in Intelligence at once."

Malcolm craned his head and rolled his eyes. "Y'all ready?"

Malaysia answered, "This is what we do, right?"

Malaysia, Malcolm, Duncan, and Dredge rode the elevator to the Elite Grand Hall and walked across the corridor to Intelligence. They entered and noticed the room bathed in red warning lights. Dredge's eyes sparkled, and his kid-like wonder could barely be contained. Tranced by the sophisticated technology he observed, Dredge couldn't close his mouth. "Oh Akan! I've died and gone on to Glory!"

"What do you mean?" Duncan asked.

Dredge responded, "You have no idea how much I've wanted an invitation from the Company. You don't just apply here. You have to be chosen, right? I never thought I'd live to see the inside of this place. It's better than I imagined."

"Well, remember you're on a trial run. Don't fuck it up by screwing us over," Malcolm sternly reminded Dredge.

"That's right," Stephanie warned as Dax and she stepped up to meet him. "We need your help, but we're not going to let you compromise us in any way without repercussions. If you fuck with us—"

"I know, I know, I'm a dead man walking," Dredge verbalized their thoughts. "Don't worry, I got you, guys. Just point me to my desk and let me get to work. Besides, don't you all have a message to listen to?"

Malaysia agreed, "He's got a point. Let's focus up. Dax, Stephanie, pull up UNN."

Stephanie crossed her arms. "Right. Dax, show Dredge where he'll be working. You guys come with me. Where's everybody else?"

"The rest of the crew is either in the quarters or down in training, probably. And Joy went to get Dredge something to eat," Malcolm reported as they took their usual seats.

Dredge followed Dax to a workstation along the wall of the third step. Dredge pulled back the chair, sat down, pulled it forward, and cracked his knuckles. "Do I need a username and password?"

"No, just your thumbprint right there on the countertop. Three-second set up," Dax flatly instructed him.

"Great, alright, let me in, I'm ready to work."

Joy walked into Intelligence with several bags of chips in her arms. "This good, Dredge?" she asked.

Dredge and Dax turned as he answered, "Yes, yes! That will work, bring them here!" Joy dropped the bags on Dredge's desk. He quickly grabbed one and placed his nose into the bag to smell the potato and salt combination. "So hungry, Akan!"

As Joy took her seat, Symone, Karl, and Daisy dragged themselves into Intelligence and stepped down to meet the team. Symone sat next to Malcolm, patting him on his back as she lowered to her seat. He looked around and noticed a member missing from his team. "Where's Alexia?"

"Oh, she went to go talk to Director Mallack. She had an incident in training," Symone relayed.

"An incident? What kind of incident?" Malcolm replied.

"I'll tell you about it later."

"That bad?"

"Certainly not great."

The screen in front of them turned to UNN. "—moments ago, this video was sent to us. We are all watching this for the first time, unfiltered and unedited. This was sent to us by whom Chancellor Croft coined 'the Outliers.' Let's watch."

The scene switched from the news desk of UNN to a map of Uri City divided into its six districts: Highgarden, Meridian, Genesis Landing, Leicester, The Underbelly, and Midtown. A voice began narrating, "Citizens of Uri City, we, the Powered Order Coalition, continue our pursuit of the powered being restored to our proper place in this state." Pictures of their last battle slowly cross-faded as the voice continued, "Your city's champions have been hired by the city to thwart our plans, but even they cannot hinder our resolve. We are holding a senator from each district hostage. We have placed them in explosive vests. These senators have stood on the side of the anti-powered, and with them out of the way, we will ensure that the numbers will fall on the side of the powered when the vote is held in the Senate chamber.

"Now, we know that your champions will do what they can to ensure that these senators are found and rescued. After all, they are funded by the very people who don't want to see us in power."

Karl rubbed his chin, "The man's got a point. A weak one, but a point nonetheless."

"So, we have done the hard work for them and will give the senators' location to the UPD, who we know will give it to their champions. But they will have to choose to either save them or save the Senate chamber itself."

Malcolm shook his head, "Wait, what?"

"Ah shit, here we go," Malaysia reacted as she rolled her eyes. "Couldn't make it too easy for us, huh?"

"We have strapped bombs to the pillars of the Senate, and they are set to blow in one cycle. So, champions, you have to choose: either save the senators or save the chamber. And, just in case you decide to send in the cavalry, be very clear: if anyone other than your champions are seen trying to assist, we will blow both the senators and the chamber to bits. Your one cycle starts now. We are the POC!"

The screen went blank, and the broadcast switched back to the news anchor. Stephanie immediately muted the holoscreen and shook her head.

"Alright, do we have anything from the Outliers?" Malcolm asked.

"UPD is sending the intel now," Stephanie replied. She tapped on the keys of her countertop, and the holoscreen switched to a map of the city. A red dot emerged from the Underbelly district.

Symone furiously stared at the dot. *This bastard.* Her mind flashed back and forth between memories she wished she could forget despite the joy she experienced when they were created. She could smell his cologne, could feel her palm on his chest. She recalled the constellations in the sky that marked the specialness of the moments spent basking in the glow of the night.

She heard Jason say, "You light up my life."

Symone recounted the rooftop they stood on when they conversed for the last time, declaring the time of death on their relationship. She recalled the chill in the air despite the perfect temperature of the day. His fury shrouded in his steely demeanor. She saw the rage in his eyes and knew he didn't want things to end despite the ice wall that stood between them. She didn't expect him to say a word, but she wished that he would show her a sign, a glimmer, a flicker of hope.

Jason's words, though, extinguished any spark that could reignite their bond. "You wanna leave? There's the sky!"

Symone and Jason ended on that rooftop that day. The same rooftop that the red dot that blinked on the holoscreen pointed to.

"I know where that is," Symone admitted to the team, fuming. "He's sending a message to me."

Malcolm asked, "What is he saying?"

"He's baiting me. He wants *me* there."

"So, what are we going to do?" Duncan inquired.

"Well, we can't just let the chamber blow. We have to de-activate those bombs," Joy chimed in.

"True, but we can't let those senators die. We have to rescue them, damn the politics or the optics. People can think what they want about us, for or against the city. This is what we do," Malaysia preached.

"Exactly," Malcolm agreed with them both. "Symone, what do you want to do? Do you want to face him? Or do you want to save the chamber? It's your decision."

"The fuck? I'm gonna kick his ass!" The embers in Symone's eyes smoldered yellow.

The team laughed and cheered as Malcolm laid out the plan. "Alright. We've got less than a cycle to handle this. Alexia's talking with Mallack, so she's out. Um, Malaysia, mind if I borrow Joy?"

Joy perked up as Malaysia jolted and said, "Sure, if she wants to."

"Yes!" Joy declared.

"Alright, Duncan, Joy, and I will go to the chamber and defuse the bombs. Symone, you, Karl, Daisy, and Malaysia, secure the senators in the Underbelly. Assume the Outliers will be there and, like Symone said, kick their asses. Dax, you and Stephanie get us aerial footage of both areas and patch them to our visors. Elite, let's get it!"

Everyone got up. Symone was puzzled. *I wonder why Malcolm decided not to come with me. I know he wants to give me space, but damn, I didn't ask for that much fucking space.*

Moments later, the Elite minus Alexia were in the garage donning their uniforms and cloaks. Malcolm looked at Joy and asked, "Can you fly one of these?" as he pointed at a free hoverbus.

Joy rubbed her hands together and said, "Absolutely!"

"Great! Let's head out. Malaysia, you good?"

Malaysia looked at Malcolm and responded, "Really?"

"Fair. Let's move out. We got 50 minutes left."

Malcolm, Duncan, and Joy loaded onto their hoverbus while Malaysia, Karl, Daisy, and Symone loaded onto theirs. Symone looked back at Malcolm, still annoyed that they weren't fighting side-by-side, and her crew was visiting the site of her last breakup. She walked to her seat and focused her attention on her target.

Malaysia lay her hands on the countertop to boot up her hoverbus. She then relayed, "Okay, let's go over the details. We will land about a block from the building. Daisy, do recon to make sure we're not walking into any booby traps. Karl and I will follow behind to help with the search. Symone, look for the triggerman. If the bombs are remote detonated, then we need to get the trigger from him in case these Outliers want to try something foolish."

"Copy that, Malaysia," Symone nodded.

"Guys, we're getting footage of the building from Intelligence," Daisy declared. "Visors on."

The team activated their visors, and the nanites covered their heads. The video footage showed the Emulator standing on the roof of a fifteen-story building, arms crossed, wearing his red and purple nanotech.

"Is that your boy, Starburst?" the Eagle asked.

"Yep," Symone groaned.

"I don't see any of his people, but we should assume they're close by. Fly to the roof to meet him, Starburst. Cause a distraction and keep him occupied until we've secured the hostages, then we'll come up to meet you and help you grind him into dust," the Eagle suggested.

"I hear ya," Starburst grumbled.

Starburst sounded annoyed to the Eagle. "Hey, Star, you good?"

"No.  No, I'm not.  Just want to get this over with.  I thought this son of a bitch was out of my life for good."

"Well, this time, we'll help you make sure he is," the Mammoth declared.

Starburst nodded.  "Let's make this the last fight of his career."

# 19

# Divide and Conquer

Joy announced, "We're descending now."

Malcolm looked out the window and noticed a large crowd protesting in the streets near the front access point of the Senate chamber. Many were waving signs, some for and others against the POC. Chancellor Croft had ordered the UPD to assist the Elite by managing the peaceful-ish protests, and the UPD built two barriers – one to keep the citizens away from danger, the other to divide the factions.

"Aw Frimas," Malcolm lamented, "looks like the crowd is giving these punks the audience they've been looking for."

Duncan huffed, "Don't they realize they're in danger? Why would they show up *now*?"

"Clout, justice, camera time, because they're dumb," Malcolm reasoned. "Either way, we don't need anyone trying to be martyrs for their causes. Joy, land the bird near the steps and away from the crowd."

"Copy that," Joy answered. She tapped on the countertop, and the hoverbus obeyed her command to drop to the Senate steps.

The chamber was a twenty-story edifice wrapped in glass. A spire fifty feet in diameter marked the apex of the building. Malcolm examined the wireframe model of the chamber on the holoscreen and stated, "This spire in the middle is holding the whole building in place. I assume they planted the bombs somewhere in or around it."

The hoverbus landed, and Joy came from the cockpit and pointed at the blueprint and said, "We should go to the foundation, where the pillars originate. That's the best place to put a bomb with minimal security detection. Let's make our way to the parking deck below."

"Speaking of minimal detection," Duncan thought out loud, "how the Frimas did they even get a bomb into this place? Security here should be tighter than a pinched water hose."

Malcolm replied, "Probably since senators are being threatened, personnel became thinner here. Let's ask Intelligence to investigate the tapes when we get back. Right now, we gotta get the bombs out of there before they blow in 41 minutes. Visors up, cloaks on. Let's get it."

"Right, let's get it!" Duncan agreed. They summoned their nanites to cover their heads. The back hatch opened, and they rushed out of the bus. The crowd showered them with a mixture of cheers and boos. The officers sternly pushed the crowd with their body shields to keep them from entering the danger zone. News crews kept rolling the cameras, and hoverbuses and helicopters swarmed the skies to capture the scene.

"Okay, Intelligence says there are four entrances to the parking garage. What should we do?" Kaminari asked.

"Let's not split up. We're stronger in numbers. All the entries lead the same way, so let's pick the closest one and travel down until we get to the bottom deck," K.C. ordered.

Ammo charged his palms as they marched toward the glass palace. The staircase that ascended to the main entrance was split by another staircase that descended to the parking garage. They walked down the steps and into the darkened tunnel dimly lit by lights in the ceiling and along the walls. Kaminari's charged hands provided more light around them.

K.C. ordered, "Delta formation."

Ammo led the way. Kaminari marched at Ammo's left side and K.C. to his right. They slowly marched in a circle, backs to each other, to ensure line of sight. About two hundred yards ahead of them was a corridor that crossed the tunnel. They made a visual on the outer rim of the glass and concrete spire.

"Okay, once we get to the break, scan for any anomalies, then we keep moving forward to the center and descend to the bottom floor from there," K.C. said.

"Copy that," Ammo acknowledged.

Their visors detected several deactivated vehicles in front of them. "Fifty feet to the break," Kaminari said.

Ammo looked ahead, and Kaminari looked to the left as K.C. looked to the right, and they both saw empty corridors. They examined the vast, slightly empty, circular parking garage that spiraled around the spire, anchored by the tunnel they were walking through. They approached the vehicles and walked past them.

"One hundred yards to the spire," Ammo declared.

Just then, an engine fired up. Kaminari, now in the rear position, announced, "Look alive, guys, one of those cars just turned on."

"Alright, keep moving toward the spire," K.C. said. "Keep your eyes open."

Then, another engine fired up. Then another. And another. High beams shone brightly and focused on the Elite. "They know we're here," Kaminari warned.

K.C. and Ammo turned around. The three stood in battle position. Suddenly, the vehicles rushed toward them. Ammo charged his hands. Kaminari charged bolts around her body. Ammo released two plasma shots while Kaminari surged an electric shockwave from her fingertips. The machines exploded, and shrapnel launched toward them. K.C. swiftly felt for them and stopped the shrapnel and debris within a few feet of their positions.

"Great work," K.C. stated. Just then, their feet detected a rumble underneath them, and they stumbled. The pavement split, and the slab beneath them rose. "They're trying to keep us away from the bombs. Ammo, Kaminari, use your flight abilities to get down there. I'll find a way to meet you."

"Okay, come on Kaminari," Ammo ran to the edge and jumped off the slab. Kaminari charged up and boosted herself off the slab and plummeted to the ground.

Miles away from the Senate chamber, Starburst, the Mammoth, the Eagle, and Blitz landed a block away from their target building in the Underbelly. The Eagle walked from the cockpit and said, "You all know your roles. Ready?"

"Let's get it," the Mammoth declared.

Starburst could only see red. "I'm ready, let's move," she growled.

"Open the hatch," Blitz said.

The Eagle pushed a button near the holoscreen, and the hatch opened. Blitz sprinted out the hoverbus and slinked through the building as she scanned for the senators and any traps their opponents might have set. Starburst blasted out of the bus and made a beeline for the Emulator. She scaled the fifteen stories and landed atop the roof, the fury of a thousand burning suns raging through her veins.

She planted her feet on the rooftop. The Emulator's red-and-purple uniform glistened in the sun as he turned to face his ex. He planted his hands on his waist and chuckled. "Symone Watson. Damn, girl, it's been a long fucking time. Gotta admit, never in a million years did I see this coming."

Starburst was tempted to take her visor off so he could see the rage on her face, but she knew that at any moment, news crews could roll up and start recording, and she did not want to risk her identity. She charged up and crafted a fireball in her palm. "Jason Xavier. What the fuck are you doing?"

"What," the Emulator held his arms wide open and flexed his fingers, motioning Starburst to embrace him, "no hug or kiss for your old flame?"

*Don't kick his ass yet. Stall until they secure the senators.*

"Stop playing games, Jason. Give me one good reason why I shouldn't eviscerate your ass." Starburst stood in battle formation with the fireball pointed in the Emulator's direction.

Jason looked at the fireball and smiled behind his visor. His eyes observed Starburst's fireball, and his mind began calculating what it would take to create a fireball just like hers. His mind began to translate Starburst's power set. Suddenly, he could feel his veins burn inside, fire churn in the pit of his stomach, his tissue hardening and softening simultaneously to withstand his rising internal body temperature. His mind commanded his body to adapt to his new power set. "Oh, I don't want to give you a reason not to. In fact, I'm counting on you trying to eviscerate me."

Starburst was annoyed. "Why are you doing this, Jason?"

The Emulator, his subconscious devouring as much intel as possible, stepped closer to Starburst as he answered, "Because the time has come for us to take our place in this world. We talked about this for years, right here on this rooftop in fact. You remember this place, right?"

"Clearly, I do, you dick! Could you be any more obvious by picking this spot, with your arrogant ass? It's like you want to get caught! What the fuck are you doing?!"

The Emulator's mind and body completely synced. He raised his hand, mimicked her stance, and summoned a star. "I'm giving you one chance, just one, to join me."

*Shit, that didn't take long at all. That's how he beat everyone so fast at NextGen. Akan.* "You're kidding, right?" Starburst laughed. "You think I want to join you? This shit you're doing is the reason I dumped you, *right here!* I told you I wouldn't be with you if you continued down this path, but you were so convinced that this was *your* destiny. So no, I think I'll pass and settle for kicking your ass instead."

"You always lacked vision, Symone. Always jumping from one place to another and never landing on anything with true conviction or commitment. One foot in, one foot out, always headed for the exit. That has always been your downfall, and it's gonna get you killed today. You know you can't win against me, right?"

Starburst had enough. She growled, swung her arm, and launched her star at the Emulator. The Emulator raised a shield out of the fireball he made and deflected it. Starburst rushed toward the Emulator and launched a series of punches and kicks at him. The Emulator grabbed Starburst's left arm and spun her around three times before releasing her. As she whisked away in the air, the Emulator flew toward her to meet her, then attempted to punch her in her face. Starburst dodged his punch and kneed him in the stomach. As he doubled over, she tomahawked his back and hurled him back to the roof. He fell flat, but then rolled over twice and stood back up in battle stance.

Blitz ran back out of the building and met the Mammoth and the Eagle. She reported, "I found the senators. There's only four of them here."

"Okay," the Eagle said. "Let's get them and put them in the bus, then we'll try to find the last one."

"Let's go," the Mammoth said.

The three followed Blitz to the seventh floor of the building and walked through the fifth apartment on the floor. There, they saw four people dressed in suits and dresses with shrouds over their heads. The Eagle said, "Senators, we're the Elite. We've come to get you out of here and to a secure location." The four responded with muffled sounds. "They might have their mouths taped. And look at the vests, they're strapped with explosives, no doubt."

"Can't risk removing the shrouds until we know what explosives we're dealing with. Let's get them and take them outside," the Mammoth said.

Blitz, the Eagle, and the Mammoth took their arms. Blitz ordered, "Everyone, hold onto somebody. We're going to lead you outside, then we'll examine you and figure out how to get you out of the bomb vests." As the senators responded with muffled noises, the Elite led them out of the room, down the staircase, and out of the main lobby of the complex out onto the street.

Back at the Chamber, K.C. broke a piece of the rising slab he was standing on and used it to lower himself back to the pavement. He ran to the edge of the spire and saw a door that granted access to the inside of it. He planted his hands on the door and split it apart. Just then, another hovercar sped quickly toward him. K.C. jumped through the entry, and the car crashed into the wall. K.C. fell about twenty feet before he caught several wires and suspended himself from them. He looked down and saw dozens of blinking yellow dots about seventy feet below him. *Those must be the bombs,* he assumed.

Ammo and Kaminari kept descending until they finally made it to the bottom of the parking garage. Before they could fully survey the area, several hovercars barreled toward them. Ammo and Kaminari stood back-to-back and unleashed a barrage of attacks against the hovercars. Their targets exploded one after another.

"Guys, I see the bombs, there's got to be at least fifty of these things set to explode," they heard K.C.'s voice ring in their visors.

"Kind of preoccupied right now. Can you move them?" Ammo asked as he shot another hovercar to pieces.

"I can't tell if they're motion-sensor activated. I'm going to see if I can get to the – oomph!" K.C. was suddenly hit with a concrete block.

"K.C., you okay?" Kaminari was concerned.

"Whoever is here just hit me with a brick. I can't see anybody here, I don't know where that shit came from," K.C. hung from the lines and looked around to see if he could catch a glimpse of who attacked him.

"Same here, these cars are not just coming from nowhere," Kaminari declared. "Ammo, I'll cover you. Get inside the spire and figure out what these bombs look like and how to take them out."

"You sure you got this?" Ammo double-checked.

"I got this. Get to the entry." Kaminari charged up and planted her palms on the ground. An electric shield shot twenty feet upward and curved to create a barrier. "Ammo, go!"

Ammo ran toward the spire as more hovercars crashed into the fence Kaminari powered. He saw the door and slipped his fingers through the crack. He then strained his cybernetic muscles to pry open the door. As he made progress, droids suddenly appeared from the left and the right and began firing laser shots at him. "Ah shit, seriously?" Ammo backed away from the door, blasted backward to keep his eyes on the droids, pointed his palms at them, and fired twin continuous rays at them, tearing some of them in half. Some of the droids dodged the counterattack and blasted upward. They continued firing shots at Ammo. Ammo declared, "Kaminari, I can't get inside. I've got company. I'm going to deal with them. Get inside and help K.C." Ammo charged his feet and blasted upward, and the droids pursued him.

"Shit, we can't let the spire fall. Okay, K.C., where are you?" Kaminari asked.

"I think I'm on the third floor. I don't want to fall into the bombs, so I'm gonna try to swing from where I am."

"Okay, I'm coming to get you."

Blitz, the Mammoth, and the Eagle got the senators outside and onto the street. The Eagle scanned their vests and noticed that they were hollow. "Wait, guys, there's no bombs on them. Their vests are empty."

The Mammoth pushed on one of the senators' vests and noticed that there was nothing but what felt like insulation. "What the Frimas?"

Suddenly, the air got crispy thin and cold, and one of the senators' hands lit up red with fire. Another senator pushed his hands outward and launched a pulse of wind at Blitz, the Mammoth, and the Eagle, and they flew backward, spinning upside down and landing about thirty feet away from them. The four senators ripped their vests and took the shrouds off of their heads, revealing that they were Frostbite, the Wave, Ignatia, and Cyclone.

*Shit,* the Eagle thought, *I should have scanned them in the building!* The Eagle yelled, "It's an ambush! Everybody, fall back!" Frostbite slammed his palm into the ground, and a thick sheet of ice rolled toward them. The Mammoth grabbed the Eagle and jumped onto the sidewalk while Blitz sped away. Cyclone took to the skies and blew a powerful, focused gust of wind toward Blitz and slowed her progression. Ignatia then combined her power with Cyclone's by launching a powerful wave of fire into his wind tunnel. Blitz was hit with a heavy wave of fire, and it launched her backward. She rolled onto the ground, and her cloak took on the damage.

The Mammoth said, "Eagle, I don't think we're gonna be able to walk out of this one. Find a perch and do what you do best. I'm gonna try to distract them as long as I can."

"Copy that," the Eagle declared. She noticed a scaffolding ladder on the side of the building in the alley. "Give me a lift?"

The Mammoth and the Eagle ran into the alley, and the Mammoth grabbed the Eagle and launched her about midway up the building. She gripped the ladder and climbed the rest of the way to find a perch. The Mammoth turned around and was ambushed by the Wave. The Wave did not hesitate and blasted the Mammoth with a devastating water strike. The Mammoth planted his feet and resisted flying backward. Frostbite took advantage of the Mammoth's instincts and combined his power with the Wave's by placing his hand in the water attack and chilling the wave well below freezing. The Mammoth flash-froze into an ice statue, saved only by his cloak that shimmered against the frost. He wriggled and strained to try to free himself from their trap.

The Wave and Frostbite then entombed the Mammoth by creating a block of ice that covered the alley from wall to wall. "One down," Frostbite growled. "Now, where's the girl?"

The Wave looked up and pointed, "There, she's climbing the ladder."

Just as Frostbite lifted his hands to deliver an ice strike, the Wave suddenly crashed into his back, and they both knocked into the block of ice they created. Blitz had recovered and rammed into the Wave. She delivered a series of swift strikes at them, backed away, whipped out her plasma guns, and rapidly fired them at her opponents. Their cloaks took the damage. Frostbite created an ice shield and pushed it forward. Cyclone and Ignatia found Blitz in the alley, and they raised their arms and launched their powers toward her. Blitz ran backward in a blur, and their powers broke Frostbite's shield and pushed the Wave and him backward.

Starburst landed on the roof and ran to the Emulator. They exchanged a flurry of punches, dodges, and kicks, and the Emulator stated, "Just like old times, huh?"

Starburst spun and swung her left fist at the Emulator's head. He ducked it and spun his right leg at Starburst's side. She blocked his leg with her left arm, then punched him in his chest. He stumbled back, regained his footing, then jumped up and kicked Starburst in the head. She stumbled backward, fell to the ground, then blasted herself back upright and delivered two stars at him. The Emulator grabbed those stars and threw them back at her. She deflected them and came back to face him. As he launched his left foot toward her torso, Starburst launched herself upward and planted her crotch into his face, spun around, and sat on his shoulders. She tomahawked his head several times as he tried to claw her off him. He heated his palms and popped her thighs, and her cloak took on the damage as she held onto him tightly and continued to try to knock him unconscious. He finally jumped and landed on his back, slamming her onto hers. Yet, she wouldn't let up. He levitated, and they rode into the sky together. She wouldn't let go of him, crossing her legs and squeezing with all her might. The Emulator created a large star above him and commanded it to crash into them. The star's impact finally caused Starburst to loosen her grip on him, and they broke apart.

Starburst was stunned and dazed. She shook herself and said, "That the best you can do?"

She zipped to him and planted her hands into his chest, and she unleashed a blast that launched the Emulator backward. He stopped instantly and zipped to her. He planted his hands into her chest and unleashed the same blast at her. It launched her backward, and she stopped instantly and flew straight toward him. Starburst realized that he was now completely her, and she was fighting her mirror image. They exchanged another series of punches and kicks in the sky, and neither one of them was able to gain the upper hand on the other. *Damn it, damn it! If I'm going to beat him, I've gotta do something different, and fast!*

Running out of time, Kaminari ran up the helix to get to K.C., with about twenty hovercars following her. She kept throwing electricity behind her to stave off the assault, still unaware of where the source was. "Intelligence, can you read me?"

"Yes, we're here," Stephanie was heard in her visor.

"We need an assist. Can you tap into the security cameras here? We can't see who's controlling these vehicles. We'd use our eyes in the sky, but she's in the Underbelly," Kaminari requested.

"We're on it," Stephanie replied.

Just then, the helix began to split underneath Kaminari's feet. "Ah shit, shit, shit!" Kaminari's body injected a fresh dose of adrenaline into her veins, and she rushed forward even harder. The path ahead of her fractured, and Kaminari blasted a pulse of electricity through her feet to launch her upward. She jumped the gap in the bridge, tumbled onto the other side, landed on her feet, and kept running. "Please find these assholes!"

"I second that!" Ammo yelled as he turned around and, while flying backward, blasted more of the droids pursuing him. "I don't know where these bots are coming from! Are these Senate's security?"

K.C. swung close to the walkway attached to the edge of the spire wall when he was hit by another cinder block. "Shit, alright, I need to concentrate." K.C. hung from the wire and stilled his mind. He opened his senses and said, "Where are you?" He sensed the energy that flowed through the wire he held onto, the composition of the spire, and the bombs below.  He said, "What doesn't belong?"  He searched below him and could feel no anomaly.  He then searched upward, and he felt a faint, yet very familiar energy source on the sixth floor.  As he concentrated harder, he recognized nanites and assumed it was a cloak.  He said, "Guys, sixth floor, opposite side of the spire.  Somebody's up there.  Get to the sixth floor and take out whoever that is.  Target is cloaked."

Ammo said with glee, "Finally, I'm on it!  And I'm bringing company!"

"Remember, try not to damage the spire's wall.  If the wall or the pillars collapse, then that's game over."

"Roger that."

"Kaminari, you here yet?"

"Opening the door now," Kaminari reported.  She charged up and blasted the door to the spire apart.  She walked in and stepped on the narrow walkway.  She looked up and saw K.C. hanging about fifteen feet from the walkway.  "Hey!  How's it hanging?"

"Oh, not too bad, I guess.  Can I trouble you for a little help?" K.C. joked.

"No problem, I got you."  Kaminari created a lightning whip and lassoed K.C.  His cloak took on damage while Kaminari retracted the whip to pull him to the walkway.  K.C. landed near Kaminari.

"Alright, we gotta get down there.  Any suggestions?"

"Yeah, let's jump!"

Malcolm snapped, "Seriously?"

"Yeah!  I'll catch us."

"Alright, Kaminari.  Catch us."

K.C. and Kaminari jumped off the edge of the walkway and plummeted to the floor in the middle of the bombs.  Just as they were about to crash, Kaminari created an electric fence and stretched it across the spire.  They bounced ten feet off the ground, which gave them enough time to find a place to land in between bombs.  Kaminari released the fence, and K.C. and she planted their feet on solid ground.

"That was fun," K.C. chuckled.

"Fun?!  Who's having fun?!  I'm glad you guys are having fun!  Because I'm not!" Ammo yelled.

The Eagle stood on the roof's edge, wielding her rifle aimed at Cyclone.  She took a deep breath, steadied herself, and squeezed the trigger.  The round struck Cyclone, and he fell backward.  Ignatia saw where the round came from, and she blasted a fireball at her.  The Eagle fell back and repositioned herself.  Cyclone regained his composure and flew upward and met the Eagle on the rooftop.  The Eagle threw her rifle and pulled out her blaster and shot several rounds at Cyclone.  He dodged her assault and threw several gusts of wind at the Eagle.  She ran behind the fire exit as the winds blew past her.  She then pulled out a dagger and gripped the handle with her right hand.  She jumped out of her hiding place and shot her blaster with her left hand.  Cyclone threw a gust of wind at the Eagle again.  The Eagle used her precise eyesight to see a gap between the gusts.  Just as the gust of wind hit her and sent her off the roof, she threw the dagger in the gap, and it latched onto Cyclone.  The dagger then sent an electric shock to Cyclone's cloak, and the cloak reversed polarity and stunned Cyclone.  Cyclone seized and landed on the rooftop, writhing in pain.

The Eagle fell seven stories, and Blitz saw her flying off the roof.  Blitz bounced off the street, onto the wall, and off the wall and caught the Eagle in midair.  They landed safely on the ground.  Just then, Ignatia launched fireballs at the Eagle and Blitz, and Frostbite and the Wave came from around the corner of the alleyway. Blitz pushed the Eagle to the side while she launched forward and planted her feet into Ignatia's chest. Ignatia flew backward, while the Wave blasted Blitz with a water attack. He then summoned all the water from the hydrants in the streets to burst forward, and a cascade of water flooded the streets. Frostbite immediately unleashed subzero ice to rain down upon the water. Before Blitz could escape, she hit a wall of ice from all sides.

Starburst landed back on the rooftop, and the Emulator chased her down. He swung his fists at her, and Starburst dodged all his attacks. He then created a star and threw it at Starburst. She rolled to her right as the star flew across the street. The Emulator lunged at Starburst, and Starburst did a split, grabbed the Emulator's legs, and twisted to plant him on the ground. She then quickly stood up, stepped on his arms, and pushed a continuous wave of star power at him, damaging his cloak. She increased her heat from yellow to white and pushed her energy into him, determined to break the cloak and get him to yield.

"Starburst, we need you down here, we're getting our asses handed to us!" the Eagle summoned in her visor.

*Shit! Not now!* "I've almost got him beat!" Starburst protested.

"Please, we need you, we can't hold them off," the Eagle pleaded.

The Emulator ordered the nanites on his suit to melt his helmet off his head. He chuckled then said, "Sounds like your team needs you down there, Symone. You got me dead to rites. What are you going to do? You gonna finish me off?"

Starburst's fury intensified, and her white locks tinted blue. She kept pushing the star power to damage his cloak more. Her thoughts flashed to the night at Switch, her teammates celebrating her becoming a Defender and officially staying with the Elite. She ruminated on their training, the battles, the fun times they've all shared. She remembered Malcolm's words:

*Be still. Take the next couple days to really think through everything. Don't make any rash decisions right now. Just take time to get the clarity you need. When you're ready, say yes to the things you want, no to the things you don't, and be at peace, knowing that everything you're doing is by choice. Still your heart, and let it be your guide.*

Starburst only got more enraged, determined that this was her only shot to kill the Emulator and focused. And the Emulator, reckoning that Starburst had fallen for his trap, smirked as he silently cheered, *Don't stop, Symone, keep pushing!*

Ammo reached the sixth floor of the parking garage and scanned the area for the cloak. Stephanie stated, "We have a lock on the target on the sixth floor. It's behind the spire, Ammo. You can either go around and meet him on the other side or go through the spire straight ahead." Stephanie patched the security camera's view of the target to Ammo's visor. Ammo and the droids flew toward the spire. Ammo eviscerated the doorway. Ammo and the droids flew through the opening and made a beeline toward the target on the opposite side. The target saw Ammo coming, backed up and ran away from the spire. Ammo rushed into and grabbed the target, and they barrel rolled onto the ground. Terra then palmed the ground, and the pavement broke apart, and she crashed asphalt into Ammo, pushing him off her. She stood up and summoned the pavement to surround and entomb Ammo. Ammo, stuck in concrete, blasted his way out of it, then shot several blasts in the air, destroying the remaining droids. He then shot at Terra, and Terra threw up pavement to block his shots and rushed at him. Ammo waited until she reached him, then blasted upward, spun around, and shot her with three cannon shots. Terra fell forward and stumbled onto the ground.

Kaminari and K.C. looked at the blinking lights. "What do you think, can we disable them?" K.C. asked.

"I'm not sure. Intelligence, patch into our visors. How do we disable these bombs?" Kaminari requested.

"Scanning now," Stephanie responded. She uploaded Kaminari's view to the screen, then analyzed the bomb. Stephanie relayed, "The bomb appears to have a motion switch within the core. The slightest internal move will set it off. I think they calibrated it to be tamper-proof, even from your powers, K.C."

"Shit, so the only thing we can do is get these things out of here," K.C. concluded.

"Damn it, there's got to be a hundred bombs in here, K.C. How are we going to do that?"

Just then, lights flashed above them. K.C. and Kaminari looked up, and hovercraft plummeted toward them. "Shit, K.C.!" Kaminari pointed upward.

"Target practice. Come on, Kaminari!" K.C. pointed his hands upward to stop as many of the hovercraft as he could while Kaminari delivered multiple strikes to blow the hovercraft apart. "If a piece of debris reaches these bombs, we're done for."

The Eagle ran behind a building to hide and pulled out her blaster. She could hear Ignatia, the Wave, and Frostbite making their move toward her. She backed up, facing the street, and got ready to strike. *Think, okay, if this is it, then go out guns blazing, literally.*

The Wave, Ignatia, and Frostbite faced the alley. The Eagle charged her blaster and put her finger on the trigger. The Wave pushed his hand forward, then was hit hard with a blast that hurled him past the alleyway. Another blast hit Frostbite and tossed him past the alleyway. The Eagle shot her blaster at Ignatia, and she flew backward and crashed into the wall across the street.

Starburst saw the ice chamber Blitz was trapped in and melted it down with her star power. Blitz shot out of the crystal dome and said, "The Mammoth, he's in the alley to the right."

Starburst flew toward the block of ice the Mammoth was trapped in and melted it down with a continuous wave of star energy. The Mammoth could finally move, and he broke himself the rest of the way out of his crystal tomb. "You good?" Starburst asked.

"Yeah. Thank you, Star," the Mammoth answered.

The Mammoth followed Starburst out of the alley, and they stood with Blitz and the Eagle in battle stance as Ignatia, Frostbite, and the Wave gathered themselves and prepared for the next assault. Cyclone's cloak finally corrected itself, and Cyclone got back up and flew down to meet his team.

Starburst's rage fueled her energy. She shot her hands forward and delivered a huge wave of star power at all four of the elemental powerhouses. The Eagle followed suit and shot blasters at them all. Not to be left out, Blitz pulled out her blaster and shot at them, too. The Mammoth ran on the sidewalk, and at the right moment, he said, "Stop firing!"

All three ladies stopped firing, and the Mammoth jumped high and swiftly clapped his hands to deliver a shockwave that sent his opponents flying fifty yards away and crashing into and sliding on the pavement.

The four Elite marched forward toward the elements. Frostbite realized that Starburst was unmatched, and they could not withstand her team's combined assault. He placed his palms on the ground, and a wall of ice separated them from the Elite. The elements stumbled to get up, and Frostbite said, "We gotta move, they called our bluff."

"Right, we're better altogether than divided. Let's move," Ignatia agreed.

Meantime, Ammo descended to the ground floor and rushed into the spire. He saw K.C. and Kaminari trying to defend themselves from the barrage above. He said, "What do you need me to do, guys?"

"Ammo, all these bombs, we can't defuse them. We gotta get them outside somehow."

Ammo looked around and saw the vast blinking lights and responded, "Shit, all of them?"

"Yeah, all of them!" K.C. said.

"But they'll blow if we tamper with them," Kaminari reminded him.

Just then, the ground near the doors of the spire shifted and blocked the way out, sealing them inside the spire. "Oh no, we're trapped," Kaminari relayed as she kept firing at the hovercraft. "Guys, what are we going to do?"

"Just keep firing, we can't let these bombs go off," K.C. said.

K.C., Kaminari, and Ammo focused their energy and effort at keeping the bombs from blasting off from the debris. Eventually, the hovercraft stopped coming. K.C. concentrated his energy and strained his hands to crunch all the debris into a super-concentrated ball and launch it to the far end of the spire, away from them and the bombs.

K.C. looked around and said, "Whoo, that was intense."

"Intense, alright," Kaminari breathed a sigh of relief.

Their victory was short lived, though, as the blinking lights started beeping rapidly. The bombs' timers shrank to ten seconds.

"Oh no, shit, what do we do?" Kaminari asked.

"K.C.?!" Ammo screamed.

"Brace yourselves, the cloaks will keep us covered," K.C. resigned.

3, 2, 1, BOOM!

The bombs all went off, and the team braced and ducked. Seconds later, K.C. opened his eyes and observed a green mist that surrounded the fire that attempted to engulf them and demolish the spire. The Elite looked confused as they tried to ascertain what was happening. K.C. looked up, and he saw someone floating above the fire. He then recognized the mist and said, "Enchantra, girl, talk about clutch!"

"Yeah!" Ammo yelled. "That's what I'm talking about!"

Enchantra rose up the spire, dragging the fire with her up to the top of the parking garage and out the tunnel. She flew out of the parking garage, and the crowd saw her and the fire she dragged behind her. Cheers and boos were heard from the crowd, and she paid the noise no attention. She rose two thousand feet in the sky, away from the buildings and the craft. She then released the fire, and the explosions completed, a massive fire and smoke show captured by the citizens below and the news crews everywhere. Enchantra swiftly flipped and descended victoriously toward the chamber's parking garage entrance.

K.C., Kaminari, and Ammo marched up the helix to get out of the parking garage. "Stephanie, any sign of our targets?"

"Shit, I'm looking now," Stephanie declared. She scanned the camera feeds and lamented, "No, no signs. They're gone, whoever they were."

"One of them was the one who controls the ground," Ammo declared.

"Yeah, I guess the other one controls electronics? They threw every car in that garage at us," Kaminari stated.

"Not to mention those droids," Ammo added.

"Doesn't matter. If they left, that means we completed the job. Let's get the Frimas out of here before another car gets hurled at us," K.C. summed up.

"True that," Ammo said.

"You guys want a lift?" Enchantra offered.

"Please, yes!" Kaminari said. Enchantra surrounded them with green mist, and they all floated up and out of the garage.

Starburst blasted into the sky to scale over the ice wall Frostbite created. She looked over the wall, and she did not see the Elements. She then doubled back to the rooftop she left the Emulator on. She didn't see him there. "Aaaaaaahhh fuck!" she cried as she knelt and punished the rooftop with her fist.

"Starburst, everything alright?" the Mammoth asked.

"They're gone, they got away again!" Starburst screamed.

"They played us, Starburst. They wanted us here, tried to divide and conquer us. There are no senators missing or kidnapped," the Eagle reasoned.

"I had him! I fucking had him!" Starburst protested, enraged. "Shit! I just needed a few more seconds!"

The Eagle knew that Starburst was pissed at her for calling her off the Emulator. "I know. And I thank you for saving us, Star."

"Let's head back to HQ. Eagle, check in with K.C.," Blitz suggested to deflect Starburst's anger.

"Hey, K.C., you guys alright?" the Eagle communicated with the other team as her crew headed back to the hoverbus.

"Yeah, we're good, the bombs have been cleared, and the chamber suffered damage only in the parking garage. We thwarted their plan. Prepared to return to base. How about you guys?"

"We're code white here. There weren't any senators kidnapped. It was an ambush. We were able to fight them off, and they've all left. Preparing to return to base." The Eagle, the Mammoth, Blitz, and Starburst returned to the hoverbus and stepped inside the back hatch.

"Great, we'll see you guys back home," K.C. said.

The insides of their visors lit red, and an announcement appeared in front of them: "ALERT: Major explosion went off in Highgarden district. Massive casualties expected. UPD, UFD, and UMC personnel headed to the scene."

K.C. looked at Kaminari, Ammo, and Enchantra. Enchantra said, "You don't think..."

"Yeah, yeah, I do think. It was them. Fuck!" K.C.'s blood boiled.

"They knew what they were doing," the Mammoth chagrined. "Let's go, y'all. We'll deal with it back in Intelligence."

# 20

# Getting Played

The clock read 01:50. Malcolm lay in his bed and stared at the ceiling fan's slowly spinning blades. He struggled with not beating himself up about the increasing impossibility of resolving the Emulator and his crew's plot. Between that and his ongoing personal investigation into the Collector's data, Malcolm's mind felt like soup. He craved a much longer break, but the Outliers ensured that a vacation was out of the question. The team decided the day before to crash in the quarters just in case the Emulator decided to unleash another assault on the city. And Malcolm knew that Director Mallack was getting the business from Chancellor Croft, so he was unsure whether an ass-kicking was coming down the pipeline.

He focused his attention on the Collector's data. He knew that he wouldn't be at peace until he knew what her intel meant. Deciding to talk to the Analyst before their debrief with Mallack, he swiftly rolled out of bed and rummaged through his drawers. He slid into a black hoodie sweatshirt and blue sweatpants, laced his black and blue sneakers, then prepared to slink out of his residence.

Symone, meanwhile, was frazzled inside. The loss didn't sit well with her, being so close to defeating the Emulator, yet letting him slip through her fingers. As she sat at her kitchen island, she ran her fingers through her locs and ruminated on Jason's words, *Always jumping from one place to another and never landing on anything with true conviction or commitment. One foot in, one foot out, always headed for the exit.*

"Is he right?" she thought out loud. *Have I had one foot in and one foot out? I have to admit, I have been acting that way, keeping my options open, not wanting to feel confined. But I don't believe I've always lacked conviction, and I'm not that afraid of commitment. Am I?*

She recalled the moment she could have eliminated Jason but chose instead to save her teammates. *I didn't want them to die. I didn't want to lose them. Had I stayed up there and killed the Emulator, they would have died. The mission would have been completed, and my team would be dead. They matter to me. I care about them.* Tears welled up in her eyes. *Oh shit, nope, tears, you stop that right now!* She pressed her fingers against her eyes to keep the dam from breaking as her heart melted from acknowledging that she had grown emotionally attached to her team, and the thought of losing them – a thought she wasn't as familiar with – was more difficult to bear than she was comfortable with. But for the first time in ages, she willed herself to feel the emotions, chalking it up to the cost of keeping them in her life. *I didn't run because I'd rather be afraid of losing them than be alone and free. Oh, Malcolm! I get it now! I get it now!*

Symone felt an overwhelming sense of relief and purpose bathing over her, and she felt compelled to talk to her boyfriend.

Malcolm closed his door and could hear a commotion in the commons. He was about to cross the threshold when Symone stepped out of her room. Unfazed, he kept walking.

Symone noticed he didn't stop and sharply voiced, "Hey Malcolm."

*Dammit, I got caught.* Malcolm stopped and turned around. "Hey Symone."

Symone was annoyed. "I know you said you wanted to give me space and all, but damn, you can still speak to me."

Malcolm thought, *Well, not going to see the Analyst now. I'll try again once the debrief is over.*

"I'm sorry," Malcolm lowered his head and crossed his arms. "I wasn't trying to ignore you. I'm just a little overwhelmed, you know, with everything that happened yesterday."

"I can tell," Symone pushed her locs behind her shoulders. "You haven't said two words to me since yesterday. You get like this every time we lose a battle."

"Yeah. I know."

"Well, you know I'm here if you want to talk, right?"

*For her to want space, she sure wants to stay tethered to me. Is she trying to get information out of me? Geez, I'm so fucking paranoid, damn it!*

"I know. And if you want to talk, I'm here, always," Malcolm turned and walked away just as Symone was about to reach out to pull him close to her.

The embers in Symone's eyes flashed red in sad fury as she struggled to understand the wall Malcolm had built between them. *Something's wrong with him. This, this isn't him. Shit, did I bring this on myself?* She couldn't bring herself to push the issue, but she worried that Malcolm may have declared their relationship on an indefinite moratorium. She reasoned that telling him what she discovered would have to wait. She walked into the commons. The others were already assembled there, and they noticed their icy exchange.

Malaysia sat alone at the kitchen island and motioned Symone to sit with her. "Everything okay?"

Symone replied, "No, definitely not."

"Is it about yesterday? You know how he is after a lost battle."

"No," Symone shook her head, "this is different. Something's really wrong with him, and he's not telling me something."

"Anything to do with the rift between you two?"

"Wait, how did— never mind. Yes."

"What's going on with you two?" Malaysia inquired.

Symone sighed. "I've just been struggling with all this change happening. It's taken me a little time to figure out what I want, and I think I've finally realized what those things are. I just hope I'm not too late."

Malaysia rubbed Symone's back, "Trust me, it's not too late. Malcolm is waiting on you. Emotions are not his strong suit, you know that. But he's different with you. He loves you, and regardless of all this chaos we're entangled with, that is not going to change."

"I know. I guess this feels different for the both of us. I don't know, something just isn't right."

"Well, at the right time, talk to him, and just tell him how you feel. I think our skirmishes with the Emulator and his goons are a lot more difficult to deal with in comparison. You got this. Just follow your heart."

Symone nodded and agreed. "You're right. That damn Emulator is a bigger fish to fry."

"Hey, I'm sorry about yesterday, by the way," Malaysia recalled.

"No, don't be sorry. You all needed me. I shouldn't have questioned you."

"No, don't feel that way. You had your mark. I would have been pissed, too."

"Not gonna lie, I was a little pissed," Symone chuckled.

"Yeah, you were.  And I'm sure Mallack is, too." She looked at the team and voiced, "Come on everyone, let's go get our asses handed to us by the director."

Everyone got up and followed Malaysia out of the Quarters to Intelligence for their debrief.

In Intelligence, Malcolm walked over to Dredge's desk and noticed a load of data whisking back and forth on his screen. "Can you tell me anything, Dredge?"

Dredge, a bag of chips in hand, turned in his chair and munched as he relayed, "I've been looking at, scanning, and analyzing data all night, man.  I've made 0.02% progress."

Malcolm rolled his eyes.  "For real?"

"I know, I'm just as annoyed.  You guys were right.  This erase job had to be ordered by Akan himself because Jason Xavier does not exist.  Even with all this tech, I'm stumped. I'm doing everything I can, so once I have something, I'll let you know."

Malcolm saw Dax and Stephanie at her desk in the front of the auditorium.  He patted Dredge on his left shoulder and walked down to meet them as the rest of his team walked through the door and took their seats.  Malcolm leaned on the desk and motioned Dax to lean closer toward him.

"Hey, Dax, is Dredge for real when he says he's stumped? Or is he playing us?"

Dax nodded his head, "He's for real, Malcolm.  He and I burned moonlight trying to figure this shit out, and we are absolutely stumped.  We are no closer to knowing who he is or where he is than we were when we first got this mission. He just does not exist, any-fucking-where."

Malcolm nodded his head, "Alright, well, keep working at it. We can't get ahead of these guys otherwise."

Dax whispered, "I will say, Dredge's method of analysis is unique."

"What do you mean?" Malcolm asked.

Stephanie chimed in. "He expanded the search beyond the typical identification databases. Like, he's digging into old news articles, entertainment reports. He investigated old video footage of sporting matches and concerts they might have attended. Even went through Symone's old prizefights to see if he was ever on camera. Dredge sifted through old photos on her stripe and found absolutely nothing. Even if she deleted them, the cloud keeps records of them, and those records are gone. Dredge even dug through social media to see if someone ever caught them together on camera."

Malcolm was stunned, unable to believe that someone had outwitted Intelligence this severely. "So you're telling me that this man..."

"...does not exist," Dax finished emphatically.

Just then, Director Mallack entered Intelligence, a rarity. The team turned around and felt a collective sense of dread enter the pits of their stomachs. Malcolm softly banged on the table twice. "Okay. Keep working." He walked toward his seat. "Director," he acknowledged Mallack and sat next to Symone.

After the team summarized the previous mission, Mallack said, "Stephanie, turn the screen to UNN."

Stephanie, sitting at her desk, tapped on keys on her countertop, and as she turned in her chair to face it, the holoscreen displayed UNN's broadcast of a recap of the Outlier group's attacks on the city. Images of destruction, citizens running for their lives, and battles between the group and the Elite flashed across the screen as someone narrated, "And despite their attempts to quell the group, more damage and destruction have occurred as the days have rolled on. NextGen, Highgarden, the Underbelly, and even the Senate building in Midtown have all come under attack. Chancellor Croft has been doing his best to assure Uri City citizens that things are okay, but many are beginning to wonder whether Croft's agenda will cost the residents more than they had bargained for. Some senators, in fact, have begun voicing their concerns regarding the vote in two weeks."

An older, dark-skinned, pepper-sprinkled haired man in an all-black suit appeared on the screen, and he stated, "Do the powered deserve the restoration of their rights, absolutely. But we have to wonder whether the vote is ill-timed. The citizens are now displaying unrest," the screen cut to the protesters outside the Senate chamber the day before, "and though we cannot capitulate to these Outliers' demands, we would be foolish to think that we can just make this decision without sacrifices."

UNN switched to an interview with Senator Dariuz. "The POC has made it clear that they will stop at nothing to ensure that the powered achieve absolute power in this city. We cannot, absolutely cannot, allow that to happen. No matter what Croft and Mitchell Daniels say, they cannot manipulate the facts. We must quell the POC and strike a decisive blow against their attempt to usurp the seat of power through fear. We are prepared to do just that in two weeks."

Daisy looked around the room, expecting to see her comrades roll their eyes and grit their teeth. Instead, she saw everyone sitting very still, attentive to the holoscreen. *Wait, nobody has anything to say? Alexia?! Wow, that's surprising.*

The broadcast replayed the images of NextGen and Highgarden, and Mallack had had enough. "Turn it off," she ordered. "Since our struggle against this group, the conversation about the vote has begun to flip. What we thought would be a relatively smooth few weeks has now become smoldering chaos. We may have won our battles, but Croft is losing his war. He is afraid he will lose not only this vote, but his seat in his reelection bid in two years if this continues. Now, where the politics swing does not concern us as far as our oath to protect the city, but we have to consider how our battles are causing unrest among the citizens."

Malcolm buried his head in his hands, then rubbed his head and slid his hands down to his neck, rubbed his neck tightly, and leaned forward on the desk. "So, what, are you saying that what's happening is our fault?"

The team looked into Mallack's eyes, all expecting a reprimand. "No, that's not what I'm saying. I recognize that the Outliers are the cause of all of this. None of this falls on us. No one has expressed that sentiment to me. And even if they did, I would've cussed them all out and told them we have been the solution."

"It hasn't felt like it, especially after yesterday," Joy admitted. "Remember what Xavier said yesterday, how we're on the city's payroll? It feels like he's lumped us in with Croft, and Uri City might be inclined to believe we're on his side."

Malaysia slid her seat back and propped her feet on the desk. Something clicked in her mind, and she could see more clearly than even her eyesight could provide. "Say that again?"

"Which part?" Joy wondered.

"The part where Uri City thinks we're on Croft's side."

"Right, well, Xavier's lumped us with Croft, and Uri City might agree with him."

She clasped her hands behind her head and stared at the ceiling. "Yeah, you're right, Joy. Which should make the city see the powered in power as a good thing, right? Right?"

Karl's gears grinded, and he sat up and reacted, "Yeah, you're right. That should be a good thing."

Malaysia declared, "It's like they want us to get out there and fight. They aren't acting like they care whether they win or lose. Just as long as after the fighting is over, somebody is arguing about it on UNN."

"You know what," Duncan's military instincts kicked in, "you're right, Malaysia." He scoffed, rolled his eyes, and clapped his hands. "Damn, why didn't I see this before?"

"Probably because your head's been hurting real bad since your one-nighter with that fine-ass bartender from Switch," Alexia chuckled.

"Haha, very funny. But true," Duncan admitted.

*Damn,* Malcolm sighed, *I forgot to tell him to get checked out after the zintol match.*

"Duncan, what do you mean?" Mallack redirected them to keep them on track.

"Oh, um, it's psyops," Duncan stated.

"Psyops? What's psyops?" Joy's curiosity piqued.

"Psyops, it's more Alexia's domain, but not in a power sense. Psyops is using propaganda to persuade people to do what you want them to do. Psychological warfare. The military uses it to tear nations down from the inside-out when sheer firepower won't do it."

Malaysia took her feet off the desk. "See, this whole time, we've assumed that the Outliers wanted to make the senators afraid of voting against the measure.  But what if what they're really trying to do is to make the senators afraid of voting *for* it?"

"That's a really good point," Karl said.  "I mean, if they really wanted to scare senators, then how come there were no senators kidnapped yesterday?"

"And none of the senators were in the chamber yesterday," Malcolm continued.  "Maintenance workers and low-level assistants mostly, but the seats of government were not in danger at all."

"Right," Stephanie's mind began piecing together their analysis.  "Even if we did nothing yesterday, it would have made no numerical difference regarding the vote."

"Exactly," Daisy tagged herself in.  "We brought this up a few days ago, if the Emulator and the Elements…"

"Wait, the 'Emulator and the Elements?'" Alexia chomped on that line.  "What are they, a band now?"

"That's actually a really good name for them," Symone voiced.  "I like it!"

"Yeah, well, if the *Emulator and the Elements* wanted the powered to be in power, they would have stopped their shit a long time ago.  Frimas, they wouldn't have even started anything up.  The vote was, and still is, in favor of the powered.  There's no conceivable reason for them to have done any of this.  Yesterday, with the Senate chamber and that skirmish in the Underbelly, they were just toying with us."

"You got that right," Symone remembered how smug Jason seemed to be during their battle and traced the theory Daisy just posed.  "The Emulator, Jason, he sent us to the Underbelly to fuck with me."

"What do you mean?" Malcolm and Mallack said in-sync.

"Jason used to live in that building. He knew that once I saw that address on the map, I would want to go there, and we would split up to take care of the chamber and the senators. Had we not gone, the chamber would have probably taken on less damage because we all would have been there. They wanted to divide us to try to beat us. They think we're the only ones who can stop them."

"No, they *know* we're the only ones who can stop them," Malcolm upped her argument. "Every time we've assembled fully, they've run away."

"I don't fully agree," Daisy countered. "Not about the ass-kicking part. We are *definitely* the only ones who can stop them. But if Duncan's right, and this is all psyops, then they *know* that we will try to stop them and, more to their point, *cause damage* along the way. The cameras will roll, capturing all of the fighting we're doing, the damage we're doing to defend the city, and then the politicians will use that footage for their own purposes. Joy just reminded us that the Emulator said, 'We're on the city's payroll.'"

Mallack sat down to process the information the Elite just lay before her. "So, let me understand what you all are suggesting. You believe these Outliers, the Emulator and the Elements, are only doing this to get the senators to vote against the bill?"

Karl rubbed his chin, "That's what it sounds like, and it actually makes sense. If they don't want the powered in power, then maybe they're not our true target. Maybe they're the distraction. It's to their advantage for the vote to go the way of the powered. So, if they're using violence to push the senators to vote against it, then someone has to be pulling their strings."

Symone shook her head. "But it doesn't make sense. Jason's whole life, at least when we were together, all he ever wanted was the powered to be in power. Frimas, he was talking to me about joining him during our last fight."

"You think that's why he picked that spot?" Malcolm asked.

"Frimas naw," Symone quipped, "he only picked it to split us up, he doesn't give a fuck about me. But if we're right, and he's not motivated by getting the powered in power, then what's his motivation? If not domination..."

"It's money."

Everyone turned to look at Dredge, who had been silently attentive. His mind had been running calculations as he made sense of their arguments, and something finally clicked. "It's always money. Money will get even the most noble person to turn dark. Everyone has a price."

Dredge stood up as Duncan bellowed, "Damn."

"Stephanie," Dredge asked, "can you put the Powered Order Coalition on the screen?"

Stephanie said, "Director?"

Mallack turned and said, "Do what he asked."

Stephanie tapped on keys and showed the list of the active members of the Powered Order Coalition. "Okay, here's the full list of the Powered Order."

Dredge said, "Now, put that in a box, and pull up all of the social, financial, and political rivals of the POC."

"Where are you going with this?" Alexia asked.

"Just trust me," Dredge stated.

Stephanie did as Dredge requested, and green lines connected the POC to sixteen different groups across the screen, each a different social, financial, or political group who was aligned against the POC. Dredge looked, then snapped his fingers and clapped his hands. "Okay, patch that through to my desk. Guys, give me half a day, and I promise you, I'll have the answers we've been looking for."

"Half a day?" Malcolm said.

"Oh," Dredge chuckled, "so you want to make this a challenge? Okay, five cycles?" he countered.

Malcolm's jaw clenched, but before they could verbally arm wrestle, Mallack interrupted them, "Doesn't matter, Dredge. Just get it done. This entire time, we've been one step behind these bastards. If you can figure this shit out, we can finally get ahead of them and maybe put an end to all of this before it's too late. Great work, Elite. Dredge, Dax, Stephanie, call us the minute you get a breakthrough. Elite, stay close. Dismissed."

The Elite stood up and filed out of Intelligence. Alexia stopped everyone when she asked, "Hey Daisy, that was some impressive work you did. How did you come up with all of that?"

Daisy rubbed her hands through her gold braids, "What do you mean?"

Everyone observed Daisy and Alexia's exchange. "I'm just saying, that was some expert-level analysis you provided today, especially for someone who's been on Dariuz's side this whole time. Your switch-up wouldn't have anything to do with Mitchell, would it?"

"Ooh," Karl chuckled as he folded his arms. Everyone's eyes beamed.

"Well, he and I did talk last night," Daisy admitted.

"Ooh, last night? Was this talk over surf and turf?" Duncan quipped.

"No," Daisy said slowly. "It was over pizza."

"Aye, so you two went on a date last night?" Malaysia cheered.

"Well, yeah, we did, and it was great!" Daisy felt a sense of relief.

The team cheered as Malcolm said, "It's about time you got a win, good for you!"

"Okay, okay, so tell us everything!" Alexia's eyes shimmered green.

The team sat back down near the top of Intelligence. Malcolm used Daisy's date story as a diversion to duck out of the room without being noticed. He left to meet the Analyst before someone, Symone particularly, could notice and try to tag along.

# 21

# My Choice

The Analyst bobbed his head gleefully to the beat of his lo-fi playlist. He sifted through the Elite's personnel profiles, training footage, and the team's last battle with the Emulator and the Elements. He ran the demographics and specifications algorithm to update their statistics. A running calculator displayed on the big screen in the front of his office, and the spinning numbers stayed blurred and scrambled as he typed to the rhythm of the song pulsating through the subwoofer. *Probably not gonna be much of a change this time around, but I have been surprised before. I can't wait to see what you reveal to me today.*

The Analyst's door lit white and slid open. *I wasn't expecting anybody today. Wonder who's coming through the door.*

Malcolm rushed in and hurriedly closed the door. The Analyst noticed Malcolm's rushed approach and asked, "Malcolm, hi! Is everything okay?"

"Yeah, everything's fine," Malcolm collected his breath, "I just didn't want anyone to see me come in here."

"Why, what's going on?" the Analyst inquired.

*Shit, Malcolm, remember, don't give too much away. Or else he's going to pull information out of me.* Malcolm composed his thoughts, remembering the lines he meticulously crafted and rehearsed for the past several cycles. He assumed his role and began, "Analyst, I need access to my personnel file and medical record." *His next line ought to be, 'Why do you need them?'*

The Analyst's curiosity piqued. "Why do you need them?"

"I'm just trying to fill in a hole in a timeline," Malcolm responded to the Analyst's question like a command prompt requiring a security answer.

"Maybe I can help? What hole?" the Analyst's gears were grinding.

*I knew he'd bite on the 'hole.'* "My training days. My mom's convinced that I didn't start here when I did, and I want to prove her wrong."

"Gotta love moms, right?" the Analyst laughed. "Why the medical file, though?"

"Well, she swears that I had a procedure done around the time I started, and I can't remember what she's talking about. She has a file at home, and I want us to compare them face to face so she can't say, 'I don't know what you're talking about.'" *Don't forget the punchline.* "I want her dead to rights over chicken and mashed potatoes."

The Analyst, right on Malcolm's cue, laughed at his corny quip. "That's funny. Okay, I'm uploading your personnel file and your medical record to you now. You'll have access to these files for one week before they become obsolete due to our updates."

"I know the drill. Thanks, Analyst, I can't wait to show these to my mom. The 'gotcha' look on her face is going to be epic!"

The Analyst tapped on keys, and Malcolm's stripe began to fill white to denote the file upload. "Let me know how that conversation goes, Malcolm."

"No worries, you'll be the first I tell," Malcolm lied. He walked normally out of the Analyst's office, then bolted for the Quarters to get to his room. When he walked in, he breathed a sigh of relief as he noticed that no one had come from Intelligence yet. He sprinted through the commons and to his residence. He locked his door and walked over to the kitchen island.

Laser focused, he sat on a stool and bellowed, "AI, activate the command center." On the opposite side of the island, a holoscreen shone from the edge. The countertop turned into an interactive screen and appeared like a black blank canvas.

Malcolm then said, "Deactivate the cameras."

AI acknowledged, "Cameras deactivated for twenty minutes."

Malcolm lay his left arm on the counter, and from his stripe, several pictures and files poured onto the countertop. Malcolm arranged the pictures of him with his family in order of time. He stared at his younger self with his parents at various locations throughout the city during different points in time. He examined times he shared with friends. Malcolm strained his mind but struggled mightily to remember when those pictures were taken and the friends he had. He saw another picture of himself holding a trophy, and he tried to remember how old he was when he won it and where he was when it happened. He banged his palm against his forehead, and it didn't help reboot his mind.

*My mind is a complete blur. Why can't I remember anything from my childhood?*

Malcolm sighed and gave up on the attempt. Shifting gears, he opened the medical file the Analyst had given him. He scrolled through the past eight years, 5716-5724, and the file had no record of major injuries or surgeries, only minor scrapes and bruises. *Thank God for cloaks.*

Malcolm then opened his personnel file, and he scrolled all the way back to 5716, the year he began working for the Company. He scanned again for a sign of a medical procedure being performed on him, and not a single procedure was recorded. Malcolm inferred that he enlisted with the Company with a perfect bill of health.

"Okay, wait, something's definitely not right here." Malcolm then opened the file that the Collector gave him and placed it in between his personnel and medical files. The Collector had given him a document that described a medical procedure done on Malcolm's head. He stared at the day he started at the Company and the day the medical procedure was completed. He saw that the medical procedure was performed on his head in 5715, a year before he started at the Company.

*If that's right, then that would mean that I was here a whole year prior to my start date. But how is that possible? I don't remember anything happening to me. How would I have been out cold a whole year? What happened to my head? Is that why I'm having such a hard time remembering anything? Is that why I had been having those nightmares and flashbacks?*

He studied the letterhead, and he noticed the unmistakable Company watermark. He examined the signature at the bottom, and he knew he had seen that signature before, though it had been years since the last time he'd seen it. He put the signatures of the medical document and his personnel file side-by-side, and he was stupefied and horrified to see Catherine Mallack's exact imprint on both. Malcolm's eyes widened, a phantom pain punched him in his gut, and he leaned forward on the desk. Malcolm's epiphany sent a shock to his system that he was not prepared to deal with. He started hyperventilating, adrenaline rushing through his veins faster than Blitz's feet carried her.

*The Collector is right?! What has the Company been withholding from me? What the Frimas happened to me?*

Malcolm's head snapped to his left as he jolted from a sudden knock on his door, his need for catharsis sharply interrupted. Symone, still reeling from their icy interaction earlier, was itching to talk to him. She was surprised that his door was locked. "Malcolm, it's me," Symone announced her presence and knocked again.

*Shit, I can't let her see me like this. Okay, get a grip, get it together.* Malcolm sat up straight and closed his eyes. He flapped his arms and breathed deeply to calm himself down. He shut down the command center, and it reverted to a kitchen island. Malcolm cleared his throat, straightened his clothes, and walked to the door. He took one more deep breath, then opened the door. He stared into her eyes and calmly said, "Hey, Symone, what's up?"

"Your door was locked. Everything okay?"

"Mmm hmm, yeah, everything's fine." Malcolm answered.

Symone noticed that Malcolm had not moved out of the threshold. "So, can I come in?" Symone asked.

"Oh, um, yeah, sure," Malcolm declared. He stepped aside, and Symone crept through the threshold. Malcolm closed the door and stood with his back to it. "What's up?"

Symone walked to the couch and sat down, then noticed that Malcolm was at the door. *Yikes.* She said, "Malcolm, come sit with me."

"Okay," he walked toward her and sat next to her on the couch.

"Malcolm, I'm just gonna ask it. Are we okay?" Symone asked.

"Yeah, we're okay," Malcolm declared unconvincingly. "Why do you ask?"

Symone laid her hand on Malcolm's knee. "Well, you've erected this huge wall between us. You're not acting like your usual self. You're acting really weird."

"How do you figure?" Malcolm acted oblivious.

"I mean, ever since our conversation on the roof, you just seem to be in this very weird, non-communicative space."

"Well, Symone, it's like I told you. You've got some things to figure out, and I've given you space to do it."

"Yeah, well, space is one thing," Symone countered, "but this doesn't feel like space to me. It feels like a regression. In fact, this feels worse than when the Collector's folk beat up on us the first time."

Malcolm stood up and slowly paced to the kitchen, annoyed with Symone because of her flip-flopping, but crushed more because he wanted to spill his soul to her about what he had discovered but was still not sure she could be completely trusted. He turned and said, "Symone, you were the one who said to me that you're scared of committing to the Company – let alone *me* – and want to run. What were you expecting from me? To chase after you? I gave you what you asked for: the power to choose."

Malcolm's words stung Symone as if one of his spears rammed through her chest. *Shit, Malcolm, do you hate me now? Akan!* "Yeah, you're right. But I feel like you're pushing me away because of that, like you're punishing me."

"How am I doing that?" Malcolm thought, *Damn, I am doing a bit too much. I probably should back up a bit.*

Symone stood up. As she walked toward Malcolm, she answered, "This. This wall between us, this isn't *you*. You've become a shell of yourself. This feels worse than how you treated me when I was your mentee."

The nanites of Malcolm's emotional cloak were shimmering brighter than his physical cloak in the middle of a battle. He wanted to pour his soul out, but until he could confirm what he uncovered, he believed he had no choice but to double down on the wall to deflect attention off himself. "Symone, be honest with me. Have you come to any conclusions?"

Symone determined not to tear up. She sat down at the island and said, "Well, I wanted to talk to you about that."

"Oh?" Malcolm breathed a sigh of relief, surprised that his deflection worked.

"Yes. When I was on the roof with Jason, the Emulator, I was this close to kicking his ass and stopping all this chaos he and his goons are causing."

"Oh yeah?" Malcolm lifted an eyebrow. "And?"

"And, just when I was lighting his cloak up, Malaysia called in saying she needed help. And it pissed me off so badly, because I wanted that kill. But I jumped off that roof to help her and Daisy and Karl."

"You said that during the debrief earlier. What does that have to do with you and me?"

"Well, I realized on the ride back here that I helped them because they are my teammates, my family. And though it scares the Frimas out of me, I can't imagine leaving them behind. I can't imagine losing them. I can't imagine losing *you*." Symone stood up and walked over to Malcolm.

"Really?" Malcolm bellowed as he stared into Symone's brown eyes.

Symone gently grabbed Malcolm's hands and declared, "Yes, Malcolm. My whole life, I've been wired to live in freedom, but being here, being with you, being with this team, all of that has taught me that running isn't freedom. My whole life, I've run from anything that felt like commitment because I've been afraid to feel my emotions and risk becoming emotional for people who I care for, and who care for me back. When everyone was telling me how much they wanted me here, I was afraid of what that meant for me, and I felt like my freedom was being taken from me. But that wasn't true. No one was taking my freedom. No one was restricting me. No one took my choice away from me. You, Malcolm, you gave me freedom tenfold. You were right all along. You helped me see that freedom is the ability to choose what I want for my life."

"So, what are you choosing?" Malcolm pulled her body into his and planted his lips onto hers, and they kissed each other slowly and deeply.

Symone pulled her head back and declared softly, "I choose to be free *and* have a place to call home. And that place, my home, is *you*, Malcolm."

Malcolm was overwhelmed with emotional bliss, overjoyed that Symone declared her love for him so emphatically. No one had ever so eloquently proclaimed their desire for him, and he was spellbound. He knew more definitively that he loved this woman, and he wanted to show her just how much with more than mere words. He swiftly spun Symone around and pressed her into the refrigerator door, and a sensation shot through Symone's spine. They then locked lips and breathed heavily. Malcolm then grabbed Symone and lifted her up, and her legs wrapped around Malcolm's waist as she grabbed his head and kissed him more. She thought, *Here he is! This is* my *Malcolm!*

Symone pulled her shirt off and over her head and threw it on the floor, exposing her skin to the crisp air. Malcolm walked them into his bedroom and gently lay her on the bed, her legs spread as Malcolm lay in between them. He noticed the ribbon they made three quarters prior while sharing their desire for each other in the cafeteria. He said, "Every time I see this, my heart smiles."

Symone lifted up and saw the ribbon he was tracing with his finger. He loosened it up, untied it, and pulled it from her torso. He said, "Just like unwrapping a gift."

Symone laughed and said, "So corny, get your ass up here!"

Malcolm laughed and kissed Symone more, their passion rising as Symone's hair and eyes began to light up. The sounds of their lovemaking were thankfully muffled by the soundproofing of the residence as they took their time reminding each other just how much they cared for each other, missed each other, and desired their bodies to explode all over his bedroom through their expressions of love.

About forty-five minutes later, Malcolm and Symone lay naked in bed. Symone, mentally exhausted from the events of past several days, was napping on Malcolm's chiseled chest, wrapped in a blanket of relief. Malcolm stared at the ceiling, waiting for Symone to hit her sleeping stride. Once she reached the point where she could sleep through a thunderstorm, he slid from underneath her, and she shuffled a little while lightly snoring. Malcolm walked to the side of the bed Symone was sleeping on and picked up her ribbon. He stared at it, then looked back at Symone, admiring her body, her mind, her heart, and her spirit. He felt the edge of eternity pierce his heart – the same feeling he had when he first met her, and her energy flowing through her veins. He pondered, *I wonder what she would think if she knew. Frimas, I still don't know what I'm thinking, knowing what I know. I can't bring her into this, not until I am certain.*

Malcolm slinked to his nightstand and carefully pulled out the drawer. He gently sifted through the drawer and pinched a tiny, weightless, transparent microdot that he had pulled from Weapons and Wardrobe. Upon pulling it out of the drawer, it slipped from his finger and fell. *Shit! I can't see this thing! Alright, concentrate.* He dialed up his senses and instantly distinguished the microdot from the fibers in the carpet. He lifted the dot from the carpet and placed it in his palm atop the ribbon. He looked at the ribbon once again and declared silently, *I hope I don't regret this.* He closed his eyes, squeezed the ribbon tightly for several seconds, then released it from his hand and watched it float to the floor once more.

# 22

# Conspiracy

The chilly air gently blew on Symone, and goosebumps covered her bare back. She shuddered from the cold and slowly awakened from her blissful nap. As she batted her eyes, she reached for Malcolm, and her hand landed on the mattress she lay on. Symone lifted and twisted her head as she steadily regained consciousness. The curtains were outlined by the light of day. Symone turned her body while she softly called, "Malcolm? Malcolm?" There was no response.

Symone pulled her locs off her chest and began braiding them into pigtails. *I wonder where he went. Is he really alright? I mean, he still loves me, but am I missing something? I can't read him anymore. Shit, he planted a kiss on me, and I let all my concerns fly out the window like a dumbass. But, he's not playing me. He can't be. That's not like him. This is too much for me to be dealing with. But I did just tell him that I choose him. Maybe I shouldn't have told him? Maybe I should have kept that shit to myself? But then he never would have come back to me. Ugh.*

She finished the last braid and pulled the sheets off her body. She gathered her clothes off the floor, piecing her outfit onto her body. She then searched for her ribbon and found it on the floor where Malcolm left it. She lowered her jeans and lifted her shirt, tied the ribbon around her waist and fastened it with a loose knot. She reassembled her pants and pulled her shirt down, then walked out of Malcolm's bedroom and went through the kitchen and his living room to the door. She let out a sigh, opened the door, and walked out.

Symone could hear her teammates past the residences bantering. She walked through the threshold and saw Karl, Daisy, Joy, and Duncan sitting in the common, while Malaysia and Alexia were in the kitchen as Malcolm was sitting at the island watching Malaysia and Alexia talking.

"I'm hoping that the zintol matches will resume next week, but shit, with all that's going on, there's no telling when they'll start up again," Alexia lamented as she opened the refrigerator.

"No shit," Malcolm acknowledged. "The league owners are probably scared one of their stadiums is next."

"Can you blame them?" Malaysia chimed. "I wouldn't want to host a match in my stadium if I knew that doing so might put people at risk." She threw a knife in the air and watched it swiftly fall and split a pineapple in half on the counter.

"Yeah," Duncan overheard them, "but they can't stall forever. The global championships start in three weeks. If they don't play to decide who will represent Uri City, then what? Does the city forfeit?"

"At this rate, we might not have a choice," Malcolm frowned. Symone reached him and placed her hand on his back. Malcolm instinctively wrapped his arm around Symone, gently cupped her arm, and squeezed her tightly. Symone laid her head on his shoulder, comforted by Malcolm's gentle, yet firm embrace, as Malcolm continued. "The league isn't going to risk another hundred thousand people for a zintol match. The only way I see them resuming play is either we catch these bastards, or they play on a neutral site outside the city."

"You're right," Malaysia, still slicing the pineapple, responded. Alexia telekinetically brought a bowl and two cartons of juice to Malaysia and sat them next to the pineapple slices. "Hey, Symone! We're making fruit punch mojitos. Do you want one?"

"Akan, yes!" Symone said. "I feel like I haven't had a good drink in a while."

"Symone, I was curious," Alexia started, "when you were up there with the Emulator, what was that like for you?"

Symone lifted off Malcolm's shoulder. She crossed her body with her left arm to grab Malcolm's hand while she narrated, "It was weird. Like, he clearly wanted to see me, but it wasn't like one of those 'I want you back' moments like you see in the movies."

"Were you expecting that?" Malaysia inquired as she dropped the pineapple slices in the bowl.

"I wasn't expecting that, but I wasn't expecting how coy he was, either," she returned. "It's like he wanted me to be there but was stalling at the same time. Even when I was about to fry him before you called for me, he was smiling the whole time, daring me to kill him."

"You think he has a death wish?" Malcolm asked. Daisy, Karl, Duncan, and Joy turned their chairs to include themselves in the conversation.

"I don't know. Jason was incredibly difficult to read. At this rate, I couldn't tell you what he wants or how he wants it, except that whole POC vote."

"And even that is up in the air now. None of this makes any sense anymore," Karl sighed.

Just then, a buzz went off in everyone's left arms. They all looked down and saw the message, "Turn on UNN."

Joy used the remote to turn the holoscreen to UNN. On the screen displayed a view of the empty Senate chamber. A woman's voice narrated, "...what can only be described as inevitable. Moments ago, the Overseer of the Senate secured a quorum, and they decided to hold an emergency meeting tomorrow at 02:00 to vote on the submission on the Powered to Hold Offices Question Measure for the General Election."

The team grumbled and sighed as their hopes to beat the Outliers were dashed by the news anchor's words.

"Guys, we've run out of time. If they're doing this, you already know which way the vote is swinging. The Emulator and the Elements won," Daisy declared. "That's game."

"Like Frimas, they have!" Alexia belted.

"Shit, Malcolm, is there anything we can do?" Joy pleaded. "Talk to the Chancellor, tell them to call it off, something, anything?"

"Naw, the Chancellor can't call off a quorum," Duncan explained. "Even if he wanted to, he can't stop them from meeting. You know how hard it is to secure a quorum? 80% have to agree to it."

"Damn," Symone's eyes smoldered in anger. "It can't end like this."

Alexia sighed, "There's no more moves, though. We have nothing to go on."

They stared at each other, then back at the holoscreen to hear more about the quorum and the subsequent vote. Malcolm thought, *Sure, this would happen right as Mallack is walking out the door and I'm supposed to be walking in. Man, just when I thought it couldn't get any worse. The Collector's saddled me with this medical file bullshit, I can't trust any-*

*body, not even my girlfriend, and I'm ending my career as a Defender with one of the biggest losses ever.*

Malaysia looked at Malcolm and thought, *Oh shit, he's spiraling.* "Malcolm, it's okay."

"Um, naw, not really," Malcolm disagreed. "But shit, what can we do?"

Suddenly, their stripes lit red and buzzed in their arms. "Great, now what?" Alexia cried.

Their stripes read, "Hey yo, this is Dredge! Get y'alls asses to Intelligence!"

"For real?" Symone chuckled. "Y'all see this, right?"

"This might be the Hail Akan we've been looking for, let's go!" Karl bellowed.

Everybody rushed out of the quarters and headed for Intelligence. They saw Director Mallack cut the corner and speed-walk to Intelligence, too.

They blasted through the door and saw Dredge standing where Stephanie usually stood at the front of the auditorium. "Guys, I figured this shit out! Sit down!"

Everyone filed into the room and sat in their usual seats. Dredge's eyes beamed, excited to share his findings like a nerd giving a book report to his classmates. Director Mallack met Dredge at the front and said, "Okay, Dredge, what did you discover?"

Dredge found a chair and pulled it up to Director Mallack and said, "You're gonna need this." Director Mallack looked at Dredge with squinted eyes but complied with his suggestion and sat down.

Dredge snapped his fingers and clapped his hands, then said, "Alright guys, I'm going to tell you a story. A story about one of the biggest conspiracies in the history of Uri City."

"The Frimas?" Malcolm asked.

Dax nodded his head. "Malcolm, let him tell the story, this shit is good! Scary good!"

Stephanie swooned. "Let him tell the story."

Dredge turned around and tapped a key on the countertop, and the holoscreen showed a picture of the Emulator and the Elements.

"Okay, when we were all in here talking about how the Emulator and the Elements seemed to be working in opposition of their own goal, it made me realize that if I was right, and it was about money, then you guys had the right idea about looking for who these assholes are, but you had been looking in the wrong direction. In a conspiracy, there are three major things you need in order to pull off what you want: a distraction, a goal, and a benefactor. We thought that the Emulator and the Elements were just terrorists. But, in fact, they are the distraction."

"The distraction?" Alexia parroted.

"Yeah, the distraction," Dredge continued. "The clue was right in our faces from the very beginning. But we were so distracted by the Emulator and the Elements that we couldn't see what was really happening. In fact, we've been directed for quarters and didn't even know it."

"What are you talking about, Dredge?" Malaysia asked. "You're saying a whole lot of nothing."

"Okay, let's start at the beginning. Where was the first attack?" Dredge asked.

"NextGen Stadium," everyone replied.

Dredge tapped on a key, and NextGen Stadium appeared on the left side of the screen. On the right appeared a write-up on NextGen Technologies.

"NextGen Technologies is a pharmaceutical and weapons technology corporation. They are contracted primarily with the city's military, have been for years now. It's been public knowledge, however, for the last year and a half that NextGen was severely tanking with the rise of better and cheaper rival companies. They've been bleeding creds, and their contracts with Uri City were not getting renewed. Last year, they had been trying to find a company to merge with and swallow their losses, and everybody they asked said, 'Frimas naw.' Then suddenly, absolute silence. No one said a damn thing about them, their future, nothing. Just silence.

"Then, as NextGen Stadium is hosting a zintol match, *boom!* The stadium falls. All of a sudden, NextGen is all over the news, the net, and the social media platforms. No one noticed that their stock prices soared, NextGen is flush with cash in a matter of days, damn near canceling all their debts, and suddenly they're in position to reclaim their stake in the arms race again."

Malcolm looked confused as he was piecing the puzzle together. "So, what, you're saying that NextGen masterminded this whole thing to get their money back?"

"No, Malcolm, it's deeper than that," Dredge replied. "In order for NextGen to even be in position to get this money, they had to stay afloat for two whole quarters without going bankrupt. And who kept them solvent this whole time? Senator Doyle out of Highgarden."

Dredge commanded the holoscreen to displayed a middle-aged, dark-skinned man with an afro in a blue suit and red tie. Underneath the picture said, "Senator Brixton Doyle, Highgarden District." Daisy gasped deeply, shocked that someone from Highgarden would be a part of this.

"The Frimas?" Director Mallack let out.

"Yeah, Director Mallack," Dredge's eyes widened. "This motherfucker. And you wouldn't believe what he owns."

"Wait, what does he own?" Daisy perked up, wishing she could, but unable to deny the evidence staring her in the face.

"He owns the 700 block of Highgarden. The same 700 block that the Emulator and the Elements blew up yesterday."

Everybody's jaws dropped from shock. "You're fucking kidding me!" Symone belted out.

"Nope. And guess who he shares that property with? This lady," Dredge tapped a key, and a picture of a silver-haired, fair-skinned woman with hazel eyes appeared. Underneath her picture read, "Sylvia Sapio, CEO, NextGen Technologies."

"What the fuck am I seeing?" Malaysia exclaimed.

Dredge said, "Because Senator Doyle is a senator, and Sapio trades on the open market, their financials are public record, and I found that they both made *heavy* payments to a company called 'JX Technologies.'"

"JX," Malcolm said, and a light bulb flashed in his head. "Jason Xavier. Dredge, I'll be damned, you found him!"

"That's right, Malcolm. I found the Emulator and the Elements."

"So, what are we waiting for? Let's get their asses!" Alexia's eyes radiated green.

"Wait, guys!" Stephanie interrupted the jubilation and anticipation. "Dredge is not done yet. That's not all he found. It gets worse/better."

"What the fuck do you mean, worse/better?" Mallack demanded. "How much worse/better can it get?"

Dredge answered, "Oh, much, much worse/better. See, I found the Emulator and the Elements, but in finding them, I found out exactly who they are and what they do. Pretend the Emulator, Jason Xavier, doesn't exist. The Elements, the six of them, I did a thorough deep dive into the archives of the global history books, and these guys have been around for about fifteen years. They are a mercenary force hired by government agencies to topple whole cities and nations across Uretha. These guys are the real deal, as in, they don't do this for money. They are usually paid very handsomely for their services, but they don't just work for hire. They work for causes. They believe in what they do, and they assume whatever characters they have to in order to achieve their missions. They are trained to be ghosts, which is why they do not exist, anywhere. They get in, destroy their targets, and get out. A psychological/guerrilla warfare hybrid."

Joy tapped in. "So you're saying this Senator Doyle hired these guys to destroy NextGen and Highgarden so they could make money? If they are believers in a cause, then why go through all this trouble so NextGen can stay in the black?"

"Because NextGen staying in the black is just a by-product of the bigger mission, what you guys said earlier today – to block passage of the measure for Uri City to vote for the powered to run for office. Thus, the goal."

Dredge pressed a key, and Senator Doyle and Sylvia Sapio's pictures slid to the left of the screen, while a box called "JX Technologies" slid to the middle of the screen, and red lines from Doyle and Sapio connected to JX Technologies.

"I accessed JX Technologies's bank records, and I saw that the Emulator's account has way more creds than what Doyle and Sapio gave them. And so, when I analyzed the account, I found several people paid loads of money into that account."

Dredge pushed a button, and dozens of pictures filled the screen, all of them arraying around JX Technologies and connecting to it with red lines.

Malcolm stood up and leaned forward on the table in front of him. Utter disbelief couldn't capture the Elite's combined emotional reaction to the familiar names and faces staring back at them – senators, city officials, moguls, athletes, entertainers, CEOs, entrepreneurs, personalities, commentators, law enforcement officers, news anchors – name after name, face after face, the who's who of Uri City flashed before their eyes.

Their heroes, idols, and inspirations instantly becoming their enemies.

"There has to be at least one hundred names up there," Symone lamented furiously.

"Three hundred forty-seven, in fact," Dredge declared.

"Three hundred forty-seven," Mallack sounded gassed. She shook her head, disappointed and angered.

"And what do they all have in common?" Dredge asked.

Daisy sighed, admitting to herself that her government had let her down, that Senator Dariuz and his ilk were wrong, that the powered in power were never the problem, and that the POC – and people like Mitchell Daniels – were never the enemy.

"They're all normal," she answered. "Unpowered."

"Exactly," Dredge clapped.

"Guys," Karl commented, "I had heard of a group of people bent on keeping the powered in check, but never in a million years did I believe it was true. I thought it was just crazy conspiracy talk."

"Which brings us to the benefactor, well, *benefactors*. Ladies and gentlemen, we found the Roots. They are the ones who, through the *distraction* Jason Xavier, hired the Elements – or whoever they are – to execute their *goal* to vote no on the measure. They are the ones who are responsible for NextGen, the smear campaign on the POC, the assassination attempt on Senator Berkeley, the attempt to destroy the Senate chamber, and the bombing in Highgarden. It's all on them, the Roots. And now, they are eighteen cycles away from achieving their ultimate goal."

"Shit! Fuck! It cannot end like this!" Alexia cried as green mist puffed from her body. "I'm so pissed!"

"We know where the Emulator and the Elements are. Let's bust their asses already!" Duncan lit his palms up.

Daisy chagrined, "It doesn't matter how many times we fight the Emulator and the Elements, Duncan. It doesn't even matter if we win against them. They completed their mission, and now they're about to get paid and get out of here. It's over. That's it. The senate will vote 'no bill' tomorrow, and that will be the end of it. We lost."

Malcolm stayed quiet, running calculations in his head faster than a supercomputer. Mallack, meanwhile, said, "Okay, team, you have done all you can. Dredge, this, this was fantastic work. I must admit I underestimated your abilities. As I promised Malcolm, you have a guaranteed spot here with us in Intelligence, provided you pass orientation."

"You serious?! Yes!" Dredge pumped his fist. *Oh yeah, oh yeah! Lana, we're moving on up, baby girl! Your daddy did it! Your daddy's working for the Company! Finally!*

"Absolutely. We need your expertise on our side. Just don't fuck this opportunity up. Now, I'm going to call Chancellor Croft and see if there's anything we can do –"

"No," Malcolm sharply interrupted her. "No, don't tell Croft. Not yet."

"What do you mean, Malcolm?" Symone asked.

"No, there's still a chance for us to make this right."

"How the Frimas can we make this right, Malcolm?" Daisy interjected, still reeling from the wool being pulled from her eyes. "Our whole government system is a farce. How can we make this right? How can we fix this?"

Alexia chimed in, "Been trying to tell you for years now, Daisy. I'm glad you finally—"

Malcolm snapped, "Both of you, shut up a minute and listen to me!" They sat at attention, slightly aroused by how he took charge. Without flinching, he continued, "It's an incredibly long shot, but there's a way for us to beat the Emulator, the Elements, and the Roots all at once, maybe even salvage the vote. And because it's the only shot we have, we can't tell Croft yet. We can't show our hand."

Mallack beamed, believing even more that she was leaving the team in good hands. "Alright, Malcolm, what do you have in mind?"

"First, alert UPD and tell them what we have discovered and give them the evidence needed to round up every single person on that list and charge them with conspiracy, kidnapping, money laundering, Frimas, throw the whole book at them. That will alert the press, and they will swarm UPD to figure out what the fuck is going on. At that point, UPD will tell them what the charges are, and the press will scramble to figure out what the arrests all mean. After that, we will then *anonymously* deliver the same information the UPD has to the media and Chancellor Croft. That will irrevocably dismantle the Roots and keep them from ever assembling again for the foreseeable future.

"At the same time, Dax, you and Stephanie *and Dredge*," Malcolm looked at Dredge and nodded, "drain the Emulator's bank account. Chances are they can't access the funds until after the job is done tomorrow. Which means if we have their money, we can control their next moves.  If Jason is indeed motivated by money alone, I'd suspect that he hasn't revealed that to his team.  We'll flush him out by telling him that his money is in another location.  Instead of us chasing him, we'll make him come to us.  He'll have to decide to either stay with the cause or go get the money.  And I'm willing to bet he will come get his money.

"Once we've separated him from his team, Malaysia, take Karl, Daisy, Joy, Alexia, and Duncan, and rip the Elements to shreds.  Symone and I will dance with Jason and take his ass down once and for all."

Symone's eyes glittered like firecrackers, and sparks flew from her hands.  Everyone looked at her and chuckled while she said, "Oops."

Mallack clapped her hands.  Stephanie, Dax, and Dredge followed suit.

"Guys," Malcolm said, "If all goes the way we think it will, this will probably be my last mission with you all for a while before I get settled in my new role.  Uri City's freedom to choose has been threatened, and we cannot let these fuckers get away with it.  At 17:00, we execute the plan, and we wait for UPD to do their thing.  Rest up and stay ready."

"Let's get it!" Malaysia screamed.

"Let's get it!" everyone echoed their leader's catchphrase.

# 23

# Uprooted

Malaysia firmly planted her hands onto her lover's bare, chiseled chest to stabilize herself, slowing lifting her ass up and down as she rode his hard, erect penis with her wet, throbbing vagina. She moaned and hissed as the ecstasy raged through her veins. Her silver eyes locked onto his as she could feel herself about to lose all control of her body. Her lifting turned into bouncing, and Malaysia pounded his pelvis faster and harder while her moans turned into soft screams. "Damn, this feels so good," she let out while she surrendered to her body's demands. He drove his pelvis deeper into her, grabbed her ass cheeks, and helped her bounce as he, too, could feel the urge to explode inside her.

"You feel so good," he bellowed. He released one of her cheeks and squeezed her left breast, softly rubbing his thumb against her nipple. Malaysia let out another hiss and scream. Her body erupted with fury. As the orgasm seized her body, the lenses of her eyes shifted uncontrollably, the maroon hues of the walls of the massive bedroom darkened by the dimmed recessed lights in the ceiling suddenly brightened and contrasted. Her eyes switched to infrared, to x-ray, and zoomed in and out. Malaysia shut her eyelids to no avail as her eyes would not let her vision go dark. As his penis knocked on her g-spot, she ignored her vision, and she grinded on him to excite her body all over again, then resumed bouncing. She was insatiable, and she would not be denied.

Her arm suddenly buzzed and lit red. "Ah, shit, ah, no, ah, not now!" she bemoaned. She ignored the buzz and kept bouncing on him.

Her lover couldn't help but notice the stripe causing her ravishing body to glow. "Are you going, mmm, to get –"

"Shhhhh," Malaysia interrupted, "not until I'm finished." *I'll be damned if I don't get every nut I want!* Without missing a beat, she grinded on him harder, knowing that her signature motion would set him off. She loved the way he felt inside her when he came and craved that feeling to make her explode at least once more. She grinded on him, and he lost it. He grabbed her ass again and slid her up and down his penis as she grinded harder.

"Shit, I'm about to cum," he admitted.

"Cum for me, mmm, I want it, ah!" Malaysia responded gleefully. He joyfully complied, the lust they had for each other ready to reach its peak. His penis grew rock hard, and Malaysia felt it hit her g-spot just like she liked it. He belted a guttural moan, and as he exploded inside her, she exploded on him, and they both seized up as they let their orgasms consume them from the follicles of their heads to their toenails.

"Ah, mmm hmm hmm," Malaysia laughed while they caught their collective breaths. "Akan, that was incredible." She regained consciousness, her eyesight returned to baseline, and noticed her body still aglow from the red stripe strobing on her arm. She shook off the gratification and read the message silently, "ELITE: Executing Operation Uproot. Be on standby." Malaysia swiftly unsaddled her lover and scrambled to the floor.

Her lover lifted off his back and stared at Malaysia's ass as she bent down to pick up her black panties. As she slid them on, he chuckled and licked his lips, "In a hurry?"

"Yeah, duty calls," she responded.

"Malaysia, when are we going to stop all this sneaking around?" he asked.

*Not this shit again.* Malaysia raised an eyebrow while snapping her bra together. "You're kidding right?"

He sat up on his elbows. "Not at all."

She placed her feet into her jeggings. "Every time we get together, you ask me that, and my answer is always the same."

He smiled, "I guess I'm hoping you will change your answer."

Malaysia rolled her jeggings up her legs and around her ass. "Stop it. No, you don't. You're enjoying this just as much as I am."

"Come on, Malaysia, let's make this official." He sat up, then planted his feet on the carpet. Malaysia stared at his impressive physique, reminded of how well-endowed Akan blessed him to be. She sharply refocused, picked up her shirt, and began sliding her arms into it.

"Official? Come on, there is no 'official.' There's just this, just sex. Secret, shameful, incredible sex."

He crept closer to her. "When will you let us become more than just sex?"

Malaysia popped her head out of her shirt and responded, "When you break things off with Emma and give up your lifestyle, Jackson, then *maybe* I'll think about this becoming more than just sex."

Jackson stood next to Malaysia. He leaned in to kiss her, and she quickly turned her head to the side, and Jackson's lips landed on her cheek.  "Aht aht," she snapped.  "You know my rule."

"Ugh," Jackson rolled his eyes.  "I know, no kissing on the lips."

"That's right."  Malaysia turned around and proceeded toward his bedroom door.

"That's a stupid rule, you know that, right?  My lips have covered your entire body."

"Not my *entire* body," she immediately returned his serve. She turned around to get one last look at his body, then said, "Good night, Jackson."

Jackson smiled and answered, "Good night, Malaysia."

As Malaysia walked through the hallway toward his kitchen, she lamented, *Malaysia, you can't keep doing this. Someone's going to find out, and your ass is going to get fried. Damn, he makes my body feel so good, though.  No one can make me feel the way he does.  This shit is going to get me killed. What the fuck am I doing?*

While Malaysia exited Jackson's condominium, Malcolm, Daisy, Symone, Stephanie, Dax, and Dredge anxiously awaited UPD's response to the information they sent to the department.  Daisy rapidly twiddled her thumbs as she stared at the big screen, noting the left side littered with small thumbnails of all the intel Dredge collected, and the right glued to UNN and the police blotter.  She wondered, "How long you think it will take them to start rounding everybody up?"

Symone replied, "I'd suspect a cycle at best."

"A cycle?" Dredge started to protest. "We have to wait a-whole-nother cycle to see some action?"

"Trust me, something this explosive," Malcolm calmed him down, "they're gonna want to make sure all their ducks are in a row before they make their moves. Just be patient."

At UPD, an exhausted Captain Stewart pushed his seat from under his messy, paperwork-riddled desk and stood up. He pulled his jacket from the back of the seat and pushed his sleeves through it. One of his detectives barged through the door, bent down to catch his breath, then emphatically declared, "Captain, you need to see this!"

Stewart was annoyed. "Akan, Dexter, I'm just about to walk out the door, can't it wait until the rising?"

"No, sir, this cannot wait. It's from the Company. Check your holoscreen."

Stewart lifted his head and unleashed a heavy sigh. He stared at his screen while tapping keys to unlock it. He swiped to his messages and found the file Lieutenant Dexter sent him. He opened it, and a wave of information flooded his screen with a damning statement from Stephanie.

"FYEO: We have found the masterminds behind NextGen, the Outliers, the kidnappings, the Senate chamber, and Highgarden. All the evidence you need is there. We secured warrants from a judge for you to apprehend every person on this list here."

Stewart clicked on the underlined "here," and the flood of names and pictures poured onto the page. Stewart's eyes widened in shock, his knees buckled, and he fell into his seat. "Oh Akan," he mumbled.

"Captain, are you okay?" Dexter was concerned.

Stewart shook his head. "No, no, I am not okay. Did you see this shit?"

"Yes sir."

Stewart looked paler than a ghost. "This is almost half of our Senate, not to mention some of the wealthiest, most powerful people in the city."

"I know, sir."

*How the fuck did they uncover all of this?* Stewart pulled his desk drawer and grabbed an antacid bottle. He shoved three tablets into his mouth and nearly swallowed them whole, hoping they would soothe his suddenly anxious, gurgling stomach. He coughed twice, looked at the screen again in disbelief, then sighed. He pushed a button on his desk and said, "Mallory?"

A woman's voice returned, "Yes, Captain?"

"Put me through to the Commissioner. I don't care what she's doing or where she's at. Tell her it's the most important case of her career."

Forty-five seconds later, an older woman's voice boomed, "Captain Stewart, this had better be good. Your assistant says it's the 'most important case of my career?'"

"Yes, Commissioner. I'm sending you the file now." Stewart hit "Send."

Thirty seconds later, Commissioner Catalina stated, "Akan, Stewart, is the Company serious?"

"I have no reason to doubt them, Commissioner. The proof is all here. The warrants are signed. I just need your go-ahead." Silence filled the captain's office. "Commissioner?"

"Operation Uproot approved. Akan, the media is going to have a field day. Captain, if this is true, show these assholes no mercy. You have my permission to use the entire force to bring them in. Authorization code 29-430. Every captain from every precinct. Get this done."

"Yes, Commissioner. Consider it handled." Stewart disconnected the call. He then stood up and said, "Lieutenant, call in every uniformed, detective, and special ops and tell them they have less than 10 minutes to bring their asses here. We will have to be swift. Move everyone that's housed in our cells to our back-up facility so we can make room for these punks. We'll strategize with the squad leaders in the command center on the ground floor."

"Yes, Captain," Dexter responded. He ran out of the office, and his voice could be heard giving orders to the team on the floor.

Stewart stood up and leaned forward with both fists planted on the desk. He tapped on the keys once more and pulled up the list. He scrolled and stopped on one name he knew very well. He let out a sigh. *I can't believe this shit.*

He pushed the button once more and instructed, "Mallory, get the deputy commissioners on the line. I want to talk to them in five minutes. I just need to handle something real quick first."

"Yes, Captain," Mallory answered.

He sighed again and said, "Okay, then." He walked from behind his desk and out of his office. He looked to his right and snapped his finger to get the attention of a detective and an officer. He motioned them to come to him. Once they walked to him, he said, "Stand behind me." He then turned left and knocked on the door next to his office.

"Come in," a voice returned.

Stewart and his backup walked in and said, "Banks?"

Captain Banks sat in an office that mimicked Stewart's. He looked away from his holoscreen and said, "Stewart, I figured you'd be home by now. What's up?"

"Brother, I hate to be the one who has to do this, but I need you to stand up."

Banks was perplexed. "Stand up, what do you mean?"

"Bernard Banks, you are under arrest for conspiracy to commit murder, conspiracy to destruction of property, conspiracy of kidnapping, conspiracy to insurrection, and a host of other bullshit I can't believe you'd ever be a part of."

The uniformed officer and detective's mouths popped open. Banks's perplexity swiftly changed to rage, incensed that he would be accused of such crimes. "You can't be serious!"

"As a heart attack. Officers, cuff him and place him in holding."

The detective and officer walked up to Banks. The detective declared, "You have the right to keep silent in protection against self-incrimination..."

"This is bullshit, Stewart!" Banks screamed. The detective and officer tried to clutch his arm, and he struggled against them. They then used force by bending him over the desk and grabbing both arms and placing them behind his back. The officer then pulled out gold bracelets and placed them on his wrists, and they glowed. A force field surrounded his hands and held them in place. Banks continued to swear, and they forcefully escorted Banks out of the office. Stewart shook his head and reached for the antacid bottle in his pocket. *This is going to be a long-ass night.*

A short time after Banks's arrest, Captain Stewart was dressed in his UPD formal black and red uniform, standing at a podium in the command center in front of Commissioner Catalina and her deputy commissioners. Several lieutenants, captains, and special operations leaders stood in the audience and awaited his orders.

He began, "Good evening. Approximately twenty minutes ago, we received word that the masterminds behind the latest attacks against the city are part of a clandestine organization coined 'The Roots.' They are responsible for the attack on NextGen, the kidnapping and assassination attempt of Senator Berkeley, the attack on the Senate chamber, and the attack in Highgarden, among other crimes dating back years. We have signed warrants for their arrests, and we are working in coordination with every precinct in the city to apprehend the suspects and bring them here to Central. Each of you has your assigned suspect uploaded to your stripe. Gather your teams and make your moves. Typically, the Commissioner asks for discretion when handling such affairs, but with the level of scrutiny this case has undergone in the press, Commissioner Catalina has given us the green light to use any means necessary to bring them in. So, if they choose to not come in quietly, bring the noise! Go get these bastards!"

Back at the Company, Malaysia got off the elevator and walked across the hall to Intelligence. She found Malcolm, Daisy, Symone, Stephanie, Dax, and Dredge sitting anxiously, waiting for any sign of movement on the UPD's part. "Anything yet?"

Symone shook her head, "No, nothing yet. Still waiting."

"Cool, I didn't want to miss it," she returned. She walked down and sat in her usual seat. "Where's everybody else?"

Daisy replied, "Probably in the quarters watching from the commons."

"Makes sense. How much longer you think it'll take before the media gets the scoop?"

"Give it about another half-cycle. The blotter just updated, look," Dax pointed at the bottom right of the holoscreen, and several red lines with white names and locations began popping up and filling the screen. "The lines will change to green once they've made contact with their suspects, then blue once they're on their way to UPD, then white once they are at the station and booked."

Dredge, with a bowl of popcorn clutched in his left arm, munched as he marveled, "Man, this is so awesome! You guys get to do this every day?"

"Maybe not every day," Symone replied, "but whenever we get action, this is part of the process in some way."

"I cannot wait to start orientation," he reacted. "I could do this stuff all day!"

"Won't lie, it's good to have you on our side, Dredge," Malcolm admitted.

"Thanks, man."

"Hey," Malcolm noticed, "one of the names is already white. Who is that?"

"Um," Dax looked closer and read, "Bernard Banks."

"Shit, you're kidding! Captain Banks?!" Malaysia lamented.

"Akan, I can't believe it. That shit's crazy," Symone said.

"Can imagine that's how everybody is going to feel once the whole list is exposed to the public," Stephanie stated.

Five minutes went by, and Stephanie, legs propped up and crossed atop her desk, heard a ping. She looked at her screen, which mirrored the big screen behind her, and saw one of the names turn green. "Guys, guys, here we go, we got action."

Everyone locked eyes on the names. One green line turned into two, then five, then seventeen. Soon, a green wave washed the red away. About a minute later, the wave shifted to blue. At that point, Karl and Alexia walked into Intelligence. "Damn," Alexia said, "still nothing?"

"UPD has just picked up several of the suspects and are now enroute to Central," Dax reported. "We're picking up chatter from the social media sites." Dax tapped on keys and displayed several live feeds from random people displaying the arrests of several prominent figures in the entertainment, sports, political, and financial spheres.

"Oh man," Karl said as he sat down in his usual chair, "this shit's about to get crazy."

"No kidding," Daisy stated. "You know what surprises me the most about this, you guys?"

"What's that?" Alexia entertained her.

"Senator Dariuz isn't on that list."

Everyone turned around to look at Daisy while Symone said, "Whoa, that is surprising!"

"Well, not really," Malaysia revealed. "Dariuz is a sleaze, but he's always been about running clean. He believes in his causes, and he makes sure that there's absolutely no way that his causes are tainted. If he gave a shit about the powered, he'd have my vote any day."

Daisy was perplexed at Malaysia's assessment of her hero. "Malaysia, I didn't know you felt that way."

"I mean, I keep up with this shit, too, you know. That's the problem with most people who are wrapped up into politics on one extreme or the other. No one takes the time to examine the people they're voting for. They look at one thing they side with and think, 'That's my guy.' Not me, I look at the totality of a man and decide whether he has earned my vote. Dariuz hasn't earned my vote, that's why I wouldn't vote for him."

Daisy reckoned, "You sound like Mitchell. And you're right."

"It doesn't matter right now. Though his name isn't on the list, look at the people who are on it. It's gotta be half the Senate," Alexia lamented. "Some of them were people I voted and stood for, too, people I thought were aligned with what I believed in. We now know who's been putting on acts just to stay in power, you know?"

Just then, Joy and Duncan entered the room. "What did we miss?" Joy asked.

"The arrests have hit social media. We're now waiting for UNN to hit us with the news," Stephanie, legs still crossed, reported. She lifted her hands and waved an air baton like a conductor leading an orchestra and led the news crew, "And here we go in 3, 2, 1."

She timed it perfectly. UNN suddenly flashed their "Urgent News" transition graphic, and a woman began, "Good evening, I am Nneka Grey. Moments ago, several key figures in the city were arrested and are being taken to UPD's Central Headquarters. These videos were captured via social media displaying popular recording artist Mecha, CEO of Titan Pharmaceuticals Donnie Wardon, and R.J. Brash, senator of the Leicester district, all being handcuffed and placed in UPD custody. Sylvia Sapio, CEO of NextGen Technologies, has also been taken into custody, along with dozens more who are being arrested and taken to UPD with no word as to what they are charged with. We have our very own Samuel Fisher at UPD now, Sam, what can you tell us?"

The broadcast switched to Samuel Fisher, a short, skinny, dark skinned man wearing glasses in a black suit and tie, standing in front of UPD. He yelled, "Nneka, several UPD hovercraft just landed about a block behind me, and a wave of officers are escorting their suspects into UPD headquarters. I haven't been given any information as to what these people have been charged with, but if you look in the sky," the camera looked up, "the hovercraft are not stopping. It's like watching fireflies light up the night. Captain Stewart, I've been told, is overseeing the operation, but to what end I have not yet been told."

"Who have you seen come into UPD so far, Sam?"

"Well, Nneka, I have been told that several people from the zintol league, recording artists, movie and tv stars and executives, CEOs of several companies, and government officials across all of Uri City are a part of this massive apprehension, and we should expect to see more hovercraft within the next cycle to bring them in. Our expectation is that UPD will make a statement to all media outlets at that time, Sam."

Malcolm looked at Dax and said, "Dax, send it now."

"Copy that, Malcolm." Dax tapped on keys, and a dialogue box opened on his screen. He typed, "Send Operation Uproot file to UNN and Chancellor Croft," then, "Execute."

Nneka and Samuel continued their exchange, then Nneka said, "Sam, let me interrupt you for a second, our news team has just received a package from an anonymous source citing details of the UPD operation titled 'Uproot.' The package includes a summary that says that the suspects that have been arrested are part of a clandestine criminal organization called 'The Roots,' and they are responsible for the atrocities that our city has faced over the past couple weeks, including the assault at NextGen Coliseum, the kidnapping and assassination attempt of Senator Berkeley, the foiled attempt to destroy the Senate chamber, and the bombing in the Highgarden district. The charges against these three hundred forty-seven suspects include conspiracy to commit murder, conspiracy to kidnapping, conspiracy to destruction of property, and the capital offense of conspiracy to insurrection, which we are being told was the overarching plan of the Roots – to sway the senators to vote no tomorrow on the bill to raise the question for the powered to be allowed to run for and hold public offices to the general election. Again, we are just now receiving this information, and we will sift through it and give you in-depth analysis of the intel over the next several cycles."

The Elite cheered as they listened to Nneka Grey narrate Dredge's findings. Malcolm clapped his hands twice, then snapped back into action as he said, "Alright, Dredge, you're up. Drain the funds."

"I never thought I'd be so happy to burn a hole in a bank account," Dredge joked. He ran to his desk, tapped on several keys, and a display of a bank transfer site appeared. Dredge typed in the "send funds from" field "JX Technologies" and the account number for it, then in the "send funds to" field "Elite Holdings" and the account number for it. He hit "Execute," and several billion creds transferred from JX Technologies to the Elite's dummy account. He then pulled out a thumb drive from the countertop and stood up. He walked over to Malcolm and said, "Here you go, 934,250,050,000 creds." He slapped the drive in Malcolm's hands.

Malcolm clutched the drive, then looked at his team, then looked at the drive. "Now, we wait."

Leaning forward, elbows on her knees, in an uncomfortable, wrought-iron chair, Samantha stared at the holoscreen in between the plans and pictures-covered whiteboards. Dread filled her stomach, and disbelief infiltrated her mind, as UNN announced that their plans officially had been foiled.

"Guys! Guys!" she screamed at the top of her lungs. "Hey, guys, get in here! Shit!"

She heard footsteps scrambling closer to the entry to their war room. Michael was the first to enter, "Hey, Sam, what's going on?"

"Guys, we're blown, UPD caught everybody, the plan is busted!"

"You're shitting me!" Quinn ran up to the holoscreen. Her eyes couldn't believe it, either.

Samantha shot up, "You see this?" she pointed at the screen. "Jason, you told us we were golden! What the fuck?"

Jason was incensed. All his dreams and future endeavors shattered before his eyes. The rug had been pulled from under him faster than his head could comprehend. There were no more moves on the board. He shook his head, "No, no, this isn't happening, this is impossible!"

Gordon pushed past Jason and looked at the holoscreen. "No, it's very possible. It's right here in full color." He turned and walked up to Jason. "The whole operation is blown, and we are exposed. They know everything."

"There's no way," Jason backed up trying to understand how the plan fell apart. "The UPD didn't have a shred of evidence on any of us, or them. There's no way they were running an op behind our backs. We would have known and prepared for this."

Jasmine's hands caught fire. "Well, clearly, we didn't account for everyone because somebody worked overtime to get this.  They pieced the whole damn thing together.  NextGen, Highgarden, the vote, they have it all!"

"What did we miss?" Otis asked.

"I don't know," Jason grumbled.

"What do we do?  The mission, how do we finish it now?" Quinn wondered.

"Are you blind or deaf?!" Samantha snapped.  "The mission is done!  We're done!  It's over!"

"No, it's not over yet," Michael pounded on a table, and it frosted.  "We just have to think.  The vote, it's still going to happen tomorrow, right?  What if we take the chamber? Hold everyone hostage and make them vote against the bill."

"How the Frimas are we going to take the chamber now? It'll be crawling with UPD, the global defenders, Frimas, they might even call in the *galactic forces* just to defend that tiny-ass speck of dirt for a twenty-minute meeting," Jasmine volleyed. "It's suicide.  I'm all for the cause, but this, this is beyond salvaging."

"Jason, come on man, what..." Michael scanned the room and realized that he wasn't there anymore.  "Where did he go?"

Everyone looked around the room.  Michael yelled, "Jason!"

Jason raced to his room and tapped on his countertop, desperate to hold onto a sliver of hope that his dreams had not been completely dashed.  His holoscreen lit up, and he opened the dialogue box and typed, "Check JX Technologies account."

The holoscreen worked and pulled up the account.  The screen displayed, "Account Balance: 0 creds."

"Son of a bitch!" Jason yelled as he slammed his fists into the holoscreen and severely cracked the glass pane.

Stephanie, Dax, and Dredge all smiled as she grinned, "We got his ass!" As Jason logged into his account, his IP address pinged, and Intelligence was able to lock onto his location and take over every camera and electronic device in their hideout.

Malcolm declared, "Patch us into his holoscreen."

Dredge and Dax tapped on keys. Dax said, "You're on."

Jason paced the floor, clawing at his head trying to understand how everything was unraveling. Suddenly, Malcolm said, "Good evening, *Jason Xavier*. We haven't fully met yet; I've only seen a glimpse of you on the battlefield. But I've heard a lot about you. I'm Kingdom Come, K.C. for short, the leader of the Elite Unit of the Uri City Division of the Company. I'll spare you the details and skip to the good part. We have your money. If you want it, you'll have to come and take it from my cold, dead hands."

"Oh shit," Malaysia said under her breath, aroused by Malcolm's bravado. "I like this."

Symone's eyes smoldered, as she echoed Malaysia's feelings. *Talk that shit, Malcolm.*

"You have one cycle to meet us at the NextGen Coliseum. Come alone, Emulator. No Elements. Just you. Or else your money will get swallowed up in the city treasury. All nine hundred billion. See you soon." The line disconnected.

"Aaaaaaahhh!" Jason slammed his fists into the countertop and splintered the circuitry. *How? How the fuck did they do this? Shit!*

Michael ran into his room. "Jason, come on man, what are we gonna do? Do we move on the Senate? Whoa," Michael saw Jason's holoscreen countertop battered, "what happened?"

"The Elite.  The damn Company did this shit.  And they got our money, man," Jason lamented.

"Money?  Jason, there's no money if we don't complete the mission.  We have to get the vote to swing against the bill.  That's what we're here to do."

"Fuck that damn vote!" Jason stopped trying to keep up appearances and revealed his intentions.  As the others crammed into his room, he continued, "This has always been about the money!  I need that money!"

"The Frimas?" Samantha was stunned but not surprised.  "I told y'all he was all talk.  From day one, he was never about the cause."

"Fuck you, Sam!" Jason screamed.  "I am about the cause. *My* cause!  And I need that money to make it happen.  Now, I just got a call from the Elite, and they said they depleted the account, and our money – my money – is in their hands.  You guys can bitch about whether to finish the mission or not, but the fact that the Elite called me means they know where we are and are gunning for our heads."

"You can't be serious!" Jasmine's eyes lit up.

"Damn right, I am!  Now, I'm gonna go get our money.  If I were you, I'd forget that fucking mission and get the Frimas out of here and find some other cause to fight for." Jason pushed through the crowd and headed out.

"Wait, shouldn't we come with you?" Gordon asked.

Jason turned around.  "No, they'll give the money away if you do.  Besides, you'll only get in my way and slow me down.  Now, your cloaks are in that box on the shelf over there.  My guy was able to modify them like I asked him.  Get them, get your affairs in order, and get the fuck out of Uri City, for good."

Malcolm looked at his team. They all stared back at him with glee, fury, and hype in their eyes, chomping at the bit to hear him tell them to suit up. Malcolm turned and looked at Stephanie and said to her, "Call UNN. Tell them to get their news crews ready for a show. A series finale they won't forget." He then turned to his team and said the three words they longed to hear him say.

"Let's get it!"

# 24

# No More Hiding

Racing through the unusually quiet night skies of the Leicester District, Jason had only one thing in mind. *How the fuck did they pull this off? No fucking way! And they have my fucking money, too! I'll kill them. I'll kill them all. They messed with the wrong one tonight!*

His visor alerted him that the NextGen Coliseum was a minute away. He revved up his black hoverbike and whisked through the cityscape, and the buildings broke away to the open sky that surrounded the ruins of the stadium. Jason pounded his head, upset with his miscalculation and determined to fix his mistake. He pushed above the stadium walls and motored toward the center of the field. He looked around and saw no one on the turf. He scanned the field with his visor and detected no life forms.

He landed his bike and unsaddled the seat. He rescanned the arena twice and saw nothing. He growled. *These fuckers played me!*

He ran to his right toward a tunnel to see if they were hiding inside. Just then, a dark figure planted his feet on the turf. Jason turned around and smirked. He joked, "So, you must be the boyfriend."

K.C. smiled underneath his visor. "If that's what you want to call me," he remarked.

"You come here to defend her honor?"

"Who, me?" Malcolm pointed to himself. "Nah, I'm *her* backup, not the other way around."

Unamused, Jason's jawbone clicked. "Enough chit-chat. Where is my money?" he demanded.

"Your money is the last thing you should be worried about right now," K.C. told him. "You've got a bigger problem than nine hundred billion creds."

"No, that's exactly the problem I have, and you are adding to it by not answering my question." Jason growled and walked closer to K.C.

K.C. stood still. "Right, because this whole thing has just been about money for you. Blaming the POC, wanting the powered in power, all of this was just a money grab for you, right?"

"Fuck you, *K.C.*," Jason roared. "You have no fucking idea what's at stake right now. You're fucking everything up. Give me back my fucking money!"

Another set of feet planted behind him. Jason looked over his shoulder and saw that Starburst had arrived. "Couldn't do the job yourself, huh? Had to sic your boyfriend on me?"

Starburst maintained her steely resolve. "This doesn't have to end like this, Jason. Surrender now and let us take you in."

"You can't be serious!" Jason laughed. "You're going to turn me in? Let me make a deal with you. Give me my money, and I'll let you live."

"Counteroffer," K.C. retorted. "Surrender, and we'll talk to the UPD about letting you serve your sentence somewhere other than the Asylum."

"Frimas naw, fuck that. I'm done talking, let's dance!" Jason double-tapped his chest, and his red and purple nanotech enveloped him. His cloak gave off a burst of power that seeped into his pores before it shimmered and disappeared.

K.C. sensed the burst from the cloak and wondered what he had done to possess Starburst's energy. The Emulator could feel his body slightly change from within and thought, *Okay, let's see how this affects me.*

Just then, the Emulator could hear helicopters and hovercraft flying above the stadium. He looked up and saw spotlights raining down on the field. The spotlights found the Elite and him, and he growled again. "Oh, so you guys wanted a show for this?"

"Shit yeah!" K.C. declared. "All the damage you've done, it was only fair that your beatdown be televised. You're a prizefighter. You should be used to it, right?"

Starburst raised her arm, and a star hovered near her hand. "Last chance, Jason. Please decline," Starburst gleefully requested. K.C. unsheathed a bo, ready for what was about to go down.

The Emulator rushed toward K.C. first. K.C. planted his feet in battle stance, and when the Emulator swung his fist, K.C. bent backward while swinging his right arm to hit the Emulator in his left side with the bo. The Emulator stumbled toward his right. Starburst blasted forward and launched two stars at the Emulator. He didn't see them coming and was hit by both. His cloak absorbed the damage while the Emulator tumbled and fell. He spun off the ground and back onto his feet. He then raised his arms and unleashed a star from each hand. K.C. shot his hand out and stopped both stars, clenched his fist to combine the stars, then swiftly shot his fingers outward to return the volley to the Emulator. The Emulator crossed his arms and braced for the attack, not realizing what K.C.'s power was but paying close attention. The stars pushed him back, and he levitated, then rushed to K.C. and launched a series of punches and kicks at him.

Starburst blasted forward and met them both, and the Emulator defended himself against them. Starburst tried to tomahawk his head, and the Emulator slid to his left and lowered his body as K.C. swung the bo twice. The Emulator exploded and punched them both in their sides. Starburst spun out of the hit to face him, then heated her fists and planted her palms into his chest, blasting him backward with star power. The Emulator stopped himself and blasted forward. K.C. quickly morphed his bo into his beloved bat. The Emulator didn't notice it, and K.C. swung for the fences and knocked the Emulator in his face. He spun off trajectory and crashed into the ground.

K.C. and Starburst walked forward to meet the Emulator as he struggled to get up. *Get it together!* He stood back up in battle stance. Starburst created a star and tossed it in K.C.'s direction. K.C. swung his bat and hit the star toward the Emulator. The Emulator made sense of K.C.'s ability to stop and start momentum. He swiftly moved to his right, stuck his left hand out, and stopped the star. He then spun around and launched the ball back to K.C. and Starburst. Starburst created another star to meet it, and they exploded in between them.

"He's learning," K.C. said.

"Yeah, if we're going to beat him, we gotta be quick, or else he's gonna have us both down pat."

"Agreed," K.C. declared.

As their battle ensued, the Elements took heed to the Emulator's instructions. In their war room, Samantha, Quinn, Otis, Gordon, Michael, and Jasmine scrambled to pull every item off the boards and toss them into the fireball Jasmine created in the middle of the room.

"Don't leave a scrap on the boards, we don't want anyone to trace anything back to us," Samantha ordered.

"We heard you the first two times, Sam, we got this," Michael grumbled while he pulled pictures of their targets off the wall. "This is some bullshit."

Samantha stared at the holoscreens and began wiping their slates clean. They began to scramble, and blue and white static was all that remained of the displays. "All the holoscreens are scrubbed," she reported.

Quinn turned to face her. "Sam, get our bus ready. We'll meet you outside."

Samantha ordered, "Everybody, we leave in 3, grab your gear and let's get the fuck out of Uri City."

Everyone acknowledged her command. Samantha ran through the corridor and pushed the bar to open the door. Twenty feet across the street from her was their parked bus. She stared at it, and the high beams flashed, and the engine roared and hummed. Samantha then went back inside and ran past three doors to her room to grab her gear like everyone else. She rummaged through the drawers and grabbed two bags. She slung them over her shoulder, turned around, and walked out of the room. She noticed everyone else walking out of their rooms at the same time.

Quinn looked around at everyone and said, "Okay, guys, we had a nice run, but let's haul ass. Samantha, you remember where we're going, right?"

"Locked in," Samantha acknowledged.

Gordon stated, "Alright, let's get out of here."

The six sprinted to the door. Michael pushed the bar and swung the door open. Michael stopped suddenly, and his eyes widened. Samantha ran into his back and said, "What the Frim–"

Samantha and the others looked outside and saw their hoverbus in flames. Standing in front of it was The Mammoth, who pounded his right fist into his left palm. Michael and Samantha looked to their left, and they saw Blitz and Ammo walking slowly their way. They looked to their right, and Enchantra and Kaminari were in battle stance, Enchantra aglow with green mist swirling around her, while lightning danced around Kaminari. They looked up, and several UNN helicopters and hovercraft shone spotlights on them, exposing the Elements to the citizens.

Michael grabbed Samantha's arm and pulled her back inside. He quickly created an impenetrable ice barrier to give them some time to strategize.

"Shit, they found us, Jason was right!" Gordon lamented.

"Alright, don't get your panties in a wad," Otis said. "We got this, we can take them."

"Damn right, we can," Samantha cosigned. "Put your suits on, attach these new cloaks, and let's kick their asses. We lost the war, but we can still beat them down."

Otis said, "Wait, you want us to put the real suits on?"

"They know who we are, there's no sense in hiding anymore. Put them on."

"Right," Michael agreed. "Let's do this shit!"

The Elements all grabbed their buttons out of their pockets and slid their arms into their shirts to install them into their chests. The buttons screwed in, and they double tapped them. Their uniforms enveloped them, and their cloaks shimmered then disappeared while releasing a pulse of Starburst's energy onto them courtesy of Jason's upgrade. Each of them could feel something changing within their bodies, but they didn't have a chance to figure out what that was.

Meanwhile, the Eagle, perched atop a fifteen-story building across the street, had her rifle aimed at the crystal wall in front of the entrance. She fired a couple rounds at the wall, and the rounds dented the ice but didn't shatter the dome. "Ammo, got anything that can blow that up?"

"Not without blowing up the whole block, nope. That wall's too thick."

"We might have to think about going around to the other side of the building, guys," Blitz reasoned.

"She's right," the Mammoth declared, "since we've taken out their means of escape, they might hole up or try to bolt through the back door."

Suddenly, the wall cracked, and the Elite could feel the air change. Kaminari said, "Okay, here we go, guys. Look alive."

Three massive swirls descended from the skies. Massive fire spikes splintered the ice wall, launched toward the tornadoes. The tornadoes devoured the spikes and became fire columns. Enchantra ran a few steps forward, spun her arms above her twice, then shot her arms and fingers upward. Shields appeared in the sky, and the tornadoes landed on them. Enchantra strained to contain them. Kaminari encouraged, "You got this, Enchantra!"

The Eagle adjusted her eyes to see if there was someone coming from the wreckage of the crystal barrier. Before she could get a lock, the building and the street shook violently, and she and her allies stumbled. The Eagle lost her footing and barreled forward and off the building. Three fingers on her right hand saved her from a date with the pavement as she dangled from the ledge.

Enchantra bent to one knee to stabilize herself, and Kaminari created a low-energy lightning whip and latched onto Enchantra to keep her up. The Mammoth stumbled backward and braced himself. He looked forward and witnessed the Elements emerging from the building.

"Guys, here we go, here they are," the Mammoth wasted no time and rushed forward to meet them.

"Frostbite, you and the Wave, handle him. The rest of you, find somebody and kick some ass," Cypher ordered.

Frostbite, donned in white and blue, rushed forward to meet the Mammoth. Blitz saw what was happening and said, "Ammo, I'm going to help the Mammoth."

"Go, I got this," Ammo declared.

Blitz tapped her feet three times, then zipped over to Frostbite. The Wave perfectly timed his attack and shot a water bomb toward her. She stumbled upon impact and tumbled on the ground. Meanwhile, Frostbite and the Mammoth met with an exchange of punches, dodges, and jabs. The Mammoth blocked Frostbite's right arm high, then hit him twice with punches to the chest. Frostbite touched the Mammoth's leg and frosted his cloak in that spot. The Mammoth then took Frostbite's arm, raised it up, and kneed him in his abdomen. The Wave planted his blue and tan nanite-clad frame and launched a water bomb at the Mammoth, and as it hit, Frostbite iced his fist and punched the Mammoth in the head, and the Mammoth stumbled backward.

Cypher looked around at every hovercraft within fifty yards of her. She summoned them to turn on and meet near her. Horns and alarms were heard all over. She then expanded her reach another fifty yards, and more horns and alarms went off. The UNN pilots could sense that something was trying to commandeer their vehicles, so they shot upward to get out of Cypher's reach. The vehicles Cypher took over suddenly rushed from every street corner and garage.

Enchantra finally reversed the tornadoes and pushed them back into the sky. Kaminari and she looked and saw the hovercars, buses, and bikes all zooming past them. A craft barreled their way. Enchantra telekinetically pushed Kaminari across the street and herself in the opposite direction before they were pummeled. They looked forward and saw the craft assembling into a forty-foot juggernaut. "Ah, shit. Okay, this isn't good," Enchantra assessed.

"I got this," Kaminari charged up, and she positioned her arms to take aim at the super-craft mash-up. Before she could launch the first strike, Ignatia's orange nanotech-clad body slid through the machine's legs and shot several fireballs at Kaminari and Enchantra. Kaminari struck back at the fireballs while Enchantra quickly shielded herself from the attack.

"Kaminari, concentrate on the fire lady. I got the robot," Enchantra said.

"You sure?" Kaminari asked.

"Yes, go, now!" Enchantra insisted.

Ammo could feel the ground underneath him shifting and said, "Alright, let's do this," and he activated his feet and began to hover in the air. Ammo was suddenly hit in the back of his head with a boulder. He stumbled forward, and then was hit with three more boulders before he could turn around. Terra's sandy silver nanotech glistened in the streetlamps as she emerged with several boulders pulled from the street floating beside her. Ammo shot his right arm forward and unleashed cannon fire from his palm toward Terra. Terra flung her hands forward, and the boulders whisked away. Ammo fired successive shots and destroyed every boulder she threw at him. Terra used the distraction to rip the ground underneath him, and Ammo fell in the pit she dug. She then seized her arms and pushed them toward each other to close the pit and swallow Ammo inside.

Three fingers turned into four, then her whole hand. The Eagle then swung her other arm to grab the ledge, and she pulled herself up and back atop the building. *I don't think they saw me. I might still have the upper hand.* Her thoughts were proven wrong as several wisps of wind pushed her backward. The wisps got stronger, and the Eagle spun violently. The Eagle became disoriented and found difficulty recognizing a green figure rising above the building and getting closer to her. He spun her more violently, and the Eagle closed her eyes to decipher how to break out of this trap. The spinning quickly ceased, and Cyclone violently pushed her with a wind tunnel into the wall of the roof access stairwell. The Eagle's cloak tried to compensate but could not give her the strength to overcome the pressure from the wind. Cyclone would not let up, determined to crush her into the wall.

Meanwhile, in the neighboring district, the Emulator planted his feet. He created a star with his right hand. Starburst, knowing that time was not on their side, blasted forward. The Emulator blasted upward, and Starburst zipped underneath him. The Emulator spun around and hit her with his star, and the impact pushed her into the ground. Starburst flipped around and braced herself in a three-point stance, then reset herself and blasted toward him again. The Emulator waited, and at the last second, he created a shield and pushed himself forward. Starburst planted her hands into the shield and tried to push the Emulator backward. K.C. got close enough and began manipulating the shield, bending it to encapsulate the Emulator in a ball. The Emulator looked around and wondered whether Starburst was morphing the energy, and before long, he was trapped in a ball, and K.C. began to harden the ball into steel.

Before K.C. could celebrate, he noticed that Starburst was still pushing the ball with resistance. The ball suddenly brightened reddish orange, and it unraveled and began to surround Starburst. K.C. saw the Emulator still pushing against the energy and belted, "Shit!"

Starburst looked around her and saw the energy about to swallow her whole, and she immediately blasted backward to escape the trap. She then blasted upward and created a star in front of her. The Emulator swiftly morphed the energy into spikes and launched them toward Starburst. She switched the star to a shield and swiped her arms in front of her to expand it just in time before the spikes could hit her. They crashed and crumbled upon impact.

The Emulator said, "Oh shit, I'm feeling it now! Can you feel it?!" K.C. took his bat and shaped it into a spear. He tossed the spear upward, caught it, and launched it at the Emulator. The Emulator saw it and stopped it midair. He laughed, "Oh, ho, ho, ho, here you go!" He then launched it back at K.C. He spun in the air and caught it. Before he could land, the Emulator morphed the ground underneath K.C., turning it into quicksand. K.C. dove into the pit. Starburst launched several stars at the Emulator. He was hit by two of them and fell onto the ground. Starburst kept firing, and the Emulator turned onto his back and stopped the stars. He got creative and morphed the energy into thin spinning discs. He then flung his hands and threw them back at Starburst. She blasted upward as the discs followed, then arced and raced downward. She pushed herself as hard as she could, aimed directly at the Emulator, and planted her palms straight into his chest. Her impact tore through the stadium turf, and they plummeted through mechanical platforms, the wiring, the tubing, scaffolding, and beams, and crashed into the concrete pad some fifty feet below them.

Back in Genesis Landing, Blitz stood up and reset herself. She blitzed the Wave and began pummeling him with punches he could not see nor stop. She then jumped up and kicked him several times before dealing a heavy kick to his chest that sent him flying backward toward the remains of the ice wall. Frostbite turned around and saw that the Wave was getting his ass handed to him. Frostbite quickly formed a glacial spear and hurled it toward Blitz. Blitz saw it coming and caught it and threw it back at Frostbite before he could make sense of it. It knocked him in his stomach, and he flew ten feet backward and fell. The Wave took advantage of the distraction and concentrated. He sensed water running underneath them in the sewers and commanded the pressure in the pipes to rise. The ground split, and through the cracks in the pavement, water burst like rain in reverse. Frostbite took advantage of the water and swiftly froze the ground just as the Mammoth regained his composure. Blitz rushed to stop Frostbite while the Mammoth took aim at the Wave.

Frostbite rolled over and stood up, only to get knocked in his back by Blitz. Frostbite turned around and swung his arm, hitting air as Blitz hit him in the back again. Frostbite turned again missed again. Blitz kicked him in his side. Frostbite then created an ice shield and swung it. Blitz jumped above Frostbite, pulled out a small stick, and pushed the button on it. The stick extended to become a bo, and she tomahawked Frostbite in the head. Frostbite crashed into the pavement.

The Mammoth got close to the Wave and beat his chest and arms with his fists. The Wave shot water cannon fire at the Mammoth, but the Mammoth was unfazed as he continued to strike the Wave with haymakers. The Wave concentrated and summoned another burst of water out of the ground, and it blasted the Mammoth upward. The Wave then backed up and released three water bombs into the air. One of the bombs made direct contact, and the Mammoth flew some thirty feet in the air and crashed near the Elements' destroyed hovercraft.

Kaminari created two lightning whips and supercharged them for maximum damage. She boosted herself forward with a lightning pulse and cracked her whip toward Ignatia. Ignatia dodged the first, then the second, then the third whip. She spun to her left and created a lava-molten ax. She got close to Kaminari and swung the ax at her head. Kaminari ducked, dropped the whip in her right hand and let out a pulse that hit Ignatia. Ignatia spun counterclockwise and swung the ax again. Kaminari backflipped to miss the ax's blade, then shot twice more. Ignatia bobbed to her right. She shot a fireball from her hand, and Kaminari shot another pulse to block it. Kaminari backed up and blasted herself into the air. Ignatia created a fire spike and threw it at Kaminari. Kaminari swiftly charged herself with a bolt from the sky and unleashed a lightning storm toward her. It disintegrated the spike and ripped the pavement apart while Ignatia blasted lava from her fists to boost herself away.

Meanwhile, Enchantra looked at the megabot slowly marching forward behind them. Enchantra clasped her right wrist with her left hand, with her right palm facing forward.

She closed her eyes, then opened them, glowing green behind the visor. Mist swiftly raced from her fingertips and seeped underground. The mist then shot out of the pavement and wrapped around the thick trunks of the machine's legs and arms. The bot tried to move, and it began to shake to try to free itself. Enchantra felt the droid's attempts and shook in resistance. Ignatia turned herself around and saw that the robot was struggling with the shackles, then turned and saw Enchantra and thought, *I have to stop her*, just as Kaminari delivered a strike to her chest and popped her across the street and into a metal wall.

Cypher used the distraction created by her droid to duck into a warehouse. She ran through the floor searching for anything that could turn the tide in their favor. She opened one of the hangars and saw a smorgasbord of defunct flying drones. "Perfect," Cypher breathed. She closed her eyes, then opened them, and her pink uniform glowed as she activated as many of the drones that were still wired to work. Engines roared and hummed, and lights flickered and flashed, signaling their readiness for Cypher's commands. Cypher said, "Follow me." The drones filed in rows and columns behind Cypher, and she walked toward the exit.

In the coliseum, K.C. morphed the quicksand under his feet and used it to push himself out of the pit the Emulator put him in. He noticed that Starburst and the Emulator were not on the turf. A spotlight shone on him, then traced a path to the hole Starburst pushed the Emulator through. K.C. waved at the hovercraft and yelled, "Thank you!" He ran toward the crater and jumped in. His visor calculated what he needed to hold onto and dodge so he wouldn't hurt himself. K.C. swung from wire vines, bounced off beams and levers, and as he got closer to the floor, he noticed Starburst and the Emulator sparring. K.C. could feel the ground underneath the Emulator and shifted the tiles to become tight tube shackles on his legs. The Emulator tumbled from his momentum, and Starburst punched him twice in his head, then heated her palms and planted her hands into his chest. The blast broke the tubes and launched the Emulator fifty feet, and he crashed into the ground.

The Emulator crafted two stars from his hands and thought, *So, I can make these things into whatever I want them to? Try this on for size!* His imagination running wild, he decided he needed some major backup. He pictured a gargantuan monstrosity would beat them down and force his money out of them. He released the stars about twelve feet in front of him, then flexed his hands and watched his ingenuity come to life as the stars swiftly expanded and morphed. Wings protruded from the big balls, then tails. Talons and arms and legs, then necks that would put giraffes to shame. From the necks, massive fangs, slithering tongues, snarling nostrils, venomous eyes, and demonic ears protruded. The skins glowed brightly as their bodies were powered by the stars themselves. The Emulator created twin raging, three-headed dragons. K.C. landed next to Starburst, and they stared at the dragons in awe and terror.

"What the Frimas?!" Starburst chagrined. "You've gotta be kidding me!" She nudged K.C. in the shoulder. "You've never thought about creating something like this before?"

In disbelief, K.C. answered, "I-I-I, never thought about it before, to be honest. I never knew something like this was even possible. Frimas, we did create a planet, though."

"Exactly! I'm gonna need you to start thinking like this from now on!" Starburst cried.

"Right?!" Malcolm agreed. "Well, let's get back at it."

The dragons roared violently, then pointed their necks and released star power from their mouths toward K.C. and Starburst. K.C. dodged to his left while Starburst blasted off to her right. She shot a continuous wave of star power at the dragons, and they roared and got bigger. The dragons shot power from their mouths at everything, and the wires, pipes, scaffolding, and field equipment started to burn, smolder, and melt all around them.

The Emulator got up, raced toward K.C., and sucker-punched him in his head. *Bitch!* K.C. was incensed yet compensated by flowing with the momentum of the punch and backflipping, kicking the Emulator in his chest. K.C. landed on his feet, then tried to punch the Emulator, but the Emulator dodged his punch, grabbed his arm and twisted it. K.C. anticipated the twist and wrapped his leg around the Emulator's torso, then headbutted him with the back of his head, elbowed him in the side twice, grabbed his head, then K.C. flipped him over his head. K.C. was then hit in the back with a blast from one of the dragons and tumbled onto the ground.

Starburst said, "We can't stop the dragons by force. K.C., I'll distract the Emulator. You stop the dragons before we melt alive in here." Starburst raced to the Emulator before he could catch wind of their plan. The Emulator spun around and flipped himself onto his feet. Starburst shot star after star at him, and the Emulator shot stars back. Starburst got close to him, lowered herself, and tripped him. The Emulator fell, but also shot another star at Starburst. Starburst stumbled back then rushed him. He resisted the push, and they levitated about ten feet.

"Just like old times, huh?" the Emulator joked.

"Shut the fuck up!" Starburst raged. She glowed from yellow to white, and she released an aura burst from her body to launch the Emulator as far from the dragons as possible.

The Eagle couldn't move her hands under the weight of Cyclone's wind attack. Cyclone pushed harder, and the Eagle crashed through the wall, and her body slammed against the opposite wall and slid down onto the stairs. Her head spun, and she shook herself to reorient. As she tried to think through what her next move would be, she heard creaking above her. *Oh shit, he's about to rip this staircase apart.* The Eagle dashed down the steps as she remembered the building was fifteen stories high. She got to the twelfth story landing when a creak turned into a crash. A tornado ripped through the roof and was sucking the staircase apart. The Eagle kept running and jumping steps to get past the tornado. *Tenth story, ninth, eighth, seventh.* The tornado was catching up, and she could feel her body armor resisting the urge to fly. *I know I'm the Eagle, but I don't have that ability!* She exited the staircase on the sixth floor and ran to the middle of the corridor. She dropped to one knee to try to regain her focus.

Cyclone was in the tornado he created, and he noticed very briefly that the sixth-floor door was opened and assumed the Eagle escaped there. He spun more violently, tore through the staircase door, and ripped through the sixth-floor hallway. The Eagle heard the wind howl and Cyclone's destructive thrashing behind her and quickly bolted in the opposite direction. Cyclone raced closer to her. The Eagle saw a window and knew it was her only means of escape. She grabbed two pistols and pressed buttons on the grips. As the wind howled behind her, she fired gatling shots at the windows and split the glass panes. With all her might, the Eagle jumped into fetal position and broke through the window. She then exploded, twisted her body, and spread her arms, her left arm toward the building across the street, her right aimed at the tornado making its way toward the end of the building. She shot a percussion grenade pulse at the tornado and a grappling hook at the building across the street. The hook latched onto the wall. She swung forward just as Cyclone ripped through the rest of the building. Suddenly, the tornado exploded, engulfed in fire, and as the building split, Cyclone flew backward toward the opposite end of the sixth floor he tore through. The Eagle noticed Blitz and the Mammoth fighting Frostbite and the Wave, then turned and braced herself for impacting the wall. She smacked into it, then lowered herself the remaining two stories onto the icy pavement. The Eagle began to run toward the Mammoth, but a sudden burst of wind slammed her through the windows of an open hangar, and she barrel rolled onto the ground, grimacing in pain.

Ammo planted his palms at the dirt and blasted himself out of the hole. He launched upward and locked onto Terra. He switched his ammunition to homing missiles and fired two of them. Terra quickly tore pavement to make a wall, and the blast backed her up. She tore the earth beneath her and rose up to meet him. Following behind her were pieces of buildings she tore. Ammo fired shots of plasma, and Terra dodged his attacks. She met him and armed her fists with cinder blocks. Ammo landed on Terra's turf and swung his fist at her face. Terra ducked. Ammo then tried swinging his left arm downward to knock her down, but Terra spun backward and to her left and swung her left arm with her momentum and hit Ammo in his side with her block. Ammo leaned over but swiftly recovered. Terra tried three punches and a kick, and Ammo blocked them all. Ammo kicked his foot forward and blasted Terra's torso with the booster, and Terra fell backward. She rolled and stood back up and launched some of the debris she brought with her. Ammo shot them to pieces, then noticed that Terra had propelled them to a high altitude. Ammo blasted off the slab and hovered underneath it. He switched his ammunition to smart demolition charges. The slab was about 20x20, and Ammo placed ten charges across the slab. Terra wondered where Ammo had gone when he suddenly returned onto the slab. He said to her, "You might want to hold onto something."

Boom! The charges eviscerated the slab into dust, and as Ammo blasted upward, Terra plummeted to the ground.

Frostbite was pissed. He grabbed Blitz's bo and quickly froze it to try to trap Blitz. She saw what he was doing and swiftly released the bo. Blitz pulled out her blasters, but Frostbite already went on the defense. He arced his hands around him and created an igloo to dome himself in. Blitz fired her weapon repeatedly to try to break through the barrier. Each blast created snow flurries and limited her vision. She didn't see the Wave's water bombs coming at her, and she was hit by three of them. Blitz flew backward and tumbled across the street. "I got her ass," the Wave signaled to Frostbite.

Frostbite turned the ice into snow and emerged from his position looking like a yeti. The Wave met up with him. "Let's finish this," Frostbite said.

"Gladly," the Wave agreed.

Enchantra held on tightly to the ropes she created. Ignatia put her feet together and blasted herself toward her. She heated her hands and prepared to knock her out of concentration. Kaminari had landed on the ground and saw Ignatia's trajectory and delivered a lightning strike to Ignatia. Ignatia shot two fireballs before being hit with the bolt, and the first one missed, but the second one hit Enchantra's hand and knocked her backward, releasing her grip on Cypher's machine. It marched forward and aimed its sights on Kaminari and Enchantra. Enchantra and Ignatia got up, and Enchantra launched green energy storms at her. Ignatia countered by throwing fireballs. Kaminari turned around and saw the droid coming from behind her. She charged up to try to overload the monster when the wall to her left exploded, and several drones flew toward her, Enchantra, and the stars above. Kaminari shifted gears and began popping the drones one by one. They exploded from her assault, and the debris fell from the skies.

Meanwhile, the mechanical juggernaut continued getting closer. Cypher ran to the machine and touched its right leg. A hole appeared, and she walked into it. The machine followed her command and rolled her toward its chest area. Cypher created a simulator gyrosphere in the heart of her monster that allowed her to move freely while being stationary. Within the gyrosphere, a bundle of wires attached to Cypher's neck, and a needle pierced her through her spine to tap into her synapses and link her to the machine. The megabot she built began to follow her movements. She marched forward.

Kaminari ran backward while taking down the drones. She tried delivering shocks at the robot, but the power was not enough to affect it. Cypher balled her right fist and slammed it into the pavement. Kaminari rolled backward while the sound of crunched metal reverberated in every direction. Some of the drones started firing lasers and bullets, and Kaminari had difficulty keeping up. Cypher raised her leg and slammed her foot down onto the pavement. Kaminari backed up again. She shot several lightning bolts in the sky to take out more of the drones, and more kept coming. Cypher clasped her fists and dropped the weight of several hoverbuses onto the pavement, tearing the street apart, making the ground tremble violently, and busting windowpanes out of the buildings next to it.

Ignatia and Enchantra kept exchanging strikes at each other, and Ignatia felt like she was wasting time. She decided to help Cypher. Enchantra threw another energy storm, and Ignatia jumped and blasted the energy storm at the last minute. She used the shockwave to propel her toward Kaminari and Cypher. Ignatia concentrated, and with one hand she rained down fire upon Cypher, while with the other shot molten lava onto Cypher's legs. Cypher ignited and became a fire juggernaut. The smell of melted pavement and heated steel reeked for miles, and Cypher became a beacon that lit up Genesis Landing for miles.

"Ah shit," Enchantra looked up. "Kaminari, what do we do?"

"I'm thinking, I'm thinking," Kaminari scrambled as she blasted backward to get out of Ignatia's purview for a moment. She landed near Enchantra and said, "Can you encase that thing?"

"It's possible, but Frimas! That thing is so big, and Ignatia keeps knocking me out of concentration. Shit, look out!"

Enchantra pulled Kaminari into her, and they spun past Ignatia's fire spikes. While spinning Kaminari out of her, Enchantra volleyed energy storms back to Ignatia. And Cypher kept marching forward, burning the pavement beneath her feet.

In the bowels of the coliseum, K.C. sensed the star power coursing through the dragons' entire bodies. As their six combined heads roared and prepared to strike, K.C. concentrated on the energy and flexed his fingers. Their necks craned, and they roared in pain. Their heads, talons, tails, and wings crunched violently, then shrank. K.C. pushed the dragons into each other, and they melded and became one. Their roars' loudness swiftly shushed, and the bright scales dissipated. K.C. morphed them back into regular star power, then shrank the power down to a concentrated star. He grabbed the star and ran toward Starburst and the Emulator.

Starburst delivered haymakers at the Emulator, and the Emulator blocked them, then uppercutted her and pushed a star into her chest. Starburst somersaulted midair, then rushed back and punched the Emulator in the head, dropped to the ground, and tripped him. As he spun, K.C. stretched the concentrated star into an unstable, explosive spear and launched it with all his might at his target. The Emulator didn't see it coming, and the spear delivered a devastating strike to the Emulator. The blast launched him to the end of the massive hangar and cut his cloak's integrity in half. He crashed into the wall and slid down to the floor.

# 25

# Overwhelmed

"Star, we're not going to beat him like this. We'll keep going on and on forever," K.C. admitted.

*What the Frimas, Malcolm?! Don't talk like that!* "No, we can take him, let's finish this," Starburst disagreed.

"Symone, he's only going to keep learning our moves. We're going to run out of plays. We have to think smarter than this. How can we beat this fool?"

"Shit! Shit!" Starburst's pride took a hit, but she knew K.C. was right. "Fine, ugh! We gotta get back to the surface. Here, hold onto me."

K.C. pulled Starburst into him. As their cloaks rubbed together, they rose back through the hole Starburst pushed the Emulator through. K.C. seriously joked, "Akan, your body feels amazing, even with all of the cloaking."

Starburst snorted, "Shut up. Don't make me laugh, I'm mad at you right now."

They landed back on the turf. "Okay, it'll be about thirty seconds before he realizes we're not down there anymore. What do we do?" Starburst asked.

Malcolm ran the calculus through his head, then thought out loud, "What's his power? Copying others, right?"

Symone agreed, "Yes."

"Okay then, let's give him a run for his money."

"How are we going to do that?" Starburst was intrigued.

"Let's run him through a simulator see if he can keep up."

"A simulator? How is that – ohhhhh, yeah, a simulator! Shit, Malcolm, that's gold!"

"Dax, can you hear me?" K.C. called Intelligence.

"I'm here, brother," Dax returned.

"We're going to need every available droid out of training to assemble here at NextGen in the next seven minutes."

"You got it, chief. Who's the target?"

"Jason Xavier. Initiate Training X42."

"Consider it done. You do realize that we're going to need to replace them, right?"

Starburst joked, "Well, we got 900 billion creds, I'm sure that'll cover the charges, right?"

Dax snorted. "Can't argue with that. An army of droids headed your way now. Stephanie, contact the UPD and UCM Air Control to get us clearance for the droids."

"Copy that," Stephanie acknowledged.

Deep in the bowels of the training floor housed a massive, brightly lit droid manufacturing and storage plant. Hundreds of thousands of machines were arranged in uniform masses. Assembly lines were waiting for instructions from the training rooms. Scraps were being cleaned up by a clean-up droid crew. Dax tapped on keys to unlock the droid bay in the ceiling of the droid bay. Hundreds of droids' eyes glowed white, acknowledging Dax's command. Their CPUs were uploaded with the training program, and they modified themselves to meet the specifications. They initiated flight sequence, and their feet boosters shuttled them upward through the tunnel toward the parking garage. The army of machines blasted out of the garage and aimed toward NextGen in the Leicester District.

"Okay, now let's get the Frimas out of here before the Emulator finds us. He can only fight like us by being around us and mimicking us. If we can stay away from him long enough, he'll lose our abilities and not be able to slice through the bots that easily," Starburst reasoned.

"Good thinking. Take us through the tunnels. AI, put the droids' ETA on my visor," K.C. said.

"Mine, too," Starburst declared. K.C. clutched Starburst again, and they zipped away through the tunnels to hide from the Emulator.

The Mammoth rolled off the ground and took a knee. He shook his head to recover. He looked up and saw that the Wave left his spot. He turned around and saw the Wave and Frostbite walking toward Blitz who lay defenseless on the ground. Adrenaline rushed through his near-immortal veins, and he exploded straight up.

The Wave aimed his hands and prepared to shower Blitz with a deluge that Frostbite would use to entomb her. Without warning, the Mammoth rammed his shoulder into the Wave with all his might and sent him through the alley. The Mammoth then jumped up and clasped his right fist with his left hand. As he prepared to tomahawk Frostbite, Frostbite turned and shot a blast of ice at him, and the blast slowed his momentum.

Blitz shook off the disorientation and stood up. She saw Frostbite's attention was turned toward the Mammoth, and she instinctively mimicked the Mammoth's move and rushed into Frostbite's chest with all her rapid momentum with her shoulder, and it launched him several feet into the air and onto his back. The Wave got up, and Blitz turned to see him. The Wave immediately shot a wave of pressurized water toward her. Blitz steadied herself and blitzed toward him.

She then jumped and spun herself around the water blast, creating a tunnel through which the water started following her through. She spun in a circle about ten feet in diameter, and the water continued to follow her in a circle.

Frostbite shook off Blitz's blow and saw her spinning around in water. He thought, *This is my chance.* He took aim, and Blitz anticipated his move. She waited for him to take his shot, and as the ice crystals materialized in his hands, Blitz ran out of the circle, the water following behind her. Blitz ran to his hand, jumped above him, ran a circle around him, then stopped and backed up six feet. Her pattern caused Frostbite's blast to freeze himself within her water trap.

Blitz raced back to the Mammoth and said, "We don't have a lot of time, Frostbite will probably break through that at any moment. We have to stop the Wave now. This might be our only shot."

"Spin me," the Mammoth said. Blitz grabbed the Mammoth's arm and commanded his cloak to bind with hers. She then spun around, and the Mammoth said, "Let me go!"

Blitz released the Mammoth, and the Mammoth crashed into the Wave, the force of the Mammoth launching them one hundred yards into a wall. The Mammoth bear-hugged the Wave and stretched his arms out. He said, "Blitz, now!"

Blitz zipped over to the Wave and punched him several times in the head until he was concussed and unconscious. His head slumped, and the Mammoth dropped him.

The Mammoth sighed in relief and said, "Intelligence, call the drone, we got one down. Take him to the Asylum."

"Copy that," Stephanie answered.

"Alright, let's deal with Frostbite," Blitz declared as she tagged the lifeless Wave.

Terra continued falling to her impending doom, unable to sense any ground below to catch her. Ammo's conscience got the better of him, and he rocketed toward Terra. He clutched her arm and boosted upward. They landed on a rooftop a couple blocks away from the epicenter of the fight. Ammo let her go and prepared a set of nullifying bracelets to put on her wrists. Before he could even fix his mouth to tell her to surrender, Terra broke the rooftop behind Ammo and sandwiched him between it and the ground he stood on.

"Son of a bitch!" Ammo screamed. Ammo reasoned that Terra could only fight at her best on the ground and thought, *Okay, I'm gonna need help. I've gotta distract her long enough. Here goes.* Ammo sent a message to Intelligence: "Send a drone to my location ASAP."

Ammo boosted himself out of the rooftop sandwich and fired multiple shots at Terra. Terra blocked, dodged, and guarded herself from his assault, lifting pieces of the roof to defend herself from his onslaught. Ammo blasted upward and met Terra, taking her on hand-to-hand. He struck his fist, and Terra crossed her arms to block it. He delivered a couple more punches, then tried to kick Terra, but Terra slid to her left and tripped Ammo, and he fell to his left. He rolled and got back up as Terra lifted pieces of the roof and threw them at him again, then stomped her foot onto the rooftop, splitting the ground they stood on. Ammo fell through the crack and into the open hangar of the warehouse they stood on. He blasted back up to meet her again, and she hit him upside his head with a beam. He grabbed the beam and blasted upward. He then threw the beam over the edge and toward the pavement. He saw Terra was trying to run toward the fire escape to get back on the ground. He shot a wired lasso her way and pulled her back. Terra felt shocked, and Ammo thought, *This is my chance!*

He blasted upward, and Terra came with him as she tried to untie herself from Ammo's grip. He shuttled faster than he ever had before and thought, *I wish Symone could see me now!* He looked below and noticed Cypher's megabot glowing like a Jubilee tree and kept climbing. Terra didn't realize what was happening, and before she could reorient herself, she couldn't feel Uretha anymore. Ammo saw two drones flying in their direction. The first one passed by him, and the second one stopped near him. Ammo unhooked the line and attached it to the drone.

"Intelligence, make sure she does not get near the ground until she is nullified by the Asylum. Drone, shield her now."

The drone delivered a barrier around the line and Terra to keep her from accessing the ground, and the drone floated away as Terra continued to struggle to break free from her bond.

The Emulator shook himself and looked at the wreckage in front of him as the room smoldered from the dragons' damage. He noted that Starburst and K.C. were no longer in the room and wondered aloud, "Where the fuck did you go?" He got up and looked at the hole in the ceiling and figured they left through there. Despite his long-term memory of Starburst, the Emulator's synapses and short-term memory began to forget K.C. and Starburst's power sets. He struggled to sustain flight and strained himself to clear the fifty feet necessary to get back onto the turf. He tumbled to one knee and breathed heavily. He created a star, but the star was deep red and could not be sustained. *Shit, where did they go?*

The Emulator examined the tunnels leading out of NextGen, and he saw the spotlights on him from UNN and the other media outlets. He couldn't decide where he should go but was determined to get his money from them.

K.C. and Starburst perched themselves in the skybox, uncloaked themselves, and told their uniforms to camouflage so they couldn't be seen. K.C. said, "So, got any plans after this?"

Starburst chuckled, "I see a date with my bed for sure."

"Mmm, that sounds nice. Want some company?" K.C. smiled as he recalled Starburst's erotic handiwork.

"I'd love some," a tingle traveled down Starburst's spine as her body and mind reminded her of K.C.'s bedroom prowess. "Know anybody who'd want to lay up with me?"

K.C. shrugged his shoulders. "I might know a guy."

"Ooh, who you thinking?"

K.C. snuck a peek at the turf below and pointed, "See that guy down there looking like a lost child? He might take you up on that."

Starburst nudged K.C. in his shoulder. "Asshole," she chuckled.

"Thought you might like that," K.C. grinned.

"No, I did not," she lied. She stared at the countdown in her visor. "Ugh, this is taking forever, two minutes left."

"Well, once they get here, it'll be game over."

They stared out of the box at the Emulator. He finally decided to try one of the tunnels to find K.C. and Starburst. He looked inside the water-damaged walkways and found no trace of the Elite. He wandered the hallways, the shopping plazas, and the food courts. He cut through some of the tape that blocked dangerous areas and still found nothing. "Where are you?! I want my fucking money!"

Just then, a black figure stood behind him. He smiled and turned around. "About damn time! I was starting to think you forfeited the fight. Wait, who the fuck are you?"

The black figure raised his hands forward, and plasma charged from his palms. Without flinching, the droid fired multiple blasts from his hands. The Emulator dodged the shots and quickly emulated what he saw. He extended his palms and shot out plasma as well, then thought, "Wait, this isn't star power! What the Frimas is going on?"

Just then, two more figures showed up. The first one had lighting swirling around it, and the second had massive muscles and tree trunks for legs. The lightning figure charged up and fired lightning strikes at the Emulator. He backed up and tried to study what he was seeing in front of him and summoned his own electricity and fired it back at the figures, missing them all. The plasma shooter blasted in the air to meet the Emulator. The Emulator quickly realized that he couldn't mimic rocket boosters for legs, and he backed up and ran toward the tunnel to get back to the turf. He stopped suddenly when nine more droids descended from the sky and marched toward him, each with a different power set, all aimed at him. He turned and noticed the first three had seventeen more with them, and each of them had a different power set.

The Emulator said, "Alright, let's dance." The Emulator tried to keep up with the few powers he had picked up, but he was unmatched as twenty-six swiftly turned into hundreds.

K.C. and Starburst saw the army arrive and move toward the tunnel opposite their skybox location.

"Alright, they're here, let's go," K.C. said.

"No, let's get it," Starburst corrected him playfully.

K.C. smirked. *I love her!*

Inside the abandoned hangar, the Eagle struggled to reset herself. She groaned, *Man, I didn't think this battle would be this hard.* She strained to peel her body off the ground. *This is probably my last shot. Okay, think, Eagle, think, what are you going to do?*

She unfolded her bow and shot several arrows at various spots on the walls, terraces, and scaffoldings. *I know his ass is gonna try to blow me away, so let me anchor myself.* She ran near the opposite side of the hangar and shot a grappling hook into the ground. She hooked herself and looped the line around her waist, then holstered the gun the line was attached to at her side. She then waited for Cyclone, and he entered through the wrecked window he shattered.

"Time's up, you're mine now," Cyclone triumphantly declared. He summoned a wind tunnel to blast the Eagle backward. The Eagle planted her legs in a defensive stance and withstood the wind. Cyclone pushed harder, and the wind intensified. Papers, dust, and debris flew across the hangar and slammed into the back of it. The Eagle slipped and fell to one knee. She tried to push herself back up, but the wind's intensity was too strong for her. Cyclone energized himself and pushed the wind even harder, and the Eagle slid and fell onto her back. The line locked into place but began to tear.

"Just a little bit longer," the Eagle grimaced. The line tightened against her cloak, and the cloak took on some damage. The hook in the ground loosened, and the Eagle could feel herself about to become an eagle for real.

The timer in her visor read, "5, 4, 3, 2, 1, Ready!" Suddenly, the sticks whirred and pointed lasers at Cyclone, unbeknownst to him. The Eagle reached for her grip, and as her line snapped, she flew away and pressed the grip. The sticks shot successive strikes at Cyclone, and Cyclone was pummeled. His cloak depleted rapidly. He tried to run back, but the lasers were locked on, and they kept firing. The wind ceased, and the Eagle fell and rolled onto the ground before reaching the wall. Cyclone's cloak shimmered and dissipated, and the lasers kept firing, slicing through Cyclone's body, piercing multiple critical organs. His soul left his body, and his corpse crumpled to the floor.

The Eagle stood up slowly and shook herself. She lamented Cyclone's demise, recalling the Defender's Oath, wishing things didn't have to end this way for him. She announced to the team, "Wind suspect eliminated. Tagging for the UPD." Her visor scanned Cyclone's body, and she then ran out of the building and back onto the street.

"Okay, Enchantra, I'm going to pull Ignatia away from here. You focus on Cypher's monster," Kaminari offered as she threw lightning bolts at Ignatia's attacks.

Enchantra started shaking her head. "No, I don't think I can do this," she doubted, worried about the powers inside her who longed to take over again.

"Enchantra, you can do this! *Alexia Montague*, you got this!" Kaminari boosted herself forward to engage Ignatia one-on-one. Kaminari released lightning daggers, and two of them hit Ignatia. Ignatia stumbled, and Kaminari charged her fists and went hands-on. Ignatia blocked Kaminari's punches, then punched Kaminari in the torso with a fire blast. Kaminari bent over and kicked Ignatia in the head with a lightning boot. Ignatia stumbled backward, and Kaminari supercharged her hands and blasted Ignatia with a shock bomb.

Ignatia screamed, "Aaaargh! Won't you give up?!" Ignatia created two lava blades and charged at Kaminari. Ignatia swung one blade, and Kaminari dodged to her right, she swung the next, and Kaminari dodged to the left. Kaminari pulled Ignatia into her, then blasted her feet to launch them into an alley.

Enchantra stared at Cypher and said, "Okay, you got this. You can do this. Just breathe." Enchantra inhaled deeply, then exhaled. She closed her eyes, and a voice said, *I bet we could do it better, come on, let us out! We can handle it.*

*We promise we won't lose control like the last time, Alexia, come on, you can trust us.*

"No, I got this! You two, shut up!" She pushed the voices into the corner of her subconscious, then imagined them in a green cage locked by her command.

Enchantra's eyes opened and glowed green within her visor. She folded her hands in a prayer stance. She then twisted her palms where the left overlapped the right, then twisted again where the right overlapped the left, then brought them back to prayer stance. She then quickly separated her hands, and a white crystalized prism ball appeared in between them.

Cypher noticed that Enchantra was about to perform some kind of assault, and she shot her left hand forward, and some of the scrap parts flung from her megabot toward Enchantra. Enchantra saw it and broke concentration. She discarded the encasement and threw energy storms at the molten scraps to evade getting hit. She then rose up and threw more energy storms at Cypher, and Cypher took damage. Cypher threw more scraps at Enchantra, and Enchantra dodged them. Cypher then activated every electronic unit within her reach, and dozens of machines, hovercraft, and drones obeyed her command to attack Enchantra. Enchantra spun a circle in front of her and behind her, and these circles became portals to a scrap heap outside the city limits. The machines all transported to the heap. Enchantra closed the portals and was met with a punch to her body by the bot that shuttled her one hundred yards back.

Frostbite shook himself as hard as he could to free himself from his own ice sculpture. He slowly manipulated the inner shell into brittle snowflakes, and he busted himself out. The Mammoth and Blitz turned the corner of the alley just as Frostbite caught them in his purview. Frostbite raised his arm to blast them both with a flash bomb when a pop hit his right shoulder and spun him around. The Eagle had fired her rifle, cocked it, and fired again, this time popping him in the chest. Frostbite aimed his arm at the Eagle, but then something white, hot, and heavy crashed into his helmet and knocked him down. Ammo then fired successive shots at him. Blitz grabbed the Mammoth again and said, "You ready for another ride?"

"Frimas yeah!"

Blitz spun him around and released him, and as Frostbite stood back up, the Mammoth crashed violently into his back and slammed his head into the pavement, knocking him un-conscious.

The Eagle called, "Intelligence, send the drone, tagging the culprit now."

Ammo landed on the ground. "You guys good?"

The Eagle said, "I'm good, how about you two?"

Blitz sped over to the group, "Yeah, I'm good."

"Ready to end this," the Mammoth declared. Everyone turned around and noted Cypher's glowing megabot.

"Alright, let's finish this," the Eagle declared just as a super-charged continuous lightning bolt descended to the ground four blocks from them.

Kaminari held onto Ignatia, and the lightning bolt dealt massive damage to her cloak. Ignatia began to charge herself and glowed with fire, dealing damage to Kaminari's cloak. Kaminari was determined not to let go, holding on with all her might and screaming, drawing more power to herself. The heavens rained down lightning strikes, damaging the ground, trash bins, and the buildings surrounding them. Ignatia dropped her swords and tried to push herself up off the ground, but she was overpowered by Kaminari's grip. Ignatia's cloak and molten lava shield were outmatched by the lightning storm. Her cloak shimmered and dissipated, and the lightning shocked Ignatia unconscious. Ignatia went limp, and Kaminari stopped the lightning strikes and rolled Ignatia off her.

Kaminari's visor warned her that her cloak's integrity was reduced to 27.3%. As she sat up, her teammates found her in the alley and ran toward her. "Kaminari, you good?" Blitz asked.

"Yes, I'm fine. Where are the others?"

"The Elements? Ice and water are tagged."

"Terrain is tagged, too," Ammo reported.

"Wind is dead," the Eagle declared.

"Whoa, you killed him?" the Mammoth inquired.

"Didn't leave me a choice," the Eagle announced.

"Well, fire is here, let's tag her and help Enchantra," Kaminari suggested.

"Here," the Mammoth extended his hand to Kaminari, "let's finish this."

The five-some dusted themselves off and rushed toward their final opponent.

The Emulator struggled to get free from the pile-up in the tunnel, but he dodged much of the army to get back on the turf. He blasted some of the bots with the power he picked up, yet more of them continued to showcase their skills. Some hit him with ice, others with fire, another grew into a giant, another teleported from one location to his to punch him in the face, then kick him in his side. The Emulator was completely overwhelmed, and his cloak's integrity couldn't keep up with the onslaught and fell dramatically. The Emulator was then hit with a continuous wave of star power, fire power, electricity, plasma, storm energy, and a host of other powers, and he fell on his back. The ground below him shifted and cuffed him to it so he could not move. The Emulator's cloak fell to 0, shimmered, and dissipated. The black bots stopped, and one bot walked up to him, shot its left arm out, and hovered a star next to his face.

Another black bot grabbed a piece of the star and hovered it over his head, also. The bots' uniforms changed colors, on the left black and blue, and the right crimson and gold.

"Yield," Starburst declared.

"So, couldn't beat me in a fair fight, huh?" the Emulator attempted to goad her.

"Who said anything about this being a fair fight? This is war. And in war, there's only winners and losers." Starburst pushed the star closer to his head. "Now, yield!"

"You do know I can feel your power coursing through me right now, right?" the Emulator taunted.

"You don't deserve my power," Starburst growled. At that moment, K.C.'s mind snapped as the echoes of his subconscious reverberated in his head.

*You don't deserve this power.*

*You don't deserve this power.*

*You don't deserve this power.*

*You deserve this power,* the sweet voice declared to him.

K.C. snapped back to reality and said, "Let's get his ass out of here. Droids, carry him to the Asylum. Barrier him, and make sure they put him in a nullifier ASAP. Kill order in place. If he so much as thinks of escaping, end him."

Four of the droids grabbed his appendages and cuffed themselves to him, then blasted away, with the rest of the army following behind like a flock of birds. Starburst hugged K.C., and he embraced her hard. "We got his ass," he declared.

"Yeah, we got him," Starburst sighed. "What about the others?"

K.C. thought to call the Eagle, "Eagle, this is K.C., how's it going on your end?"

The Eagle raised her fist to signal to the team to stop moving. "We've got one last big problem and we'll be code white."

"Need help?"

"No, *Director Bennett*, we got this," the Eagle declared. "You two finished with Xavier?"

"Yeah, he's on his way to the Asylum now. Finish the job, we'll see you back at HQ."

"Copy that." The Eagle disconnected the call. "Alright, Elite, let's get it."

Enchantra shook off the blow and continued throwing energy storms at Cypher. The rest of her crew turned the corner. The Eagle said, "Okay, Ammo, go up to the head and attack the beast from the top. I'll blast this thing from behind here. Blitz, use this line and bind the bot from moving. We'll chain it to this post here." The Eagle pointed her rifle at the asphalt beneath them and shot a spike into the ground. "Kaminari, take the front and blast him backward. Mammoth, anchor Enchantra. Enchantra, can you hear me?"

Enchantra threw more energy storms and said, "Yes, I can hear you!"

"Listen to me. I know you're scared. I read up on what happened to you the other day. You can do this. Don't worry about the past, we can't do anything about that right now. Focus on what's in front of you. End this shit now! Everybody, move!"

Blitz took the line from the Eagle and speedily jumped over parts of hovercars, lamp posts, ATM machines, microwave ovens, and the like to wrap the line around one leg, then the other, then the right arm, then the left, then the torso, then the head, then spun from head to anus, then back to the Eagle and latched the line. "Secure," she answered.

Ammo blasted upward and began firing at the head of Cypher. Cypher looked upward and tried to swing her arm but was stuck in Blitz's line. The Eagle drew her bow and fired several arrows at the megabot, and pieces fell off bit by bit with each successful shot. Kaminari blasted in front of the megabot and unleashed a lightning storm at the front of the machine, and more parts fell off the machine. The Mammoth ran quickly to Enchantra and said, "I got you, do your thing, Enchantra!"

Enchantra closed her eyes and breathed deeply once more. She opened her green-glowing eyes and placed her hands in prayer stance. She twisted one palm over the other, then the other over the first, then put them back in prayer stance again, then popped them to where the prism appeared once again. "Mammoth, throw me between her legs!"

"The Frimas?"

"Do it!"

The Mammoth grabbed Enchantra by her elbows and spun around ten times, then let her go. Enchantra whisked past Kaminari, slipped in between Cypher's legs, and yelled, "Encasement!" She threw the prism upward, and Cypher's bot was enveloped until there was nothing left but a white crystal prism ball twelve stories high. Blitz caught Enchantra and slowed her momentum. Enchantra, with her arms still wide, strained her arms, and the prism began to shrink. She strained until the ball became the size of a zintol.

The Elite walked up to the prism. Enchantra said, "Hey, Ammo, got anything that can hold this?"

Ammo opened his left palm, and a black box released from his hand. He gave it to Enchantra, and it increased in size to fit the parameters of the prism. Enchantra closed the box with the prism inside it, then said, "Intelligence, send a drone, tagged at this location. Cypher's inside."

"Wait, Cypher's inside it?" Ammo wondered.

"Yeah, I felt her, or at least her cloak anyway, inside the giant."

"That means—" the Mammoth started.

"Intelligence," the Eagle said with a sigh of relief, "we're code white. Elite, let's get the Frimas out of here.

# 26

# The Verdict

Snores broke the silence in Karl's bedroom. The gentle giant slumbered, his mind requiring a shutdown his body rarely needed. Karl lay flat on his back, starfished across his bed, ignoring the sunlight of the three suns flooding his room as he slept. His arm buzzed, and the stripe lit blue. Karl rolled his eyes as his lids cracked. He slipped into consciousness and slowly lifted his arm to see who was disturbing him. The marquee scrolled, "CALL FROM JENNA."

Karl retrieved the call and through a soft, cracking voice said, "Great rising, Jenna."

The voice on the other side of the call chuckled, "Great rising, indeed, Karl."

Karl closed his eyes and resumed his motionless position in the bed, "How are you? How are the kids?"

"I'm great, the kids are great. How are you?"

"Oh, I'm good, still in bed," Karl yawned.

"I figured as much, I saw the news, that was you and your team out there last night, right?"

"Yes, ma'am, that was us."

"You guys kicked ass, I'm so proud of you all. You could have called last night, though, to tell me what was happening."

Karl cleared his throat, "I know, but it was late, and I didn't want to worry you."

"You know I'm always going to worry about you, Karl. I know what..."

"...you signed up for," Karl finished, "I know. I'm sorry. It was an incredibly long day and night, and by the time all the fighting was finally done, I crashed."

"Yeah, well, I'm glad you're okay. The news anchors can't stop bragging on you guys. You all put on a Frim of a show, apparently."

Karl chuckled as he shuffled his legs a little, "Yeah, well, that was all Malcolm's idea. Since they kept putting themselves in the spotlight, figured what's one more show."

Jenna laughed, "True, gave them their money's worth. So, what are you guys doing today? Debriefing?"

Karl rolled and looked at his clock on the right nightstand. It read 01:49. Karl replied, "I don't think we're debriefing, not with the vote happening today. But I probably should be glued to the holoscreen with the crew soon to see how that vote goes."

"Well, then, you should probably get out of bed so that you don't miss it. It's going to begin in ten minutes."

Karl fought against gravity to drag his massive torso upward and planted his feet on the cold tile. "Ugh, fine," he stretched his arms and back. "Kiss the kids for me."

"Karl, we miss you. I miss you. When are you coming home?"

"After today, I'll ask for some time off so we can be together, I promise."

"I'm gonna hold you to that, Karl. I love you," Jenna declared.

"I love you, my queen. I'll call you later tonight."

"Alright. Have a great day, my king."

The call disconnected. Karl methodically rolled his shoulders then his neck. He stood up, grabbed his robe from the bench, slid into his slippers, and proceeded out his residence. He heard bantering in the commons. Symone was stretched across the couch on the right, sitting in between Malcolm's legs with her locs against his chest. He softly caressed Symone's exposed stomach with his fingers while she ran her fingers through his hand. Malaysia, Joy, and Duncan sat on the couch facing the holoscreen, while Alexia and Daisy anxiously awaited the start of the Senate meeting in the recliners on the left. Malcolm and Symone were dressed in street gear while the others were in pajamas and gym clothes.

"Did I miss anything?" Karl asked.

"There he is!" Malcolm joked. Everybody cheered as he continued, "No, just UNN talking about us and the vote that's going down in the next few minutes."

Karl sat in the recliner next to Malcolm and Symone's couch and said, "Turn it up, I wanna hear what they have to say."

Malaysia lifted her bare arm and turned the volume up on the holoscreen.

UNN displayed scenes of their last battle as the news anchor narrated, "...as the Company's Elite dispatched the Outlier group who was allegedly hired by the Roots to sway the vote against giving the city the opportunity to decide whether to allow the powered to hold offices in Uri City government. One of the Outliers was killed in the incident, the others were all apprehended and transported immediately to the Asylum for the Uncontrollable, and miraculously, no civilians were hurt in the attack."

Karl declared, "Yeah, we put in that work last night."

"Damn right, we did," Duncan agreed.

"Shit yeah!" Joy put her hand up, and Duncan slapped her a high-five.

UNN continued, "Now, we are moments away from what remains of the Senate entering the chamber and beginning their emergency meeting. As we've reported earlier, over half the senators were arrested on several charges. Only forty of the ninety senators remain in the Senate, and they will decide the fate of the bill in just a few minutes."

"Guys," Alexia spoke, "what if it was all for nothing? What if they decide to kill the bill anyway?"

"We did everything we could, Alexia," Malaysia answered as UNN cut to the street view of the Senate chamber. People picketed along a secure barrier line erected by the UPD. "All we can do now is hope that they do what's best for the city. Whatever they decide, Uri City will be fine."

"True that. We kicked ass and protected the people. Hopefully, that was enough," Symone chimed in. "And even if it's not, people like Mitchell will keep fighting the good fight until we win."

"Alright, here we go, here we go," Karl pointed at the screen as UNN cut to the live feed of the senators entering the chamber. The chamber was round, and the seats cascaded from the blue illuminated walls. Two crossing walkways split the seats into four quarters. A massive desk with three seats and a podium demarked the end of the vertical walkway. The senators entered the chamber from the three entrances and took their seats. The majority of the seats in the chamber were barren, noticeable to even the most casual viewer of UNN.

"Now entering the chamber is Vice Chancellor Royce, Overseer of the Senate," the UNN news anchor narrated. "He will take the middle seat at the desk, with Senators Wimberly and Dariuz, who are walking down the middle aisle now, sitting to his left and right respectively. This meeting is on the heels of the victory scored by the Company's Elite last night, and many wonder whether that battle, the arrests of the Roots organization, and the intel received by the Uri City Police Department will have any sway on the Chamber one way or the other. Here's Vice Chancellor Royce, who is now ready to initiate the meeting."

Vice Chancellor Royce, a slender, light-skinned man with a crew cut hairstyle, slid his chair forward and began speaking. "Greetings, salutations, and great rising to you all today. If there are no objections, this meeting is considered in session. Before we get started, I want to personally thank you all for attending this meeting, and I want to thank those of you who are watching today, as we continue to demonstrate to our enemies, both foreign and domestic, that we will continue the essential and necessary work to uphold our oath to govern Uri City to the best of our ability.

"I want to thank Commissioner Catalina and the Uri City Police Department for their incredible work to thwart the efforts of, who we have just learned last night are, the Roots. Chancellor Croft and the Executive Office of Uri City are working in collaboration with the UPD to ensure that these criminals are prosecuted to the fullest extent of the law, and we will not rest until every piece of the Roots is dismantled and, as they said last night, uprooted.

"Lastly, I want to thank the Uri City Division of the Company and their Elite Unit of Defenders, who, once again, have successfully defended this city from the tyrannical efforts of the Outliers hired by the Roots to undermine the work that we have been doing for their various benefits. We owe an incredible debt to the Elite Unit, and I believe I speak for everyone in this chamber, as well as Chancellor Croft, when I say that if not for the efforts of those eight individuals, we would not be here today. We salute you, and we thank you."

"Damn, what an endorsement!" Joy leaned back in her chair and played with her hair. Her team nodded and whispered in agreement.

"Today, we are meeting to vote on whether to put Proposition 1 – 'Should the powered citizens of Uri City be allowed to run for any office and hold any position within in the Uri City government?' – on the ballot in the general election. Despite the bevy of intel we have received from the Uri City Police, and the arrest of fifty of our very own senators, this Senate still believes it is prudent to discuss the matter, make final recommendations, and vote to put this matter to rest once and for all. We have agreed that the two bastions of the subject – the Gentlewoman Senator Deborah Wimberly from the Leicester District, and the Gentleman Senator Martin Dariuz from the Highgarden District – will each speak. Afterwards, we will pause for a five-minute break, then reconvene for the final vote on the matter.

"If there are no objections, we recognize Senator Wimberly, who will take the podium and speak."

Senator Wimberly got up from her seat and walked around the table to the podium about ten feet ahead of it. She pressed a button on the podium, and her face shone on the oversized holoscreen on the wall behind them for everyone in the chamber to see her clearly. The UNN camera zoomed in on her.

Senator Wimberly began, "Great rising, Senators, and thank you Vice Chancellor Royce. These past couple weeks have been among the tensest in Uri City's recent history. We have witnessed violence and the threat of violence on a level we could not have foreseen nor expected, and it is the work and dedication of our police department and our contract defenses that have kept our citizens safe. For that, I am personally grateful and say thank you to everyone who has stood in the fray for the defenseless.

"Make no mistake, the Outliers who terrorized our city were not some mere blip on the radar. They were part of an orchestrated attempt to maintain control of the population birthed from division among us. We have evidence now that there are many people across the economic, political, and social landscapes who want to keep the powered under submission, and their beliefs infiltrated our work here in this Senate and created a divide between us. We were so blinded by that divide, we couldn't see the emergence of the Roots and their deployment of the Outlier group who wrongfully, sinisterly guised themselves as the Powered Order Coalition to further the agenda that the powered should be controlled, not celebrated.

"Some of us in this hallowed chamber fought tirelessly to keep the powered in 'their place,' shamelessly using the events that took place over a century and a half ago as the weak, feeble justification for keeping the powered in check. But these same people then ask, no, *demand* that the powered entertain us with their skills on the zintol field, fight in our wars when artillery alone can't win our battles, and defend us *with their powers* when other powered individuals try to impose their will upon us. No one can explain to me how it makes sense for us, the unpowered, to demand that the powered answer our every request, but then tell them that they cannot speak for themselves – as if we, the unpowered, are the final authority over their lives.

"When we were at the mercy of these Outliers over the past couple weeks, it wasn't ordinary, unpowered citizens who stopped them. It wasn't the UPD's firepower that stood in the gap. When Senator Berkeley was kidnapped, none of us in this chamber picked up a gun to hunt them down and rescue our fellow lawmaker. The biggest military force on Uretha couldn't intervene when the Senate chamber was under threat of demolition. And not a single unpowered person could have done a damned thing about the Outliers last night.

"No, it was the Defenders, the Elite Unit of the Company, the *powered*, who saved us *again*. Sure, they're contracted, and the city pays them for their services, but they still *willingly* put themselves in harm's way time after time without hesitation. They, too, have sworn an oath to use their whole might to defend this city with their lives, and they keep their oath, despite being treated as second-class citizens by their government and the very citizens they fight for."

"That's what I've been saying for years!" Alexia broke her silence.

"For decades, we have acted like the powered are the ones who should be held in check. But let's be honest. After yesterday's devastating revelation, the unpowered clearly aren't any better, and maybe we're the ones who should have been held in check all along. Just because we don't have superpowers doesn't mean we don't wield power, and many of the unpowered flexed their power to influence us to bend to their will. Here's the reality: it's not powers, special abilities, money, or influence alone that corrupts a man. The heart of man, the character of the man who wields the power, that is what sways him to corruption.

"Let me say it again. It's not superpower alone that corrupts, but the character of the one who wields it."

"Damn, talk about bars!" Malcolm's eyes widened.

"I second that," Symone agreed.

"I declare," Wimberly continued, "that we must restore full rights to the powered. We cannot continue to hold the powered to the same laws and statutes as the unpowered while denying them the ability to speak for themselves and be represented by those who are powered like them. I, therefore, recommend to the Senate chamber that we vote 'yes' to put Proposition 1 on the ballot during the general election. Thank you. Vice Chancellor, I yield the floor back to you." Wimberly pushed the button on the podium to silence the microphone, and her body disappeared from the holoscreen.

Alexia, Malaysia, and Symone clapped their hands as Vice Chancellor Royce said, "Thank you, Senator Wimberly. We now recognize Senator Dariuz, who will take the podium and speak."

"Here we go," Alexia rolled her eyes and leaned back in her chair.

Senator Dariuz rose from his seat as Senator Wimberly walked back to hers. Dariuz walked to the podium, and after pressing the button, his face shone on the holoscreen. He began, "I want to thank the Uri City Police Department and the Elite Unit of the Uri City Division of the Company for their valiant efforts to keep this city secure. Theirs is not an easy job, but they have taken it on, and we are forever in their debt.

"Despite everything that has been revealed to us over the course of the past several cycles, my position on this matter remains unchanged. I do not believe that the powered should be allowed to enter city government. The events of over a century and a half ago cannot be overlooked or ignored. I fear that we have not learned the lessons from the past and are rushing to give the powered more power than they can handle.

"But that has been my problem, and apparently, the problem of several of our contemporaries in the Senate and across the social, economic, and political landscapes of Uri City. And instead of using the proper mechanisms to exercise judgment from legitimate concerns, they used those concerns and manufactured fear, then weaponized that fear to maintain power and control. I do not believe in that."

"Wait," Alexia popped up, "what is happening?" The team stared at the screen trying to make sense of Senator Dariuz's statements.

"No way," Joy murmured.

Malaysia's eyes flickered. "Yeah, I think it's happening."

"Don't you dare speak like that," Daisy challenged Malaysia.

"It's no surprise that some of us in these seats of power are corrupt and will do anything to stay in power. The Roots is proof of that. And we cannot tolerate anyone who takes advantage of the people of Uri City for their own agendas. Regardless of what side of an issue we stand on, we must always stand for the people we represent and never use our power to oppress anyone. I realized after last night that I, too, have been an accomplice to keeping the powered oppressed, and so today, I decide to drop my fear of what might happen and side with the powered."

"You're fucking kidding me!" Daisy screamed.

"You, *me!*" Alexia's jaw dropped.

"Though I am afraid that we may see what happened 150 years ago transpire again, I'd rather swallow my fear and do what is right than to continue nursing my fear and be a part of a scheme to oppress the very ones who have fought to keep us safe from all evil, both powered *and* unpowered. I, therefore, recommend to the Senate chamber that we vote 'yes' on Proposition 1 and allow the matter to be decided by the citizens of Uri City in the general election. Thank you.

"Vice Chancellor Royce, I yield the floor."

The Elite was stunned. The Senate chamber was silent as a morgue. Vice Chancellor Royce looked just as stupefied and took a moment to regain his composure before saying, "Thank you, Senator Dariuz. The Senate chamber is now in a five-minute recess. We will reconvene in five minutes to vote on the matter."

The UNN news anchor narrated, "The Senate is now in a five-minute recess after an unexpected and explosive twist in the Proposition 1 saga. Senator Dariuz just recommended to the chamber that they vote in favor of Proposition 1 going to the general election ballot, after fighting for years as the face of the opposition of the bill. He stated his fear was weaponized to oppress the powered in Uri City and will no longer allow it to be. We can imagine that he will vote 'yes' on the bill, but it is still anybody's guess whether the chamber will agree with Senators Wimberly and Dariuz."

"I'm just, just, shocked right now," Daisy stammered, exasperated and stunned. "I never would have guessed he would side with Wimberly. I'm so confused."

Malaysia reached over and tapped Daisy's arm. "I told you, Daisy, Dariuz is a good man. He doesn't choose sides just to choose sides."

"But he's allowing the powered to hold offices again. What if what happened back then happens again?"

"Then we'll stop them," Duncan declared. "It's that simple, Daisy."

"Yeah," Karl concurred. "The eight of us, the Elite, we are unstoppable together. There's no opposition we can't overcome. Period. Let a powered Chancellor try to take the city over. He or she will have to go through us to do it."

"Without hesitation," Malcolm said.

Daisy buried her head in her hands. She didn't want to hear it, nor did she want to admit to them that they were right. She blitzed to her residence, bitter that her hero had let her down. She jumped in her bed and planted her head in a pillow.

The five-minute recess ended, and the senators returned to the chamber. Wimberly and Dariuz were now among the waned crowd of forty, and Vice Chancellor Royce sat alone at the desk. "The meeting is back in session. In the next two minutes, your holoscreens will display the question, and you will have ninety seconds to make and confirm your vote. After the ninety seconds are up, the results will instantly post on the holoscreen behind me, I will read the results, and we will have concluding remarks and adjournment. The vote reads as follows: 'Should Proposition 1 – 'Should the powered citizens of Uri City be allowed to run for any office and hold any position within in the Uri City government?' – be placed on the ballot in the general election of 5724?' The options are 'yes,' 'no,' and 'undecided.' Senators, the vote is on your screens, and your ninety seconds begin now."

The forty senators scrolled to their choice and voted on the matter. The Elite sat with anxiety churning in their stomachs, aching to know whether their hard work over the past two weeks was worth it, or if the Emulator and the Elements had indeed completed their mission.

Ninety seconds expired, and the vote instantly appeared on the holoscreen. Vice Chancellor Royce looked at his holoscreen and read, "On the matter at hand, the Senate voted 40 yes, 0 no, and 0 undecided."

Alexia roared, and Malaysia, Duncan, and she jumped from their seats. The others roared loudly, knowing that the Senate just delivered the deathblow to the Emulator and the Elements' plan.

Royce continued, "Proposition 1 will be included on the ballot of the 5724 general election, and the citizens of Uri City will decide whether to allow the powered to run for offices starting in the 5726 Senators Elections, as well as allowing the powered to apply for positions within the city government. These results will be entered into the record and are viewable on the Uri City government website. If there are no objections, this concludes our meeting, and we are adjourned."

"Yeaaaaaaaaaaaaaaaaaaaah!" Alexia cheered along with her comrades.

Malcolm leaned his head back and sighed, relieved and excited. He sat in gratitude to Akan that their work, from NextGen to their final confrontation, was not in vain. Malcolm tapped Symone, and she lifted off him. Malcolm lifted his leg and twisted to get up from the couch. "Hey, where you going?" Symone inquired.

"I'm going to talk with Mallack real quick, see how she's feeling about all of this. I can't believe it, we won, babe, we actually won!" Tears welled up in his eyes.

"I know, we did it, Malcolm, we did it!" Symone agreed. She noticed his eyes slightly tinting red. "Aww, are you about to cry?"

Malcolm sniffed and said, "No, no I'm not. I'm just really happy for us all. I'll be back."

"Okay," Symone leaned in and kissed Malcolm's lips, then whispered in his ears, "It's okay to cry."

Malcolm got up and walked to the exit. He looked back at the team and noted their jubilation, but also noticed someone was missing from the celebration. "Hey, somebody check on Daisy, make sure she hasn't passed out on the floor or something."

"I got her," Karl said.

# 27

# Parting Ways

Malcolm hesitantly traversed the corridor to Director Mallack's office, his gut churning, injected by a bottomless supply of anxiety. His mind was deeply submerged in paranoia, unsure whether this conversation was even worth having with his boss. Keeping up appearances was the only play he had in his book, and he was terrified that someone would recognize that he wasn't acting like himself and call him out on it. *Don't fall apart. Not today. Hold it together just a little while longer. We're so close to getting answers.*

Malcolm knocked on the door. "Come in," Mallack answered on the other side. Malcolm slowly swung the door open, and Mallack recognized him, "Hey, Malcolm. I knew I'd see you today."

Malcolm noticed the emptiness of her office. Most of her trinkets and books that personalized her office were removed from her desk and bookshelf, her years of directing and leading the Uri City Division of the Company reduced to a shrinkbox on the floor. Surprise flushed Malcolm's face, and Mallack noticed it immediately.

"Yeah, not what you're accustomed to seeing, right?" Mallack inquired.

Malcolm fought back tears and ran his fingers across his textured hair. *Damn, she's really leaving.* "Right, this is so weird. Director, are you sure about this?"

"Never been surer. I'm going home! This is the best feeling I've had in a long time," Mallack answered as she pointed to Malcolm's favorite seat in her office. Malcolm sat down as she continued, "Brilliance isn't as exciting as Uri when it comes to battles and all that—"

"—because nothing bad ever happens in Brilliance, boss," Malcolm blurted out.

Mallack chuckled, "You're right. But I get to be among my family and friends again. I love you all, *and* I'm excited as Frimas to be going home."

Malcolm nodded his head and smiled, "I'm happy for you, boss, really."

"Speaking of happy, outstanding job on the Emulator and the Elements yesterday. That was an incredible show of force and precision, impressive on a level I can't begin to describe. I've gotten calls from the Chancellor, the UPD Commissioner, and the lawmakers – the ones we have left, anyway – and they all can't stop raving on how pleased they are that things went so well."

"I can't imagine they are pleased about learning that half the who's who in Uri have been plotting against the powered like this."

Mallack nodded. "You are definitely right about that, and the fallout from rooting out the Roots we've barely begun to feel. But Uri has been through far worse than this, and I'm sure it will recover stronger than it ever has before."

"True. Thank you, Director, for believing in us," Malcolm put his hands on his knees.

"Thank you, for letting me lead you. You always stand for what is right and what is best for the city, and it shows. When you take my place in a couple days, I'm confident that the Company *and* Uri City will be in excellent hands."

Malcolm grimaced as he slowly tapped the left armrest twice with his fist. Mallack knew that Malcolm wanted to get something off his chest. She squinted her eyes and peered at him. She then inquired, "Malcolm, what's wrong?"

Malcolm's emotional reservoir was bursting as he struggled with his feelings. He wanted to spill his guts but wondered, *She couldn't be, but she might be. I can't.*

"Mallack," Malcolm began, "I have to do something, but I don't know if I should do it."

"Why aren't you sure?" Mallack pressed to help Malcolm arrive to the conclusion he needed to get to.

"If I do this, then I run the risk of changing everything, messing everything up. What I have to do could change my whole life and the lives of everyone I'm connected to."

Mallack raised an eyebrow. "What do you mean, Malcolm?"

"Well, if I decide to do this, I risk everything I've worked so hard to accomplish in my life, everything I have, all of my relationships. I could ignore it and just pretend that what I know is just a figment of my imagination, but I would always second guess everything and wonder 'what if,' and that, I am sure, I couldn't sit with forever."

Mallack noticed the tension rising in Malcolm's chest, could see lines forming along his forehead. She recalled the first day meeting him several years back and realized that those same fissures had become more defined as the years went by. *Malcolm will always have a terrible poker face. He can't help but show his emotions, even when he's trying to hide them. He'll never fully trust me, but it's good to know that he's leaning into the fact that he doesn't have to struggle alone.*

Mallack responded, "Malcolm, I know you are struggling right now, and for your personal reasons, you're not going to tell me what you're struggling with or why. All I have to offer is this." She leaned forward and planted her elbows on her desk. "One thing I have always admired about you is your instinct. It has never steered you in the wrong direction. Even when all has looked bleak and grim, your instinct has always led you right. So as your boss, your colleague, and your friend, I advise you, trust yourself. Trust your instincts and go with Akan. Do what you have to do, and trust that no matter the outcome, you will be fine. Even if everything goes to shit, you have the power to climb out of the pit."

Malcolm's eyes watered. *How does she do that? Know exactly what to say? Every single time?* His voice cracked as he said, "Thank you, Director."

"Come here, Malcolm," Director Mallack stood up and waved her hands toward her. Malcolm walked to the other side of her desk, and they hugged each other. The dam burst, and Malcolm shed a few tears. Mallack heard him sniffle, and a tear started falling from her eyes. "You're going to be fine, Malcolm. You got this, okay?"

"Yes, Director," Malcolm reacted. They backed up from each other, and Mallack wiped the tear from her face. "Now, get out of here before you make me cry for real. Go do what you have to do."

Malcolm composed himself and asked, "Hey, are we debriefing today?"

"No, I figured I'd give the team the day off, and we'll get back together tomorrow," Mallack answered.

"Okay. Then I'll see you tomorrow, Director," Malcolm walked away from her desk and headed out the door.

"If Akan wills it, Director Bennett," Mallack responded.

Malcolm stopped at the door, turned to look at her, and smiled. He then opened the door and walked out of the office.

Mallack sat back down. She closed her eyes and sighed. She opened her top left drawer and retrieved a silver pocket watch with nine Chioro symbols etched on the front and back sides. She popped the clasp, and inside, the watch ticked frenetically, with several hands rotating counterclockwise at various speeds. She nodded at the watch as she mentally counted the denominations, closed her eyes, then softly, slowly declared, "And here we go."

Malcolm turned to the right and was surprised to see Symone walking down the corridor from the quarters. Symone saw him and sped up to meet him.

"Hey babe," Symone said.

"Hi Symone," Malcolm returned. They met at the elevator, and Malcolm squeezed Symone tightly and kissed her fervently. Symone was shocked and nearly turned into a puddle from his surprise embrace.

She pulled her lips from his and shivered delightfully. "Well, somebody's happy to see me! Did you just leave from Mallack's office?"

"Uh, yeah," Malcolm replied as he released her, "just finished talking to her."

"Okay," Symone hit the down button. "How did that go?"

"It went fine, just did a debrief. She gave us the day off and said she would meet with all of us tomorrow."

"That's great, I know the others will be happy about that."

"Got that right. Hey, how is Daisy? Still recovering from shock?" Malcolm chuckled as the elevator door opened.

Symone laughed as they walked through, "Man, listen, I'm sure Karl used his *Mammoth* power to peel her off the carpet, her pitiful self."

"I can imagine it's hard to watch your hero lose like that, huh?" Malcolm analyzed.

"Lose?  What do you mean?" Symone pondered.

"Anybody with enough sense could tell that Dariuz didn't want to say any of the shit he said at the podium."

"Damn, for real?  You think he was playing with Uri City?"

"Damn right, I do.  He lost all his allies last night, so to re-coup his losses – and get ready for the next election – he made it *sound like* he didn't want to be viewed as an oppressor. He voted yes so that his district remembers him in the next election when his seat is up for grabs."

Symone laughed, "I never even considered that, Malcolm. How do you come up with this stuff?  That's genius!"

"It's politics," Malcolm reasoned, "and politics is theater. It's all one big fat show.  What do people with power want? More power.  And when that power is threatened, people will do whatever they need to do and say whatever they need to say to keep it.  Martin Dariuz hasn't changed.  He just showed people like Daisy that all it takes is the right set of circumstances to push a person in a particular direction, just like the Emulator, the Elements, and the Roots all tried to do."

"You think we did all of this for nothing?" Symone sec-ond-guessed the team's efforts as the elevator stopped at the garage and the doors opened.

They walked out as Malcolm continued, "Aww, Frimas naw, we did the right thing by exposing their asses and getting them locked up.  But we can't think for one minute that it's over.  We caught this group, but there's another one coming.

And they'll trim the loose ends that the Roots left dangling for someone like Dredge to find and pull on. And before long, we'll find ourselves in a similar situation again. And when that happens, we'll do what we always do: respond in kind."

Symone's eyes flickered, and a tingle rode down her spine, "Damn, Malcolm, I love it when you talk dirty to me."

"Oh, ho, ho, is that right? Come here," Malcolm pulled Symone into him and planted a long, deep kiss on her lips. Symone wrapped her wrists around Malcolm's neck while Malcolm wrapped his arms around the small of Symone's back. Malcolm longed for this moment to last forever and grew terrified all over again that he might be ruining them by chasing down his lead, even with Mallack's blessing. They locked lips for a few seconds, then backed their faces away from each other as they held onto each other. "Wait, we're in the garage, you going somewhere?"

"Yeah," Symone answered, "I'm going to the Asylum to talk to Jason."

"Man," Malcolm lifted his head up and smiled as he looked back at her, "I wish I could be a fly on that wall when you give him the business one more time."

"You could come with me, though I don't think he'd be as forthcoming with you there. I wouldn't mind the company," Symone said as they began swaying in each other's arms.

"No, no, I'm actually going to my parents', we're overdue for a 'lunch and chat,' so I'm gonna head out there since we have a free day."

"Oh, cool, cool. Well, listen, once we both get back, let's take the rest of the day, just you and me. We can do whatever you wanna do," Symone looked at Malcolm, her eyes aglow from a heart filled with joy and peace.

"I'd love that.  Let's meet back here in the quarters," Malcolm agreed.  He released Symone, circled his wrist, then drew a line from his wrist to his elbow, summoning his hoverbike.  Symone did the same.  Their bikes met them.  Symone pulled Malcolm into her and kissed him passionately one more time.  They then released each other and straddled their bikes.  Their bikes revved up, and they blasted out of the Company's garage bay into the bright skyline.  They separated, Malcolm pushing toward Meridian, and Symone in the direction of the Leicester district, toward the outer rim of Uri City.

## 28

# Symone × Jason
# Redux

Symone soared high, bathing in the suns' rays as they kissed her body. Her mind vacillated between the joy reverberating in her chest from an echo chamber of love growing between Malcolm and her, and the frustration brewing in her mind from the mystery behind her ability to enhance others' powers. But she wouldn't let that vacillation ruin the thrill of motoring through Leicester's skyline. She breathed deeply and revved up her bike to propel faster.

The skyscrapers lessened in their height, and soon, Symone saw the outer rim of Uri City. The one-hundred-foot wall marked the separation between the city itself and its outer municipalities. Symone got in line behind others who were leaving Uri City through one of its gates and noted the UPD guard, a scanner a few feet high, and the security gate that scanned the vehicles as they passed through. Both the scanner and the security post repeatedly lit white for approval.

Eventually, it was Symone's turn. The UPD guard looked at Symone and attempted to not imagine strip-searching her as she gazed at her supple form. She requested, "Lift your arm up to the scanner, please."

Symone briefly examined the officer's uniform's red and white color scheme and thought, *Hmm, that color pattern would look good on me. Maybe not the white, though. Silver, maybe?* She lifted her arm to the scanner, and it scanned her stripe. The scanner sent the information immediately to the guard's holoscreen. She lifted it up to match the ID to Symone's face. The guard then stated, "Alright, Miss Watson. You are clear. Just hover through the gate and enjoy your time outside of the city."

"Thank you," Symone answered. She rode through the gate, and it lit white to signal to security that she was not carrying contraband. She then zoomed through the fifty-yard tunnel underneath the wall. She revved up once again and blasted above the lush green hills and farmlands of the outer rim. She inhaled the crisp, damp, grassy smell in the air and could tell that it recently rained. Herds of beasts tilled and consumed the land they tread upon, bellowing sweet melodies of life outside the hustle and bustle of the city. Symone briefly turned her head and marveled at the translucent dome that cloaked the city, seated atop the wall. She then refocused her attention to the road ahead of her and shuttled toward her destination.

Two miles ahead was the Asylum of the Uncontrollable, one of the most feared incarceration centers and most lauded training academies on Uretha. It was built for the sole purpose of containing those whose powers were considered extremely difficult to manage, or those whose motives were deemed a threat to society. The Asylum was a solid white fortress that stood three stories high, covered five square miles, and was buried twenty stories deep into Uretha's crust. The Asylum's security measures were heavily reliant on nullification technology – rumored to have been created to defeat and permanently subdue Chancellor Holland over a century prior – to render powered persons incapable of activating their abilities, for some a delight, while for others absolute torture.

Symone rocketed to the parking lot and landed toward the entrance. Symone walked toward the blacked-out glass panes that stretched twenty feet wide and scaled ten feet, and they slid automatically. Twenty feet in front of her was the reception desk surrounded by a translucent cloak. To her right and left were benches attached to silver walls. The room itself was bathed in white light, with black marble flooring touching her feet. She walked forward, and she was immediately greeted by a receptionist. "What can I do for you?"

"I'm here to see Jason Xavier. I'm with the Company," Symone answered.

"Ah, yes, my boss relayed to us that Director Mallack said he would be seeing someone from the Company today. We have him housed in Suite D. I'll let Sgt. Hibbett know you're here. He'll escort you to him. Just have a seat on the bench."

"Thank you," Symone responded. She turned and sat on the bench to her left and waited.

A moment later, a tall, slender man with a crew-cut fade walked from the corridor behind the desk. He was wearing a black cargo uniform and a tan-colored field jacket. His beady eyes locked onto Symone, and he asked the receptionist if Symone was the woman he was looking for. The receptionist nodded, and he walked around the desk to meet her.

"Symone Watson?" he posed.

"Yes, that's me," she stood up.

He extended his right hand and said, "Very nice meeting you, I am Sergeant Dante Hibbett." They shook hands as he continued, "You're here to see Jason Xavier, correct?"

"Yes, that's right," she replied.

"Great, come with me. I've cleared you for thirty minutes with him before he has to finish processing. We have him in a general nullified room, so you will not be able to access your powers in there, not that you would need them since he'll be behind a cloak. Come with me, please."

"Thank you, Sergeant."

Hibbett and Symone walked through the brightly lit corridor and passed by processing and classification rooms. Symone noticed through the windows to her left a small boy sitting at a kiddie table coloring pictures with markers. She grabbed Hibbett's arm. "Hey, wait, is that Jacob?"

"In there? Yeah, that's Jacob, from the Mega Mall incident."

Symone's mind flashed back to the incident and felt a sting in her heart. "Have they decided what they're going to do with him?"

"Not yet. He still has to go through classification. Psych is going to talk with him today and decide whether to send him to the academy or to lockdown."

"Oh geez. Any idea what direction they're swinging?"

"It's looking like the academy, but it's going to take him a while to process everything that happened to him that day before he gets to use his powers again. Killing his parents, a whole host of others, that's not easy for a kid to accept, especially since it's not his fault, you know?"

Symone sighed, "You got that right. The most I ever did was burn half my house down. I can't imagine going through what he's going through."

"Not to mention how the news anchors are painting him out to be some uncontrollable freak, like most of us in Uri City haven't gone through something similar when we first got our powers. They make us out to be monsters when we're really just beings in discovery of our whole selves."

Symone blinked twice. "That was very well put."

"I figured a lot of my shit out during my departmentally-mandated therapy sessions." They walked farther down the corridor and reached an elevator. Hibbett pushed the down arrow, and the elevator door opened. They walked in, and Hibbett pressed 3. He continued, "My therapist constantly reminded me, 'No matter what anyone tells you about who they think you are, their opinion of you cannot outweigh your own. *You* control the narrative of you. You, and no one else.'"

The elevator rushed down to the third floor below them and swiftly stopped. The door opened, and Symone and Hibbett walked down the white and gray corridor. Symone responded, "Well, we can only hope that someone drills the same sentiment into Jacob's heart. The world is going to try to rip his soul from him."

"Let them try. If the academy has anything to say about it, Jacob couldn't be in a better place to define himself and shape his destiny."

"Well, aren't you just a journal of wisdom!" Symone swooned.

They stopped at the fifth door to their left as Hibbett chuckled, "I do what I can. Anyway, here we are. You have thirty minutes to talk with him. Do you need help in there?"

"No, Sergeant, I'm good," Symone declared.

"Alright." Hibbett placed his hand on the palm reader, and the scanner lit white for approval. Mechanical locks whirred then popped, and the thick, heavy white door unlocked from the wall. Symone stood back, and Hibbett grabbed the hinge and slowly pulled the door open. "There's a red button on the back wall to your left. When you're ready to leave, press that button, and it will open the door."

"Thank you."

Symone walked inside the cyan room bathed in white luminance from the recessed ceiling lights about fifteen feet high. The door sealed shut, and she heard a low hum flowing through the walls. Symone felt slightly chilly and wondered where the air vents were. She looked up and noted the ducts in the corners of the room weren't blowing anything. She suddenly felt the fire in her veins cool down. *The nullifier,* she shivered, *it's doing its job.* She lifted her hand toward her face and attempted to create a star. Her palm barely glowed, and only two sparks shimmered then disappeared. She shivered and rubbed her arms, a frost she hadn't felt in decades chilling her bones. She lamented, *My Akan, I pray I'm never imprisoned, this is awful. I'd lose my shit if I ever ended up in a place like this. They'd have to put me in the psych ward. Let me hurry up and get my ass out of here.*

"Well, isn't this a nice surprise," a familiar voice quipped. Thirty feet in front of Symone, Jason stood behind a thinly veiled cloak, dressed in a red tracksuit and black boots. He stared at Symone and smiled. He licked his lips and slowly pranced toward her. Symone took note of his bravado and thought she was going to be sick.

He leaned onto the cloak in the middle of the room. "You missed me? Want to give me a conjugal visit before they lock me up for good?"

Symone noticed chairs along the right side of the room, picked one up, and sat it five feet from the cloak. "Give me a break, Jason. That ship sailed years ago." Symone sat down and crossed her right leg over her left as she ran her fingers vigorously through her locs.

Jason chuckled, "Clearly. I'm over here, and you're over there. So, what do you want?"

Symone sighed. "Jason, I know you have no reason to answer any of my questions, so all I can do is ask you and pray that you do. Were we ever real?"

Jason was stunned. He sat down in the seat on his side and responded slowly, "Were we ever real?"

"Yeah, Jason. Were you and I ever real?"

"How could you ask me that? Of course, we were real! You were the realest thing that ever happened to me!"

"Then what happened between us, Jason? Why did things fall apart the way they did?"

"Oh, you have got to be kidding me." Jason tapped at the cloak, pointing at Symone. "You. You're what happened to us."

Symone pointed at herself. "Me? What does that mean?"

Jason chuckled again and rolled his eyes, "Symone, everything about us revolved around you. Everything was always about what you wanted, and how you wanted it. *We* were never about us. You were the master and commander of our entire relationship. You talked a really good game about not wanting the spotlight, but you'd be damned if you didn't take it."

Symone was dumbfounded. She skimmed over the high- and lowlights of their relationship and couldn't figure out why he felt that way. "That doesn't make any sense to me."

Jason grew agitated. "Symone, when I wanted to move us out of Uri City, you said *you* didn't want to leave because your whole life was here. When I wanted to get out of prizefighting, *you* were the one who convinced me to stay because *you* didn't want to leave it behind. When I finally understood my purpose and wanted you to join me, *you* were the one who chose to live in mediocrity."

"Jason, your definition of 'purpose' required snuffing out people who didn't have powers. You were gifted, but you were never destined to lead people, let alone a revolution. I didn't want to leave Uri City because you didn't have a plan that made me feel safe. You wanted to leave prizefighting, but you hadn't had any money saved up to leave it behind, and I never felt comfortable being in a situation where I had to support the both of us, so, no, I didn't feel like it was the right choice to make."

Jason scoffed and threw his hands up. "That was always your problem, Symone. As much as you loved to be 'free and spontaneous,' you were never willing to take the leap, to take a real risk, a real chance. You always lacked faith in me."

"For someone who felt that way about me, Jason," Symone uncrossed her legs and leaned forward, "you sure did stick around for a long time. What, you thought I was going to change my mind? Had I not broken things off with you, would you had ever built up the courage to call it quits with me?"

Jason shot up out of his seat and paced away from Symone. "I didn't want to leave."

Something didn't add up in Jason's equation, and Symone was determined to pry the missing variables out of him. "Why not, Jason? There was nothing special about me that should have bound you to me. If I caused you that much misery, you could have just left me behind. Anything that I was to you, you could have easily found in another person. What made me so damn special that made you stay?"

Jason did the mental calculus, bent his head downward, and chuckled again. *She must think I'm stupid.* He then turned around and said, "So, you figured it out, huh?"

"Figured it out? Figured what out?" Symone pulled on a loc of her hair.

Jason turned around and walked toward Symone. "Don't play coy with me, Symone. You figured out how I evolved, didn't you?"

*Shit, I've been made. Okay, roll with it. Make him give it up!*

"Of course, I did. I'm not an idiot." Symone crossed her arms. "You figured out that my star power in its various forms caused you to change. But rather than tell me that, you kept that shit to yourself. And even though you wanted to run for the hills, you couldn't risk losing me – the source of your evolution."

"Damn right," Jason revealed.

"How long did you know?"

Jason scoffed. Symone was getting riled up, but her eyes didn't ember, which infuriated her even more. "Damn it, Jason, how long did you know?"

"I figured it out the second year of our relationship."

"Shit," Symone lamented. "So, for five fucking years, you siphoned as much power from me as you could, becoming better at emulating people and their powers. You gassed my ass all the way up, calling me your 'Guiding Light' and 'Lighthouse' and 'True North,' when all the while, you were just stealing from me. You fought me, shit, *fucked* me, just to level the fuck up!"

"Damn, Symone, you make me sound so heartless," Jason quipped.

*Fuck you, you prick!* "I'm still confused as Frimas because you tapped out. Your evolution reached max around, what, year four of our relationship? And that was around the same time you started talking all that shit about being superior to the unpowered. So, what were you still doing with me?"

"I wanted you to come with me. Don't you fucking get it? I wanted to run this town. And I knew that you were the key."

Jason's answer threw Symone slightly off track. "The key? The Frimas does that mean?"

Jason's annoyance with Symone's needlepointing made him want to put her in her place. "Symone, you're so fucking shortsighted, only concerned about what happens from one day to the next, one fight to the next, one relationship to the next. You can never see the bigger picture. Just like how you fucked everything up with our plan to get the vote to swing against the powered." Jason banged on the cloak. "You fucked the whole plan up!"

"What fucking plan, Jason?!" Symone screamed.

"Global domination! We had a plan to take the whole world. There are things going on behind the scenes that you can't even begin to fathom. The Roots, they're just one of several organizations and groups that are seizing control of the powered in this world, and we're tired of this shit! But as long as people like you are so fucking oblivious to this shit, we'll continue to be dominated by people who have for too long been allowed to run a world that is no longer theirs."

"That still does not fucking explain why you stayed with me all those years, Jason!"

"I stole your fucking energy! I figured out how your stars were affecting cloaks, and I found ways to reverse the polarities of the cloaks to cause others to evolve. For years, I did it to myself, and that's how I evolved. After I peaked, I started selling my cloaks to people who were part of the cause. That's what we needed those creds for, to manufacture the cloaks in a lab so that we would no longer need your star power to evolve. And once we had enough firepower in our arsenal, we were going to launch an assault on this world unlike anything anyone had ever seen before, and the unpowered would never again enslave us to do their bidding at our expense. You, your fucking boyfriend, and your team fucked that all up, and now we have to wait another decade to try again. There's a war coming, Symone. A war between gods and demons, unlike anything we've seen in the history of this galaxy. And you've just ensured that when it comes, we'll be three steps behind the opposition and fighting an uphill battle. And the blood will be on your hands. Can you live with that?!"

Jason's heavy breathing filled the void of silence as his voice reverberated off the frosted glass panes encasing the room. His eyes pierced Symone's body as he ached to snuff the life out of her. Symone's demeanor changed, no longer appearing as a spurned ex-lover. She melted the sadness off her face and stood up. Walking to the cloak, she smiled and said, "Thank you for your cooperation."

Jason was perplexed. "Wait, what?"

"What you did was fucked up, Jason. I had no idea that you did what you did. But now that we do, we now know how to dismantle the entire network of people who are using people like you to undermine the harmony of our globe."

Jason shook his head, confounded by Symone's assessment of how he assisted her. "I don't understand."

"Exactly, Jason. See, *you're* so shortsighted, you believe that people can't change. You're absolutely right. When we were together, I was living from day to day, moment to moment.

And sometimes, I still feel that way. But I have changed. And I, now, see the bigger picture. As long as there are people like you who believe that people should be dominated – powered or unpowered – there will always be people like me who will stand in the gap to stop them, powered or unpowered. No one should have their choices taken away from them. And now, knowing that there is a whole network of people like you in the world who are trying to dominate the unpowered, we can make our stand to ensure that if you're determined to try it, you're going to have to go through the *powered* to do it. And like you found out last night, you will lose. Every. Single. Time. Kay?"

Symone spun slowly and walked away. Jason realized that he was entrapped, and he took the chair and threw it at the cloak. The chair bounced off the cloak, and the cloak shimmered and sizzled in the place the chair hit. "Fuck you, Symone!"

Symone quipped, "You already did that, and look where it got you." She cracked a wry smile and lifted her left eyebrow as she pressed the red button. The door opened, and Symone pushed it slowly and stepped out of the room. She then closed the door and looked around. The corridor was empty, and Symone walked to the elevator. She pressed "UP" on the wall, and the elevator met her. She entered the elevator, and once it closed, she pushed the emergency stop button. She sat down, and she buried her head in her lap. Her thoughts and emotions flooded her all at once, and she let out a muffled whimper. The pain of knowing how Jason used her crystalized her belief that she may indeed have been the cause of known and unknown destruction within Uri City.

*It's my fault. It's all my fault. My power made him this way. Who else knows? Who else has used me? How has my power caused others pain? Why didn't I see it? How was I that blind? Was I really that self-absorbed? So self-centered that I couldn't see what was happening right under my nose? Damn it, Symone!*

Symone could feel her powers returning, and pain and fury churned in her veins. She quickly stood up and hit the emergency stop button again, and the elevator reached the first floor. The rage and fire continued to boil, and Symone's eyes began to ember, and her locs began to glow. The doors opened, and Symone levitated and swiftly flew through the corridor to the front door. The fire in her eyes began to singe around her eyelids, and once the front door slid open, Symone swiftly flew straight, then blasted into the sky. She climbed a mile high, and once she felt it was safe, a white aura emerged from her body, and her hair turned white. Her eyes widened and shined, and she unleashed a burst that ignited the sky, incinerating the clouds. Birds instinctively flew away from the heat wave, oxen and cows bellowed, and sheep shrieked from the thunderous boom.

Symone's hair color swiftly changed to jet black, and the aura around her body dissipated just as rapidly. She lost consciousness from the massive energy loss and plummeted toward the grassy terrain. Her stripe noted that she had blacked out and searched for her cloak button and found that Symone had placed it in her chest. Her stripe scrambled to decode the cloak, and once it cracked the code, her stripe simulated a double tap, and the cloaking nanites surrounded Symone's body just as she pounded the grassy knoll and bounced twice before landing chest down.

A cycle later, a couple zintols nudged Symone's lifeless body and nestled next to her. Symone could hear a ringing in her ear as the stripe pulsed a sonic signal to try to wake her up. Her eyes rolled, and she struggled to crack her eyelids. She noticed the grass she lay in and the suns still riding high in the sky. She felt the furry bodies lying next to her and could smell the crisp, clean air around her. She heard the wind rustling around her. She slowly rolled her body to sit up, and the zintols whined as they shuffled and sat next to her again. Symone held her head and noticed her body was in pain. She looked at her stripe and noticed what time it was. She tried to stand but realized that she was completely wiped out. She looked at her stripe again and asked it to shoot her with adrenaline.

About twenty seconds later, Symone felt energy rush through her veins, and her eyes widened. She stood up, and the pain subsided substantially. She then remembered all that Jason had told her, and she determined to return to the Company and talk to the Analyst. She summoned her hoverbike to locate her.

*That Affinity Theory is bullshit. I AM THE THEORY.*

# 29

# Homecoming

The Meridian district of Uri City was abuzz from the hustle of transit between the hovercars, buses, mass transit lines, and the powered-in-flight all zooming to their various destinations. City planners designed Meridian to be a series of neighborhood hubs nestled in between shopping, recreation and parks, and entertainment plazas throughout the district. They intended to make the hubs walkable, thus minimizing the need for heavy vehicle traffic. The planners, however, didn't anticipate the popularity of Meridian's spaces, and as the population swelled, so did the traffic – a beautiful problem in the eyes of the district managers that they did not concern themselves with trying to solve.

Thus, Malcolm zoomed deep into the heart of the Meridian district along with the thousands of patrons, employees, teenagers, and passers-through who shared the skies with him. As he drew near to his parents' home, he released the left handlebar and descended out of the main traffic line. He could see his neighborhood and floated down to street level. He passed by several picturesque driveways, then saw a familiar figure spraying water onto a red and purple flower garden. Sandra, Malcolm's mother, was wearing a spaghetti-strapped shirt and loose shorts, their light blue hue contrasting greatly with her ebony brown skin and short, wavy brown hair. Malcolm inhaled the smell of crisp grass and looked at the house he grew up in, the two-story brick-and-mortar home that served as a backdrop for many blurry memories Malcolm still had trouble unearthing.

Malcolm unsaddled his ride and disabled his cloak. Sandra turned to the side and noticed Malcolm walking toward her. "Malcolm! Well, what a surprise!" she exclaimed. She released the water nozzle and dropped it on the ground while walking over to him. "How are you?" She opened her arms, and they bear-hugged each other.

"I'm great, Ma, how have you been?" Malcolm returned.

"Wonderful, simply wonderful." They released each other, and Sandra held Malcolm's hands. "I am so happy to see you. Come on, let's go inside, your father will be so happy to see you, too!"

"He's here? Okay, good," Malcolm replied. Sandra released Malcolm's hands, and he followed her up the porch steps and through the black front door into the house. They stepped into the living room with the staircase about ten feet in front of them. The kitchen behind them was separated by a bar. His father's office was to the left of the front entrance.

"Alex?" Sandra called as she walked into the kitchen. "Your son is here!"

"Oh yeah?" A gruffy voice bellowed from upstairs. "I'm coming down, give me a minute."

Malcolm looked at the family pictures scattered across the walls of the living room. He motioned toward the couch, staring deeply at several moving snapshots of himself: on a swing set at a park, winning trophies at a school competition, molding sandcastles with his powers at a beach, standing with his family at graduation. He tapped his head a couple times as he grumbled, *Why am I having such a hard time remem-*

*bering all these things? I know I was there. Clearly, I was there for all of this.*

Soon, steps scurried down the staircase, and a husky, six-foot juggernaut yelled, "Malcolm! So good to see you, son!"

Malcolm turned around and saw his father Alex, who donned a grey t-shirt, shorts, and a pair of socks his wife made him wear to keep from catching a cold from the icy hardwood floors they walked on. They embraced each other. "Good to see you, too, Dad."

They let each other go, and Alex continued, "We saw you on the news earlier`, that was some legendary stuff, my boy! I am so proud of you."

Malcolm scratched his head, "Really, this time around we didn't do anything spectacular. Intellect won out."

Alex patted Malcolm's shoulder and motioned him toward the kitchen, "A win is a win, however you achieve it. Brute strength, intelligence, however you manage to keep this city safe, you do it well. We are all indebted."

"We really are proud of you, thank Akan every day for protecting and keeping you safe while you and your friends take on the problems in the city," Sandra added as she pulled bowls from the refrigerator.

"Thanks, guys," Malcolm said, the little kid in him appreciating his parents' pat on the back. As he slid his stool back from the bar, he watched his mom pull plates from the cabinets. His dad mimicked him, and they sat side-by-side.

"So, to what do we owe the pleasure, my boy?"

Pride swiftly turned into dread. Malcolm felt a void deep in the pit of his stomach, like he had been punched, scared to open the can of worms, but fully aware that there was no turning back. "Well, Dad, I've been trying to figure something out, and nothing I've come up with has made any sense. So, I wanted to ask you guys and see if you can help me out."

"Okay, what's the problem?" Alex asked.

Malcolm placed his left arm on the countertop, and from his stripe flowed several documents he had compiled since the night the Collector confronted him. Malcolm cleared his throat and began, "Okay, so, I started working with the Company in 5716, eight years ago, right?"

"Yes, that's right," Alex confirmed. "I remember when you called us to tell us that you got the call, we were so happy for you. It had been your dream to defend the city."

"Right," Malcolm declared while Sandra prepared the plates with leftovers from the night before. "Well, I grabbed this report from my job the other day, and there seems to be a discrepancy with my time there." Malcolm shuffled the pages and found a document with the Company's "C" watermark at the top right corner. He pointed at the top of the page, and he noted, "There's my name, and the date is stamped for 5715, not '16."

Alex examined the page on the countertop. He saw the date stamped for 5715. He said, "I don't understand."

"Right here, it says that I was in the Company's medical unit in 5715. I don't remember ever being in a medical unit in 5715. Do you?"

"I can't recall you being in a unit for anything," Alex scratched his head and rubbed his eyes. "Sandra, do you remember anything about that?"

Sandra shook her head. "No, honey, I don't. Malcolm, maybe it was just a mistake? A typo? The year had just started, you know how sometimes they can write dates wrong."

Malcolm shook his head. "Yeah, see, I thought, that, too, but these medical documents stretch the entirety of '15.

Something about a 'severe head injury.' How could you not know about something like this?" The pages kept flipping. One after another, Malcolm's full name and credentials were listed atop the Company's letterheaded medical files with the year listed as 5715. "I wasn't discharged until the end of the fourth quarter. And I don't remember any of this!"

Alex looked like he had swallowed a frog. Malcolm noticed that Alex wasn't surprised by the news. Instead, Alex stared at Sandra, who had stopped mid-plating. She had the same look of fear on her face, like they had been caught red-handed by their teacher for cheating on a test. Malcolm saw their non-verbal exchange and probed, "You know something? Somebody, please, tell me what I'm missing here."

"Well, son," Alex placed both hands on Malcolm's shoulders, "we had no idea how badly things had really gotten for you. You see, you actually didn't start with the Company in 5716."

"Right," Sandra sounded like the wind got knocked out of her lungs. She stopped plating and walked to meet them. "You enlisted with the Company in 5715. You told us that they wanted to start you right away, and they immediately thrusted you into action."

"Yes," Alex continued, "and your first mission went sideways, and it concussed you. For a whole year, we were concerned that you would never wake up, and then, like a Jubilee miracle, you did. And you didn't remember anything that had happened, so rather than tell you everything that did, we kept you in the dark."

"We're so sorry, Malcolm. We should have told you what had happened," Sandra hugged Malcolm.

Malcolm pushed his mother off him, and his mom's eyes widened in shock. Her consolation was not enough to calm the flames building up in his veins. Malcolm rationalized, "So, you're telling me that I went on a mission with the Company and got concussed? And rather than tell me what happened, you chose to bury it? Whose idea was that?"

"Um," Sandra paused, "well, it was–"

"It was the Company's idea," Alex finished.

Malcolm shot out of his seat and vehemently paced the living room floor, "Wait, the Company? No, no, that doesn't make any sense! There's no way that the Company would decide to keep me in the dark about this. No one would be able to hold a secret like this from me for that long, not even the Analyst!" Malcolm was bewildered and seething.

"I'm sorry, son," Alex stood up and calmly stepped toward Malcolm. "We wanted to tell you. You told us that the mission was too important an opportunity for you to miss out. And after everything that happened, the Company informed us that it would be better if we didn't tell you because if you knew, it might have ruined your shot at staying with them. To them, you were too valuable to be jarred by the mishap."

Malcolm stared at his parents, then pounded his head with his palms three times as his logic tried to reboot, "Wait, is that why all of my memories are so fuzzy? Why I can only remember back to '16?"

"That's what they told us. They fixed it so that you would forget anything that happened."

"But why would they do that *and* take all my memories before then?! I've lost *over two decades* of my life! I can't remember anything that those photos on the walls represent!" he screamed as he pointed to the pictures of his younger self. "You're telling me that the Company ordered you to say nothing?"

"It was for the best, Malcolm," Sandra reasoned. "Look at how much better you've become since then."

Malcolm ran his memory back eight years. He didn't recall waking up from a hospital bed. His first vivid memory wasn't of him lying in the Infirmary of the Company. *In fact, my first memories are of me waking up in my apartment in Genesis Landing and getting ready for my first week of orientation at the Company. I got "the call" a few days prior. Everything was normal that day.*

*In 5716.*

"There's no way that what you're saying is true," Malcolm growled.

Alex and Sandra stared at each other, puzzled. Alex looked at Malcolm and asked, "What do you mean?"

Malcolm knew the Company's protocol thoroughly. Something smelled dodgy, and he was not going to back down. "The Company never sends out rookies to handle missions without going through orientation. Not even I would have been able to bypass that, no matter how 'valuable' the Company may have thought I was back then. Orientation is necessary for anyone entering the Company. You're lying to me! What the Frimas is going on?"

Alex twitched. "I-I-I'm sorry, son," he hugged Malcolm, "We wanted to tell you. You told us the mission was too important an opportunity for you to miss out, and after everything–"

"You already said that, Dad. Tell me the truth! What the Frimas is going on? Whose idea was all this, specifically?"

"Um," Sandra stated, "well, it was–"

"It was the Company's idea," Alex finished.

"What the Frimas?" Malcolm perked up. "What's going on with you two?"

"Nothing, son," Alex tried to assure Malcolm. "We're just trying to help you understand what happened."

Sandra got close to Malcolm. "Come on, Malcolm, I've almost got lunch ready, why don't we just eat, and after we all have food in our bellies, we can hash all of this out, huh?

Malcolm's mind scrambled as he walked back to his stool, his senses dilating from his anger. *Wait a second, something is not right here. The Company put me on a mission, and I got concussed. The Company did a surgical procedure that took my memories from me, and then held me in a hospital bed for a year. My parents knew that I was in a coma for a year, and the Company asked them to keep that a secret from me. I "woke up" a year later like nothing happened, and everybody was okay with this? Hold up!*

Malcolm sensed something grinding in the room, a noise he had never heard before in all his years of visiting his parents' home. It was faint, but distinct, mechanical-like ticks. *What is that ticking, grinding noise I'm sensing?* It sounded like gears turning in multiple clocks. He looked at the digital clock on the wall and thought, *Nope, that's digital.* He dilated his senses even more, scanning the room to determine where the grinding was coming from. To his surprise, he sensed it inside Alex. He then sensed the same twisting and clanging inside Sandra.

*What. The. Fuck?!*

Malcolm flexed his fingers and grabbed the gears. They grinded to a halt. Alex and Sandra seized, and Malcolm screamed, "You have five seconds to tell me what the fuck is going on! Who the fuck are you, and where are my parents?!"

Glitched, Alex stuttered, "What a-a-are you doing, Mal-al-alcolm?"

"I asked you two a question, who the fuck are you?!" Malcolm lifted them two feet off the ground and floated them both into the living room.

"Ple-e-e-e-as-s-s-s-se, Malcolm, wha-wha-wha-what are you do-do-do-do-do-doing? Put us down!" Sandra yelled.

Incensed, Malcolm demanded, "Last chance, who in the fuck are you, who are you working for, and where are my parents?!"

"Malcolm, we are your parents!" Alex yelled. "Put us the fuck down now!"

Malcolm dialed his senses up more intensely, and he felt a holoscreen-like computing system where their brains should have been. He searched and noticed that they didn't have hearts, veins, or arteries. Their spines and bones were metallic, and their skins were pure silicone. He could feel the electric pulses and signals racing through their bodies. Malcolm's rage for their faulty decision-tree logic responses boiled inside him. He thought about the Collector's data, being in a coma for a year, being lied to by these machines, and wondered if the Company indeed had anything to do with his coma at all, and what all of this meant. Malcolm fought to remember something, anything that could shed light into what happened to him, but his memory was still a swirl, and not one memory could give him an answer. Malcolm's head hurt in the same spot Sonic ignited the year before in the parking garage, the same spot it always hurt when he struggled with his nightmares and visions.

Malcolm saw red, and he could contain his emotions no longer. Malcolm stuck his hands out and seized his fingers to clutch the gears grinding in their chests. He then swiftly pulled his hands back, and the gears seized and whizzed, then tore through their bodies. Sparks burst from their eyes, ears, and chest as parts of their mechanics exploded from the assault. Black ooze gurgled from the holes Malcolm ripped, and Alex and Sandra's heads, eyes, and arms twitched before falling to the floor.

Malcolm's frustration enlarged. He stared at the pictures and fought to remember the memories and failed again. He looked at the house, stared at the kitchen, reflected on the staircase, and couldn't remember anything. He ran through the rooms, and not a single memory sparked. He ran upstairs and turned to the right to enter his room, and he stared at the walls and couldn't see a thing in his mind. He hit his head three times, and it produced nothing but a worsening migraine.

Malcolm's heart palpitated. The pit of his gut was gored by the void of his soul. Malcolm hyperventilated. He dropped to his knees and buried his head in his hands. Tears streamed down his face, and flashes of red appeared around him. He immediately tried to contain himself, but he couldn't bring himself to begin his grounding techniques. The rage overtook him, and as his hands planted onto the floorboards of his childhood room, his senses kicked into hyperdrive. He could feel the cells of the floors and the walls. Malcolm's anger flowed through his veins hotter than Symone's star power through hers.

Pissed about everything that was revealed to him, he hollered at the top of his lungs to attempt to release the rage, unconcerned about what his powers might do. He sensed every single molecule in the house. The more he thought about the past eight years, and all the years he lost, the more enraged he became. And Malcolm, with the fury of a dying star, set off a shockwave from his body that eviscerated his parents' home into shreds, splinters, and dust. He fell through the air that replaced the floors and landed on the foundation while pieces of the house fell around him.

*Fuck me!*

Malcolm had completely unraveled and now knelt ashamed for losing control of his powers. Malcolm lifted his head and realized what he had done. His anger turned to dread. *Oh shit, oh shit! What did I just do? How do I fix this? What can I do now? I can't trust the Company. I don't know who did this. Are my parents alive? Did Mallack have something to do with this? She had to have. I don't know who to trust. I don't know what to do.*

He slowly stood up and looked around. He knew that it would be a matter of time before the neighbors came outside and UPD showed up. He scanned the driveway and saw his hoverbike untouched and thought to walk in that direction when his stripe lit up. *Not now, shit! Not now!* He looked at his arm, and it read, "Unknown Caller."

Malcolm answered the call. A sweet voice responded, "Don't speak."

*You deserve this power.*

*We are destined for this.*

Malcolm's mind almost slipped into a trance as his senses remembered the cadence of her sound.

She continued, "I don't have time to explain anything to you. I am sending you the coordinates to where I am. Memorize them. Then rip your stripe off your arm, leave your cloak and uniform, and destroy your tracker. I know you know where it is, you're the only one who can sense it. Do this now, or else the UPD will lock your ass up in the Asylum, and you'll never get the answers you're seeking. You have thirty seconds." The call disconnected.

Malcolm breathed heavily, adrenaline racing through him faster than Joy's lightning piercing the sky. He looked down at his stripe, and the location the voice gave him appeared. He memorized the location, then used his powers to rip the stripe off his arm. He grimaced as his arm bled slightly from the holes the stripe screwed into. He dropped the stripe onto the ground. He unscrewed his uniform and cloak from his chest and threw them into the ruins of his parents' house. He then searched for the tracking chip inside his left thigh, pinched his fingers to clutch it, then pulled it out of his thigh, groaning from the pain it produced.

Malcolm then looked through his hoverbike and found the tracking device embedded within it and destroyed it, too. He saddled his ride, turned the bike on, and revved it up. He wiped his eyes and rose into the sky.

*My life is over.*

# 30

# Debunked

The Analyst stared at Symone's avatar, demos, and stats on the holoscreen in the front of his office. On the right of the display, video footage of Symone's solo fight with the Emulator played. Symone, still recovering from her burst, sat at the desk in the middle of his office, holding a burrito in one hand and her head in the other. The Analyst studied the film. As Symone unleashed star power on the Emulator and his cloak took damage, the Analyst paused the footage. "Is this what you're talking about?"

Symone swallowed the food in her mouth, then said, "Yes, that's what Jason said, that when the cloak takes damage from my star power, the nanites absorb the energy."

The Analyst faced Symone. "This is incredible! So, your star power is changing the molecular structure of the nanites? I wonder why Weapons and Wardrobe never caught onto what was happening with the cloaks."

"It can't be as simple as structural change if Double W never caught on," Symone posited. "The nanites are pro-grammed to resist all types of powers, changing on a whim. Maybe they're just holding the power within themselves?"

"You might be right," the Analyst assumed. "The cloaks themselves never enhanced, so the nanites might be acting as storage containers that hold the energy, then release it upon reactivation of the cloak."

Symone took another bite of her burrito in angst, then declared, "That means that every person I've ever battled has potentially gotten stronger because of me. If anyone ever took a cloak off and put it back on, he got a boost from my power, even by the tiniest degree. The team, when they fight with me, residue from my power is latching onto them and their cloaks. Enemies who got away, they have taken on some of my energy."

"Whoa," the Analyst backed up, "when you add up all the people who may have benefited from fighting you, Symone, the list could be in the hundreds."

Symone growled and rolled her eyes, "Yeah, don't remind me. I've done a *lot* of fighting in my life. I always said that every person should fight a person like me. Now I'm eating my words. And what's worse, Jason enlisted help to maximize the energy output, and that person reverse-engineered this shit and knows that I'm the 'key' to power evolution."

The Analyst looked at the screen again. "That's putting it mildly, Symone."

"What do you mean?" Symone said as she took the last bite of her burrito.

"Well, after you sent me the information a cycle ago, I looked at your powers again. It's going to take me a few days tops to really get a grip on this, but your power is more than just light, heat, and energy."

"Right, last time we talked," Symone recalled, "you said my star power might be like an engine."

The Analyst nodded, "Yes. I revisited that engine theory, and I truly believe that your power is literally what powers the universe."

Symone scratched her scalp. "What are you talking about?"

"I went back to your last fight with the Emulator. When he mimicked Malcolm's morphing abilities, he changed your star power into dragons. Living, fire-breathing dragons! Last year, Malcolm and you created a micro planet in the training room. I assumed Malcolm evolved and expanded his powers to craft the planet, and judging from how much he has excelled, there's truth to that. But in the right hands, Symone, your power can become literally *anything*. The same energy that brought the universe to life lives *in you*. There's no telling what your energy is capable of!"

Symone was more furious than amazed. "Great, so you're telling me that anyone who can capture my power – by cloak or residue or some other contraption – can not only use it to evolve, but could use it to do other shit, too?"

The Analyst was surprised by Symone's reaction, expecting her to be just as awestruck as he was with his reasoning. He cleared his throat. "In sum, yes."

Symone stared at the holoscreen as it played her facing Jason. The footage captured Jason's smirk, and Symone knew in that moment, Jason was happy that Symone was pummeling his cloak with her power. Symone's eyes embered red. *Damn it! This can't be true. But it is. I've made people stronger. Who else knows? Who else figured it out? Of course, no one would tell me, because it wouldn't benefit them to tell me.*

The Analyst continued, "We should talk to Weapons and Wardrobe and discuss our findings, see if they can figure out how the nanites are interacting with your powers."

"Fuck that, no!" Symone abruptly shot his idea down. "Don't tell Double W a damn thing. Once they find out what's happening, Mallack is going to have me poked and prodded. I'm already on the fence as it is with training newbies. The last thing I need is to become a guinea pig for you guys *again*. No, don't tell Double W shit, not until I've had a chance to process all of this."

The Analyst lifted his hands, "Okay, I understand. I won't say anything."

Symone cut her eyes at the Analyst, knowing full well the Analyst's tendency to speak when he should stay silent. She stepped to him and stared into his beady eyes. "Listen, I know you. You can't hold water. So, I am asking you, *begging* you," she slowly enunciated every syllable to emphasize her dire request, "*don't tell anyone what we've learned today*, not at least until I can understand it better myself. All my life, people have been taking shit from me without me knowing and I, for once, finally feel like I am one step ahead of everyone. Let me keep this for myself, just for a little while, until I'm ready for people to know. Hold the line, please."

The Analyst knew what Symone was asking of him. He computed that staying silent would be in his best interest, lest he face the wrath of a creator of the universe. He stared into her eyes and declared, "I promise, I won't say a word."

Symone said, "Thank you." She walked toward the exit, then turned around and said, "So, what does this mean for your 'Affinity Theory?'"

The Analyst turned and looked at the holoscreen again, "I don't know. I'm still a believer, but I honestly don't know anymore. I thought we had figured it out. But I have been wrong before. Maybe it's just been you all along."

"Right. I'm the theory," Symone cracked a wry smile, and her left eyebrow raised. She walked out of the office.

The Analyst stared at Symone's avatar, and a light bulb went off in his head. "She's right!"

Symone walked down the hallway and opened Intelligence's doors. Stephanie was at her desk at the bottom of the auditorium. Symone walked down the steps to meet her.

"Symone, hi!" Stephanie's eyes beamed.

"Hi Stephanie. Got a minute?"

Stephanie could tell that Symone wasn't her best self. "Sure, what's up?"

Symone leaned and planted her elbows on Stephanie's desk. She moved her locs out of her face as she began, "Okay, so I talked to Jason today, and he told me that he evolved using my powers."

"Just like you said the Analyst predicted, shit, Symone!" Stephanie said.

Symone nodded, "Uh huh. What's worse, Jason found a way to harness my power in the cloaks themselves and most likely sold several cloaks to people while we were together. While I don't think that matters now since it was so long ago, I'm not sure if the power boost is a one-time thing or a continuous thing, like if there's a shelf-life to my power in the cloaks? I don't know."

"What are you thinking, Symone?" Stephanie asked.

"We need to find the person who built the cloaks for Jason. Since we now have Jason and the Elements in custody, is there a way to trace his contacts? Between the people I know and the people he knows, there has to be a connection somewhere. Maybe this person can tell us who he built the cloaks for."

"That makes sense," Stephanie scratched her head in agreement. "It may take some time, but I think I can cross-reference your connections and compile a list of possible targets."

"Take your time, it's no rush. And, can you keep this between us for now? I don't want to sound any alarms."

"I got your back, Symone, whatever you need," Stephanie lifted her hand, and Symone slapped her a hi-five.

"Thank you." Symone lifted off the desk, turned, and left the auditorium. Stephanie tapped on the keys on her counter and created a ghost file called "S × J."

Symone walked inside the quarters and saw Karl, Duncan, and Joy sitting in the commons watching the holoscreen. "Hey guys, any of you seen Malcolm?"

Karl turned around in his seat and said, "No, he hasn't been through here yet, not since he left earlier."

"Okay, I'm gonna go in my room. When he gets back, let him know where I'm at?"

"Sure will, Symone," Karl replied.

Symone walked into her residence, plopped on her couch, lay sideways, and closed her eyes.

Meanwhile, across town, Ashanti rushed through the door to Nova's office, eyes widened. "Boss?"

Nova turned in her chair, looking away from a holoscreen she was gleefully monitoring. "Yes?" she responded.

"He's here."

Nova's pearly whites flashed in the light, sparkles shining in her eyes. "Fantastic. Right on time."

"I'll never understand how you get shit done."

"Never underestimate me, Ashanti."

Nova was dressed in a white crop top and a pair of black jeans. She stood up and walked around her desk toward Ashanti. Ashanti noticed that Nova didn't pick up her mask from her desk.

"Don't you want to put on your uniform?"

"No, not this time. Get Mason and meet me at the entrance."

Ashanti raised an eyebrow in concern. "Are you sure? He could expose you and, worse, try to kill you."

As Nova walked out of the office, she declared, "If that's the case, then this was my fate all along. What is meant to be will be."

Ashanti obeyed her leader and summoned Mason. She heard Mason's voice in her ear say, "What's up?"

"Get ready, he's here. See you in three."

"See you there."

Nova and Ashanti marched down the corridor to the elevator. Mason ran down the hallway and met them. Mason asked, "Xander and Heinrich are still on mission?"

"Yes," Nova replied, "but we won't need them. We'll be fine." Ashanti hit the up button, and the elevator rode down the shaft to meet them. The silver elevator doors parted. Nova walked in first, then Ashanti, then Mason.

Nova declared, "Lady and gentleman, destiny awaits."

Ashanti and Mason nodded in agreement. They looked forward and awaited reaching the top of the elevator shaft. The elevator slowed to a halt, and a ding indicated they reached their destination. The elevator opened, and they stepped off. They walked down the brightly lit corridor as the black marble floor echoed with every step they took.

They reached the entrance of their lair. Nova said, "You two ready?"

"Ready," Ashanti declared and double-tapped her chest. As her uniform enveloped her, she silently wished for something to go wrong so she could unleash a lightning storm.

"Ready," Mason said as he, too, double-tapped his chest. The nanites enveloped him, and he locked his tentacles above his head, ready to strike.

*Okay,* Nova took a deep breath and began encouraging herself, *everything you've worked for now hinges on this moment. Do not fuck this up. You will not get another crack at this.* Nova placed her palm on the reader on the right wall near the door. It scanned her print and lit white for approval. The door popped backward about half an inch, then slid to the right into the wall. The brilliant light of the three suns flooded the hallway. Streak and Mygalo's visors adjusted immediately so they wouldn't be blinded.

Malcolm stood outside the door, emotionally drained and physically fatigued. His eyes were red from crying and the wind he couldn't shield from since he rode uncloaked. He recognized Streak and Mygalo from their previous battles almost a year ago. He then looked at the petite woman standing in front of him and stared into her eyes. His mind flashed, his senses uncontrollably dialed up, and they latched onto Nova like a child gripping his mother. Nova could feel Malcolm's powers surrounding her and stood unfazed and unafraid. Malcolm's consciousness drew blanks, but his body vividly, deeply, and foundationally remembered her deep brown eyes, her infectious smile, and her beautiful, wavy hair.

Nova slowly slinked toward him while Streak and Mygalo craned their heads at each other in disbelief. Nova softly asked Malcolm, "Why are you here?" Malcolm's splintered mind could barely form words. The voice he heard triggered echoes of the nightmares he fought so hard to push away, flashes of red and black once again dominating his headspace. Malcolm heard that sweet, soft voice reverberate, *You are destined for this. You deserve this power.*

Malcolm dropped to one knee and struggled to recall when and where he heard her voice. He bellowed, "Answers."

Nova methodically squatted to match Malcolm's level and touched his shoulders. "It's okay. Shhhh, it's okay."

Malcolm fought through his choked throat and teary eyes to look up and face Nova. He stared into her eyes again, and the echoes continued to rattle his skull. "Who are you?" he stammered.

*Don't fuck this up.* Nova gently touched his face with the palm of her hand. Malcolm's senses flashed again with faint memories of her touching his face the same way. Nova looked around and noticed sand slowly floating off the ground and swirling around them. Streak noticed it, too, and charged up. Nova heard sparks fly and swiftly shot her left arm toward Streak, pointing a finger to signal her to wait.

Nova answered Malcolm, "I am Adrienne. Adrienne Nova Ling."

*Adrienne. Adrienne. Adrienne.* Malcolm's senses continued to knock against his soul as Adrienne's name rang like a siren in his ears. His mind feverishly tried to assist him but was useless in giving him a clue as to how his body remembered her so vividly. The more he tried, the more vigorously the sand swirled behind them, shifting positions across the pavement slab.

Adrienne looked into Malcolm's eyes and said, "It's okay. Calm down. Breathe. Tell me, what are five things you can see?"

Malcolm's heart nearly burst from the shock. *How the fuck does she know about my grounding technique?* "How? How did you know?"

Adrienne didn't skip a beat. "I taught it to you, so many years ago. Now, what are they? Five things?"

Malcolm focused his eyes and embarrassingly admitted, "Your eyes. Your hair. Your white shirt." He breathed in and out more slowly and didn't want to finish.

"What else?" Nova wouldn't let him stop.

*Dammit.* "Um, your black pants. And, um, your brown skin."

"Good. Four things you hear."

Malcolm tried to concentrate. "I can only hear one thing. Your voice. Your voice is all that I hear." Malcolm fell onto Adrienne's shoulders.

"That's it. That's it. Breathe. You are okay. You are safe now."

Malcolm's heart and mind steadied, and the sand responded in kind and settled onto the ground. Adrienne noticed that some of the rocks Malcolm raised were in different locations than where they started from. She silently cheered, *Yes. The plan is working, just like I knew it would.*

Malcolm, buried into Adrienne's shoulder, asked, "Who am I?"

Adrienne held onto Malcolm, and as she stood up, Malcolm stood up with her. She grabbed his hand and said, "There's so much to catch you up on, but first, let's start with your name."

# Epilogue

Cycles went by, and nightfall neared. Symone groggily arose from her much-needed refresher nap. She noted the time on the clock read 13:42 and wondered why no one had gotten her up yet. *I bet they forgot all about me. Can't blame them, we're all tired.* Symone looked at her stripe and noticed she had no missed calls or messages. She called Malcolm, and she only got a humming noise for about twenty seconds. *That's weird.* She sent him a message, "Hey Malcolm, where are you?" Symone then got up and walked out of her residence to the commons, finding her comrades all where she left them.

"Hey Symone, you're up!" Malaysia cheered.

"Hey y'all, have you seen or heard from Malcolm?" Symone inquired.

The team looked at each other as Joy answered, "No, he hasn't come through here."

"Nope," Karl continued, "he hasn't come through those doors. We've been here watching 'Leicester PD' the whole time."

"Here, let me try to reach him," Malaysia got on her stripe and called Malcolm. The team waited, then Malaysia responded, "Nothing."

Symone sighed, "Alright, well, I'll go check the building, see if he's in Intelligence or training or something. See if any of you can get a hold of him."

"Okay, we will," Alexia replied.

As her teammates began calling and sending messages to Malcolm's stripe, Symone ran through the cafeteria and noticed Malcolm wasn't there. She left and walked down the corridor to the conference room. No Malcolm. She flew to Intelligence. Malcolm wasn't there. She revisited the Analyst and didn't see him there. She peeked in Weapons and Wardrobe, no Malcolm. She tried calling him while floating to the elevator and got no response.

She pressed down, and waited for the elevator to climb to get her. The elevator opened, and she walked in. She pressed "T" for the training floor, and the elevator raced down while Symone, arms crossed, tapped her foot in frustration. She tried calling him again and got no answer. She then texted him again, "Where are you? Why aren't you answering my call?!" The elevator opened, and she flew through the entire training floor and did not see Malcolm's name scrolling on any marquee. Symone growled and huffed, then flew back to the elevator, went inside, and rose back to the Elite Grand Hall.

Symone opened the quarters and saw the whole team sitting frantically in the commons. "Anybody heard from him yet?" Symone asked.

"No," Malaysia replied, "He's not responding to any of our calls or texts."

"Anybody know where he last was?" Karl wondered.

Symone replayed her last conversation with Malcolm. "Yeah, he said he was going to visit his parents."

"Anybody know how to get a hold of them?" Malaysia posed.

"Nope, not even an address," Karl declared. "I've never met them."

"Neither have I," Symone said.

"I alerted Mallack," Daisy stated. "She's on her way now."

"Where can he be? This isn't like him to not respond to us," Alexia pondered.

Symone scratched her scalp and frenetically ran her fingers through her locs. Mallack soon entered. Symone turned around and said, "Director, have you found him?"

Mallack sighed, "No, nothing. I can't even get a hold of his parents."

"You serious?" Joy asked.

"Yes, no response from either of them."

"Let's ask Intelligence," Symone reacted.

"Great idea," Mallack said. "Let's go."

The Elite sprinted out of the quarters toward Intelligence. Symone was the first in the room. Stephanie, Dax, Dredge, and a couple other analysts looked at Symone and the Elites' urgent faces. Stephanie instinctively asked, "What's wrong, what's going on?"

"We can't find Malcolm. Can you locate him for us?"

"What do you mean you can't find Malcolm?" Dredge asked.

"I'm on it," Dax declared. He ran to his desk and tapped keys to pull up tracking information. "Okay, his tracker has him in Meridian. The address is his parents' home."

"That's where he said he was going, but why isn't he or anyone else picking up their stripes?" Mallack asked.

Dax rang Malcolm's stripe, and no one answered the call.

Mallack ordered, "Pull up the satellite footage."

Dax tapped on keys again, and the live feed showed his parents' house in utter shambles. The team was horrified and shocked. UPD and UFD were on the street assessing and processing the scene. Dread filled their chests as their worst fears infiltrated their minds.

"No, no, no, what the Frimas?" Alexia blurted out, her eyes flashing green and green mist puffing from her body.

Mallack demanded, "Where is his uniform? His cloak?"

Dax, trying to keep it together, frantically tapped on keys, and the holoscreen pulled up the information. "His uniform and cloak are in the rubble, Director," his voice cracked as his eyes began to well up.

"Impossible, no, not Malcolm!" Malaysia could barely contain her tears as her throat closed up. Duncan banged on the table in saddened rage. Daisy and Karl buried their heads in their hands.

"Who? Who could have done this?" Mallack cried. "Who is capable of carrying out a hit like this?"

"I don't know, Director," Stephanie could barely breathe. Her voice cracked, "I don't know." She slumped in her chair.

Symone stared at the wreckage on the screen. Her mind was running a mile a minute through her skull. She looked at her crew and saw them unraveling. *No, he's not dead. He's not gone. Something's not right.*

Symone listened to her reasoning and asked, "How is his stripe still active?"

Stephanie sniffed and said, "What?"

"His stripe, how is his stripe still active? If he were dead, his stripe would not still be active. Where is his stripe?"

Dax tapped the keys again and located his stripe. "It's in the wreckage, but Symone is right. If he were dead, the stripe would have been destroyed along with him."

"Get an exact location on the stripe, I want to see it on the screen," Mallack stated.

Dax zoomed in on the footage, and he located the stripe in perfect condition on the driveway next to the untouched green hovercar. Dax reported, "The stripe is right there. Looks like it got ripped out of his arm."

"You can't just rip a stripe out of someone's arm. You'd have to rip out the bone to do that," Duncan recalled.

"Right. Where's his hoverbike?" Symone asked.

Dax panned the camera and noted, "It's not there."

Symone breathed a sigh of relief. *He's not dead. Okay, Malcolm, where the fuck are you?*

"Okay, so his stripe is a dead end. But his bike, can we get a read on the bike?"

Dax tapped keys again and said, "Tracker on the bike is either disabled or destroyed. His thigh tracker is pinging on the driveway pavement, too. We have no way of locating him."

"Yeah we do," Duncan countered. Offering his military expertise, he countered, "Rewind the satellite feed footage. We can at least track where he went."

Dax rewound the satellite feed, and as it got closer to Malcolm's departure, the feed suddenly went black. "The Frimas?" Dax questioned. He continued rewinding the footage, and the black screen finally went away, displaying Alex and Sandra's home untouched. He then pushed the footage forward, and the screen went black again. "No way," he declared.

"What? What's happening?"

"The footage, the sat feed's been wiped for a three-cycle stretch," Dax declared.

"Okay, so go back to when Malcolm left the Company," Stephanie reasoned.

Dax tapped on keys again, and the satellite feed showed black at that time, too. "It's wiped, blacked out."

"Well, what about his uniform camera feed?"

Dax tapped once more, and the footage was missing from the archive. "There's nothing here."

"Wait a damn minute," Mallack said, "now that's impossible! How did that footage just go missing?"

Without warning, the whole room was bathed in red while an alarm blared. Everyone was immediately irritated and annoyed. "Shit, not now!" Malaysia yelled.

A red block with yellow letters read, "From Company HQ. PRIORITY ONE TO THE ELITE: TRENT SALAZAR."

"No fucking way," Symone declared. "I thought we killed him!"

"You think he's behind this?" Daisy asked.

"I don't know," Karl admitted.

The holoscreen then showed the Elite a picture of Malcolm, and they all gasped. Suddenly, the name "Trent Salazar" appeared underneath his picture. Then, the holoscreen placed his picture next to a picture of the Collector, Streak, Hex, Sonic, and Mygalo in their uniforms, and arrayed them side by side.

"No, no, no, no, there's no fucking way," Mallack lamented.

"Wait, Malcolm is Trent Salazar? How is that possible?" Malaysia was puzzled.

"He's working with the Collector? Since when?" Alexia demanded.

Underneath their pictures, HQ announced, "ELIMINATE ALL SUBJECTS. KILL ORDER IN EFFECT."

While the team deliberated over HQ's intel and order, Symone sat down in complete disarray. Her mind split in several different directions, and her heart splintered. The red in the room masked the embers in her eyes. She remembered what she said to Malcolm just a day ago.

*I choose you, Malcolm.*

A single tear escaped her right eye and streaked her cheek.

TO BE CONTINUED...

# Acknowledgements

I still sit in awe as I write these words, in disbelief that I wrote a book, again! There are so many people who helped make this possible, I'm sure I'm going to miss someone. But I'm going to try my hardest to mention everyone who impacted my life and helped propel this book and the Affinity Saga in a major way.

First, I truly thank my Savior and Lord Jesus Christ. As I said after crafting *The Affinity Theory*, neither this book nor the saga would exist without Him guiding me every step of the way. The Holy Spirit orchestrated every single decision that has been made, from what to put in the book, to who to entrust on my team to bring it to life. I am forever grateful for His love, grace, guidance, patience, and care throughout this process. He is the reason that I live, move, and have all being, and this book is but a tiny demonstration of his power and might over my life.

To you, the reader of this book, I thank you for entrusting me once again with your mind, ears, and page-flipping fingers as I've taken you on this journey! To every single person who bought a book, read the book, loved/hated the characters, hyped the book up on your media pages, DM'd me about the book, celebrated every win, THANK YOU!

To my alpha and beta readers of *Echoes*, thank you for giving me your guidance on sharpening my writing. Your fingerprints are all over this book, and I am grateful for your assistance in ways that will impact the rest of the series.

I thank my editor Kamiyah Crawford (IG: @kamshappyplace), who was the first person post-completion of the book to lay eyes on it outside of my wife and give me not just a polished revision, but the most positive feedback about the story. I'm so glad we met on TikTok and look forward to our continued relationship!

I am incredibly grateful to Brit (@britandherbooks), Storm (@blackgirltiredbooksanddrinks), Megan (@vigilantevibespodcast), Shaunkeese (@shaunkeese), DeeAnn (@hijabi_booklover_), Yasmine (@yasie0324), Nicole (@bookedandbizzie), Stephanie (@booksandbounty), R.K. Renton (@somethingsweet1277), my cousin and fellow author Candi Usher (@candiusher), Olivia Linden (@olivialindenauthor), Sovereign Jane Jenkins (@the_healing_agent), and a host of other authors, readers, and influencers who have leveraged your platforms to help catapult my book to heights of success that I hadn't even imagined getting to in such a short amount of time! Your encouragement, words of kindness, suggestions, and shout-outs are priceless, and I cannot thank you enough for what you did and continue to do for me.

A.A. Lewis, my "auntie," thank you for giving me the push to launch my book in October 2024. I didn't think I was ready, but you knew I was ready, and your timing was nothing short of divine. Thank you for your encouragement and guidance. I wouldn't be here without you telling me what to do and where to go to make this book happen.

To my best friend Lavona Gantt, I cannot emphasize enough how your incessant push sparked the ambition to write this series. The debt of gratitude owed to you for recognizing "all this talent sitting behind these gray walls" is immeasurable.  Both I and the readers owe you big time!

I thank my children, Marie and Allison, who continue to show me love and support, ask me questions about the book, give me song suggestions, show suggestions, and keep encouraging me to keep writing and working to get this book on TV.  I love you both, and we will keep pushing until we make the entire dream a reality.

I thank my parents Charles E. and Evelyn D. Vinson for just existing!  You two have been the biggest supporters of everything I've ever done, no matter how silly or ambitious. You've always believed in me, encouraged me, and hyped me up.  It's taken me some time to fully appreciate you for all you've done for me and been to me, and I thank God for opening my eyes to see just how amazing you both have been to me!  Thank you for supporting me and supporting the saga.  I love you both to life!

Last, but certainly not least, I thank my wife, my great love, and my best friend, Nicole.  You have DEVOURED both books, sat up with me and listened to every word and correction, questioned motives, helped me tease things out, celebrated every win, let me go LIVE, packed up books, stood by my side on every trip, supported every purchase, and the list goes on.  I am eternally grateful for your love, your support, and your grace. My Symone Watson, my Eve, I love you, so much, and I thank you for loving me the way you do. Your loyalty, your support, your scalding hotness!

I love you all!  To destiny!

# Glossary

## The Elite Defenders Unit

| Real Name | Code Name | Power | Color Scheme |
| --- | --- | --- | --- |
| Bennett, Malcolm | Kingdom Come | Molecular Manipulation | Black and Blue |
| Watson, Symone | Starburst | Energy Generator | Crimson and Gold |
| Jones, Malaysia | The Eagle | Multi-focal Eyesight | Purple and Black |
| Luther, Karl | The Mammoth | Rapid Healing | Black and Gold |
| Montague, Alexia | Enchantra | Mystic Arts | Green and Blue |
| Parker, Daisy | Blitz | Hyperkinesis | Red and Black |
| Blake, Duncan | Ammo | Cybernetics | Silver and Black |
| Olivier, Joy | Kaminari | Electricity Generator and Conduit | Yellow and White |

## The Collector's Army

| Real Name | Code Name | Power | Color Scheme |
| --- | --- | --- | --- |
| Adrienne Nova-Ling | The Collector | Power Siphoning | Black |
| Ashanti ******* | Streak | Electricity Generator | Blue and White |
| ****** *** | Hex | Mystic Arts | Purple and Red |
| ******** ***** | Sonic | Sound Amplification | Magenta |
| Mason ********** | Mygalo | Man-Spider | Green and Red |

## The Emulator and the Elements

| Real Name | Code Name | Power | Color Scheme |
|---|---|---|---|
| Xavier, Jason | The Emulator | Ability Mimicry | Red and Purple |
| Biggs, Michael | Frostbite | Ice Manipulation | White and Cyan |
| Blythe, Jasmine | Ignatia | Fire Manipulation | Orange and Black |
| Crews, Gordon | Cyclone | Wind Manipulation | Green and Black |
| Jameson, Otis | The Wave | Water Manipulation | Blue and Tan |
| Parsons, Quinn | Terra | Terraforming | Sandy Gray |
| Tyson, Samantha | Cypher | Electronics Manipulation | Neon Pink |

## Other Characters (Ordered by Last Name)

- The Analyst – a cybernetic algorithm split into several bodies, one for each unit/team; responsible for collecting and analyzing training and battle data to determine evolution rates for each defender

- Captain Banks – one of the captains of the Uri City Police Department

- Stephanie Banks – Head of the Intelligence Division of the Elite Defenders Unit

- Alex and Sandra Bennett – Malcolm's parents

- Senator Berkeley – senator of Uri City

- Chancellor Winston Croft – elected leader of Uri City

- Mitchell Daniels – leader of the political advocacy group the Powered Order Coalition

- Senator Martin Dariuz – senator representing the Highgarden District, political rival of Chancellor Croft

- Dredge – a computer hacker and recovering gambling addict

- Dante Hibbett – sergeant who works for the Asylum of the Uncontrollable

- Chancellor Holland – a ruthless powered individual who 150 years ago, as Chancellor of Uri City, attempted to rule the city as a king, but was stopped by a coalition of powered individuals and sent to the Asylum for life

- Jacob – a boy who activated his powers and accidentally killed his parents Kenya and Lance, and countless others, and caused massive damage to the Uri Mega Mall

- Catherine Mallack – Director of the Uri City Division of the Company

- Dax McHill – Assistant to Stephanie Banks in Intelligence Division

- Vice Chancellor Royce – Vice-Chancellor of Uri City and Overseer of the Senate

- Jackson Santana – Malaysia's ex-boyfriend and an Underbelly gang co-leader with Emma Leslie

- Captain Stewart – one of the captains of the Uri City Police Department

- Senator Deborah Wimberly – senator representing the Leicester district, an ally of Chancellor Croft and the powered population

## How Time Works on Uretha

- Year > Quarter > Week > Day > Cycle > Minutes > Seconds

- 60 seconds = 1 minute

- 60 minutes = 1 cycle

- 28 cycles = 1 day

- 9 days = 1 week

- 10 weeks = 1 quarter

- 4 quarters = 1 year

- Rising (first of Uretha's three suns crosses the eastern horizon) = 00:00

- Nightfall (last of Uretha's three suns crosses western horizon) = 14:00

## Terms

- Affinity – according to asheologists, where a person's powers originate along a spectrum between darkness and light

- Affinity Theory – a power theory authored by leading asheologists which posits that when two powered individuals are biorhythmically synched to each other holistically – spiritually, mentally, emotionally, and physically – they will enhance, alter, morph, and transform each other's powers exponentially

- Akan (ŭh-kăn′) – god of all creation, brother of Bashko

- Asylum for the Uncontrollable – a massive institution situated miles outside Uri City which houses a training facility and a prison for powered individuals who have been deemed too dangerous for society

- Bashko (bŏsh′-kō) – ruler of Frimas – the bonsam world, brother of Akan

- Benny's Emporium – a premier weapons and ammunition store in the Underbelly district

- Commissioner Catalina – commissioner of the Uri City Police Department

- Chioro (shē-ōr′-ō) – The dominant world religion

- Cloak – transparent armor constructed with sophisticated nanotechnology built to adapt in real-time and withstand various powers and weapons; not indestructible

- The Company – one of several contract city defense organizations dispatched by the city to manage crisis situations beyond law enforcements' capabilities

- Cred – short for credit, unit of money

- Cycle – a unit of time on Uretha; sixty (60) minutes = one cycle, twenty-eight (28) cycles = one day; sunrise = 00:00, sunset = 14:00

- Defender – a powered individual sworn to protect Uri City when called upon by the government

- Defender's Oath – the oath every defender in Uri City must swear to; crafted from the Three Laws of the Uri City Contract Defense Agreement

- Divine – one of the pantheon of supreme spiritual guardians of Uretha created by Akan; sworn to protect and direct the will of Akan for the affairs of man

- Elite Defenders Unit – A specialized group of powered Defenders in the Company who are called upon to handle crisis cases that no one else (powered or unpowered) can

- Frimas (frē'-mŏss) – Bashko's domain, also the nickname of the Frostlands due to freezing temperatures

- Holoscreen – next-generation CPU that displays information and other media with high-resolution, four-dimensional graphics; comes in various sizes

- Hovercraft – vehicles that use propulsion technology to transport via flight

- InCiP – The Inter-City Police, the international police department in charge of handling global and multi-city matters of law enforcement

- Jubilee – week-long holiday celebrating the beginning of the new year

- Maldola – one of the eleven city-states on Uretha that suffered a genocidal civil war twenty years ago; Joy Olivier's home of origin

- Medinure – the hardest material on Uretha

- Nanotech/nanites – microscopic fluid metal used in shielding technology; applications include cloaking, uniforms, bonding, and barrier defense

- NextGen Technologies – a pharmaceutical and weapons technology corporation and sponsor of NextGen Coliseum, a zintol stadium in the Leicester district

- Nullifier – a device designed to suppress the power gene in individuals and normalize them

- Powered Order Coalition – political advocacy group dedicated to restoring full citizen rights to the powered population in Uri City

- Prizefighting – mixed martial arts fighters competition in which a combatant battles to disable his/her opponent's cloak in a set number of timed rounds

- Proposition 1 – Chancellor Croft's signature platform bill which, if passed, will take the "Powered to Hold Offices Question" to the General Election

- The Roots – a clandestine group of the most powerful, richest, and connected unpowered people in Uri City who use their resources to keep the government from restoring full citizenship rights to the powered population

- Stripe – identification, communication, and applications device attached to a person's arm that connects to the nervous system and can relay and transmit information wirelessly

- Uretha (yo͞or-ē′-thă) – small planet in distant galaxy

- Uri (yo͞or′-ē) City – one of eleven city-states on Uretha, broken up into six districts – Midtown (government seat), Highgarden, Meridian, Genesis Landing, Leicester, and the Underbelly

- UCSN – Uri City Sports Network

- UFD – Uri City Fire Department

- UMC – Uri City Medical Center

- UNN – Uri City News Network

- UPD – Uri City Police Department

- UZL – Uri City Zintol League

- Zintol (zin'-tall) – a small, round, furry, docile animal with wings; also, a sport in which two teams attempt to throw a zintol into their opponents' rings. First to eliminate all opponents' rings first scores a point. First to seven points wins the match.

# About the author

Eddie Dee is a born-and-bred native of Valdosta, GA. He is a devoted Christian, husband of sixteen years to his wife Nicole, father of two daughters Marie and Allison, and babysitter of his daughters' dogs Cristal and Chelsea. He works as a Licensed Marriage and Family Therapist, specializing in acute and chronic trauma, relationships, and sexuality. His parents are Dr. Charles E. Vinson, Sr. and Evelyn D. Vinson, and he's the oldest of five siblings – Darius, Latoya, Erica, and Eric.

He draws inspiration for his writing from his faith, his study of relationship and interpersonal dynamics, and various TV shows and movies like the Mission: Impossible series, Power Rangers, the Marvel Cinematic Universe, Brooklyn Nine-Nine, and the Ocean's Eleven series. He released his debut novel *The Affinity Theory* on October 25, 2024.

# Also by

*The Affinity Theory*, an Adult Superhero Romance Thriller, is **X-Men meets Hancock meets Twilight meets the Avengers**. On a distant planet in a faraway galaxy, Malcolm, the leader of the Elite Unit of the Uri City Division of the Company, Symone, the newest member of the Elite and Malcolm's mentee, and their superpowered teammates are racing against the clock to stop a serial-killing menace and his team of assassins from wiping out the powered population and murdering one of their own. The threads that bind Malcolm and Symone's hearts and powers may prove the key to the survival of the Defenders, their organization, and all of Uri City.

Scan the QR Code or visit www.theaffinitysaga.com to enter The Affinity Saga Store!